ANOMALY

Anne Fleming
ANOMALY

RAINCOAST BOOKS

Vancouver

Raincoast Books gratefully acknowledges the financial support of the Province
of British Columbia through the BC Arts Council and the Book Publishing
Tax Credit and the Government of Canada through the Canada Council for
the Arts, and the Book Publishing Industry Development Program (BPIDP).

Edited by Lynn Henry
Cover design by Bill Douglas
Interior design by Teresa Bubela

Library and Archives Canada Cataloguing in Publication

Fleming, Anne, 1964–
          Anomaly / Anne Fleming.

ISBN 978-1-55192-831-9 (bound)
ISBN 978-1-55192-942-2 (pbk.)

          I. Title.

PS8561.L44A76 2005   C813'.54   C2005-903304-5

LIBRARY OF CONGRESS CONTROL NUMBER: 2007926762

Raincoast Books	*In the United States:*
9050 Shaughnessy Street	Publishers Group West
Vancouver, British Columbia	1700 Fourth Street
Canada V6P 6E5	Berkeley, California
www.raincoast.com	94710

Raincoast Books is committed to protecting the environment and to the responsible use of natural resources. We are working with suppliers and printers to
phase out our use of paper produced from ancient forests. This book is printed
with vegetable-based inks on 100% ancient-forest-free, 100% post-consumer
recycled, processed chlorine- and acid-free paper. For further information, visit
our website at www.raincoast.com/publishing.

Printed in Canada by Transcon.
10 9 8 7 6 5 4 3 2 1

With apologies to Duncan O'Brien

A man could spend a lifetime looking for
peace in that city. And the lives give way around him — marriages
founder, the neighbourhoods sag — until
the emptiness comes down on him to stay.
But in the city I long for men complete
their origins. Among the tangle of
hydro, hydrants, second mortgages, amid
the itch for new debentures, greater expressways,
in sober alarm they jam their works of progress, asking where in truth
they come from and to whom they must belong.

— FROM "CIVIL ELEGIES," DENNIS LEE

Part One

AIR PHOTO A25945-62
TORONTO, 1982
1:6,000
(FROM THE COLLECTION OF GLENN RIGGS)

A TINY PATCH OF CITY, a close-up of the northeast quadrant of a local hub, Yonge and Eglinton, lower left. Upper right is the grey wash of Sherwood Park, cut by that thin field-hockey stick of a stream, that brown, sewery tributary of the Don his dad skated on as a child.

Quiet day, little traffic, office lots empty, church lots full, shadows showing midday. A Sunday.

The southern two-thirds of the eastern half is all high-rise, low-rise and parking. The high-rises are buildings to live in, apartment buildings, slim as dominos; the older low-rises are walk-ups; the newer ones are buildings to work in, offices, commercial buildings, unflippable as Olympic wrestlers in the table position. Ratios of building volume to parking space are constant. (How they *think*, these humans! All the time *thinking*.) In the blocks with high buildings are only two to three talls or possibly two talls and a shortie, taking up in total perhaps a quarter of the land area. That's it. The rest goes to parking. The blocks with low buildings take six or seven buildings that collectively cover, say, half the area, with parking not in great slabs but wedged between buildings.

The residential areas to the east and north run fifty buildings to a similar-sized block, the rest of the block's land area taken up with yards and trees (bare: it's spring), little wee driveways. Mere pencil lines of space separate the Sen Sen tabs of domicile lining the block's edges. Median Homes of Toronto.

People there are none. People disappear in air photos. Even in large-scale ones like this, even with a magnifying glass. Air photos'll show you where a man has been — one soldier cutting through a field gives away the best-camouflaged gun — but except by inference (that car turning into the Sunoco, there, on Mount Pleasant, someone must be driving it) they don't show you where anyone is now. Everything in the picture is evidence of their doings, but the existence of people themselves you have to take on the evidence.

Or on faith.

In the past, he has liked this.

Standing out for their rounded rectangles of running tracks, the only buildings allotted substantial bits of free land (versus land in service to the building) are the high schools, of which there are two. The elementary schools (there are also two) are half the size and get half the land.

Each day, children from an area roughly the size of this photograph, but centred on the school, make their ways to the elementary schools. Each day, children from an area easily ten times larger than that pictured here make their way to the high schools. His older daughter is no longer among these children.

His older daughter is somewhere else in the city.

Where, he has no idea.

1972

Glynnis

MR. RIGGS DIVVIED UP the roast strings, crisp with fat, between his two daughters.

"No one can accuse Lawrence Park Church of giving up on its young people. They want guitars instead of organs? They want jeans instead of grey flannels?" A slender pink roll of beef fell away from his knife. "By all means! By all means!" He repositioned the carving fork with a neat jab. "Let them mob the altar in their peasant get-ups. Let them hammer out freedom …"

"Wo-o," his son said into his napkin. Mr. Riggs gave no sign of hearing.

"Let them hammer out justice." Another pink slice nestled into the pile heaping up on the platter. Glynnis, salivating, was glad she had the roast strings to suck on. She wondered when her father was going to stop.

"Let them hammer out the love between their brothers and their sisters."

"Aw-awl over this land," said Jay. His father eyed him sternly for a moment, then went on.

"One Sunday a month. What can it hurt?" He swung a broad smile around the table to each of his children. He gave them an even broader wink. His aren't-I-a-fun-with-it-kind-of-Dad wink. His isn't-your-mother-an-old-stick-in-the-mud wink.

He waited for them to smile back. Glynnis concentrated on the roast strings. Jay played with the fall harvest centrepiece. It was Carol, eager to please, who popped her father a wet-lipped grin. He slipped her another piece of crisp fat.

What their mother had said to bring on tonight's monologue was that she hardly felt like she'd been to church at all. It was a neutral statement, not a judgement. If it did stray to the critical, it was only to say, *This will take some getting used to, this love and flowers and Jesus on a first-name basis.*

For Glynnis, the opposite was true. She had felt more than ever like she was in church, watching the teenagers up there singing, beating their tambourines, tossing their long hair. She was more aware of the hand-me-downs she wore — a stiff baby-blue frock and white leotards with the crotch halfway down her thighs and shiny shoes with buckles that dug into her feet.

"Next week can we wear jeans?" she asked.

"You don't have jeans," her mother said.

"We could go to Thriftys."

"One more time, and that radio goes."

"It's *my* radio," said Carol.

"Pants, then."

"If your mother wants you to look decent at church, you'll look decent at church," their father said. "This drop-in centre for the young teens, this 'Odd Spot,'" he went on. "Now, there's a solid idea. Off the streets. Away from drugs. You give them a place to fool around and work off their energy, give them a young guy to get them talking, and you give them a chance to go right in the world, to grow up to be the men they were meant to be."

Men? Glynnis thought.

⌒

GLYNNIS LOVED THE ODD SPOT. She loved how the youth worker talked over her head about Vietnam and Quebec and communism when nobody showed up to the rap sessions, and taught her to do back flips off the stage onto the gym mat. She liked to be able to say at school, "Oh, yeah, the other day at the Odd Spot ..." She liked the way other seven-year-olds admired the casual authority with which she spoke about this hangout for thirteen- and fourteen-year-olds.

So it was with longing that she passed the ground-floor rooms of the Odd Spot on her way into Brownies the following Tuesday. Her throat was dry, it was a hot September afternoon, as hot as June but not so humid, and she was dying for a Lola. She had her weekly dues — her Fairy Gold — in her brand new Brownie purse. If it weren't for two things, she would be sucking on that pyramid of frozen syrup right this minute. The main thing was that getting in trouble with Brown Owl was no regular matter of getting in trouble, but doubled at least, or quadrupled, because of who Brown Owl was: Mrs. Riggs herself. Pretending to go to the washroom and ducking into the Odd Spot instead to buy a Lola with the Fairy Gold her mother had given her moments ago — a plan she was half-formulating on the way in — would not wash. It would take too long, and besides, Glynnis was on her best behaviour.

Today was Glynnis' first day as a Brownie. A year ago, on Carol's first day, Glynnis had been consumed with envy. For as long as she'd been coming to Brownies with her mother — which was as long as she could remember — Glynnis had wanted her own uniform, two neat rows of badges to be sewn down the arm, a white scarf with orange maple leaves knotted at her throat. She'd been convinced that if only her mother would advocate on her behalf, the Girl Guides of Canada would give her a test proving what exceptional Brownie material they were letting slip by for lack of a single year of life, and would grant her special advance Brownie status. Today, in Carol's old uniform, cinched in with her new Brownie belt where it was loose, Glynnis didn't much care.

Nonetheless, Glynnis was acting particularly helpful. This was not because she aspired to the heights of virtue, but because she knew she would get in big trouble later that evening and hoped to soften the blow with advance good behaviour. She knew it would have little or no effect, and in fact might have the reverse effect of proving that she knew she'd been bad, and was trying to shirk her just punishment, but she couldn't help herself.

Lawrence Park Church had two gyms, a smaller one upstairs and the large one down. Attached to the downstairs gym was a large, modern kitchen to service the father–son and mother–daughter banquets held each year, the church dinners and pancake breakfasts and festive teas. Going from the kitchen to the upstairs gym was a dumbwaiter, allowing the kitchen to serve two do's at once, presumably, or an especially large do that overflowed upstairs. With the Odd Spot and the youth group, Scouts and Cubs, Guides and Brownies, the UCW, the Bible group, the church was in use every afternoon and evening. Tuesday afternoons it was Cubs downstairs, and Brownies up.

The gym floors were refinished every second summer. This year, the upright piano had been shuffled about in the process, so that it blocked the cupboard under the stage where the Brownie equipment was kept, the mirror pond and electric campfire and cardboard toadstools. Mrs. Riggs, Glynnis and Carol set to pushing it out of the way.

The piano was on castors that, when they deigned to roll at all, crunched, groaned and squeaked in succession. One spot in their revolution — the groan — was particularly sticky and required a good heave each time they came to it. Where Carol halfheartedly leaned against the piano as if pushing a shopping cart, Glynnis threw her weight into it like a Roman slave in a quarry, Christianly heaving a chunk of granite off her sworn enemy. Who happened, today, to take the form of Carol's teacher, Mrs. Harris.

"Come on, girls, one more good shove," said Mrs. Riggs.

Crippled, but grateful for her life, Mrs. Harris would realize how wrong she'd been about Glynnis. She'd kiss her feet, gratitude oozing from every pore. Except the thought of Mrs. Harris actually kissing her feet, that thick face with its pursy lips bent over her nether appendages, was not a pretty one. Glynnis fell back for a moment to regather her strength, then pushed again from the bottom of her toes.

The castors crunched, and started to groan. Glynnis felt that sudden euphoria that comes with knowing you're using the whole strength of your body, and using it well. Just as she was swelling into the heart of this euphoria, feeling with each step the line of her body go from bent leg, coiled spring, to full extension, spring uncoiled, the piano lurched as the far castors snapped off, then screeched to a halt as the remaining metal stubs dug into the newly refinished floor. The hammers crashed in great ringing discord against the strings, and Glynnis slammed into the piano face-first. She biffed it with the heel of her hand. Stupid piano. Stringing her along, letting her push her guts out, when the whole time it sat there waiting for the right moment to prove it could move perfectly well on its own. After hitting it she felt better, and she noticed that the after-hum of the piano strings made a satisfyingly ethereal sound. If she hadn't been on her best behaviour, she would've made a peace sign with her fingers and said, "Ooo, psych-a-*del*-ic!"

What Glynnis was going to get in trouble for was something she did not think was wrong.

She had been planning, for show-and-tell at school that day, to take the beefeater doll her mother had brought back from England that summer, to talk about the beefeaters and the Tower of London, and executions and the princes in the tower. But last evening, Camper Barbie had knocked the beefeater's head off playing kung fu fighting.

A glitch, headlessness, but a rectifiable one. All she needed was a paper clip to fish out the elastic inside the body and snap it over the hook that stuck out of the lower end of the head.

"Glynn-is!" Her mother called her to set the table.

She rummaged in the drawers of the desk she shared with Carol. Carol's drawers were neat and tidy: no paper clips. Glynnis' drawer was crammed to the top.

"I'm not asking you again," called her mother.

"I'm coming," Glynnis yelled.

Glynnis turned the drawer over on her bed and spread out the contents like Halloween candy. So many things she'd forgotten she had. A broken watch found in the park. One Labatt's IPA beer cap amid a whole box of Blue and Export caps. A set of Snoopy pencils. A crochet hook? She didn't know where it came from, but it would certainly do the trick.

Carol marched into the room. She had two walks — a bobbing, long-strided one when she was happy or she felt in charge, and a slouching shuffle when she felt sad or put-upon. Today it was the bob. "Mom says if you're not downstairs in less than a minute, your TV privileges are suspended for a week." She turned smartly on her heel and bobbed two steps, swinging her arms, before bobbing right onto the beefeater's head, smashing it into plastic shards.

Carol. "Clumsy Carol," as their father had taken to calling her lately. (Glynnis was "Glamorous Glennis," after the plane Chuck Yeager flew to break the sound barrier.) That week Carol had already broken a good china teacup, a lamp and the towel rack in the bathroom. Now it was the beefeater's head.

"I'm telling," Glynnis said.

"Go ahead. It's your fault for leaving it on the floor."

"Fine." Glynnis started for the door. "Mom!" She pitched her voice loud enough to sound like she meant it, but not loud enough for her mother to hear.

Carol caved in. "Don't! Please, Glynn? Pretty please? I'll ... I'll ... give you my allowance."

At dinner Mrs. Riggs asked if Glynnis was ready for show-and-tell.

"Of course," Glynnis said. She was annoyed at the tone in her mother's voice that implied she expected her not to be, and at the look that followed, implying she did not believe her when she said she was. Glynnis didn't have to rehearse everything the way Carol did. If she knew what she was talking about, she could make it up on the spot, which she did now.

"This is a beefeater doll." Glynnis held up the imaginary doll. "The beefeaters were guards at the Tower of London, which was a prison. They're called beefeaters because they ate beef when not everybody had enough money to eat it. The Tower of London is where Henry the Eighth's wives were kept before they were beheaded, about which there is a song that goes, 'With 'er 'ead tucked underneath 'er arm she walked the bloody Tower.' It's also where the Princes in the Tower were kept, who were heirs to the throne, but they were put there by Richard the Third, who was their uncle and who people think killed them."

"Well!" her mother said, beaming, "I *am* impressed."

There was not much to be impressed about, but Glynnis accepted the praise anyway. History was her brother's hobby, British history in particular. He could recite kings and queens for days. When they were younger they'd pretended he was Richard the Third and Carol and Glynnis the Princes. They had also pretended that he was Henry the Eighth and they were his wives. Glynnis had loved being the feisty Anne Boleyn laying her head on the chopping block. Dying could be just fine if you knew ahead of time you'd get to carry your head around in your hands and haunt people.

After dinner Glynnis wanted to put Camper Barbie's head on the beefeater, but it was Carol's and Carol wouldn't let her since it would involve cutting off Barbie's hair to make the beefeater hat fit over top of it. They tried stuffing her hair under the hat, but it wouldn't stay on, and it looked stupid with an elastic holding it in place.

And then it came to her, what she could take instead.

"Carol," Glynnis said to her class the next morning, pointing her sister out with a wave of outstretched palms like the ladies on *The Price Is Right* showing off a fridge, "is a genetic anomaly. She is an albino."

Glynnis liked these words. Anomaly. Albino. Albino she knew already. 'Anomaly' came from the talk their father had given them the week before, trying to convince Carol she was neither adopted nor a foundling. Their father's talk ran to red- and white-eyed fruit flies, and the girls did not entirely understand it. Glynnis wished that she were the albino. She wanted something that special to recommend her.

'Anomaly' was not in the *Random House Children's Dictionary*, which was the classroom's main reference work, so Glynnis had to explain it. Except now that she was put on the spot, with the whole class waiting and the teacher smiling at her, she was at a loss.

"It means ..." She couldn't say 'special.' Special was not quite it. She couldn't say 'weird' either, because Carol was sensitive.

"It means like ..." She knew what it meant. It was a scientific word, a scientific weirdness, which was not the same as regular weirdness. "... you know, like ..."

And then she had to wonder if she did know what it meant, since the test of knowing was being able to say, and she couldn't. She hated when this happened to her. How do you describe in *other* words what a word already says all by itself?

"An irregular occurrence?" suggested the teacher gently.

"Yeah," she said.

A snicker came from the back of the class, and she hurried on to explain what pigmentation was, and how Carol had none, which made her skin and eyes extremely sensitive; in fact, she was legally blind. The class was rapt again. Glynnis went on about how a lot of mammals had albinos — rabbits and rats and mice — and how albino pigs had no sense of smell because it was the pigment in their nasal receptors that made them work. This had also been part of their father's talk. "You won't find truffles with an albino pig," he'd chuckled.

Carol stood by with a small smile now, her eyes blinking behind the bulbous lenses of her pink plastic glasses. Being on the pudgy side, and having an air of squishiness about her, Carol resembled nothing so much as the Pillsbury Doughboy — albeit with bottle-bottom glasses. Their brother had been the first to notice the likeness, and Carol had been flattered enough that she had perfected the Doughboy's giggle. As her finale for the morning, Glynnis poked her sister's stomach, and out came that bashful titter. Carol was a hit.

But when Glynnis caught up with her on the way home that afternoon, Carol was crying. She cried a lot these days. Before Glynnis could even ask what was wrong, Carol swung her Loblaws bag at her.

"Everybody hates me, and it's all your fault," she said. Her lower lip looked extra-pink turned out like that, and her glasses started to fog up from her tears.

Glynnis got an ugly feeling in the pit of her stomach. "Is not," she said.

"Is too. Everybody knows you used me, and they all think it's terrible. You were just using me for your stupid baby show and tell."

"No, I wasn't."

"Yes, you were. Even my teacher thinks so, and she's going to phone Mom and tell her what you did."

She would, too. Mrs. Harris had hated Glynnis ever since she'd caught Glynnis pulling down Kevin Money's pants to prove he didn't wear underwear. Mrs. Harris had pegged Glynnis then and forever as a bully.

Carol and Glynnis had to go straight home to change before going to the church to set up for Brownies before everyone else arrived. Glynnis dragged her feet. Maybe Mrs. Harris had already phoned. But Mrs. Riggs was in brisk good spirits, and did not even scold them for being late.

"ROWENA, HONEY, are you all right? I heard a terrific noise coming up the stairs, it was like an elephant with hay fever, oh, good Lord, the piano? Well, what were you doing, pushing it all by yourself? At least no one was hurt. My luck I'd have been lying on top, singing 'Am I Blue,' I'd have toppled right off and spilt my martini." This was Mrs. MacDonald, the unlikely best friend of Glynnis' mother, and the mother of Glynnis' best friend, Sandy. Also the mother of Carol's former best friend, Alison, whom Mrs. MacDonald pushed forward now. "Alison? Don't you have something for Carol?"

Alison MacDonald had short, curly blond hair and a chipped front tooth from hitting the diving board at their cottage last year. The MacDonald kids were known for being bad. Sandy was the exception. One older brother had been arrested for possession of marijuana. Another had been sent to private school in an attempt to straighten him out. The oldest girl had run away from home at sixteen and lived with a man in his thirties for almost a year before she came home.

Glynnis missed Alison coming over to play with Carol. Alison always wanted to *do* stuff. "Let's go climb the willows and spit on people in the park," she'd say. Or, "Let's go to the ravine and pretend we're lost, and we have to live off the land." Glynnis and Carol were not supposed to go to the ravine at all, day or night. Alison had brought adventure into their lives.

Now Alison handed Carol an envelope without looking at her. "Here," she said. "It's an invitation to my sleepover."

"She forgot to give it to her at school today. What will you forget next? Your feet? Your teeth? Your fingernails?"

"Maw-awm." Alison shrugged her mother away from her.

"They're all attached," said Sandy, laughing. "She can't forget them."

Alison sighed impatiently.

"All right, all right, I'm going," said Mrs. MacDonald. "Good luck, Rowena. I don't know how you do it, all these girls. You're a saint."

"Pshaw," said Mrs. Riggs. She had a seemingly endless store of expressions nobody else used.

A pink look of pleasure had spread across Carol's face when Alison gave her the invitation, even though Alison had clearly not forgotten to give it to her, but was being forced to by her mother. Glynnis looked away.

That night, without being asked, Glynnis set the table, chopped the beans, washed the lettuce and pared the carrots. After dinner, she got right to work on her project on caves, down in the basement, thumbing the 1930 encyclopedia set they were allowed to cut things from. Stalactites hung from the ceiling, stalagmites came up from the ground. "That's the spirit," Mrs. Riggs said, meaning the Baden-Powell spirit.

By nine o'clock, up in the kitchen eating the snack she was allowed because Mrs. Riggs was in a good mood, Glynnis started to think she was home free, that her good deeds had paid a cosmic dividend, that Mrs. Harris had decided not to call after all. Precisely at that moment, the phone rang.

GLYNNIS WAS MARCHED straight upstairs to Mrs. Riggs' bathroom, where she was smacked five times with the back of a hairbrush. Then she was held in a vice grip on both shoulders facing her mother.

"You," Mrs. Riggs said, "are a deceitful little show-off."

Glynnis turned hot. Her palms sweated, her neck itched, her eyes stung as if she had gotten insect repellent in them.

"I'm embarrassed and ashamed. Now I want you to tell me what it is that you did wrong."

Like walking through a maze of prickle bushes blindfolded, this enforced confession. You edged up one avenue, hands out like a sleepwalker, wincing at the dead ends, sidestepping and trying again. You ended up saying things you didn't believe. Glynnis still did not feel she'd done anything particularly bad, but now she had to guess all of what her mother would think was bad about it, and tell her. And then her mother would think that she'd known all along it was bad, and that she was malicious as well as deceitful and selfish. She also had to look at her mother through all of this, look her in the eyes. That was what the hands were on the shoulders for, to keep her from turning away. But Glynnis found when she looked into her mother's eyes she could not say anything at all. She started to shake and cry. Her mother let go and waited for her to finish crying. "I can wait all night if I need to," she said.

"I should have told you … I … I … broke the beefeater's head."

"And?"

"I shouldn't have taken Carol to show-and-tell."

"Why?"

"I don't know."

"Yes, you do."

"Kevin Money took his sister."

"She was an infant, it will not affect her life. Now, why?"

"It's not my fault Carol has no friends."

"Glynnis Riggs, stop this right now and tell me the truth."

"But she …" Glynnis was still sniffling, and she felt a sob surge up her throat. She tightened her jaw muscles and narrowed her eyes, trying to keep it down, she tried to swallow it, but it was too big to swallow. It washed out of her like a wave.

"All right, then, if you can't control yourself, I'll leave you alone to think of your sister and what you've done to her. You can come downstairs when you're ready to tell me why it was wrong."

Her mother left, closing the door behind her. Glynnis felt the unfairness in her muscles, and the guilt in her glands, below her ears, behind her jaw. She sat on the floor and wrapped her arms around her knees.

Unfair: Carol hadn't minded at first. *Carol* broke the beefeater. Glynnis had not told on Carol. Carol should learn to be proud of being different. Carol *had* been proud, up there, doing the Pillsbury Doughboy. *Glynnis'* teacher never said anything about it. *Glynnis'* teacher never said it was mean, or that she was using Carol. She wrapped her knees tight, squeezed her feet together, and rocked forward and back.

Guilt: She shouldn't have been playing kung fu with the beefeater. Or Camper Barbie. She shouldn't have told her mother she was taking the beefeater when she wasn't. She'd lied. It made it hard to swallow.

She unfurled herself slowly and pulled at the fringes of the red oval bathmat, braiding them. Time passed, she had no idea how much. Her mother's voice outside the door said, "Glynnis, I'm waiting." Her wet innards were hardening like limestone into stalactites.

At Brownies her mother said to new girls who stared or giggled at Carol, *Carol is an ordinary girl like you. I won't have her stared at …* Glynnis could feel it starting to come, what she would say. When she could repeat it again and again in her head, she went downstairs.

Her mother sat at her desk over pattern books.

"I should not have taken Carol for show-and-tell because she is not a sideshow attraction, she is an ordinary girl like anybody else."

"And?"

"I shouldn't have lied."

"And?"

More. There was more.

"Did it make you feel important showing off your sister?"

"I shouldn't have used my sister to make myself feel important." Glynnis felt like she was going to cry again. She concentrated on her calcified innards.

"That's better. See? You did know, if only you thought about it. It's very important to me that when you are punished, you understand why you are being punished. It does no good to slap a child and not tell him why."

This had happened to Mrs. Riggs as a child, she'd often told Glynnis, slaps with no explanations, and she'd sworn she'd never do that to her own children. She took Glynnis' face in her hands, then chucked her on the nose with an index finger.

Carol was already in bed, listening to the CFTR Top Ten countdown on her clock radio. "Did you tell her I broke it?" she asked.

Glynnis got into her pajamas without looking at her sister. "What do you think?"

"She's going to kill me."

"I told her I did it."

"You did?"

"'Course I did." Glynnis went to brush her teeth.

"Thank you, thank you, thank you," said Carol.

When Glynnis got back from the bathroom, Carol was up on the bed singing, "You put the lime in the coconut and shake it all up." They had done this every night for a week, danced to this song on their beds, jumping back and forth. Glynnis got into bed. Carol jumped over to it. "You put the lime in the coconut and call de doctor," she shouted. Glynnis answered by turning to the wall.

"Carol, in bed, right now," their mother said, coming in to kiss them goodnight. A car door slammed in the driveway. Their father was home, and would be wanting their mother's company at dinner. She turned the radio off and gave Carol a kiss. She had to pull back the blankets from over Glynnis' head to kiss her, and Glynnis pulled them back up again right away. Mrs. Riggs turned out the big light, leaving them with the bedside light.

"Hello, hello, hello," called their father. "Nobody interested in greeting the old man?"

"Hi, Dad," Carol yelled. "Hi, Dad," said their brother from his desk. Glynnis said nothing.

"Glynnis?" Carol said finally, "Aren't you going to read?" Carol was not allowed to read at night. It was too hard on her eyes. They were in the middle of *My Friend Flicka*.

"No."

"Please?"

"No."

Carol begged. Glynnis was resolute. Finally Carol turned off her light. Glynnis could hear her sniffling in the dark.

"I hate you," she said.

"I hate you more," said Glynnis.

"Do not."

"Do too." It always made them laugh in the end, Do not, Do too, they couldn't help it. It was so stupid, and besides, somebody always got mixed up eventually and said the wrong one, so the other could say "Aha! See? I was right, you just said 'Do too.'" By then they would almost have forgotten what it was they were arguing about.

MRS. RIGGS FAVOURED sensible gifts for girls. Not Barbie dolls (the ones Carol had were gifts from their Aunt Helen), not anything advertised on TV, not boy-gifts like trucks or Tonka toys or hot wheels, but craft kits or skipping ropes or Doris Day records. Today, for Alison, Carol had a make-your-own model birchbark canoe kit, and Glynnis had a Girl Guide whistle.

Strictly speaking, Glynnis had been invited as a companion for Sandy, not as a guest of Alison's, but Mrs. Riggs had thought it polite for her to take a gift also. There had been some doubt, given that Glynnis was still in disgrace from the show-and-tell incident, that she would be allowed to go at all, but Mrs. Riggs had at last given her assent.

The MacDonalds' house, just one street over, was much like their own, a large, sturdy brick square set down in a comfortable margin of green. It felt strange to go to the front door, glossy green and formal, with its stone porch. The side door, scratched up and ordinary, was the proper entrance, where they could chuck their boots and coats down the stair to the right before coming in. The MacDonalds' house was brighter and messier than their own, and it was easy to be there.

They played games in the garden and ate hot dogs and cake. Carol dropped the egg off her spoon more than anybody else, and even Alison couldn't make up for it. Glynnis' team won, and in the next race she found herself on Alison's team. Carol cried three times and was cheered up twice by Mrs. MacDonald and once by Sandy before it came time for the presents. Alison tossed aside the kit with barely a glance. The whistle merited a couple of exploratory blasts before it, too, was set aside. She got two pairs of toe socks, a Frisbee and an Elton John album. They played more games, and then they got into their pajamas and brushed their teeth.

Glynnis and Sandy were supposed to sleep in the den and let the others have the run of Alison and Sandy's room, but they snuck upstairs because Alison was planning a séance. More specifically, a levitation. They planned to levitate Carol. She was the heaviest, and the difference between her regular state and her levitated state would, therefore, be the more marked.

How levitation worked was this: the girls arranged themselves around Carol's body as she lay on the floor on her back, Alison at her head. The lights had to be low or off. Each of the girls would put two fingers of each hand under the portion of Carol's body that was in front of them. "Ready? One, two, three, lift," Alison said. The girls strained and heaved and could hardly lift Carol off the ground.

"She is dead," Alison began, and the next girl intoned the phrase in turn, "She is dead," then the next, all the way around the circle. *She is dead. She is dead. She is dead.*

"Clouds come close to the earth," said Alison. *Clouds come close to the earth. Clouds come close to the earth.*

"Spirits, seeking their own." *Spirits, seeking their own.*

"The fog swirls round her head." *The fog. The fog. The fog.*

"The fog *is* her head." *The fog is. The fog is. The fog is.*

"The fog is her body." *Her body. Her body.*

"She is lost to the mist." *Lost to the mist.*

Morning dawns. The mist rises. The fog lifts. The new day begins.

"She is light as a feather, now RISE!"

And they lifted her as easily as a cardboard box. They got to their feet and lifted her higher, above their heads. Seventy-five pounds above their heads, like it was nothing. Carol giggled, and suddenly she became heavy again. Glynnis thought she saw Alison and her new best friend, Bridget, pull their hands away altogether before Carol crashed to the floor, but she wasn't sure.

"You dropped her," Sandy said.

"She laughed. You break the spell when you laugh," said Alison.

"She's dead. Dead people don't laugh," Bridget said.

"I felt like I was dead," Carol said. "It was weird, it was like …"

But Alison and Bridget and the others ignored her. "You guys know the ghost of the bloody fingers?" asked Alison.

"Tell it! Tell it!" the others said.

"Everybody knows that one," Carol said.

"Did you hear anything?" Bridget asked. "I thought I just heard the body say something."

"How could it?" Alison asked. "It's dead."

"She's dead," Glynnis said, her skin quivering with suppressed laughter.

She's dead. She's dead. She's dead, the others repeated.

"You guys," Carol said.

"Do you think it'll start to smell?" Bridget asked.

"You know, you're right, it probably will." Alison sniffed the air. She was so good at being serious it was funny. Glynnis laughed harder.

"I think it's starting to already," said someone else.

"It is, it *is*."

"We'll have to bury it tomorrow."

"Come on, you guys."

"Why not tonight?"

"You know, that's a good question. Why *not* tonight?"

Glynnis was splitting her side. Even her own laughter seemed funny to her. She didn't know if she'd ever stop. It was starting to hurt. Sandy poked her.

"It's not funny anymore," she said.

"Poor Carol."

"Poor Carol."

"She had her whole life ahead of her."

"Not a very promising life, but still."

"I didn't really like her, did you?"

"Of course not, but it's sad anyway."

"You guys, I'm alive." She jumped up and down and waved in front of Alison's face. "See? I'm alive."

Glynnis stopped laughing. She had no pride, Carol, it was embarrassing.

"So sad."

"Leave her alone," Sandy said to Alison.

How weak Carol was here, how easy to hurt. At home it had always gone the other way — Jay hurt Carol hurt Glynnis, never the other way around, at least not in any lasting way. But here it had turned around for a night, and Glynnis had loved it.

All night Glynnis had been having the time of her life while Carol had the misery of hers, and that had made Glynnis' night even better. Alison *liked* her, Alison wanted *her* on her team, Alison wanted to make *her* laugh. Alison despised Carol, she could see that, too, and it had made her happy. It had made her giddy until now, when Sandy tried to stop it, and she knew her friend was right.

"Yeah. Leave her alone," Glynnis said.

"Leave her alone? Of course we'll leave her alone. She's dead."

"You know what I mean. Come on, Carol, sleep downstairs with us."

"I don't need *you*," Carol said with total condescension. As long as no one came to Carol's defence, she could pretend the rest of them were teasing her the way they'd tease any of their number. Now that someone had — someone younger, someone's *little sister* — she couldn't pretend anymore.

"Isn't it past your bedtime?" she went on. "Little kids need their sleep."

There was an awkward pause, then Alison said, "Good night, John-boy," sealing their fate. They went downstairs.

"CAROL IS A FART," wrote Glynnis on Sandy's back with her finger. "ALISON IS A POO BALL," Sandy wrote back, but Glynnis didn't believe that for a minute.

⌐

NOBODY WANTED TO be a Fairy. Fairies were gay, like cat's-eye glasses, pointy sneakers and flowered wicker bicycle baskets. (Carol had one on her girl's bike, a white basket with pink and purple flowers on it. Alison had a banana bike with a metal basket. Glynnis didn't have a bike.)

This was how Brownies was divided up, into sixes: Fairies, Pixies, Elves, Gnomes and Sprites. Each six had a little song they had to sing at the beginning of each meeting, holding hands and skipping in a circle. The Sprites' went, "Here we come, the sprightly Sprites, brave and helpful like the knights." And the Gnomes: "Who are we? The laughing Gnomes, helping others in our homes." Elves helped others, not themselves, and so on.

Some people had to be Fairies, that was just the way things were, and since you had no choice in the matter, you could not really be held accountable. Unless you were gay to begin with, being a Fairy wouldn't count against you. You had to make a show of not wanting to be a Fairy anyway, of which Glynnis did a passable job, though she actually wanted nothing more. Alison MacDonald was a Fairy.

Her mother read out the names. Sandy was made an Elf. Another friend was made a Pixie. This boded well. Her mother would not put her in the same group as friends she saw every day, thinking it important to expose her to a wider range of people. She didn't know anyone in the Fairies except for Alison, and this boded well, too.

"Glynnis Riggs?" her mother read out. It sounded funny, the whole name, because she usually only said it that way when Glynnis was in trouble. "Fairies."

Glynnis slouched over to join the Fairies, feigning disappointment, but feeling, in fact, gay. "Oo-oo," she said when she got there, "I'm a Fairy." She flopped her wrist for effect. Mrs. Riggs looked up from her list, her sharp blue eyes especially piercing between the black of her reading glasses and the dark brown of her thick eyebrows. Alison laughed behind her hand.

When it came their turn to sing, Alison and Glynnis skipped up a storm. "We're the Fairies, glad and GAY," they sang, swinging their arms high, "Helping others every day."

It became a thing, acting gay.

"Yoo-hoo," Alison took to saying. "Fairies over here." And Glynnis would skip over, "What is it, darling, what is it?" They acted like a combination of Alison's mother and Felix Unger on *The Odd Couple*.

Mrs. Riggs did not catch on for several weeks, but when she did, she gave them a talking to. "Gay is a perfectly good word," she started. "And Fairies are older than the hills." It seemed to pain her that Glynnis found being a Fairy laughable.

She explained that 'Brownies' itself was another word for Fairies, that every country had a traditional belief in them, the Irish had 'the little people,' the English had 'the Brownies' and so on. "Brownies," this time she meant the institution, "leads you into the world of imagination. Or it would, if you would let it." This did not strike Glynnis as being true. Brownies was about knots and semaphore, Morse code and first aid, sewing and knitting and being good as gold. Imagination, she and Alison had. Brownies had a round mirror, flagstone-shaped construction paper and cardboard mushrooms. Brownies had props. It did not have imagination.

Mrs. Riggs grew more severe as she ended her talk. "I don't think you realize how you look when you prance around like that. You look ridiculous. You sound ridiculous. You are ridiculous. Every *bit* as ridiculous as the people you are mimicking. Homosexuals are sick, sick people, they are *not* funny, and neither are you," she said.

Homosexuals? thought Glynnis.

"Glad she's not my mother," Alison said after she'd walked away, and Glynnis got an itchy feeling in her throat, as if she might cry. She did not want to cry, and this turned the itch into a fury that she felt on her skin of her arms and neck like a sunburn, tight and hot. She wanted to hit her mother, to whack her sturdy panty-hosed calves with a hairbrush.

"Yoo-hoo, Fai-ries," Carol called out to them, because of course now that Alison and Glynnis did it, everyone did. Mrs. Riggs was too late — the tradition had caught fire, and would not be easily stamped out. "Come and practise semaphore with the Pixies."

"Shut up, Carol." Glynnis and Alison said it exactly together.

That night in bed, Carol said to Glynnis, "She'll get bored of you next week, you know. She does this to everyone."

Glynnis didn't say anything because she knew it might be true.

⮌

THE CUB SCOUTS THAT RAN at the same time as Mrs. Riggs' Brownies were led by one of the younger fathers in the neighbourhood and his bachelor brother. They were lax, these two, and didn't care much what the boys knew so long as they could light a fire, tie a couple of knots, play hard and not be sucks. Cubs consisted, as far as the Brownies could see, of making an astonishing amount of noise while playing floor hockey. Glynnis and Alison were not the only ones who would have preferred to be Cubs. Mrs. Riggs had an ongoing battle with Brian and Dover Smith. More than once she'd left the Brownies in the large, fluttery hands of her young assistant, Tawny Owl, to bawl them out.

One week the Cubs threw beanbags at Brownies from behind the stage curtain. As soon as Mrs. Riggs' neat brown figure huffed out of the room — Glynnis noticed she walked a little like Carol did when she was happy, that bob — Glynnis leaned over to Alison and asked if she wanted to go play foozeball.

"Foozeball?" Alison asked. "What's that?"

"You don't know what foozeball is? Come on." And she took her to the games room in the Odd Spot. No teens were around. There rarely were.

"Oh, this game," Alison said. "I didn't know what it was called. I've always called it Soccer Guys on Sticks." She spun the defence line like an expert.

It was 7-4 for Alison when Tawny Owl found them. "Here they are," she sang. "Boy, are you two ever in trouble. We've been looking all over for you. Didn't you think we'd miss you? Come on. Boop-boop!" Boop-boop meant hurry up. It was an expression she'd picked up from Brown Owl.

The fifth whack of the hairbrush that night stung as much as ever, but the confession was easier to come up with. "I shouldn't have snuck out of the Brownie room to play foozeball because nobody knew where we were, and everyone was worried about us." It still made her want to turn away when her mother took her by the shoulders. What she was looking for was contrition, which Glynnis wasn't sure she felt. Ruefulness she felt, and dread, and a very small feeling, a comma in the middle of her stomach that might be contrition. She looked her mother in the eyes, and the comma, the sense of having done something wrong, grew bigger, though in her head she was still thinking it was *their* fault for being worried when there was no need to be. She and Alison were fine. Of course they were. What was there to worry about? And why did they always say, We're not angry, we were *worried*, when it was clear they were angry? But the comma swelled to the size of her chest, and she clenched her jaw not to cry. Her mother let her go.

Carol had been listening to her parents downstairs. "Alison's a bad influence on you," she said when she came to bed, "you shouldn't be allowed to see her. You're too easily led."

"I'm the one who said we should go play foozeball."

"You only did that to impress her."

"Did not."

"Did too."

"Did not."

"Did too." There was a giggle in Carol's voice, as if she was hoping Glynnis would start to laugh soon.

"Go stuff it, Carol," Glynnis said.

Carol jumped out of her bed and onto Glynnis'. Glynnis tried to kick her away, but Carol grabbed her feet and sat on them. Then she worked her way up so she was sitting on Glynnis' stomach, pinning her hands above her head while Glynnis struggled. She let a piece of drool hang over Glynnis' face, then sucked it back up. "Say you're Alison MacDonald's little monkey."

"You're Alison MacDonald's little monkey," Glynnis said.

Carol gripped her wrists tighter and drooled again. She sucked it up. "Say it."

Glynnis stopped struggling for a second before gathering all her strength into her hips. She bucked Carol off her, head first into the wall. Carol started crying and kicking in a pink-faced fury, until their father flung the door open and roared at them to stop that racket.

They didn't read that night, either. The next day Carol taped a line down the middle of the room, just like she'd seen on *The Brady Bunch*.

⌣⌐

THE RIGGSES AND the MacDonalds had a party in common to go to on Friday night. Alison and Sandy's older sister, Mary, made popcorn and let the four of them watch *The Wizard of Oz* while she and her best friend smoked hand-rolled cigarettes in the backyard.

Alison and Sandy had seen the movie before, though Sandy only remembered the wicked witch and the flying monkeys and kept covering her eyes when the woods grew dark and scary. Carol was scared, too. Every time Sandy drew her legs up on the couch, Carol did the same. They watched through their fingers. Alison and Glynnis remained scornful, though it was a stretch for Glynnis during the scene with the poppy fields doping the adventurers into sleep. She didn't like the thought of plants exerting that much power over a person, of being in thrall to something that strong, of sleeping when you desperately needed to be awake. But Glynnis didn't let on and Carol and Sandy did.

During the commercials Alison pretended to be the Wicked Witch of the West and Glynnis her evil flying monkey minion.

"Quit it, you guys," Sandy kept saying, "I mean it." She appealed to Glynnis specifically. "Come on, Glynn."

"Eeee-eee," Glynnis replied, swooping down on her from the top of the couch, until Sandy finally said she didn't like Glynnis anymore and she thought she should go home.

"You can't send her home," Alison said.

"She's my friend and I can send her home."

"Okay, so now she's my friend, and I can invite her back."

"What's going on down there?" Mary called from the top of the stairs, without really seeming to care. "You're both staying till your parents come to get you."

Later, when Glynnis' parents were saying goodbye to the MacDonalds in the front hall (which took forever, as always), Alison said to Glynnis, "Too bad you're not your sister's age. Then you could really be my friend." Carol heard this and went outside. Glynnis found herself smiling at Alison, then felt terrible and hurried out to sit on the steps with her sister. She wanted Carol to say something or punch her arm, but Carol hugged her knees against the chill and was quiet.

Monday and Tuesday at school, Sandy wouldn't talk to Glynnis or play with her at recess, and neither would their other friends. Sandy had got to them first. Alison, of course, rarely did more than say hi at school. Glynnis had never expected anything different.

On Monday, Glynnis played on the monkey bars with the boys. She noticed Carol by the tree-well at the girls' end playing with a girl from Brownies with cat-eye glasses. Last fall Carol had been part of a group that skipped every day at recess. This year it was just her and the other girl, playing their little games. It was sad, and in a way it wasn't fair.

Of course, in another way it was totally fair. Carol was a suck, and a liar, and a cheater. She was all these things because she needed to be. She couldn't win fairly, so she cheated. She was clumsy and awkward, so she lied. She was an albino with bad vision and sensitive skin and chubby legs, so she was a suck.

She *was* ordinary. And because she was ordinary, she didn't know how to milk her difference. For a minute, in the classroom, seeing her do her Pillsbury Doughboy, Glynnis had thought Carol had got it, had understood the way out. She hadn't. She probably never would. She was doomed.

Glynnis thought maybe she should play with Carol and the girl with the glasses, whose name, she found out yesterday, was Daintry.

"Hey, what're you doing?" she asked.

Carol blinked suspiciously and didn't answer, but Daintry said they were playing house, did she want to play?

"House?" asked Glynnis. She noticed Alison MacDonald and Bridget swinging themselves under the chain-link fence back into the schoolyard not twenty feet from where she was. "House?" she asked again louder. "Are you kidding?" She walked over to the monkey bars.

Later that afternoon at Brownies, the Cubs shot spitballs at them from the dumbwaiter. Mrs. Riggs bobbed out again, not before whispering some sort of admonishment to Tawny Owl.

"All right, everybody," Tawny Owl said, clapping her hands. "Let's ..." No one paid attention to her. Two girls at the piano — now propped up on bricks at the broken end — showed another how to play a simple one-finger duet.

Another group was over at the window, misting up the cold October panes with their breath so they could draw happy faces and make impressions of feet with the heel of their fist. Others were playing jacks, some were tying knots, some were even practising semaphore.

"Let's what?" said Daintry.

"Let's you and I play Paper, Scissors, Rock," Tawny Owl said.

Alison started a game of frozen tag. No one would unfreeze Carol. She was still frozen when the game petered out, and Alison and Glynnis jumped from behind her, pretending to be Flying Monkeys.

She shrieked and ran behind the piano, and then she tried to be a Flying Monkey herself. Alison promptly became the Wicked Witch, and chastised her for not bringing back Dorothy. She pointed at Sandy. "There she is! Get her!"

"I'm not Dorothy," said Sandy. "I'm Toto."

"And your little dog, too," said Alison, bearing down on Sandy, who ran away barking.

"There's Dorothy," Carol shouted, going after Glynnis.

"I'm not Dorothy," Glynnis said. "I'm somebody else."

"You are too Dorothy," Carol said. It was not playful, Carol's voice.

"Am not." She ran up to the piano and slid underneath it so her legs stuck out the front.

"Hey, Alison," she yelled. "Hey, Alison, who am I?"

Carol ran after her. "You're Dorothy, and I'm taking you to the Wicked Witch of the West." Carol tried to drag Glynnis out by her shoulders.

"No, I'm not." Glynnis hooked her feet on the front of the piano so Carol couldn't pull her out. She felt the piano shift a few millimetres on the bricks. Carol's knees were behind Glynnis' head while she tugged. Glynnis pulled her head forward, then bashed it back against Carol's knees. Carol yelped and jumped away. "Alison!" Glynnis slid back under the piano and called again. "Alison! Who am I?"

"I don't know, who are you?" Alison asked.

"The Wicked Witch of the East. Get it? The Wicked Witch of the East."

Alison laughed. Glynnis could hear her on the other side of the piano. She started to laugh, too. She was just pulling herself out from under when a chubby brown leg swung past her.

"No you're not, you're Dorothy because I say so!" Glynnis had never heard Carol's voice like that. It sounded broken, like a dream she'd once had about a Chatty Cathy doll that went mad. She watched her sister's foot kick the bricks.

Rowena

ROWENA SPOTTED THEM, the boys crouched in their box chewing wee wads of paper, phwooting them through straws. Eight year-olds playing in a dumbwaiter: an accident waiting to happen. The Smith brothers should be shot.

Quick word with the shrinking violet. Blithely ignore finger-pointing Pixie. Nip downstairs, catch the little beggars in the act.

"Oooowop, ooowop," went a boy's voice like a submarine siren as she pushed open the kitchen hallway's swinging doors. Sentry. How fully children participated in their escapades — it was a serious adventure indeed that needed a sentry.

"Brown cow alert," the voice added.

But gosh, there was something wrong with children these days. Honestly. The *cynicism*. Glynnis seemed to want to be a teenager. At seven. She looked up too much to Jay.

In the kitchen, two boys hurriedly lowered the dumbwaiter, while the sentry stood in front, arms at four and eight o'clock as if he could shield them, but he had no choice but to give way before Rowena. "I'll take over, thank you very much," she said, reaching for the ropes.

The boys tugged on the rope to lock it into place before backing off. "Hey," came a shout from the dumbwaiter, accompanied by banging on the bottom of the platform and threats to break the legs of the boys below if they left them hanging. "Leave us here and you're dead, Bialystock. D-e-d dead."

Rowena lowered, mad chatter from the box stopping before the door was even open, boys appropriately dumbstruck to open the door to Brown Owl's face instead of their friends'. With a grim sense of satisfaction, she led the bunch of them into the gym, where the rest of the Cub pack gathered around Brian Smith as he and his brother demonstrated wrestling moves. No, that was being generous. They were just wrestling, the boys just watching.

In the past, Rowena had been careful to call the Smiths out into the hall to give them a piece of her mind. Children should not see their leaders called to task. Now she didn't see any reason to stand on principle.

"I'll thank you, sirs, to keep your boys in this room. They do not have the run of the church. If you cannot control them, I will ensure you lose the privilege of this hall."

Brian Smith had the decency to hop up and look embarrassed. Dover just sat up on the mat. "Wo," he said. "Brown Owl, Brown Owl. Take it easy ..."

"I will not take it easy, this is your last warning. How many boys have to go missing before you even notice? Your whole pack could fall down the sewer. I have five boys here, five boys, gone at least ten minutes, and here the two of you are, wrestling each other like children yourselves. They could have garroted themselves. They could have run into traffic. They could have had eight seizures."

"Yeah, but they haven't, have they?" Dover Smith said.

Gah. "They were playing in the dumbwaiter. They could have killed themselves. People entrusted with the care of other people's children should not let them play in dumbwaiters. You are not fit to run a bath, let alone a —"

But she was interrupted by a crash — brief — and a howl — long and high, just on the edge of being human. A speared animal. They ran. Brian Smith, Rowena, Dover Smith, bursting open the first set of swinging doors like a floodgate at a dam, then the second set, cubs streaming behind them. Rowena's reading glasses, on a strap around her neck, hit each shoulder in turn. The howl became discernibly human, a child's wail, then after a sucking in of breath went animal again. *Not Carol, not Carol, please God, not Carol,* her heart went, at the same time that she offered up a fierce prayer that it not be anyone else's child, either. How idiotic. How hubristic. *People entrusted with the care of other people's children ...* And she addressed God again. *Please, no. Please, no.*

She followed Brian through the final set of doors and saw a prone figure lying by the piano inside a ring of Brownies. Thank God. Not Carol.

They ran to the figure's side. And not anyone else's child.

Both her prayers had been answered.

She felt faint. She saw the scene as if she had suddenly retreated through a culvert. Sounds were hollow and echoey. At the other end, close, but far away, Lyddie, who knelt at Glynnis' head, turned back from where she'd twisted in order to throw up, wiping her mouth. Brian Smith, at Glynnis' left shoulder, asked Glynnis her name. Dover Smith, at Glynnis' left knee, said, "Holy shit, what the hell happened," while his brother said, "Dove," and shook his head and told Glynnis it would be all right. "Mitchell," he called to a Cub, though Alison MacDonald was standing right there, "call 911." Why not send a Brownie, who knew what had happened?

And then she whooshed back through the culvert and was in the scene with the rest of them.

"Alison. Go with him."

Rowena discovered she was gripping Glynnis' hand, that a stream of comfort was issuing from her lips and had been all along. "That's right, Glynnie, you'll be all right, Glynnie, that's right, my Glynn, we're here, we'll take care of you, that's right, shh, it's okay, it's okay, it's all right."

It was not, however, all right. It was not all right at all. The lower part of Glynnis' left leg was visibly *flattened,* the sole of her shoe flat on the floor, foot limp and lifeless. Sock and skin had shredded away on her ankle-top, revealing glimpses of bone white as new baby teeth, tendon like a dead chicken's, ripped from bone. All up the shin, bits of tibia shone through the shredded sock, literally, bits. Incongruously, the elastic that held up Glynnis' knee sock was intact.

Lyddie sputtered something about her head only being turned for a minute and who'd have thought the piano and oh dear with a hand over her mouth and we did pull her out. This made Rowena aware of the rest of the girls

"Daintry," she said to the first girl her eyes lit on. "Fetch the first aid kit. Quickly."

But someone else was bringing it already, handing it to Brian Smith, who was acting like he was in charge.

"A coat for her head," Rowena said.

"And one to cover her," said Brian. "She's —"

Annoyance shot through Rowena. "In shock," she said at the same time he did.

"We need to elevate that limb."

"Tourniquet?" said Dover to Brian.

Brian whipped off his Scout's scarf and reefed it just below the knee, above Glynnis' wound. He eyed the wound. "What do you think? Tensor bandage?"

"I can't see wrapping a tensor bandage around *that,* can you?" said Dover. Rowena had to resist an urge to break his nose with her elbow.

"It's okay, Glynnie, yes, it's all right, you'll be fine, now, everything will be fine, you're a brave, strong girl."

"Here," Mrs. Riggs said to a group of girls. Sandy stepped forward with large eyes. "You take my place. Reassure her." She shifted, reaching into the first aid kit and ripping open the big packages of gauze bandages, dropping each one, when open, neatly in a row on top of Glynnis' wound. Then she shook out a triangular bandage, folding it in half.

"What are you doing?" asked one of the Smiths.

She explained herself. Lay the pads on the shin. On top of that, a triangular bandage folded into an oblong. Then on top of that a bandage pressed tight to the sides of the leg.

To lift the leg, they could slide a third bandage under the knee and worm it down beneath the entire lower leg, then bring it up around the top bandage at the same time as they lifted.

"Brilliant," said Brian, getting to work on the underneath bandage. He was quick and deft, and suddenly she was grateful to him. All the same, Glynnis began howling again. Sandy's voice rose. She was doing perfectly. Rowena must remember to praise her later.

Plasma had grabbed ahold of the gauze pads and fixed them in place, blobs of blood blooming through the white. Dover Smith laid on the next row. When it came to pressing the bandage tight to the sides, Dover sucked in his breath and said he didn't know if he could do it, and Rowena's hatred of him dissipated. She pressed the bandage into the knee side of the injured part, and he pressed it into the sides of the ankle side, while his brother drew the sides of his underneath bandage up around theirs. He lifted, and another coat — Rowena's, she'd insisted — was placed underneath the crushed leg. Brian continued to hold the bandage. He could keep the best tension that way. Dover released the tourniquet.

They heard sirens. They had done all they could do.

The other girls must go home, Rowena realized. They must be cared for, their parents must be called. Shock might take hold of them, too. Three huddled together, fists up over their mouths. Another two held hands, crying. What they had seen was the worst injury most of them were likely to see in their lives. Sandy sat by Glynnis' waist, facing her head, holding her hand and saying, "It's going to be okay," over and over again.

Still, something was undone, something needed doing. Ambulance called. Lyddie gathering the girls together and taking them downstairs to call their mothers. Brian at Glynnis' head, Sandy on one side, she herself on the other, Alison standing behind. Ambulance siren nearing.

Suddenly she looked around. "Where's Carol?"

⌣

How did this happen? Rowena thought in the ambulance. *How did this happen?* She did not go on to the next thought, but let this one replay. *How did this happen?*

In her stomach was a sickish lump that was the answer. The answer was no use to her. The answer was knotty, the answer was mundane. The answer was a thick, clotted bolus in a stew of digestive juices. In the answer was the bottom dropped out of her world, in the answer was raw terror. She clung instead to wonder, to disbelief. *How did this happen?*

The technical details were not what she meant, how the piano fell, how Carol was involved (where was she now?), why Glynnis' leg was under there in the first place, how it could possibly even fit beneath the low-lying upright. Her question was much larger. *How did this happen? How does anything happen? How* this? *How?*

Glynnis looked a twig on the big adult stretcher. Her eyes were closed now, but behind the lids they darted. Two vertical lines kept vigil between her eyebrows. Poking out from the wrap of blankets, her hand gripped Rowena's as the ambulance wailed and roared across the streets and down the broad, damp avenues.

How did this happen? To a child? Meantime her mouth never ceased its string of words. "That's my brave Glynnie, yes, yes, that's it, Glynnie, breathe now, be a strong girl, that's it, Glynnie. What an adventure, we're going through all the red lights. Not much farther now. That's it, Glynnie."

They pulled up at Emergency. Rowena went to let go of Glynnis' hand as they unloaded the gurney. Glynnis wailed, "Noooo," and clutched at Rowena's arm.

"Take her hand, Mum," the ambulance attendant said, but Rowena already had. The need in Glynnis was like nothing she'd felt before, not even the need of her babies as newborns. It was a gift. It was everything.

"I won't let you go," she said, feeling it as a promise. "No, I won't. I've got you. I'm right here. I've got you."

They saw a doctor right away, a man so lean his cheeks had seams. The surgeon had been paged, he said. The nurses — one moved in as he said it, beginning to undo the first aid — would set up a drip.

"So she will need surgery."

"Oh, she'll certainly need surgery." He gestured for Rowena to follow him to the area beyond the curtain edge. She understood him to mean he wanted to talk out of Glynnis' range of hearing, but she could not let go of Glynnis' hand. A promise was a promise. In front of a doctor, this felt like weakness — Glynnis would be all right — but Rowena honoured her promises.

"She doesn't like to let go of me," Rowena said apologetically.

The doctor cocked his head, then came forward and spoke to Rowena in a low voice.

With a crushing injury like this, the doctor said, the limb might or might not be salvageable. It depended on the amount of vascular damage. If the blood vessels were badly damaged, Glynnis would not be able to get enough blood to the foot to keep it free of infection, and it would have to be amputated. The surgeon would be better able to tell when he did his exam whether this was the case for Glynnis or not.

"It all depends on the vascular damage, as I say. We'll have to cross our fingers and wait." He assured her that Dr. Fisher was the best there was and if anyone could save the limb it was he. The grammatical correctness — "it is he" — seemed to hang in the air like something that could fall, a ceiling or a guillotine blade.

The doctor went on to other patients and Rowena sat there numbly. One girl hurt, the other missing. She needed to phone Jay. She needed to phone Glenn. She needed to phone June MacDonald. She needed to know where Carol was. She needed to do something, not just sit. But here was Glynnis' hand. Here was her pact.

She kept still. Her mind raced.

Carol blindly running from whatever she'd done or thought she had done — for she must have done something or thought she had — or she would not have run. Carol darting across Bayview, car horns blaring, lights veering as they banked away from a ghostly little figure in brown in the headlights. Carol running through the woods, down the hill, snot coming out her nose, tears blinding her. Carol tripping on a stick, falling face down on a mat of slick leaves.

But how silly, how melodramatic. Carol was not so adventuresome. Her hiding places were not inventive. She'd be somewhere in the church or somewhere at home, easy to find. In fact, she was probably found by now.

Again the yawning feeling of something dropping out beneath her feet came on Rowena. She could not keep her children safe. She was a mother who could not keep her children safe. She was a mother who had let things go horribly wrong. Perhaps she had handled Carol wrongly from the very beginning. Perhaps she had handled sibling relations wrongly. It did not seem possible, even now. But it was possible. Look what had happened.

Suddenly she realized the assumption she'd been operating on: Carol had run because she was somehow responsible for the piano shifting; Carol's responsibility had been a result of the two of them continuing their fighting of the last couple of months. What if the assumption weren't true? What if the piano shifting had been an accident, plain and simple, nothing to do with the sisters' relations at all? What kind of a mother was she to assume the worst of her poor children?

After the wash of guilt came a creeping of shame. Oh! Think of herself with the Smith brothers! *You are not fit to run a bath!* Who was not fit to run a bath? What was an accident waiting to happen? The dumbwaiter was in perfect working order. The boys playing in it were safe as houses. But the piano! The piano! She had let the piano sit there, unrepaired, propped, merely, on two rotting red bricks.

What a cruel irony. She vigilant and careful, proud of her vigilance and care (oh, now she knew the meaning of hubris!), the Smiths lax and carefree, no, care*less*, care*less*, they *were*, she was not wrong about that, or maybe she was, perhaps she was wrong about everything, perhaps she was utterly wrong about how to live, only if she was, how was she to do anything differently, how to change, how to learn a new way to live, and what new way might that be, where and how might she find it?

The shame reached her cheeks. How proud she'd been. How certain that she could handle any emergency, how assured of her own superior competence. But when it had come down to it, she'd felt faint. She'd felt as if she might lose consciousness, she'd retreated through that culvert. She'd been idle, incompetent, not up to the task, out of it, while two nincompoops put her to shame.

She recognized now, with a deeper, horror-stricken shame, that she had only come out of her culvert because of her prideful need to prove herself, herself and her girls, her Brownies. She had only come out because she had to compete. She had to prove girls can do things, and do things as well as, if not better than, boys.

Another part of her retained this pride. She might have felt faint, but it had only been for an instant, and then she was back, then she performed beautifully. The nincompoops respected her in the end as they ought to have from the beginning. Once they did, they stopped being nincompoops and became part of her team, flawed members of her team, with redeeming qualities, such as calm and a knowledge of first aid.

What would she tell Glenn? One daughter about to lose a leg, possibly, the other missing.

What kind of mother let that happen?

And she thought of her two prayers as she'd run up the stairs. *Please God, let it not be Carol. Please, God, let it not be someone else's child.* Combined, it was as if she had prayed for Glynnis' injury. And now Glynnis clung to her hand as if to a saviour, a cliff edge, a life buoy. Rowena would not let go until she had to.

IN THE SAME WAY, though less rationally, Rowena did not want to let go of the telephone later, so she rested her left hand on the receiver as she had between each call when drawing a new dime from the row she'd laid out. Could she call anyone else, simply to be able to keep her hand attached to something concrete? No. She had reached Glenn. She had spoken to Jay, she had spoken to June. Carol was safe. Beryl would go to the house in the morning.

Her wait might be three hours or it might be six or more, said the surgeon. They were going to try to save the leg. He thought they had a sporting chance. Nothing like young bones for growing and healing, he said. He described the plates and screws and pins that they would use to try to piece the bones back together so that they could begin to knit. There would be later operations to take the hardware out. Several more to graft skin onto the wound, as it was too damaged to regrow on its own.

Rowena was not aware of how frightened she had been at the prospect of Glynnis becoming an amputee until the surgeon spoke of what measures they would take to spare her, which she nodded to, nodded to, everything he said, the long and labour-intensive surgery, the multiple operations, the plates and screws installed, the plates and screws removed, the skin removed, the skin grafted. He seemed almost happy, the surgeon. She nodded and nodded, biting her lip, wincing for the pain Glynnis would undergo, wondering if a leg was worth it, after all (of course it was, of course, the operations were only now; an amputated leg was forever, was Glynnis' whole life) and off he went with Glynnis, who howled, leaving Rowena alone with the queer feeling, the one that kept raising the hair on her arms and making the world turn wonky. Carol was safe, Glynnis in the best hands possible, she knew this, but the feeling said no. The feeling said, *Nothing is as you think it. The wall is not wall, the floor is not floor, but gap in the vacuum of space.* Only moments ago she had not known herself.

"What is it?" Glenn had asked from Vancouver.

"Did they not tell you?"

"They told me a piano fell on Glynnis. Broken telephone, I thought. Had to be."

"A piano fell on Glynnis," she said. In an alternate universe she broke into laughter.

Glenn shouted through the receiver. You don't have to yell, she went to say, and then realized that it was not in an alternate universe at all. She was laughing.

All at once she stopped.

"Rowena," he barked. "Get hold of yourself. You're hysterical."

"Sorry. Sorry. Sorry. Sorry. No," she said. "No. No. I'm fine. I just — I'm fine."

"How. Did a piano. Fall. On Glynnis." He spoke as if to an imbecile. Had they been happy up till now? she wondered.

"Brownies, Brownies, at the church. The upright was broken, she was underneath, and down it came on her legs." She wanted to laugh again and bit her lip.

"What was she doing underneath the piano?"

"That is something we do not yet know."

"You weren't there?"

"Of course I wasn't there, do you think I'd let one of the girls crawl under a piano in the regular course of events?"

She told him the extent of the injuries. He wanted to talk to the doctors.

"They've spoken to me, Glenn."

"But what kind of a state were you in?"

"I'm fine," she said.

"You don't sound fine."

"Oh, who would?" she said savagely.

There was a silence until he said, "I'll be on the next flight."

Then she had wiped it from her mind and dialled Beryl.

Now, finally, her hand let go the receiver. She walked — her legs moved under her, amazingly — to the chairs and sat down.

June was coming. June would be a distraction. She would let herself be distracted by June, not because that was what she wanted but because it was what June wanted. She could anticipate the exact note of exasperation she would feel at having to be distracted, at not being able to think her thoughts in private, and also the exact flood of the relief contained therein. She was not sure relief would be good for her, however. A good bout of hard thinking — that would be good for her. A change of clothes she did look forward to. Already she'd had one nurse tell her she'd always wanted to be a Guide but never was because her mother couldn't afford the uniform, another nurse tell her she'd loved being a Guide but her children hated Brownies, the doctor tell her being a Scout was the best thing that ever happened to him, and three mothers talk about accidents they had heard of occurring at Scouts or Guides.

Also, for the moment, she did not feel worthy of the uniform, of the gold cord slung so proudly through her epaulet and across her breast.

She sat, ankles crossed, the ball of her left foot grazing the floor. The same woman who had told her all about her family's history with the scouting movement, whose child had chronic asthma, now leaned forward and said, "Don't feel bad, honey. Everyone's bound to go a little off the deep end when —"

Rowena found herself on her feet. "Please don't talk to me," she said. "Please don't. I know that's rude." She looked at her watch. June would be here soon. Let June and this woman talk. She had to escape.

She found an empty hall and paced it several times before noticing the sign.

The chapel was quiet and still, as she expected, with a simple altar laid in green and a plain wooden cross hanging from the ceiling on clear fishing line. Fishers of men, she thought, almost laughing again — visions of Jesus in a pocket vest, casting with 50-lb test, visions of the cross as giant fish whipped out of the sea by God. Had she laughed, her absurd laughter might have immediately flopped to tears. But two men — grandfather and father? father and brother? — knelt together in the front row. Rowena knelt in back.

When her mother died — finally, after eighteen months of bizarre behaviour classed first as "nerves," then as madness and at last, when the seizures came, as what it was, a tumour — Rowena had found comfort in three things: her brothers, the Guides and her church. (Strangely, things were easier after the death — worst had been the "madness" phase, when they were ashamed and had to hide their mother — but the flood of sympathy after she died was pure and easy and allowed her many feelings she had not been allowed before. Though she felt guilty availing herself of people's leeway, she took it all in and pretended, for a while, to be grief-stricken. Later, when the memory of her mother's madness faded and the grief truly set in, the period of leeway was over. The only one who still let her feel bad then was Miss Balls.) At home there had been her grandmother, her father's mother, who gave them smacks without saying why.

"*You* know what that's for," she'd say. But Rowena didn't. She'd guess and wonder and spend afternoons in tears while her mother slept, or called out the window to an imaginary suitor. Later Grandma Cameron let it slip that she didn't know, either. "I'm sure you did *something* you shouldn't have." By that time, Rowena had stopped crying. Her mother died, Rowena turned thirteen and Grandma Cameron moved back to Peterborough, where she could torment Rowena's cousins.

And Rowena went to church. Sunday School and the junior choir provided activities and camaraderie. The church itself, the building, the nave, provided solidity. Solemnity. The simple grandeur a reminder that the life of the spirit is large, not small. The minister told her she was welcome any time. He treated her specially, as people did. She took him at his word, and for a time stopped in at church every day, sometimes more than once. She would pray. First for her mother's soul. Then her brother Lloyd's. Her other brothers' safety. Her father's ease. For the poor. For her friends. For refugees. And finally for herself, that she might know thankfulness and humility, that she might recognize generosity and good intentions in the actions of others.

Now, in the hospital chapel, she could not even begin to pray, or rather, she could not get past the beginning. *Dear Lord*, she tried, *I pray for* — "Wisdom," she wanted to say, but that felt suddenly presumptuous. Wisdom! How can one *ask* for wisdom? Wisdom is either human, won from experience, or God's, his own. How ludicrous to ask the Almighty for what makes him Almighty. The wisdom of God was God's. You could not ask for it.

She tried to pray in turn for strength, for humility, but each time, the same thing happened. The prayer went wrong, got derailed, made no sense. Once again she had the feeling of solid things dissolving, revealing their true nature as tiny atoms in space — the kneeler under her knees, the pew against which she leaned her forearms. Prayer, as familiar and comfortable to her, as sturdy and constant as furniture, suddenly seemed as foreign as practising a whole different religion.

It seemed wanton and idolatrous, like Catholic indulgences.

It was borne in on her that she *had* prayed and that her prayers, both of them, had been answered, and in that fact was great significance. One did not expect one's prayers to be answered. They never were. They were not meant to be answered. They were meant to be uttered, not answered. That was the nature of prayer.

Of course, her prayers had not been answered by God but by coincidence. Accident and injury had happened by the time she prayed them. Rowena's prayers could not have changed the fact that it was Glynnis underneath the piano. Had she prayed it be Lyddie emitting the cry of the wounded animal, that prayer would not have been answered because it could not be answered, given the logic of time and event by which the world was governed. But prayers answered by coincidence are prayers answered nonetheless. There is God in coincidence as there is God in everything. And so this shuddering dissolve.

Why had she prayed those prayers? Why had she prayed that it not be Carol? The answer was simple, too simple, and therefore, Rowena was certain, suspect. There had to be something rotten in the core of it. The answer was that Carol was too easily hurt, that Rowena thought that Carol *needed* her prayers. That Carol bore the burden of difference already.

But from God's point of view, what was the plea that Carol not be smitten with greater misfortune than she already bore but the plea of a selfish mother? What was all prayer but plea after plea of the selfish? God meted out fortune and misfortune. The godly accepted it, however it came.

What reason then to pray at all? And yet if there was no reason to pray, how could there be a God, a God involved in the lives of humans, a God who cared, a God who was born and died human? And now the prospect of a godless universe yawned before her horrifyingly and she recoiled from a kneeling position to a seated one on the bench of the pew.

She had prayed that it not be someone else's child because she knew she could not stand to be responsible for an accident that hurt someone else's child. It was not the parents' blame she feared, but the obliteration of her public and private self. Rowena Riggs was above all competent. Things did not go wrong under Rowena Riggs. Rowena Riggs could fly a plane, hang a door, reglaze a window, bake a soufflé. Keep a family clothed and fed. Strong and healthy.

Accidents happen, she might say to Glynnis and Carol when this had all settled down (Horrors, Glenn might say to her). But this was not an accident, not in the sense that people mean when they say that accidents happen. When people say accidents happen, they mean that unexpected, unavoidable things happen, and that we must neither chasten ourselves nor affix blame to others for their happening. A true accident was one in which, say, one person was crossing a room carrying two glasses of wine and someone else turned suddenly and ran into them so the wine spilled. It was not wrong to carry wineglasses across a room. It was not wrong to turn. Both happen at the same time? Accident.

In a true accident there was no wrongness. In this event, wrongness was everywhere. It was wrong of Glynnis to be under the piano, wrong of Carol to — as June reported from Alison's version, which she did not entirely trust — kick the bricks that supported the piano. It was wrong of Rowena to have been out of the room, leaving children in the care of Lyddie, who could not begin to control them. It was wrong of her to have been berating the Smith brothers. It was wrong of her not to sort out the animosity between Carol and Glynnis before it escalated to this point. And so the wrongs extended back into history, on and on. She thought of the Middle East, of Ireland, of slavery in America, blacks and whites.

If the surgeon could not save the leg, Glynnis would have to live with an amputation, a phantom limb, her whole life long. If Glynnis' leg was amputated, Carol would have to live with knowing she had caused it. And Rowena would have to live with the knowledge of both.

Watch out, part of her mind went. *You are in the Slough of Despond.*

You're right, she answered. *Take me, take me.* She pictured herself in quicksand, sinking. When gone, she'd be gone, and this agony would end.

Glynnis, Glynnis, poor Glynnis. She'd never seen such pain. What had got into Carol? Could she be the thing Rowena most feared? Damaged? Already? Because people are, people do become damaged, she had seen it. It can happen very early. It can happen early and go unknown for years and years.

No. She could not believe it. Not of her daughter. Not of Carol. Carol was an ordinary little girl. So she always said. It was not just by the force of repeating it that it was true. It would be true if she never said it. But she seemed to be the only one quite certain of that, which is why she had to repeat it so often.

But if Carol were to become damaged ... this might be the thing to do it.

Rowena felt stretched over a gap, fingernails on one side of a chasm, toes on the other, arms shaking. The possibility that her own life — and by extension, the lives of all people, life itself — had absolutely no meaning was what yawned beneath. She shook.

⌐

AS SOON AS ROWENA saw her daughter's face in the recovery room — the small, refined not-quite-replica of her own — meaning gathered itself from the air and like a genie sucking in breath whooshed into her chest, walloping heart and lungs. Life had meaning. It did. Its meaning was this: daughter-and-mother. Also: children-and-adults. Brethren. Man and man. Woman and woman. Woman and man. *This* was God's gift to man: others. Beings with whom we can communicate. Beings with whom we are connected.

The idea of Jesus as God's gift to man took on new meaning. Jesus was the same gift as every human on the planet, only more so. Jesus was the reminder that the bridge between God and Man was crossable, that there even was a bridge. That there was a God. That every single person on the planet was a gift.

Rowena wept. Glynnis' eyes flickered open. Rowena wiped her eyes, took up Glynnis' hand again and kissed it.

After an hour or so, Glynnis was moved to a room on the ward where three unknown children slept, Glynnis making the fourth. From time to time one of them would whimper. The nurses told Rowena she should go home and get some sleep, but she could not leave before Glynnis woke and knew she was there. She slept sitting up in the clothes June had brought her, in the chair by Glynnis' bed. Every half hour a nurse came in to check Glynnis' pulse and blood pressure and temperature, the drip that kept infection at bay.

As the hours passed, the elation she'd felt at the rekindled flame of her faith did not dissipate, but other things crowded in on it, the same things as before — not her prayers being answered or not, but her culpability, her pride, her venality.

Morning came properly. Glynnis rose from unconsciousness, dropped again, rose, dropped. Breakfast arrived for the other children in the ward. The mother of the black girl in the body cast dashed in on the way to work and dashed out. From being a sanctuary, the hospital became a workplace again. A school. A dispensary. An orphanage.

Late in the morning, Glenn came through the door, doffing his cap and kneeling beside her with one arm round her and one across Glynnis' chest. Rowena had heard him first, his voice like oak, inquiring at the nurses' station. Then he entered, tall and broad. The strong one. She would let him be the strong one. She would let herself be weak. A kind of penance.

Miss Balls

BERYL TIDIED HER DESK in preparation for bed, stowing for the fiftieth time the box of writing paper, unwritten-upon. She felt very badly about it, very badly indeed, but there was nothing she could do. Every start she made led to the business with Judy. And that was the end of it. That was as far as she could go.

What Minnie must be thinking! Beryl sick or dead. Or, after fifty years of constancy, changed.

But how ridiculous. The business with Judy was silly, she couldn't *let* it stop her from anything. She drew the paper out again.

Dear Minnie, she thought, picking up her pen. *Do you know, the oddest idea keeps popping into my head. Memoirs. I shall write my memoirs. It occurs just that way: 'I shall write my memoirs.'*

'Shall I really?' I respond to myself. 'Shall I really?' And, do you know, I really think I shall. The History has lost its appeal.

She wrote this, and then she went on composing. *I apologize for not having written these last months. I did get your second letter, thank you, and the latest. How is Robert? And little ...* She could not remember the new baby's name, Minnie's latest granddaughter. One of those impossible-to-remember African names, Nbosi or Nyasi or Nafuna.

The new baby is thriving, I hope. New paragraph. *There is something I want to ask your opinion of …*

No.

A curious thing happened to me in the spring and I have long wanted your opinion of it, but feared to ask …

Words to follow these lurked in her mind, unformed. In case you should …

… confirm …

… agree with …

… share the opinion of …

They are saying I …

You see, there are words and there are things and ideas and we have only words to express the things and ideas. Sometimes we have the right idea but we use what someone else thinks is the wrong word. Should we be dismissed for our words, which are loose, flippant things, changeable from year to year and age to age (think of what gay once meant and what it means now — perhaps in your part of the world it still means what it used to), or for our ideas, which are the real thing, the true thing?

I wonder, can you guess what they have accused me of? I think you would be shocked.

But possibly she would not be shocked. Night after night this possibility kept Beryl from writing to her pen pal of fifty years, her friend, Minnie. She fretted over this, too, along with the rest of the business, and slept badly, with ill dreams.

She sighed and pushed with two hands up from her desk to go to bed. The telephone rang, giving her a start. Who, so late?

"Hello?"

Rowena Morgan. Riggs, rather. She had not heard from her since … could it really be? … no, no, Rowena had called just after Labour Day. "Rowena, how lovely to hear from you," she said. And what was Rowena saying? Oh, dear. Oh, dear. The poor wee thing.

"Yes, yes, of course. Yes, I'll be there first thing, don't you worry."

Beryl hung up the phone, tapped the receiver with her finger and went not to her room but back to her desk and drew out a new sheet of vellum.

Dear Minnie, she wrote.

So many times I have picked up my pen to write you these last months and so many times I have then put it down. I went through a bad patch there in the spring. Someday I must tell you all about it; it seems not so important now. The details aren't important. The important thing is that I've retired at last from leadership of the 14th Toronto Company. I had rather hoped, like Lord and Lady B.P., to have kept going until the very end, but of course their circumstance and role and my own are quite different. In keeping going, I have kept others from positions of leadership. It is time to step down and make way for younger folk to shine. When I stop to think of it, I have had whatever small influence I have had over hundreds of girls over the years, possibly as many as a thousand! What an awful lot of lives to have touched and been touched by. And of course it's not me, personally, but the experience of Guiding that is the most important influence I've been lucky enough to pass on. Oh, I think of our early camps, the mishaps and foul-ups and wonderful self-reliance with which we pulled through it all. The confidence I've seen girls gain after just one weekend in the woods! I don't need to explain to you. You have seen just the same thing. Every Guider has.

I've just had a call from a girl who started with the 14th, went on in Guiding and has become a firm friend (how I thank the Girl Guides for so many great friends!). She's now a 'Brown Owl' — what we call the leaders of the youngest girls here. There has been a terrible accident and she's called for my help!

Carol

CAROL HAD NEVER FELT before quite the way she did when Glynnis whacked her head against Carol's knees pretending to be the Wicked Witch of the East. It was amazing. She *did* see red. Her blood *did* boil. The heat of the moment was *hot*. But none of these things really said it. None of them mentioned the thickness of it, the way her body and head were absolutely full of the redness, the thick, churning redness, bubbling up to that explosive boil. Frothing, seething, roiling, bursting suddenly into gas — bam! — that hammered on the lid of her pressure-cooking noggin. Zammo! Head and body were one, and what they knew was action. They took in stimulus: Glynnis-shape under piano calling to Alison-shape, Glynnis-shape ignoring her, Glynnis-shape and Alison-shape ha ha ha ha-ing. Action: red roiling surged down back, down butt, into leg, into toe, red roiling flashed through lungs to mouth. A yell, a run, a kick, red roiling directed right through the bricks. "No you're not, you're Dorothy because I say so." Clunk, clunk, bricks toppled. The piano lurched, castors screeched, piano smashed, Glynnis screeched.

Slowly the red receded, drained, something like that, ebbed away. Carol felt cold now in the pit of her stomach. Cold, white, like porcelain on a toilet. Everyone rushed toward Glynnis. Rush, rush, shouting,

63

ordering themselves around the piano, hands underneath, feet planted ready to lift. Everyone turned to look at her for a second. Why? What were they looking at? Then they turned back to their task. They lifted together. Tawny Owl pulled Glynnis out. Carol turned and ran. She ran down the back stairs. She ran through the hall and out the door. She ran all the way home and up to her room and into her closet, where she closed the door and clutched her "Happiness Is …" laundry bag to her chest and cried. Soon her eyes adjusted to the dark, and she pulled a dress off the hanger above her and draped it over her head. That was better. Darker. She was not meant to be able to see at all. Something was wrong with her. She should have been totally blind, that was what she was meant to be, not partially blind like this, with enough sight to see bricks, piano, Glynnis, bricks, piano, Glynnis, bricks, piano, Glynnis, foot-in-motion, screech, crash, screech. Carol put her hands over her ears as well as the dress over her head. Herself crying sounded funny inside her head, hollow and distant, like in a cave, the red cave of her head. She pictured herself walking around in the cave, fearful of goblins and cave things and the laughter of witches. She started to sing a brave song to ward off the things in the cave, to ward off her fears. Like "Follow the Yellow Brick Road" or "If I Were King of the Forest," only she couldn't remember those, so she sang "Oh They Built the Ship Titanic" while she cried in the closet with the dress over her head and her hands on her ears.

CAROL KNEW SHE'D been asleep when light broke in on her. She knew she'd been crying because the underside of her skull pounded, ba-boom ba-boom. But where was she?

"Here she is," her brother yelled. "She's in the …"

Closet. That's what the smell and feel of the place was. She pulled the dress off her head.

"… closet." The shape of her brother was crouched down in front of her. He held out his hand. She took it and stood. Her toes hurt.

Sandy and Alison MacDonald ran into the room, followed by their mother. "We've been looking all over for you," Alison said snottily.

"Oh, thank Christ," Mrs. MacDonald said, putting one hand to her chest and leaning the other on the dresser. "Thank Christ, you're found. That's one less worry."

Jay's hand was on Carol's back. She turned her head into his shoulder and whimpered. Smears on her glasses broke the light open and her eyes hurt. She could smell Mrs. MacDonald's perfume as she crouched down beside her.

"Listen, sweet pea, Carol, you're going to come stay with us tonight, I need you to pack a bag, all right?"

"I want to stay here."

"You can't stay here. Your mother is at the hospital with Glynnis and your father doesn't get back until tomorrow at the earliest."

"I want to stay here with Jay."

"Jay is going to Rodney's house. You can't stay alone. Help me out, here, Carol-Marrill. Come on, where's your bag?"

Carol liked it when Mrs. MacDonald called her that, but she couldn't stop whimpering as she got her overnight bag out from under the bed and stuffed her pajamas into it. She could feel them staring at her. Sandy and Alison. What a stare felt like was air on a really hot day, thick and wavy, only just on your back and not your front (not always your back, of course, but whatever part of you was getting stared at while the rest of you felt cold). If she put Reginald in her suitcase they would see: Carol's bringing her teddy bear.

"Come on, Carol, what else do you need? Brush? Toothbrush? We need to get home before your mother calls from the hospital or she'll be frantic, not knowing what happened to you, on top of everything else."

Carol stood with her legs against the side of the bed, not wanting to move except to get in it and lie next to Reginald and tell him how everybody was going to take Glynnis' side just because she got hurt, and how that part was an accident, and how nobody ever saw how Carol got hurt, and how sorry she was, and how everything she ever did came out wrong no matter what. Then Reginald would make up a song to distract her and punch her in the nose with his soft, soft paw and do somersaults until he got tired and fell asleep beside her.

"Carol? Did you hear what I said?"

"Earth to Carol," said Alison.

Carol yanked her suitcase, forgetting it wasn't shut. Her pajamas spilled out. She picked them up, then got her brush and then her toothbrush from the bathroom. When the others were on the stairs in front of her, she ran back into her room and got Reginald.

"Where has that girl gone?" she heard Mrs. MacDonald say.

"She's coming," Jay said from her doorway.

Jay. Jay. Please let her stay with Jay. But no, he was leaving the car, she was left with the enemy. Her breath went in and out more thickly again, her voice box vocalizing it as it went, though of neither of these things was she particularly conscious, only of being sorry and of hating Alison and of hoping Glynnis was not too badly hurt. Glynnis bruised easily, though not so easily as Carol. In the summer when they wore shorts, they would sometimes compare, and Carol almost always won. This'd beat anything Carol had had, though. This'd be the daddy of all bruises. A doozy of a bruisy. Carol felt her knees, where Glynnis had smacked her with the back of her head. Yup. Bruises there. On her toes, too. They throbbed away inside her shoe.

Glynnis had to be okay. If she wasn't, the two of them wouldn't be even. They'd always ended up even before, or close enough.

CAROL RUBBED HER FINGER along the groove in the vinyl door handle, front to back, back to front, and didn't look up when Mrs. MacDonald got in again or when they pulled into the MacDonalds' driveway and the girls hopped out the back, and Mrs. MacDonald's door slammed shut. She didn't look up a few seconds later when Mrs. MacDonald's form filled the car window beside her, her knuckles rapping on the glass, her voice saying, "Open up! Police!"

She did look up when Mary MacDonald shouted out the side door to her mother that Mrs. Riggs was on the phone. Mrs. MacDonald's mouth hardened into a line as she opened the car door and grabbed Carol's wrist, dragging her up the driveway and through the screen door, not stopping to notice Carol didn't need dragging anymore.

Mrs. MacDonald picked up the receiver from the top of the kitchen wall phone. "Rowena? How is she?" Carol came closer to try to make out the expressions on Mrs. MacDonald's face.

"Oh, *she's* fine. We found her hiding in the closet. Made a beeline for home."

Carol felt her face go pink. She wondered what her mother was saying. *I could shake that girl. That girl is going to drive me to drink.*

"Well, she's safe now, that's the main thing. Jay is at the Friedmans' for the night, so that's all settled. How's Glynnis?"

There was a long pause. Mrs. MacDonald sucked in her breath and bit her lip. "Oh, no," she said. "Oh!" She put a hand to her heart. "What if it doesn't? When will you know?" Carol's heart clunked harder.

"We all have our fingers crossed here. Listen, can I get Doug on anything for you? No? Have you heard from Glenn yet? Well, you can't wait all by yourself! No! Listen, I'll get a thermos of coffee, I'll get you a change of clothes, Mary can look after the kids here. I'll be there in an — Rowena, I'm coming whether you like it or not. I'll be there in an hour."

"What's going on?" Mary asked her mother.

Alison slid into the kitchen on her socks and beat her mother to answering, "Carol knocked a piano on Glynnis."

"What?!"

"It was an accident," Mrs. MacDonald said.

"No, it wasn't," Alison said. "She *lined* up those bricks, I saw the whole thing ..."

"Alison," her mother warned.

"I did not, I did not, I did not," Carol yelled. Again the red surge flooded her. She wanted to whale on Alison with the heels of her hands.

"Carol!" Mrs. MacDonald said.

"But I *saw* it," she heard Alison say. "She was going to *waste* 'em."

"Alison," Mrs. MacDonald barked. "Shut. Up."

Surprisingly, Alison did, and Carol knew suddenly that Mrs. MacDonald believed her daughter, that she was shutting her up not because she was angry with Alison or disagreed, but just to get her to shut up, so Carol would shut up, too, so Carol wouldn't go off the deep end again. There *was* something wrong with her. She was flawed. Defective. Like Hymie on *Get Smart* when he got reprogrammed by Kaos. Only she wasn't a robot, so nobody could fix her. She thought of the albino in *My Friend Flicka*. Loco.

Carol ran to the bathroom, planning not to come out ever again. She curled up against the wall, putting her face behind the towel that hung down from the rack. Then, as she was sucking breath into her chest between teary outflows, she heard Alison shout, "Op-er-*a*-tion!" like the ad for the game. Operation? Were they talking about Glynnis? Was she going to have an operation? Carol's breath burst and spilled out of her in waves. Eventually there was a knock at the door and Mrs. MacDonald came in wearing her coat. She lifted up the towel.

"Carol? Honey? I know you feel bad, but you've got to be strong and cross your fingers for your sister. Mary'll get you some supper and make you up a bed in the basement. Come on." She stretched out a hand. Carol pressed herself against the wall.

"Suit yourself, kid. I'm off to the hospital. Should I tell your mother you're a blubbering mess or a good girl?"

Carol sobbed anew.

"All right, Carol, never mind about that. Stay in here if you like." She hesitated before leaving.

"Is it broken?" Carol asked. As soon as it was out of her mouth, Carol knew it wasn't what she meant. She meant: *How bad is it, don't tell me.*

Mrs. MacDonald said, "Yes, Carol, it's broken. It's … very broken. It's about as broken as a leg can get." Then in the same breath but a completely new tone, as if she'd suddenly realized she'd been talking regularly when she should be using adult-to-child talk, she switched gears, saying, "Come out when you're ready. If I'm not back by morning, Gloria will get you breakfast and off to school."

⌐⌐

CAROL WOKE HEARING the exact pitch of Glynnis' scream inside her head. It made her want to duplicate it, just to see if she could. Instead she cupped her hands over her ears, adjusting them to hear that burr of air pocket between ear and hand, not quite a hiss, not quite a roar. Then, flattening her palms against her ears, she created enough suction to make a slight pop as she removed her hands. Burr, suction, pop, burr, suction, pop, until the scream was gone. She listened to the sounds from upstairs, dishes and footsteps, voices crabbing, a crash, scurrying. She wondered if she had to get up. Feet on the stairs, a flap and slap on each step.

"Who's the lazy bones still in bed?" Gloria's voice. They were Gloria's feet, now at the bottom of the stairs. "Hmm? Who's the big lazy bag of bones?"

"I'm not lazy, I'm sick," Carol said.

"O-ho, I've heard that one before." Gloria pulled the sleeping bag off Carol. Gloria was the MacDonalds' housekeeper. She always seemed mad to Carol. Carol didn't think Gloria liked her and had come to the conclusion that Gloria ignored her because she couldn't be bothered with her, but every now and then she wondered if it wasn't because she, Carol, always ignored Gloria. Part of the problem was that she didn't know what to call her. If she called her Gloria like the MacDonalds did, Gloria looked extra mad, but Carol didn't know her last name, and so couldn't call her Mrs. Whatever, either.

Carol sat up.

"That's better," said Gloria. "I'm glad I didn't have to light you on fire like I thought I was going to."

Carol went to get dressed and realized she had nothing to put on but her Brownie outfit. She was unprepared. She was always unprepared.

— HOW COME CAROL'S wearing her Brownie uniform?

— Didn't you hear? Glynnis Riggs is in the hospital, she may lose her leg.

— I don't get it.

— What happened?

— Did you actually *see* it? The leg? Was it really gross?

— Oh, yeah. All red and sorta ... pulpy ... and blood everywhere and bones poking out, and ...

— Oh, God, I think I'm going to be sick.

— Tawny Owl *was* sick.

— So was Daintry.

— What happened? How did it happen?

— Was it, like, hanging by a vein? My sister caught her finger in the door and it was hanging by a vein and they sewed it back on.

— Eww, gross.

— No, but it was backwards. You know like normally your knee goes like this, right? It only bends one way. And it was going like that. The other way.

— You guys! What happened?

— It was the piano. At Brownies. It fell on her leg.

— How?

— I don't know, I was *playing* the piano. It's up on bricks, right? At one end? And Glynnis is lying underneath it —

— What for?

— I don't know.

— She's pretending to be somebody ...

— Yeah, and then all of a sudden, the piano goes like errrr-clung-ung-ung, and Glynnis is screaming, and Carol's just standing there like an idiot with her hand up to her mouth, like 'Oh, did I do something wrong?'

— Do you think she did it on purpose?

— Who?

— Carol, duh, who do you think we've been talking about?

— I just heard her yell and then Glynnis is screaming and Carol's standing there, and we're all like freaking, and trying to get the piano off her, and Carol takes off.

— She musta done it on purpose.

— Sh. Sh. Here she comes.

— Why's she wearing her Brownie uniform?

— Why don't you ask her?

— Shut up!

— Why don't you just ask, Hey, Carol, why are you wearing your Brownie uniform and oh, by the way, is it true you knocked a piano on your sister?

— Shut up, I said. She can hear you.

— Okay, I'll ask her. Hey, Carol, um, we were just wondering, is it true you knocked a piano on your sister? 'Cause if you did, you know, that's not very nice.

— Of course, if you didn't do it on purpose, that's totally different. Did you do it on purpose?

— Carol, it's not very nice not to answer people when they ask you questions.

— I'd say it's rude, in fact.

—We just want to know: accident, or on purpose?

— Or maybe: accidentally on purpose?

— I bet she did it on purpose.

—What's wrong, Carol? Aren't you going to sharpen the rest of your pencils?

— Oh, look, she's crying. The little Brownie's crying.

⌒

"LOOK WHO'S HOME," Miss Balls said, looking up from chopping onions as Carol slouched into the kitchen at lunch. "What are you doing still in your uniform? Off you go and change."

Miss Balls was a friend of the family, an old lady who had been Mrs. Riggs' Girl Guide leader when Mrs. Riggs was a motherless girl.

"Milk?" Miss Balls asked when Carol returned. Carol nodded. Where was her mother? She didn't trust her voice to ask.

Miss Balls patted the tall stool at the counter for Carol to come sit on.

"Terrible turn of events, isn't it?" she said, not sounding at all like she thought it was. "When I think of it! Your poor sister. And your father clear across the globe! I guess it was a bit of excitement for the girls, though, eh? My goodness! Had you done your First Aid yet?"

Carol nodded again, taking the cold glass from Miss Balls' long, tendony hands. She put her elbows on the counter and tipped the glass toward her mouth while resting the bottom on the counter between elbows.

"And did you use it?" Miss Balls stopped chopping to open a can of soup for their lunch.

Carol nodded one more time without taking her mouth from the glass before she fully realized what she was nodding to. The milk piled up against her lip, then fell back, up, back. She decided that Miss Balls meant the collective you, not the individual you.

"At least there's that," said Miss Balls. "The poor wee thing. But your mother says she was brave as General Wolfe. And by the sounds of everything, she'll keep the leg."

The bottom of Carol's glass slid out from her grip and what was left inside sloshed her in the face and ran down the front of her top.

Miss Balls made a clucking noise, snagging the dishcloth from the sink. "What is it we say about spilled milk and crying, now? Come on. Mop up."

Carol ferried the sopping cloth from counter to sink, thinking of Glynnis with one leg, then herself in juvenile detention. She wailed.

"Really, Carol. It's only milk. Off you go again and change."

Carol ran up to her room and threw herself on her bed. Glynnis would come home in a wheelchair. Or on those metal crutches, her stump swinging. She would really hate Carol instead of just pretending to. Everyone would hate her. Jay, her mother and father, Miss Balls, Mrs. Harris, her aunts and uncles and cousins, the neighbours, even Sandy MacDonald, and they'd be right to, it was all her fault. They wouldn't want to live with her. They'd make her a ward of the court and after she got out of reform school, she'd live in a group home. They'd tell her she really was adopted like she'd thought all along and send her back to her parents, who were criminals who lived on the worst part of Jarvis, and she'd deserve it all, all the hatred, all the punishment. She might as well die right now.

She dwelled on this thought for a long time, her lungs convulsing with sobs, until without realizing it she'd begun to imagine another scenario, in which she devoted the rest of her life to caring for her crippled sister who hated her. There was a Sunday afternoon movie sort of like that about a crippled rich girl in Switzerland and the cheerful nice, poor girl who helped her.

Every day would be a punishment, a punishment Carol would embrace, and gradually Glynnis would see how meek and stalwart and good Carol was, caring for her year after year, turning down marriage to the handsome man who loved her passionately and went and devoted *him*self to missionary work in Africa since he couldn't marry his one true love.

Carol's eyes were sore and her head hurt. She wanted to sleep but Miss Balls was banging a pot and yelling, "Soup's on!" Carol changed her shirt and washed her face and cleaned her glasses with the special fluid and special cloth. Then she went into her parents' bathroom and took two aspirins and went downstairs.

"Crackers or toast?" Miss Balls said like there was nothing wrong in the world at all. Carol began to cry again. Was it Glynnis? Miss Balls asked. Carol nodded and cried harder. "There, there," Miss Balls said. "I'm sure she'll be all right. Why, it's wonderful what they can do these days. They can sew limbs right back on, did you know that? Not like in my day when the best you could do sometimes was cut the wretched thing off so it didn't get worse ..." She faltered for a moment. "Mind you, if the war was good for one thing, it was developments in surgery. I'd bet you the shirt off my back they wouldn't be sewing limbs back on now if not for the groundwork laid then.

"And then, too, sewing a limb back on is predicated on having the limb to sew. Most of those boys in the war didn't bring in their missing parts on their stretchers. When they lost legs, they lost 'em. Unless it was gangrene. There's nothing you can do for gangrene except get out the bone saw, quick as you can." She shook her head. "Even if it is the most beautiful part of you. There was a boy. A beautiful boy, the most gorgeous head of curls, the boys always get the curls, don't they? We were a little in love with him, even our hard-bitten old matron, who disapproved of emotions. He seemed familiar to me, this boy. So many of them did. Why, it's the butcher's youngest, I'd think until I took another look. And in fact I did meet boys I knew from town, even one I'd known in Toronto growing up. But this fellow seemed doubly familiar. It wasn't until prepping him for surgery that I realized why, and once I remembered I was surprised I hadn't made the connection earlier. You see, he looked exactly like Michelangelo's David, and I had already remarked that once — when I'd seen him onstage at the Royal Ballet in London. He was a dancer, a great sensation, heir to Nijinsky, everyone said. And he, this great dancer — and young, so very young — had got so frightened and desperate he had shot his own toe and the toe had got infected. The most beautiful leg on the most beautiful boy had gangrene." Miss Balls sniffed and pulled a hanky from her cuff and wiped the corner of her eye. "And that was that." Carol's toe throbbed in sympathy with the beautiful boy. If her toe could get gangrene and fall off, it'd even things up with Glynnis. She determined to neglect it and see what would happen.

Whenever they knew Miss Balls was coming over, Jay and Mr. Riggs made a bet. How long before she referred to the war? Jay always went for the shorter time, Mr. Riggs for the longer, and until she unwittingly obliged them, everybody but Miss Balls (and Mrs. Riggs, who tried to pretend it wasn't happening and sometimes took Miss Balls, of whom she was protective, away into the garden or kitchen in order to avoid them) was watching the boys work their angles, tempting her or distracting her, then countering each other's temptations and distractions. Their one rule was they could make no direct mention of her war — the first — or any other. Sometimes they varied and complicated their bets, working out odds. Fifty cents on Girl Guides, four minutes, even odds. Group of Seven, Algonquin Park, Tom Thomson, twelve minutes or less, 2:1 for mention of one, 3:1 for mention of two, 4:1 for mention of three, 10:1 if you added in mention of another particular member of the Group of Seven.

Mr. Riggs exaggerated, Mrs. Riggs said. And even if he didn't, Miss Balls had a heart as big as a house and had been very kind to Mrs. Riggs when she'd needed it as a girl and the old lady *had* had many wonderful adventures all those years ago and who could blame her for clinging to them, everything must seem a bit dull after that. What kind of example was it to the children to make fun of her? It wasn't Christian.

After they'd finished eating, Miss Balls chopped and floured and browned the beef for tonight's stew, while Carol measured and poured and kneaded dough for biscuits, and Miss Balls told Carol about her Guide troop's first accident. The way she said it was like a chapter from an Enid Blyton story: Our First Accident. Miss Balls was from another world, Mr. Riggs often said, but Carol liked that world. Things in it seemed clear cut.

Miss Balls' troop was one of the Very First There Ever Was. This was in England, before the war. She'd been born in Canada, but her father had shipped her and her brother Tom back to England after her mother died, when she was just the same age as Mrs. Riggs had been at her mother's death. She knew what it was like to be motherless. That's why her heart had gone out to poor Rowena.

In the village where Miss Balls lived in England, people didn't take kindly to girls dressing up in uniform and parading about the streets. They thought they should be indoors, knitting and sewing, keeping their feet dry and their skin pale and their hands dainty. But oh, they were full of fire, the girls in Miss Balls' troop, the fire of youth and patriotism, and they wouldn't be held back. They *wanted* to do their bit, they were *going* to do their bit, and nobody was going to stop them.

It was different back then. They never stayed within doors if they could help it. Outdoors, rain or shine, tramp, tramp, off we go.

They'd take turns picking a spot to meet each week, scouting it out with a compass and then delivering bearings and course to each Guide. What a thrill it was to see each new pair of Guides come over the lip of the hill to the meeting place (of course they always worked in pairs for safety). One felt so accomplished, part of the finest crew of the finest land, ready to leap into the whatever breach yawned before one. Well, and as it turned out, what a breach. The War, the War.

What the troop did each week depended largely on their enthusiasms. Miss Balls had been a great one for Florence Nightingalizing and going on marches or scouting the enemy. As they tramped through the woods, they would take turns at being the injured party. Just when everyone least expected it, a girl fell over clutching her forehead or her stomach or her ankle and moaning, and the rest hopped to it, applying first aid, rigging splints and stretchers, sometimes even building bridges to carry the stretcher over a creek. More often than not, the injured party would jump up to help at a barrier like this — no reason she should be kept from learning for the sake of play-acting. One time, an old gentleman fishing a stream — an ally, they'd decided, on spotting him — had just about fallen over to see the girl in the stretcher leap up and help the others, then lie back down and be carried over the stick bridge.

"Well, weren't we excited one day when we heard a shot and a terrible shout. A hunter — poacher, actually — had accidentally shot his foot. Off we went at a run, and found him in agony, poor man. We tried not to be too gleeful as we bandaged him up. He must not have known what was happening to him, suddenly surrounded by a battalion of girls with haversacks and bandages and blankets, ordering him to bite hard on one of his own bullets. He was a good deal heavier than any one of us, I can tell you that. But we got him into the village on the stretcher and marched him right into the doctor's house. 'I was wrong about you Girl Guides,' said the doctor. 'You've done a bang-up job here, a bang-up job.'

"Well, weren't we pleased. I decided right then and there that I *would* be a nurse, no ifs, ands or buts. I *would* and no one would stop me."

"Who would have stopped you?" Carol asked.

"My father, that's who."

"Why?"

"He had an idea it was like being a nun. Only girls that never wanted to marry would do it. And he wanted me to marry, and be nice and quiet and delicate, like Mum. He said I had my looks against me already, I couldn't afford bloody aprons and opinions. Well, he may have been right, but marriage looked very dull to me, and I was willing to take a chance. And nurses at the time, well, there were two sorts, the Nightingale sorts from good families and the girls that had to earn their living, who were rougher sometimes, but no worse for that. Funny now, but working girls of any sort — except governesses, I suppose — were quite looked down on."

"When's Mom coming home?" Carol asked.

"She didn't know for certain when I spoke to her."

"Did Glynnis have an operation?"

"The first of many, I suspect. She's very lucky they didn't have to amputate right away, with an accident like that. A piano on a child's leg! You'd think it would be utterly crushed. What I don't understand is how the piano fell in the first place and how on earth it fell on her leg. Pianos don't just up and topple on people in my experience." Miss Balls pretended to be more absorbed in her stew than in what she was saying. "Were there children on top of the piano? Were they trying to tip it over? A whole gang of children might do it, I suppose." She glanced sideways at Carol, who stared at the floor. "That's it, isn't it? And you were one of them."

Carol froze. Oh, God. Oh, God. Nodding would be a lie. So would shaking her head. Please, please, please, she thought, not knowing exactly what she was pleading for.

"Oh, pet, didn't you know better?"

Carol let a breath out. That would do. Miss Balls went on in her sternly gentle we-must-learn-a-lesson-from-this voice, and Carol just focused on breathing in and out, in and out until Miss Balls said, "There. I think I've said enough."

That night, Carol wanted more than anything to sleep. Her brain was driving her nuts, circling and circling around everything people had said that day. It was like picking at a scab. Made it worse, but you couldn't stop doing it. She tried all her going-to-sleep tricks, but the clock-radio kept flipping over its numbers, and she kept being awake.

In that kind of sleep that you don't realize is sleep until you really wake up, the kind in which you can be snoring and hearing exactly what's going on around you at the same time, her mother — who she'd heard come into the house and greet Miss Balls and Jay — came and sat on her bed. Trying not to tense, Carol whimpered and rolled away from the light, certain that Mrs. Riggs, in that omnipotent way of parents, would know she was faking and would tell her to give it up, she was fooling no one, and she'd better get a good sleep because tomorrow she was going to have to account for her actions. But Mrs. Riggs just stroked her hair, sighed and said, "Oh, Carol. What are we going to do with you, eh? What are we going to do with you?" Then she kissed her on the temple and went out, stopping in the light of the doorway to stretch.

꙳

STEPPING OUT THE front door to go to church on Halloween, Carol could feel the wind through her leotards and the cold nudging her feet in their shiny black buckle shoes as she stepped out the front door ahead of her mother and father and brother. Her eyes watered, making the frosted walk and lawn blur so it almost looked like there had been a light snow. On the second step, her right foot in its shiny shoe shot out from under her, her bruised toes mashing against the end of the shoes, and her bum catching the edge of the flagstone step. More water flooded her eyes.

"You all right there, sport?" her father asked.

She nodded. *Watch me walk,* went the song her head had been serving up the last few days as she willed herself not to limp, *I can walk and walk.* So far, no gangrene, although the bruising had hit its purplest and green was showing at the edges, so you never knew. It looked like she might lose the nail on her second toe, which was longer than the first and had got the worst of things. Normally she would have shown the progress of her injuries to Glynnis night and morning. Normally she would have shown it to anyone who would look, normally she would have wanted everyone to know and sympathize. But nothing was normal anymore, and possibly never would be again. Glynnis was not at home. She was not with them on their way to church. They were not walking to church the way they usually did when there wasn't a rainstorm or snowstorm, they were driving so that they could go straight to the hospital afterwards, where Carol would see Glynnis for the first time since the accident and have to apologize.

What would happen to Glynnis? What would happen to Carol? Her father had said he didn't know if there was a suitable punishment for what she had done, or if there was, what it was. "You can't court-martial an eight year-old," he'd said.

"That's not funny, Glenn," her mother had said.

"I didn't mean it to be," he said. "I didn't mean it to be."

Carol would have welcomed a court-martial. Then maybe it would all become clear, why she had done what she had done, how the blame could be measured out and to what parts of her. In the meantime she could do little but cry. Her eyes looked like they had styes, her heart thumped all day near her throat, her throat burned, her chest constricted unexpectedly and convulsively. She had blubbered so much during her "talk" with her parents on Thursday morning that her mother had let her stay home for the day. Her father worked on his canoe in the garage, and she lay in bed with a headache, sleeping and waking as if she really were sick, except that no one brought her ginger ale or comic books. In the late afternoon, Miss Balls came to make dinner and Mr. Riggs went off to the hospital. Mrs. Riggs said that Glynnis was lucky, that you never knew until something went wrong how lucky you were. She said no matter how bad things were, there were always people worse off, and one had to count one's blessings. Glynnis would leave the hospital under her own steam, but not all of the other children would. Some would not leave at all. She felt so sorry for the mother of one girl in Glynnis' room. To start with, the girl was a mongoloid, and then she had been in a car accident. She just didn't understand why everything hurt and why she had to have all these operations. The mother was there every day, a lovely woman, playing the child's favourite games, singing her favourite songs. There was another girl, a little Black girl in a body cast. Mrs. Riggs wasn't certain what her diagnosis was. The mother did not talk. The last girl was a Portuguese girl who had broken both her ankles trying to jump from one garage roof to another. Her parents did not speak any English.

The church was very bright with the sun coming in the high windows behind them, lighting up the banners hanging by the choir loft. "God is Love" said one. "I am the Light and the Life" said the other, and it seemed to make sense that the light streaming in was God, that God was that bright and good. The church seemed like a place where people *were* good, where goodness was a natural state of being, and it seemed to her that she could be good, too, if she tried, if she started right that minute, though she would have to start by rooting out a feeling she had at the core of her that made her feel reckless and hopeful and free and sick all at the same time. Unheard words whispered around that feeling like long grass around her knees in the summertime. She had felt them, the words, the tickling and snicking grass, before, but she had not heard them, and she didn't want to hear them now, when goodness seemed within her reach and the words were so scratchy and the feeling so dense and embedded. Light. She had to concentrate on the light, to feel God in it, to feel the weightlessness of it.

I am sorry, she said in her mind to Glynnis, who sat like a king in her hospital bed. There was a long pause. *I forgive you,* said the imaginary Glynnis, with a slow nod of her head and a long blink of her eye.

And then the grass whispered, *She deserved it.*

Carol flushed, her heart tapping the inside of her chest like a metronome on presto. She glanced at her mother beside her, saw her slide herself forward on the pew, ready to stand, her finger already slipped into the new red hymnbook at the appropriate page.

"Good morning!" the minister said. "The congregation will stand for Hymn Number 274."

Carol hummed along with the hymn, not really listening, feeling the evil thing in her that no longer made her feel reckless and hopeful, but just sick. "Let there be light," sang Carol's mother and father and brother. "Let there be understanding, let all the nations gather, let them be face to face."

Glynnis

GLYNNIS GOT MOST of her leg out before the piano fell, giving the same distant and ethereal crash as before. At first she couldn't believe it. Her *body* knew it — her eyes, after all, had zinged a message to her brain and her brain had flooded bone and sinew with a great sucking riptide of action, but too late — bam, it fell, and now her leg wouldn't come out. She tugged. No result. It was pinned by the fallen piano, her left leg, from mid-calf down. Her right leg was out, bent up, foot planted and braced in the motion of pulling the left. Tug, tug. Nothing. Tug, tug.

The world turned huge and white, the largest thing she had ever felt. Her leg was a club eight times its regular size. She was surprised it hadn't tossed the piano off all on its own. But the nature of pain is weakness, she realized. Incapacity. She also realized that that high, thin wailing noise was coming from her own throat. Her mind was so behind her body it was astonishing.

People crowded around her. All the Brownies, and Tawny Owl crowding around the piano. "Get it off me," Glynnis bellowed, "get it off me." They put their hands under it. Everyone lifted. Someone pulled Glynnis out, tugging her by the armpits. Beautiful instant, no weight, nothing, nothing, beautiful instant. A blur of grey and green ran in followed by a blur of blue, Mr. Smith and Mrs. Riggs. Then bam it was back, worse. She heard kids saying "Oh, my God," and Tawny Owl retching, and then things got blurry and weird and weirder and all she knew was someone was holding her hand and if she let go she was doomed. Doomed.

There was a stretcher. A ride in dim light and her mother's voice, saying, "There's a brave girl, now, Glynnis, there's a brave girl." The hand was her mother's, strong and neat around Glynnis' own clenching one. Doom was at bay.

⌣

THERE WAS A bright room — hospital, Glynnis' mind told her — and a lot of faces looking into hers and mouths saying comforting things amongst other things that were a murmury formal wash, like prayers in church. And her mother's voice saying, "That's my brave girl, now, that's my brave girl, Glynnie. Yes, yes, that's it, brave Glynnie." And then saying other things to other people. And then saying something to her in a slow, careful voice. Glynnis didn't care about whatever got said in that voice, that voice didn't matter, the hand did. The hand was a talisman, an amulet. And it was letting go now. "NOOO!" shouted Glynnis as they wheeled her away. "NOOOO! I'M DOOOOOMED!"

After the hand dropped, Glynnis was wheeled. Down corridors, around corners, up elevators, around more corners, down more corridors. They were taking her somewhere deep, deep in the heart of the place this was — hospital, her brain prompted, another part of her brain saying no — deeper, deeper, till they came to a cave with a bright centre and dim corners, voices whispering and singing from the cave's walls — radio, her brain said; says you, said the other part of it. People moved unhurriedly around her, out-of-time figures in soft matching costumes. Here, the secrets of the universe would be unfolded to her, here her quest would be made known, what she had to do back in the outside world to earn her place in this pantheon of the Calm and the Wise. The softest voice imaginable spoke her name. How could they know her name if this wasn't the magical world to which she truly belonged and which had been waiting for her all these years while she was fostered with the Riggses? "Count backwards from ten," the voice said. What this really meant was, "Accept the mantle of your heroic destiny." Glynnis took a breath and counted. At seven she tasted onions. At six she fell into a deep rest.

A room blurred into view, a bright room, with a clock on the wall that split into two if Glynnis didn't look right at it. This is what they are trying to show when they put cameras out of focus, Glynnis thought. They're getting it wrong. Edges are not uniformly blurred; some are sharper than others.

The light hurt her eyes. She closed them and immediately her body ballooned up into a huge grey blimp of pain. She opened her eyes again. The pain scaled back into her left leg, not that she felt it as an actual leg, more like a force field of pain, a block of ice enclosing a leg-shaped thing.

She went on closing her eyes, opening them, closing them, opening them, each time astonished by the weird metamorphosis between blimp and force field. It made her feel sick.

After a blankness, she found herself in a small room, lying on a bunk, experiencing something like a movie or a play; sometimes she was in it, sometimes she was watching.

"Ruckin-fruckin' muck!" A voice from the bottom bunk said. "Your muckin' sister, man, I could ruckin-fruckin' kill her, I swear, I'll bust her puny little pale bones. I'm so hurt, you don't know."

Glynnis leaned over the edge of the bunk. Below her was a leg, her leg, the bottom half, from foot to knee. It had little bulbous eyes on the kneecap, and a wide, thin-lipped mouth just below them. Its head was broad and bald with two knobby semi-spherical bulges on each side that made up its cranium. It looked crabby, but fine.

"She gets that way sometimes," Glynnis said.

"*Gets* that way sometimes! *Gets* that way sometimes! What's *that* supposed to mean? Is that supposed to be an *excuse*? Is that supposed to make everything just *okeydokey*? Oh, yeah, she just gets that way sometimes. You might as well say Charles *Manson* gets that way sometimes. Jack the *Ripper* gets that way sometimes. Lucrezia *Borgia* gets that way sometimes."

"No, you don't get it," Glynnis said. "It's not like that. She's — She's — "

"She's vengeance personified, that's what she is. Listen, kid." The leg suddenly changed tone, pitching its voice lower, "none of that matters now. We keep arguing, we'll never get out of here, and we gotta get out of here."

"We do?"

The leg leaned forward and turned its head as if listening. It had a little hairy ear nestled underneath the bulge of its cranial lobe. Glynnis looked around the room. It was a jail cell. Bars for one wall, beyond it a corridor with bright lights and beyond the corridor the darkness in which the audience sat. In the room — or was it a stage? — were a bunk, wooden stacking chair, sink, toilet. Small window high up on outside wall, barred.

"Here," the leg said, gesturing with its head toward the window. "Boost me up. I think I can squeeze through the bars there."

"What about me? You can't leave me here."

"Listen, kid, I may be a lot of things, but I'd never leave a comrade behind. Hear that? I'd rather die than leave a comrade behind."

She boosted the leg up and it balanced on the window ledge between the bars, looking out. "Woo. Man," it said. "I'm getting — I'm getting dizzy." It teetered, then righted itself and told Glynnis to start tying bedsheets together. And then it was gone. It disappeared from the window. Glynnis heard only a faint, faint screaming that was more horrible because distant. It was gone. Destroyed. And there was nothing she could do. He was dead now, dead and gone, and Glynnis' heart felt bent, worse than broken, bent like a stepped-on tent pole, irreparable. She sobbed her grief and then realized she was awake and the thing with the leg had happened somewhere else, when she was asleep. Only it hadn't been a dream, either. Partly it had been her creation, though she couldn't control it in the end and the leg, the cranky, brave leg had fallen. She missed him. His griping, his bossiness. Closing her eyes, she tried to go back to where it all started, that room at the centre of the hospital, the labyrinth.

Too bright, it was too bright. Her eyes opened. She was in a bed. Her mother beside her. Noises behind them, carts and voices and whimpering. The sounds hurt. Her head was very little and everything else was very big, especially her left leg, which felt as big as a refrigerator, but also very far away, at least as far the next room, maybe further, and not a refrigerator after all, but rather a big hunk of meat trapped in a freezer, inside of which the sharpest, coldest winter wind blew on her exposed limb while six grey foxes gnawed on the near-frozen flesh.

IN GLYNNIS' SCARIEST DREAM, the one she had when in a high fever or in other extremity, there were no people at all. All that happened was that she lay face-up six inches below an infinitely wide and long grey-black thing like a cloud, but a cloud dense as felt, dense as felt and seething and infinitely thick. And though it did not touch her, it weighed down on her, it oppressed her. One instant of it was unbearable, but to wake up was to lose it, and that, too, was unbearable. She always felt if she could just dream it one more time or a little bit longer, then she would be able to describe it in a way that did its terror justice. Now she dreamed it over and over, waking exhausted then falling back into its thick, heavy nothingness, never able to say how infinite and beautiful and terrible it was. The only other thing she had heard described that way was God. She tried praying to it, but it didn't care, and that seemed like God, too, not the God-is-Love God of church, not the God who was a who, but the God who was an it, a force with the power to make out of nothing everything there was, a force on which human suffering, big-bellied, fly-covered children in Biafra and people kidnapped and locked in car trunks and people with their skin burned off them, registered not at all.

GLYNNIS DIDN'T KNOW how long it was before she got used to day and night again, to things coming after one another in a regular way, light, meals, shots, pills, bedpans, voices, darkness, hands probing, lifting, stroking, tearing. All that regular life happened vaguely and distantly like a fly buzzing in the next room. The warm, firm hand came and went. The adventures of her and the mustachioed leg continued, with bizarre variations. He was a leg. He was a toe. He was attached to her just like her real leg was. He danced on the end of her bed. His flesh slumped off its bones in oozing clumps, beetles scuttled over the open wound, little writhing worms rose out of it, and she woke panting and desperate. Her leg. Her leg. Her real leg: there it was: clean, bugless.

Gradually she became aware that the hand was her mother's and the people who came in and out were not random, but the same ones over and over, nurses and doctors and orderlies. Gradually she became aware that she shared the room with others.

One nurse was very tall and skinny with red curly hair, buck teeth and a soft voice. She walked bent forward at the hips as if always leaning into her destination. Another was solid and sturdy, with thick glasses and a mole on her cheek right next to the dimple of her smile.

There was a black lady with flat hair and a strong African accent who came and emptied Glynnis' bedpan, and changed the sheets and plumped the pillows. She always looked tired and talked so little Glynnis came to think of her as unable to say anything but Up, Down, Roll right, Roll left and Done your business? And there was a man with a very round, shiny head and big black glasses, who always came with a crowd he called "all the king's horses and all the king's men." This was the surgeon. The crowd was his students.

"Morning, Humpty," he would say to the person in the bed across from Glynnis', a girl she could only glimpse past two white casts suspended on pulleys just like on cartoons when someone jumped off a cliff and ended in hospital.

"Morning, Dumpty," he would then say to Glynnis. Then one of the king's horses and men would try to distract her by asking her what grade she was in or how she liked her teacher while another began to unbandage her leg so they could examine it and Glynnis would concentrate on holding the leg up for him, her eyes sprouting pain-tears. It still felt like a club, her leg. Inside it was a deep ache that made her think, for some reason, of the core of a carrot, how it was tougher and stringier than the outside of the carrot and how, if you peeled off the outside with your teeth, what was left was this spine with ganglia radiating from it at intervals. This was the inner pain. The outer pain was like someone had taken a giant vegetable peeler and peeled off her skin. All of this was just the regular pain, which was sometimes worse and sometimes better, but always there. The pain when even the very gentlest nurse, the tall, quiet one, took off the bandages was indescribable. The sturdy one, her name was

Kerry, told Glynnis it was okay to yell, told her to yell into her pillow, took it out from behind her first and put it in Glynnis' hands.

If Mrs. Riggs was there, the doctor would say, "Hold her hand, would you, Mom?"

"It hu-u-urts," Glynnis would wail.

"I know, dear, I know," her mother would say, letting Glynnis' tears run onto her knuckle.

Today Mrs. Riggs was not there, and tears ran into Glynnis' ears. The doctor asked if Glynnis could feel a series of what might have been pinpricks or might have been random hot spots on the flesh. He asked her to wiggle her toes, on which she had to concentrate immensely. "That's it, good girl." Then they wrapped her back up. The tall nurse came with another shot, and Glynnis fell again into the jailbreak scene with the leg.

She woke with the dream howl just a whimper like a sliver in her throat. Her leg, her real leg, pounded along with her heart. Someone else was whimpering, too, very quietly, and in a way it was worse than the dream. Glynnis panted, quieting. The whimper, coming from the other side of the curtain next to her bed, turned into a moan.

"Are you okay, Lilah?" a child's voice asked.

"Poor Lilah," said the moaning voice, sounding as if her speech came entirely from nasal passages at the back of her throat and only passed through the mouth as a wind. "Poor Lilah, poor Lilah, poor Lilah, poor Lilah, poor Lilah."

"God," said a third voice, Humpty's. "I wish she'd stop that." Glynnis propped herself up on her elbows to look at the speaker, but all she could see was the two casts.

"She can't help it," the second voice said from the bed kitty-corner to Glynnis'. This person she couldn't see either, since the bed was flat and the girl was lying down.

"What's wrong with her?" asked Glynnis.

"Is that the new girl?" said the second voice.

"She's a retard," said Humpty, answering Glynnis.

They both went off into a fit, repeating, "'Is that the new girl?' 'She's a retard.'"

Glynnis folded her tongue over her lower front teeth and tucked the tip of it behind her lower lip. "Yuh, I'm a re-tahr," she said.

"Am no' a rwee-tar, am no', am no', am no', am no', am no'," the first girl said in a loud, hurt voice. Glynnis wanted to hide under the bed.

"Way to go," the lying-flat girl said. "It's okay, Lilah, we know you're not. Some people just don't know any better."

Lilah whimpered and then began to moan. It was a rhythmic moaning, almost like a car turning over in the cold as someone tried to start it.

"Want me to buzz a nurse, Lilah?" the lying-flat girl asked.

Now Lilah latched onto this word. "Nurse! Nurse! Nurse! Nurse …," she went. Humpty counted each repetition. There were six.

"You're right. Six times."

"Told ya."

"Did you buzz?"

"Yeah."

"Poor Lilah, poor Lilah, poor Lilah, poor Lilah, poor Lilah."

"Five," said lying-flat girl.

"Is it true a piano fell on you?" Humpty asked Glynnis.

"Sort of."

The tall nurse came in at her usual tilt and headed for the far bed.

"It's Lilah," lying-flat girl said. "She's been doing that thing again."

"What thing?"

Humpty imitated Lilah's throat-and-nose intonations just as Glynnis had done: "Poor Lilah, poor Lilah."

"Lucy, don't, I mean it," said the nurse.

"Sorry."

But Lilah had already joined in. "Poor Lilah, poor Lilah …"

The nurse asked Lilah what was wrong. Hurts, said Lilah. Bones, said Lilah. Glynnis felt the same way. She wondered what had fallen on Lilah. She imagined that everyone there had had something fall on them.

Just then Mrs. Riggs walked in, talking to another lady dressed in a grey suit. This lady trotted quickly ahead as she saw the nurse at Lilah's bedside. "What's wrong?" she asked the nurse.

"Lilah says it hurts."

The woman hurried behind the curtain. "Poor Lilah," Glynnis heard her say. "Mommy's here now. It's okay."

"You're awake!" Mrs. Riggs said to Glynnis. "How are you feeling?"

"It hurts," Glynnis said. Wait. That's what Lilah had said. "It kills."

"I know, dear, I know. Boy, it's good to see you more alert. You've had a rough go of it the last few days."

Glynnis liked having her mother there so much of the time, having her hand to hold, connecting her to something alive outside her torpor, letting her know that something other than her was flesh and blood. They played double solitaire and hangman and the game where you join dots on a grid with lines and claim each box you close with your initials. Her mother handed Glynnis water, and kleenex, and books that Glynnis ended up not being able to concentrate on, and when that happened, she read to her. Right now they were two chapters into *Kidnapped*.

Lucy's (Humpty's) mother and father and brother and grandmother came at four-thirty every day. They spoke in low voices in another language and Lucy's personality changed almost completely. Erica's (lying-flat girl's) mother came at six; Erica stayed the same.

Mr. Riggs showed up around the time it started getting dim outside. He kissed Glynnis on the forehead and called her sport, which normally she hated because it showed how clueless he was, but now she was glad he was there, too. She was glad he was in his casual clothes and not his uniform. When he was in his uniform, she felt like he wanted to be leaving, that's what the uniform was about, leaving, flying off somewhere, being airborne. He had a slightly different personality in uniform than out, in his open-necked shirt and v-neck sweater, a drink in his hand.

After he'd asked her how she was and put the flowers he'd brought on the bedside table, he didn't seem to know what to say, he didn't seem to know he could just sit there and read to himself and she'd be happy. He sat in the chair, leaned forward with his elbows on his knees, clasped his hands together and looked around the room.

"How's the room service here?" he said. "Pretty good?"

"Oh, yeah," she said, making a face. "Just great."

"Is there anything you want? Anything I can get you?"

Glynnis wanted to be at home, with a regular leg, not a smashed-up one, but there wasn't much her father could do about that.

"Poor kid," he said. "I bet it hurts like heck, eh?"

She nodded. He reached out to stroke her hair off her forehead. She closed her eyes as his fingers gently took a strand of hair and pushed it to the side. His knuckles brushed her forehead.

Erica and Lucy played twenty questions.

"*Everything* you pick is smaller than a bread box," said Lucy.

"So?"

"Is it smaller than a *slice* of bread?"

"Yes."

"Smaller than a *crumb* of bread?"

"Depends how big the crumb is."

"Oh, big help."

Her father raked his fingers lightly through her hair. *Don't stop,* Glynnis thought.

"Is it a bug?" Lucy asked.

"Yes," said Erica.

"My turn!"

"No, you have to guess what bug."

"Forget it! Who cares?"

Glynnis breathed more deeply. With the backs of his fingers, her father stroked her cheek.

"Is it a flea?"

"Nope."

"A ant?"

"Give up?"

"Spider?"

"Uh-uh."

Termite, Glynnis thought. *Housefly. Blackfly. Mosquito.*

"I don't want to play anymore."

"You giving up?"

"No, I just don't want to play anymore."

"You're giving up."

"No, I'm not. I just don't want to play."

This was what she and Carol sounded like, the old Glynnis, the old Carol. Pushing at each other, pushing, pushing. But needing each other, too. With no one to push, you just fell over. Or you didn't even start, you were immobile, a doll sitting on the floor with splayed legs.

Glynnis breathed deeper still, almost asleep. Then her father withdrew his hand and she was awake again, though she didn't open her eyes. She heard him get up and pace, heard her mother come back and ask if Glynnis was asleep, heard her say, "Oh, Glenn, how could I have let this happen?" Heard her voice catch and rasp in her throat, heard her breath come out in rushes. Heard her, for the first time ever, cry.

Even though she didn't want them to know she'd heard something she wasn't supposed to hear, she couldn't help herself, she had to look. She slitted open her eyes. Her mother's face was against her father's chest and her shoulders were shaking. He held her tightly, his broad hand bunching the fabric of her top. She pushed away from him slightly, pulled a kleenex from her sleeve. He was about to look up, Glynnis could sense it, and she quickly shut her eyes.

Microbe, she thought, with the sudden certainty she always got when she had the right answer.

⌒

THAT THEY TRIED to simulate Halloween at the hospital just showed how pathetic hospital life was. (Before actually being in the hospital, Glynnis had had fantasies of hospital stays, part of a series of no-parent fantasies she had — boarding school, summer camp, orphanage. The reality was much more tedious.) If you didn't go out of doors in the dark wearing a costume and knocking on doors, you hadn't had Halloween. Halloween *was* being outside in your costume, long johns and a sweater underneath and the air chill against your cheeks, your fingers cold at first around the handles of the plastic bag, then warming up as you warmed. Halloween was marching down the street shouting *Shell out! Shell out! The witches are out!* and feeling almost like it was true, you were that in control of things, and that dangerous. Getting the scoop from other groups of kids on where the good and bad houses were, like the dentist's house that gave out toothbrushes instead of candy, or the house that was giving out cans of pop, or the houses with the most theatrical displays (houses that could also generally be relied upon to give out the best candy — name brands instead of those gross chewy things in the orange wrappers), the ones with creepy music playing or graveyards on their front lawns or doors rigged up with skeletons that zinged down the stairs at you when the door opened. And then coming home and dumping the bag upside down on the living room floor, spreading it out to pore over and sort before choosing three treats to eat that night.

Halloween was not doctors and nurses and patients (the things normal people dressed up as) dressing up as witches and fairies and convicts. It was not being bedridden and forced to do gay crafts with construction paper. Only Linda, the red-haired nurse, made her feel better. What Linda did was not try. She acted like it was any other day. Only when she moved from bed to bed she made a weird slapping sound. Glynnis peeked over the edge of the bed as Linda took her vitals. Clown shoes.

"What?" Linda said.

"You're wearing clown shoes."

"No, I'm not."

"What are those?"

"What are what?"

"Those."

"Penny loafers."

With her clown hair, it was as if she were not wearing a costume at all, as if this were her true self: clown. Glynnis was almost starting to enjoy herself when her family, in church clothes, filed in, Jay first, then Carol, held by the shoulders in front of Mrs. Riggs, with Mr. Riggs behind.

The sight of Carol was a shock. Glynnis had somehow imagined Carol would look different, but she didn't, not at all. In fact, the whole family looked the same, which made them seem unreal, as if they were robots in the shape of her family. Her mother, for one, she knew to be changed; how then could she look the same, slip back into the selfsame groove she'd leapt out of for that long moment, weeping in her husband's arms?

Seeing her mother cry like that had shifted something. Glynnis grew afraid. Everything seemed suddenly less certain. That the leg would be fine, that people would always like her, that what she thought of herself was true, that her version of the world was the only version, that she had greater insight than most people seemed to have.

For as long as she could remember, Glynnis had felt herself to be in opposition to her parents. They were people to hide things from, show one face to while hiding another, to rail at the unfairness of. This was possible because they were, if not gods, then not simply people, either. Their frustration was not the same as other people's frustration, their temper was not the same as other people's tempers. They made no mistakes. They were wrong a great deal of the time, of course, but that was not the same as making mistakes. Even the possibility that they might err had not seemed to exist. Her father was a professional pilot, for whom one small mistake could cost hundreds of lives. Her mother was Brown Owl.

But now her mother had revealed herself not only to think herself capable of making mistakes, and not only so capable of making mistakes that she would blame herself for having made one, but actually to be making an enormous mistake. Her mistake was thinking that the accident might be her fault. It was not her fault. It was Carol's.

Mrs. Riggs had said the previous afternoon that Carol was terribly upset and terribly sorry and that she hadn't meant to hurt Glynnis. Bull crap, Glynnis had thought. That's exactly what she meant to do. Glynnis knew it because she could still hear the tone in Carol's voice when she'd said, "You're Dorothy because I say so." It had been as full of intent to hurt as a voice could get. She knew it, too, because there were times when, in remembering the accident, she'd felt the exact same thing, and she recognized the feeling from times she had played British bulldog and had someone crack their elbow on her chin, say. You feel this sudden rush where meanness runs pure and clean inside you and you want to punch or kick or elbow or tighten the headlock. Only afterwards does your meanness become shameful and dirty, when the person is crying and saying *I hate you*. Then you think you didn't mean it. But Carol had. And Glynnis did now. And Mrs. Riggs wanted Glynnis to forgive Carol. She had asked Glynnis if she understood what was meant by forgiveness. She had talked about God and Christ and had said the Lord's Prayer and made Glynnis say it with her.

Glynnis did understand the concept. The word she had only ever used when she was joking, but she understood the concept. She just didn't know if it had any validity, if it actually worked. As a philosophical concept it had a certain beauty, but it seemed like it would never be fully applicable in practice, like dividing by zero or multiplying by one. What was the point? You got either something weirder than nothing or the same result.

Nor was she certain she had ever been fully forgiven herself. For anything. Or if she had been, that it wasn't conditional and temporary and thus not the thing her mother described in her little talk. Glynnis did something wrong, was found out, made to describe her own wrongdoing, punished, and then in disgrace for a length of time that varied with the seriousness of her misdemeanour. Being in disgrace didn't end in forgiveness so much as taper off into a wariness that awaited her next misdemeanour. There had been times, however, when she had felt truly, truly sorry, and these times her mother was almost gentle, almost kind. Maybe that was it.

She had run the line from the Lord's Prayer over in her head as her mother talked. Forgive us our trespasses as we forgive those that trespass against us. Forgive us our trespasses as we forgive those that trespass against us. If you ran it all together, it was just a lot of hissing and humming.

Her family seemed nervous and trying not to be.

"Hey, kid," Jay said.

"Well, well, well," Mr. Riggs said. "If it isn't Glamorous Glennis herself."

"Happy Halloween," said Mrs. Riggs, kissing her cheek. "Do you remember what I said about forgiveness?" she said in a low voice close to Glynnis' ear, and Glynnis nodded. Her mother backed away.

Carol said nothing, but kept twisting the sheet. She didn't look like a person capable of yelling, "You're Dorothy because I say so," like a maniac. She looked like a sick rabbit, weak and nervous. She looked like she wanted to run out of the room crying. Mucus bubbled in her nose, you could hear it.

Glynnis despised her.

"Carol? We're waiting," Mrs. Riggs said.

Carol flicked her eyes up at Glynnis a few times before she really looked at her, genuine distress apparent in her distorted peepers. "I'm sorr-ee-ee-ee," she wept, her mouth morphing into that sort of rectangle that happens with crying. "I'm sorr-ee-ee," she repeated. Glynnis looked at her, feeling nothing but an empty cave inside her so cold it burned, eclipsing for an instant the core carrot pain of her leg. Then she saw her mother's hands shift and tighten. She was about to be told to say something to her sister, and suddenly Glynnis couldn't stand the thought of their mother's words between them.

"I know," she said. "I know."

Rowena

ROWENA MADE A grocery list for Beryl as she rode the subway down to the hospital, while in the back of her mind she composed another list. Spend time with Carol (suggest Snakes and Ladders). Spend time with Jay (try Mastermind). Ask Jay about Crusaders project. Be home for dinner. She mustn't let them feel they were less important than Glynnis.

Carol seemed relieved after the visit with Glynnis. Her apology had gone over well, Glynnis had not objected or accused or blamed but had accepted it, graciously, even. A touching scene, in which Rowena felt herself regained. This was not going to destroy both girls' lives, it was not going to destroy their relationship as sisters. There would be difficulties still, but they would work through them together. See how well they had responded to the talk about forgiveness? They would be open. They would continue to talk. They would come out the other side.

She and Glenn had not spoken, really, about the accident. On the phone, yes, that embarrassing time in hysterics. On the way home after the first day at the hospital, but then only the strict how of it — the dumbwaiter boys, the report she'd got from June of some game to do with the Wizard of Oz, Carol being a bad sport and lashing out at the bricks. He had run his hand over his face, something he did in disbelief or emotion, taken in a big breath and let it out, then picked up her hand as he drove (too fast, as always) and kissed it. This gesture was intended to mean what the embrace in the hospital had meant: Do not blame yourself, or rather, I have forgiven you: blame is irrelevant. He never said it out loud and she did not want him to. He did not understand the nature of her self-blame, its subtleties. She did not tell him about the world falling apart, breaking up into atoms. It was not relevant and she didn't know how in any case. Except about the children, they had a habit of communicating in ways other than words. They did speak. But one of the things they liked about one another was that they didn't have to chatter, chatter, chatter all the time. That they were in tune.

They were not in tune now. If she let it be so, they would be again.

"We'll have to hear the story from Carol," Glenn said in the car, both hands on the wheel now, draped on top. They'd talked from there about the children, how this might affect them, what they must do to ensure it did not, or not any more adversely than it must, and it was about that and surgery and doctors and treatment they continued to talk.

How familiar the hospital was becoming. The nurses greeted her with bright smiles, other parents smiled and exchanged pleasantries. There was Libby in consultation with the sandy-haired doctor now, and Mrs. Nunes faithfully parked by her daughter, working away at her lace.

"Hello," Rowena said brightly to her. The poor dear couldn't speak English, but Rowena for one would be friendly anyway. Then "Hello," brightly to Glynnis, intent with a colouring book. Hello to all the children, Erica in her body cast reading a comic book, Delilah breathing noisily through her nose, Lucy smacking a baseball into a glove while listening to a transistor radio. Hello to Libby, coming into the room now, but no response. Bad news?

After a time bowed over Delilah's sleeping form, Libby rose. Her eyes were wet and her gaze passed quickly over Rowena's. In the hall her footsteps broke into a run.

"Will you — ?" Rowena nodded to Glynnis, making it to the hall in time to spy Libby pushing open the door to the parents' lounge. Even from this distance, she could hear the sob burst out as soon as the empty room was gained. Oh, dear. It must be very bad news.

Strangely, she felt a pull toward Libby, the opposite of the feeling she usually had at other people's sorrow, which was to walk quickly in the opposite direction. Perhaps it was all those years of being shut up in a house with her morose father, who fed his grief with Gooderham's and then was not content until he'd spilled it all over somebody. She was not that kind of woman, the sympathetic kind. But here she was, drawn down the hall toward sorrow, opening the door.

"Do you — " She didn't know what she was going to ask, but it didn't matter. Libby fell on her as soon as the door shut.

"Oh, Rowena," she cried.

"Sit down, Libby. Sit down."

At last, Libby sat. She blew her nose into her handkerchief, said "Oh, dear" a great deal, occasionally lapsing again into sobs. The reason Delilah's bones were not healing was because she had bone cancer.

"Oh, Libby!" Rowena said.

No, no. That was not the worst of it, said Libby. She had raised Delilah on her own. Her husband had left because he could not stand looking at Delilah and seeing the physical resemblance to him while knowing there was no mental resemblance. Libby loved Delilah, loved her like crazy, there was no one sweeter, Libby would do anything for her, but there was an evil, corrupt part of her that knew what he meant, that felt the disconnect between normal and not, felt that there was an essentially unbridgeable gap between them, no matter how great the love. And now, now with this new diagnosis, well, the first thing she'd felt was … well, fear first, that was the first thing, but next was a little sort of plea, a little voice inside her that went, "Oh yes, oh please." And she hated herself.

This took, actually, a very long time to come out but Rowena felt a sort of exquisite patience. She knew there was something more, something very deep, eating away at this poor soul — even as she had been eaten away the night of Glynnis' surgery. The night she had come to think of as the dark night of her soul. With a brightness in her heart, she told Libby about it and about the peace she felt now. The brightness in her heart was powerful, almost painful. Afterwards, in Glynnis' room, watching her daughter eat, knowing Libby was comforted, it came to her that this was a religious feeling, a feeling of God. She had been speaking of God with God in her heart and it had helped Libby.

This seemed, actually, not possible, a foolish notion. And yet there it was. What she had done was God's work. God was the feeling that compelled her to turn and follow Libby. God was the feeling that gave her real compassion where previously she had only recognized she ought to feel compassion.

She felt no compulsion to do anything more than rest in the glow of this. Libby sat at the next bed, holding Delilah's hand.

Carol

DAINTRY HAD THIS WAY of just sort of shutting down that Carol envied. She'd go all still and blank when someone said her name the way the name seemed to invite — with a rise in the middle like they were imitating something prissy — Da-ain-try. Then, after they were gone, she was back, picking up wherever she'd left off, in the middle of spooning out porridge, say, if they were playing house, or in the middle of being Jesus raising Lazarus from the dead if they were acting out Bible stories as Daintry liked to do.

During school the day after the accident, Carol had tried it. She imagined, as she shouldered her way past barbs and prods to the pencil sharpener with her blunted Laurentians, or huddled in her seat amid waves of giggles and whispers, that she had a button in the middle of her back and that God leaned down and shut it off. His enormous ghostly hand floated behind her, long knubbly-knuckled index finger neatly flipping the switch. Snap.

Instead of a rush of wind scooping her up and depositing her on a vast snowy plain, though, everything continued just as usual: yellowish light hit yellowish desk, casting shadow on Carol's knees. Her map of Canada still lay half-coloured, pencils arrayed around it. Her ears kept hearing pencils scratching and whispers and sighs, her heart kept pumping a beat to her hot ears, flushing her face. Snap. Same again. Nothing changed.

You are not here, she tried saying to herself, waving her blue Laurentian back and forth over Hudson Bay like a hypnotist's pendulum. *You are not here.*

But that didn't work, either. She was there. She was so there that when Roger Meaford leaned forward and delivered his loudly whispered pass-it-on message with mock innocence, sloppy hand whipping up to cover his Oops-shaped mouth, her reaction was immediate and involuntary. "I did not!" she spurted, on her feet, arms and legs straightened and tense, hands in fists.

Quiet dropped on the class. Three heartbeats later it broke in intakes of breath and shuffles just as Roger shrugged and Mrs. Harris stood, tugging down the top of her skirt suit. In her scary ultra-polite voice, she said, "Did not what, Miss Riggs?"

Carol was still aboil, her face pink with it. "I did not kill my sister!"

"I should hope not," Mrs. Harris said in the same voice. "Who suggested you had?"

Roger's name spilled out past Carol's quivering chin.

"I was only passing it on," Roger said.

Carol wasn't a noisy crier except for her sniffles and big gasps of breath, but inside her own head, crying took up a lot of space. It was not equivalent to switching off altogether like Daintry, but it did make everything feel farther away. Mrs. Harris seemed as far away as a minister in a pulpit as she waved her fingers toward the back corner of the classroom where people were sent "to contain themselves."

Strangely, it was only a visual effect. Mrs. Harris' voice sounded crisp and close. "Yes, Suzanne?" she said. "Don't look smug, Roger, I haven't forgottten you."

"Excuse me," came Suzanne's voice. "It's true Carol didn't kill Glynnis, but she did push a piano on her and she is in the hospital and she *might* die ..."

At this, all the girls in the class who had been at Brownies gave their version of the story at once, making Mrs. Harris blast "Quiet!" in her foghorn voice. She never crescendoed, she never even seemed to take an extra breath, she just went from level voice to thunderous boom that flattened everything in its path. As usual, she paused in the glory of her effectiveness, then went back to her regular fake sweetish voice. "I'm sure it's all very exciting, and we're *all* concerned for Glynnis, but I don't want to hear a single word more of this, do you understand? Not a single word."

Then she told Roger to trade seats with Corey Smythe and invited Carol, who had indeed been able to contain herself if not to shut herself off, back to her seat. At recess Mrs. Harris asked Carol to stay behind for a moment. She asked if what Suzanne had said was true and if Carol knew how her sister was, and Carol had to say yes, it was true, but she hadn't meant to, it had been an accident, and she didn't know how Glynnis was, all she knew was she'd had to have an operation. No one had said anything about dying. Panic licked at Carol's insides.

"She's not going to die, is she? She can't die, she's not going to die."

And Mrs. Harris said, "There, there, Carol. There, there. I'm sure she's not going to die." Then she sent her to the nurse's office for the rest of the morning.

Back at school the day after next, reassured that Glynnis would not die, or even, despite Miss Balls' chirpy allusions, lose her leg, and relieved at last to have bawled her heart out in front of her sombre parents, she forgot about shutting down until a big boy slowed down as he rode his bike past her on the sidewalk next to the schoolyard and said, "Hey, you're the psycho-killer albino, aren't you?" He sped on down the sidewalk, then stomped on his brake and spun out, yelling, "One-eighty!" as he did so. Back up on his pedals, he hauled on the handlebars and accelerated straight at Carol, veering at the last second. "Whatsa matter, killer? Chicken?"

Carol stayed stuck to the pavement until he'd ridden into the schoolyard, then she ran to the steps next to the teachers' parking lot, up into the schoolyard and straight to the doors, where she waited for the bell to ring.

At recess she wasn't any better prepared when a crowd formed around her, chanting, "Ki-*ller*! Ki-*ller*! Ki-*ller*!" She closed her eyes, summoning God's long finger again. Flick. "Ki-*ller*! Ki-*ller*!" Flick-flick. Busted. It was never going to work. She opened her eyes. A dozen kids bent in toward her, their eyes bright, their heads bobbing in the rhythm of their chant. Suzanne, Janet, Gordie, Roger, Mike, kids from the other grade three class, kids she didn't know, smirking and bobbing. "Ki-*ller*! Ki-*ller*! Ki-*ller*!" Something huge and bottled up in her, like a genie or diarrhea, wanted to get out. She let loose, arms flying, legs spinning her round in a circle, lungs launching an enormous howl. Hunks of the crowd broke away in shrieks, scattering.

As her lungs cacked out, her spin slowed and her arms dropped. The few remaining kids took off at the sight of the teacher on duty, strolling purposefully in their direction, hands behind her back, as always, where they held the bell, but seeming, as always, like they held something scarier. She slowed, giving Carol — alone now on the asphalt — a long look before turning on her heel and taking up her regular slow troll.

Carol edged her way around a group playing Mother-may-I over to the chainlink fence at the south edge of the asphalt, clutching it in her cold fingers and peering through two diamonds like another pair of glasses past the big grassy hill down to Blythwood Road to the bare treetops of Sherwood Park beyond it, looking peaceful and wild. All of a sudden she sensed someone behind her and spun around quickly. One skinny little boy stood facing the school about twenty feet from her, and about thirty feet behind the others playing the game. "Mother may I cross the river!" he shouted. "No you may not," shouted back the leader. The boy stood there mute, waiting for his next chance.

Carol stretched her arms out and snagged the fence with two fingers on each hand as she bounced her bum against the chainlink. Her brown buckle-shoes appeared and disappeared beneath the hem of her duffle coat. When, after a long while, she glanced up again, the skinny boy still had not advanced. Daintry was playing in the horseshoe-shaped treewell abutting the fence to her left.

Looking again at her shoes, and running her left hand along the chainlink, Carol scuffed slowly, as if aimlessly, in Daintry's direction, then bounced again a few strides away from her. Shoes, coat, shoes, coat, shoes, coat. Daintry played X's and O's with a stone on the top of the wall around the treewell. Carol sidled closer. Shoes, coat, shoes, coat. Daintry wasn't in the habit of asking people to play. She'd invited Glynnis, once, that time Glynnis got all snotty about playing house. That was the only time Carol could remember. Her eyes stung at the corners, thinking of it, and of Daintry saying nothing now.

"Can I play?" she asked finally.

Daintry looked up. "My mother says I can pray for you but I can't play with you." Whump, went Carol's stomach. What Daintry's mother said was final. So that was that. Carol officially had no friends.

She told Reginald so that night. My family hates me and I have no friends. Everybody hates me except Miss Balls, and she would too if she knew the truth. She bent Reginald's worn white head forward to say, *I'm your friend, Carol-Marrill. I know you are,* Carol said, stroking the greyish tufts of his ears.

Day after day she tried to shut down, to go someplace inside herself. She tried it when Julie Rice said she'd only been nice to her out of charity because she wanted to show Alison and Bridget that people shouldn't be mean to other people, but now that Carol had been mean to Glynnis, well, she didn't deserve for people to be nice to her. She tried it when little kids on dares ran up as close to her as they could then tore off squealing. She tried it when big kids yelled out, "Hey, Crusher! Who'd ya flatten today?" She tried it when her former friends Suzanne Wells or Wendy Gold would pretend to be making up with her and get her talking while somebody else knelt on all fours behind her so that when Suzanne or Wendy gave her just a little push, she went tumbling backwards. She tried it when people stuck out their feet to trip her in class. She tried it when a note 'accidentally' landed on her desk, saying "What does C.A.R.O.L. stand for?" on one side and "Crazy Albino Rips Off Legs" on the other.

She failed.

And then she discovered a place she could go: the washroom. She was careful not to go too often or to stay too long, but sometimes, sitting there on the toilet, with or without her skirt up and leotards down depending on whether she actually had to go or not, she would get lost in thoughts of being a stewardess on her father's airline and flying all over the world, or of going to Wyoming and living with the wild horses, patiently taming them one by one, or becoming more and more wild herself, growing fur to keep her warm in winter and finally joining them as an accepted member of the herd.

The first several times this happened, Carol would be startled out of her reverie by the sound of children's voices as they entered the washroom, and would hop up, flush the toilet whether she'd used it or not, stick her hands under the tap and race back to class. Then one time Mrs. Harris actually sent Julie Rice to get her and Carol had to limit herself to one visit per morning and one per afternoon, plus of course recess and lunch.

On the second Friday morning after the accident, she was hearing the thundering of hooves as the herd swept down the valley. Flicka nickered urgently underneath her, and trotted in place with eagerness. Carol reached down a calming caress onto Flicka's shoulder, keeping the reins steady in her left hand. And then she froze.

"Ca-rol. Oh, Ca-rol," a voice said quietly. There was no other sound. Carol's feet were tingling from having dangled so long over the edge of the toilet seat. She slid, easily because she hadn't taken her leotards down this time, forward on the seat so her feet were flat on the floor. "Ca-rol," the voice called again.

Carol peered through the crack in the cubicle door, but saw nothing. She decided to pretend she was just finishing and tugged toilet paper off the roll, balling it up, then turning to drop it in the toilet and flush. BAM-BAM-BAM-BAM-BAM went the walls of her cubicle. Her heart thundered like the horses' hooves. The banging seemed to come from all sides, but she saw no feet out front, no feet in the cubicles on either side.

"Ca-rol, oh, Caaa-rol," the voice called again, trying to sound far away, but identifiably now coming from the cubicle to her left. BAM-BAM-BAM-BAM-BAM went the walls again. Her heart galloped away in her chest. "Go away," she forced herself to say. "Leave me alone."

No one answered. Carol wondered if anyone was on the other side of the door, waiting for her. She didn't think so. She put her hand on the door lock, preparing herself to turn it, pull and race from the bathroom into the relative safety of the hall. One. Two.

"Ha!" two voices yelled at once on either side of her, the shapes of their heads popping up above and behind her. Carol jerked the door open, banging it on her forehead and then against her shin before managing to get the opening and forward movement coordinated so her body could get through. She ran from the bathroom, down the hall, slowing on the stairs to pull the cuffs of her shirt over her hands and dig behind her glasses to wipe her eyes. Laughter burst through the steel doors behind her and feet pounded up the steps as Alison and Katie raced past. After taking the second floor doors at a run and tearing down the hall, they slowed just before the classroom door, straightening their posture and gaining their composure. They snickered in their seats as Mrs. Harris greeted Carol.

"Nice to have you back, Miss Riggs. As you can see, we are practising our writing."

On the board were sentences Mrs. Harris had printed that they were to put into writing. Don't be a quitter. Pick up your litter. See the yellow warbler puff out its chest and sing. Sally loves to take trips to the zoo. Freddy Flute is a fine fellow, though a show-off. Every egg in the basket broke.

She was on the line of capital effs she had to do to practise for Freddy Flute when she felt her bladder begin to strain. Eleven o'clock. One hour to go before lunch. She concentrated on forming the letters on the page. Carol liked writing, how slow and careful it was, how the capital *T*s and *H*s and *Q*s were so fancy and how everything had fancy tails on them. Mrs. Harris' handwriting was beautiful, very elegant. Carol's generally started well but went wrong. She still had to consult the big cards posted up above the blackboard for the capitals.

Her leotard elastic pressed against her bladder. She shifted in her chair, crossed her legs and started on her practice capital *E*s. *Every*, she wrote, but her *v* looked like a *u* and she had to start again. When she'd finished the sentence, she raised her hand.

"Yes, Carol?"

"May I please go to the bathroom?"

"What time is it, Carol?"

"Ten after eleven."

"And what time did you get back from your last trip to the washroom?"

"I don't know."

"Would you like me to remind you?"

There was no right way to answer that.

"You returned at ten minutes to eleven. Now, if you returned at ten minutes to eleven, and it is now ten minutes past eleven, how many minutes is it that you have been with us?"

Somebody else shouted out the answer. "I'd like Carol to answer, please."

"Twenty," Carol said softly.

"Twenty minutes since your last washroom visit, Miss Riggs. That's not very long, is it?"

"No."

"You will wait until lunchtime for your next."

Carol had it on her tongue to say *But I didn't go before*, but she couldn't let on she'd asked to go to the bathroom when she hadn't needed to. Mrs. Harris turned her attention elsewhere and Carol crossed her legs the other way, squeezing her thighs together. The next sentence was, Gary grabbed the grasshopper. She laboured on her row of capital Gs, pushing her pencil slowly up the slope of the first stroke, speeding on the first loop and the dip over to the next loop, then slowing again to round the letter's belly. It was one of the capitals she didn't really get, it was so unlike its printed counterpart. Little and big zed, either. *G G G G*, she wrote. Quarter past eleven. The *Ee, eff, gee* part of the alphabet song went through her head. *Aitch eye jay kay ell em en o pee.* Keeping her thighs tense, she wiggled in her seat, remembering the joke where the teacher won't let the kid go to the bathroom until he's sung the alphabet and he leaves out pee so the teacher goes, "Where's the pee?" and the kid goes, "Running down my pants." She put up her hand again.

Mrs. Harris ignored it. Carol bent her arm at the elbow then flung it to its full extent repeatedly. "Mrs. Harris, please, I really have to go."

Mrs. Harris looked over her reading glasses at the clock, then back at Carol as if to emphasize her disapproval. She sighed. "All right, Carol —"

Carol uncrossed her legs. Then went rigid.

"— but I'm sending somebody with you. Julie?"

Julie heaved a petulant sigh and stood, but Carol remained seated, eyes bugging out. Between her clenched thighs, a hot spurt released itself, wetting underwear, soaking leotards, creeping through jumper beneath, funneling forward to the edge of her seat and over.

"Carol?" Mrs. Harris said. "Are you going or not?"

"She's going all right," Roger Meaford said. "Going all over the floor."

Roger's voice barely reached her. Everything was muffled, as if her own Cone of Silence had descended from the ceiling. People's shapes and colours fluttered around her like leaves in the wind. She was there and not there at the same time. Nothing touched her but clothes and hair and air. She was free.

Not that she was conscious of any of this at the time. It was only afterwards in the nurse's office as she shifted her position, sending the droopy crotch of her leotards slapping like a cold tongue against the insides of her thighs and the newspaper lining her chair crinkling underneath her, that she realized she'd done it, gone the place Daintry went, which was nowhere, really, not a place after all but a way of being. She felt uncomfortable — her skin was itchy on the parts that had started to dry, and the temperature differential between wet and warm and wet and cold made her not want to move at all and therefore more aware of the discomfort of her position, huddled on the chair with hands wedged beneath moist thighs, more aware of the sogginess of the centre of the newspaper and crinkliness of the edges — but she felt calm and rested, as if waking up between two sleeps.

At the sound of voices in the outer office, she rose, more of the cold wet knit slapping her legs.

"I run a tight ship," went Mrs. Harris' voice. "I *can* cut slack for a girl in Carol's situation, and I *do*, but comes a time when the jib has to be trimmed."

"I don't understand it," came the other voice, her mother's. "Eight years old!"

Carol folded the newspaper the secretary had spread on her chair and dumped it in the waste basket. A newsprint-marked smudge of moisture remained on the seat. She pulled her sleeve over her fist to wipe it.

"With nervous children it does happen," Mrs. Harris said. "I've tried very hard to strike the right balance with Carol, firm yet gentle, but perhaps I've erred on the gentle side. It's a weakness of mine with the awkward children. The danger is that they won't learn limits. I fear with Carol —"

"I beg your pardon, Mrs. Harris," Mrs. Riggs said briskly. "Perhaps we can save the discussion for another day."

After a moment, the door opened and Mrs. Riggs came in carrying Carol's duffle coat and a plastic bag with a change of clothes. Mrs. Harris was gone. "Here, let's get you changed." She helped Carol off with her jumper, then waited as Carol peeled off leotards and underwear. While Carol put on clean undies and a pair of pants, Mrs. Riggs rolled up the soggy bundle and put it in the bag. "Coat," she said, holding it open for Carol to slide her arms into. Then she held out her hand for Carol's, not caring if it was wet or smelled like pee. With just the right tightness, she led Carol by the hand to the car.

"Eight years old." Mrs. Riggs clucked and shook her head as Carol climbed into the front seat. The clean clothes felt good against her skin and the warmth of her coat over them, too, felt good, protecting against the nip in the air that made her think of orange leaves with frost on them in the morning. Even her mother clucking and shaking her head at her felt good. "What is going on, Carol?" It was all good and right.

"Carol? I asked you a question."

She hadn't known she was supposed to answer it. She would rather have not answered, she would rather have not spoken for a week, but she breathed out, "Nothing."

"Something must be going on. This is not like you."

"Mrs. Harris wouldn't let me go to the bathroom."

"Why not?"

"I don't know."

"Yes, you do."

Oh, Carol thought. She knows. Mrs. Harris told her. "'Cause I already went."

"Why do you have to go to the bathroom so much?"

"I don't know."

"Did you go when you were there?"

"Ye-eah."

"Carol. Did you go when you were there?"

"No."

"Why not?"

"They were being mean to me."

"Who?"

"Alison."

"Who else?"

"Katie."

"Who else?"

"Everybody, they're all mean to me. The whole school hates me. They go, 'Ki-*ller*! Ki-*ller*!' Or else they go, 'Here comes Reggs, watch your legs,' or they go, 'Hey, come get me, Killer,' or —"

"Were they doing this in the bathroom?"

"They banged on the door of my stall and wouldn't let me out."

"Oh, Carol," her mother said in a shocked voice. "I will definitely be having a talk with Mrs. Harris. And she will be having a talk with those girls. Mr. Riley will hear about this, too."

The calm feeling seeped away. Carol looked out the window. "Where are we going?"

"Miss Balls' car is in the shop today. We're picking her up so I can get to the hospital."

In Miss Balls' neighbourhood, both the houses and the trees were smaller, and to Carol they seemed more alike than in her neighbourhood. Mrs. Riggs sent Carol to ring the doorbell of Miss Balls' bungalow, and though she'd been there before, she hesitated at the door with its three diamond-shaped windows, feeling like she was in a dream she'd forgotten she'd had. The door opened without her ringing the bell, and there was Miss Balls, tall and lanky, and looking odd with a purse, though Carol couldn't have said why. "Hul-lo," Miss Balls said, and suddenly it clicked with Carol that was the way the word was meant to be said in Enid Blyton books, as if you were greeting a surprise, not a person. Glynnis had been saying it the regular way when she read aloud and Carol had one of those moments where she recognized her own stupidity, in this case for never even thinking it strange that the children said hi to wooden crates in caves by the sea or to footprints in gardens outside broken windows.

"Sorry I'm late," Mrs. Riggs said to Miss Balls as she got in the front seat and Carol in the back. "Carol had a wee incident at school."

A flash of how Glynnis would laugh at that made Carol's throat ache. *A wee incident,* she'd say, mimicking their mother, but turning her more Scottish like the MacDonalds' grandmother, *A wee, wee incident.* It was a line that could keep Glynnis going for weeks. Carol felt a lump in her throat.

"It seems news of Glynnis' accident has spread all over the school and children are taking advantage of it to bully Carol. Even the older ones who should know better."

"I don't follow," Miss Balls said.

Carol sat forward in her seat, leaning in the space between headrests. "They all gang up on me. They go, 'Killer,' 'Crusher,' 'Hey, you gonna get me, Killer?' They go, 'Hey, Killer, what's your favourite song? *Chop*-sticks?'"

"I still don't follow," Miss Balls said. "Do they do this to *all* the girls involved in the accident?"

"All the girls?" Mrs. Riggs asked, pulling up to a stop street and waiting for the car on the right to come to a complete stop before proceeding.

"Surely they don't just single out Carol."

"Now I'm afraid I'm the one not following."

Carol slid back in her seat, looking at her hands. Oops.

"There were several girls playing on the piano when it fell. Wouldn't they all come in for this kind of treatment?"

Mrs. Riggs turned to Carol. "Did Carol tell you there were several girls?" The other car in the intersection honked. "Go! Go!" she shouted, impatiently waving the driver through before stepping on the gas.

"The day after the accident. How on earth would a piano fall on someone's legs, I'd wondered. There must have been some serious roughhousing for that to happen and Carol said yes, there had been, and the whole crew of them had put their first aid to use. I thought they all must have felt awful, the girls involved, I mean, but at least they knew what to do in an emergency, and there must be some consolation in that."

Carol felt impaled, like a worm on a hook.

"I do *not* have the energy for this on top of everything else," Mrs. Riggs said as she pulled up to a stop at Bayview. "I just do not have the energy." With a contradictory display, she slapped on the turn signal with a sweep of her left hand and punched her head forward to check for traffic. Miss Balls grazed Carol with a questioning look before focusing again on Mrs. Riggs, who jerked them into the northbound flow of traffic. Carol kept her eyes down and toyed with the toggle on her duffle coat.

"Carol?!" Mrs. Riggs was glaring at her in the rearview mirror. "You want to tell Miss Balls what really happened? Why don't you tell her just how well you put your first aid to use? Hmm? And when you're done that, you can tell me what on earth you were thinking about when you lied to her."

But I didn't lie, Carol was thinking. You don't know. This time the questions did seem rhetorical. There was no answering them, not right now, there was no saying how innocent it had seemed to let Miss Balls go on thinking what she thought. There was no breaking the thick silence of the rest of the drive.

In the driveway, Mrs. Riggs turned to Carol before getting out of the car. "I'm serious, Carol Ann Riggs. I want Miss Balls to hear from your lips exactly what happened."

Impossible. She'd never be able to say exactly what happened. Every beginning led away from the truth. The truth itself was like looking at branches through a ripply window, shift a little and what seemed like a crook in the limb ran up or down it. Apart from not being able to get it right, she simply didn't want Miss Balls to know. It had seemed more than halfway fair that there be someone in the world who didn't know, who took her as she was in the moment, not how she'd been on the worst day of her life. The idea that she could just refuse, hold out forever, pricked at the back of her brain.

Lunch was a tight, stiff meal of crackers breaking and of spoons clinking bowls. Glynnis was having another operation that afternoon, a skin graft. Miss Balls talked about the wonderful advances of medicine in the last fifty years. Glynnis would be just like new before you knew it.

Mrs. Riggs cleared away the dishes. Then she leaned against the cupboards with her arms folded and said, "Well?" to her daughter, waiting for the explanation.

Carol opened her mouth. Her brain was blank. Miss Balls' hands were folded on the table, one index finger tapping. Her long face was bent slightly down, with her eyes looking over the tops of her glasses. Carol still couldn't say anything. She couldn't get her mind to even think about Glynnis and the piano and what had happened. She was too aware of being where she was, in the kitchen with the smell of vegetable soup still in the air and two stern faces waiting, one finger tapping, and herself full of mush or of nothing, she couldn't have said which.

"All right. I don't have time for this. I'm going to the hospital now and when I get back, I want to hear that you've told Miss Balls exactly what you did from beginning to end, do you hear me? In the meantime, go to your room."

Carol trod slowly upstairs, pulling herself up with the banister, her half-off socks dragging against the dull green carpet in the hall. Without thinking about it, she went and lay on Glynnis' bed, curling up on her side and staring at the neat row of pink, white and green gum stuck to the underside of Glynnis' end of the desk between their beds. Glynnis'd get in trouble when Mom saw that. Carol picked at the gum.

Carol herself was in worse trouble than she'd ever been before, but she wasn't feeling it like she usually did, like she had ever since the accident, all tender and sore as if each jibe from the other children, each self-blaming thought in her head — dozens for each mention of her mother's vigil at the hospital, of Glynnis' injuries and bravery and progress, of the doctors and nurses who cared for her, the children who shared her room — were a finger pressing hard on the centre of a bruise. Now she could have a thought like *I'm in trouble*, and feel nothing, feel like the gum, stuck there, hardening. She would tell Miss Balls what happened. But not now. Not just now.

She woke to a dark room and voices downstairs. Reaching automatically for her glasses, she found air instead of desk. Her heart sped. Hand groping further, she hit wall. Panic. Where was she? Whose voices were they? Wildly, she swept the air on the other side of her.

Ahh. Desk. Glasses. Glynnis' bed, that's where she was. The voices were the usual ones, the deep one of her father, the rusty one of her brother, the barky one of Miss Balls, the smooth and low one of her mother. She was about to get up to check the clock radio when she heard feet mounting the stairs. Stuffing herself under the covers then whipping them over her head, she turned on her side and slumped into stillness. The door opened and the light came on.

"Miss Balls is going," her mother said. "Time to get it over with."

Carol didn't move.

"I know you're not asleep."

Yes I am, Carol thought, trying to make it true. Her mother sighed and came forward to sit on the other bed. "I can wait all night if I have to."

Carol wanted to move then, but something held her back, something heavy inside her bones. Her mother shifted, then shifted again. Silence except for the banging of pots and muffled voices from downstairs.

The arch of Carol's foot cramped and her leg jerked involuntarily, making a noise against the sheets, which she decided to turn into a yawning stretch of the just awakening, turning her toes up to work out the cramp and rolling to her other side while tugging the covers off her face, flickering open her eyes and seeing her mother, not perched on the bed as expected, but curled up on it. Carol lay still again, listening. Her mother's breath came out in slow puffs after long, quiet inhalations. She was asleep. That's how she was always able to tell whether Carol was or not, by the way her breath sounded.

She heard feet on the stairs again, this time her father's slower, heavier tread. She folded her glasses onto the desk again, and resumed her fake-sleeping position, matching her mother's breathing. The footsteps came toward the doorway, paused, made off down the hall and returned, coming into the room, to the bed her mother slept on. There was the rumple of an unfolding blanket, the soft whush of its settling over a body. Then the footsteps retreated, the light went off, the door closed and Carol continued to match her mother, breath for breath, until she felt herself slipping sleepwards.

THE HOUSE WAS dark and quiet when Carol woke the next morning, and her mother was no longer in the bed. It was Saturday. Carol used to love Saturday mornings. As the earliest riser, she had the house to herself, the TV to herself, nobody to answer to or argue with for that wonderful, dim couple of hours that almost felt like a separate reality from the bright, hubbubby rest of the day. Sometimes she didn't even watch TV, but sat on the back patio listening to the birds or picking dandelions in the backyard if it was warm, or at the dining room table with a colouring book or a magazine if it wasn't.

Today, however, TV seemed like the one right thing to do. Slip down to the basement, curl up under a blanket and watch cartoons bounce across the screen. Except she wasn't allowed, and with that knowledge of what she wasn't allowed, the bruisey ache of her life since the accident was back.

She went to the bathroom, where the prick of pleasure in relieving her full bladder brought back the horror of the day before when she'd peed in the classroom, when she'd been completely helpless against the physical release. Even amid her horror, she had had a spark of the same pleasure.

How could she go back to school after that? It would be better to stop existing.

Back in her bedroom, she lay on the imprint of mother's body on the bedspread and tried to stop breathing. Not to hold her breath, but to stop it, just cut it dead in the middle. One-thousand, two-thousand, three- … She sniffed in a little more accidentally, started counting again … one-thousand, two-thousand, three-thousa … She made it to nineteen, then twenty-eight, then forty, but she could not stop altogether. "No fair," she whispered to Reginald. "You don't have to breathe."

"Silly Carol," Reginald said, fake-punching her chin with his soft paw. "Stupid Carol. Stupid, stupid Carol."

She lay there clutching him and letting the tears run into her ears.

Finally she heard sounds of her parents getting up. Her father knocked, then poked his head in her door.

"Wakey-wakey, up and at 'em," he said. She thought he was going to withdraw, but he came in, which meant one of his talks. He never came in otherwise. He sat on the other bed.

"Your mother," he said, examining his hands for a long time before going on, "is hurt. Your mother is angry, your mother is embarrassed, she's hurt, she's disappointed. She's angry that you refused, out of sheer stubbornness, to tell Miss Balls the truth yesterday. She's embarrassed that she can't trust a child of hers, that she can't trust *you*, to tell the truth in the first place. She's hurt that you have so little respect for her that you would lie to her friend, to Miss Balls, who's not only like family to her, but like it or not, like family to you. She's disappointed that you simply don't seem to have the courage to come out with the truth." He arched his fingers and bounced his fingertips together as if giving her time to absorb what he'd said.

"Do you have anything to say?"

"But I didn't mean to lie, it was an accident ..."

"We know it was an accident, Carol, that's not the point here."

"No, you don't understand, I didn't lie to Miss Balls, I didn't say anything ..."

"Did you not hear what I just said? Face up. Own up. Smarten up. That's what you're going to do from here on in, understood? Starting with apologizing to your mother. Five minutes. You've got five minutes to wash the tears off your face and get downstairs and tell her you're sorry."

After Carol was done, Mrs. Riggs nodded in acceptance and told Carol that once she'd had her bath she'd be going to Miss Balls to do today what she hadn't been able to do the day before. Confess.

⌇

THE DAY WAS BRIGHT and crisp and Miss Balls was in navy pants and an old wool plaid shirt with a navy cardigan, raking her front lawn. She'd drawn the leaves straight back from the low hedge, so there was a rectangle of red and green and yellow inside the hedge's rectangle. It looked like the lawn had a border, like it was a picture and the hedge was the frame. Now Miss Balls was raking diagonally along the rectangle, erasing it and leaving rake-marks in the grass beneath like combed hair. She told Carol to fetch a second rake from beside the back door and get started on the other side of the lawn, giving no indication that she thought Carol was there for any reason other than to help.

As she copied Miss Balls' method, drawing the leaves out of the hedge-bed into a line, she snuck a few glances at the old lady to see if she seemed to be wanting a confession now or not wanting it till later. Absorbed in her task, Miss Balls was all efficiency and energy. Mrs. Riggs always said how amazing Miss Balls was for seventy-five, and Carol saw what she meant. She looked happy. She looked as if, on a day like this, a bright fall one with a rich blue sky, she liked nothing better than to rake. She also looked a person alone. A person happy to be alone. The confession would definitely wait.

Carol tried to be as thorough as Miss Balls and made slow progress. She'd only done a quarter of the first side of hedge when Miss Balls interrupted with a request for help bagging her finished piles. Then Miss Balls moved to the backyard, leaving Carol to continue alone.

Under the top layer of dry leaves was another layer, wet, glommed together, that needed a jerk to get hauled over the lip of the lawn's edge. Pausing after several of these she saw a small, half-pink worm writhe in the sun, trying to poke its head — or tail — into the earth. Crouching above it, she stuck out her index finger, rolling the worm back and forth. She picked it up. Its mucus sparkled in the sun. Tiny clods of earth clung to its ends. Tongue out, she brought the pink end of the worm to the tip of her tongue. It didn't taste like much. A little earthy, the way it smelled. She opened her mouth and tossed the worm in. Cold and wriggly, it made her want to giggle, as if she were being tickled, though it didn't actually tickle. She threw her head back like she was taking a pill and swallowed. Cool sliminess slid down her throat, but not all the way down her gullet. A wriggling at the back of her mouth, behind where the tongue could do anything about it, made her cack. Then she swallowed again, and felt it go down. Now she was part earthworm, silent and pink and happy in the rotting leaves and dark earth. No one would know it to look at her, but she'd done something most people couldn't do. *Yum yum yum.* A gleeful shudder passed through her. She was free. She had made herself free.

They spent all morning raking and bagging leaves, without saying anything more than needed to be said.

For lunch Miss Balls made ham sandwiches, mixing up hot mustard for herself from a powder. She didn't have any regular mustard. The bread was brown and dry and the texture of the ham made Carol think of the worm and she had to take a sip of milk after every bite in order not to barf.

"Now," Miss Balls said, when she'd polished off her sandwich. "Business."

Carol was only three-quarters done hers, but she left the last bit and hoped Miss Balls didn't make her finish it later. She looked at her hands as she talked, locking her fingers together and twisting the palms one way then the other. "So, um, Glynnis? She was under the piano. And she wouldn't be Dorothy. We were playing Wizard of Oz and I was taking her to the Wicked Witch of the West, only she wouldn't go, she bashed my knees with her head. And that made me mad, so I sort of just kicked close to her, to scare her? But, um,

I hit the bricks instead, the bricks that were holding up the piano
'cause it was broken? And they all fell out and the piano went crash,
right on Glynnis. It was awful."

She looked up and quickly down again, fingers intertwined, hands
twisting.

"So you didn't use your first aid."

Carol shook her head.

"You ran away instead."

Carol nodded.

"In the war —" Miss Balls made sure she had Carol's eye, then
continued. "— my war, they shot deserters." Stab. "They had to make
an example of them, you see, or others would get the same idea.
Nobody *wanted* to go back to the front. They had to. They had to
draw on the depths of their courage to face the German lines, to face
death every day, all around them, everywhere. You could understand
some turning coward when you heard what they faced, when you
saw it with your own eyes …" She trailed off and was silent for a few
seconds, as if seeing it now. "But you couldn't forgive it, not when
so many others went back, and went back, and went back, again and
again, not when so many fought so bravely and so well."

Carol thought her situation was different, but snuffled anyway,
wiping her nose with the back of her hand. The sound seemed to
nudge Miss Balls out of the little world her words had created. She
took Carol's plate without even asking if Carol wanted to finish.

"Of course, it's one thing for a man to be frightened and run away
and quite another for a child. So we won't shoot you, not today, anyway."

She turned to Carol with an expression Carol only recognized
after it faded, upon Carol's snuffles exploding into sobs, as a grin.
Miss Balls' eyebrows drew together in apparent puzzlement. "My
goodness, Carol, you are a crier, aren't you?" She gave Carol a handkerchief pulled from her breast pocket and tidied the kitchen as
Carol cried harder still.

Glynnis

GLYNNIS WAS DISCHARGED from the hospital three days after her last skin graft and more than a month after she'd entered it. She'd imagined a grand exit, everyone crowding round for a teary farewell, doctors and nurses and Erica and Lucy following her down the hallway to wave a sad goodbye as the doors to the elevator closed. But Lucy had just said, "Catch you on the flip side, sister," before being taken down to Radiology, and Erica had been discharged the week before. The girl who'd taken her bed was conked out, so there was just Delilah, grinning and sticking out her fat tongue and saying after her mother told her to, "Bye, Gliss, bye Gliss, bye Gliss," as the orderly wheeled Glynnis out past the nursing station.

Glynnis had never in her life been indoors for so long. Four weeks with only two short outings in a wheelchair with her father, who had insisted she needed fresh air. The last outing, a week or so ago, had been bright and there'd been a delicious faint warmth in the sun, a blip, a sharp, sunny sliver of summer compared to the world she saw through the glass doors today. This world harrumphed November at her like it was clearing its throat to spit. This world was dim and windy and wet and she wasn't sure she wanted to go out in it. When she did, though, taking her crutches from the orderly as she saw her mother pull up into the bay, she noticed the air felt more like air, even with exhaust jetting out from idling cars and taxis. She could feel it going in and out of her lungs. She could feel wind and cold on her bare hands where they clutched the crutch handles, on her cheeks and neck, and whispering down the collar of her thin fall jacket and whooshing through her knee sock and up under her skirt to the bare skin of her right leg. None of these sensations were pleasant, but she liked them. They weren't pain.

Glynnis stretched her leg across the back seat and twisted around to look out at the world that had gone on without her all this time. That always went on without her, really, all these hundreds of thousands of people who lived in the same city and didn't have a clue she existed just as she didn't have a clue they existed, until now, watching them hunch down the street, collars up and heads down, half-jogging to the subway entrance holding newspapers over their heads with one hand and clutching briefcases with the other, and who went on existing, hunching, jogging, clutching, riding subways, when she was thinking only of herself, and they were long gone from her mind.

An umbrella-topped woman crossing College was suddenly exposed by a gust of wind that snapped her umbrella like a shut flower above her head. Her hair lifted as if it, too, might fly off, and Glynnis got a glimpse of her mouth mashed into a thin red line as she turned to pop the umbrella back into shape. It seemed utterly remarkable that this woman should continue to exist all the time, that she should do other things than cross the street and get mad at her umbrella, but she must. She must have brothers and sisters who she liked or didn't like, or children who made her laugh, or friends who loved the way she said a certain word, the way Glynnis loved how Melanie Rusk said balloons. *Balloowans*, Melanie said. Glynnis made her repeat it over and over.

It seemed just as remarkable that the same must be true for the people in suits and trench coats going in and out of the Parliament buildings and the university students cutting across the park behind them and all the kids piling off the school buses lined up outside the Planetarium and the Museum.

Glynnis watched University turn into Avenue Road and wondered if the people inside the Hare Krishna church were different since they were brainwashed. Maybe not. They still had to have lives, however shadowy and weird. According to Jay, if you said "Hare Krishna" a thousand times, that was it, you were a zombie and would do whatever they told you. Sometimes they played it as a game, Hare Krishna zombies. "Now, my children," Jay would say when she and Carol were in a zombie state, "you must fetch the sacred Chips Ahoy from the kitchen, bring them back and prostrate yourselves before me." Or Glynnis would say, "To prove your devotion to the great Glynnis, I mean Krishna, you must do the chicken walk out to the street and back." Sandy's sister Mary said it wasn't true, but she wouldn't say the thousand Krishnas to prove it.

At UCC, Avenue Road turned into Oriole Parkway. Glynnis peered at the muddy boys playing rugby in the rain and was reminded what it was like to be out on a day like this, playing some hard-played game. First your hands got raw and red, and then they warmed up from the inside as you played, and skin became this amazing thing, so sensitive and resilient on your swollen, sausagey fingers. You were out there in the bluster, braver than anyone else and maybe a bit crazy. You were more alive than anyone who stayed inside and you felt that aliveness in your skin.

She thought about the skinlessness of her leg before the grafts, how appallingly ugly it was, how it oozed and burned, how raw it was, how at the mercy of the slightest thing, a negligible draft, not to mention bacteria. She thought of skin now on her leg that had previously been on her bum and the backs of her thighs and how much it had hurt to have it taken off, like it was the wrong thing to do, unnatural, not meant to be, but how it was wonderful, too, that somebody had thought this up and tried it and it worked.

By the time they turned down Eglinton at the end of Oriole Parkway, Glynnis had a feeling like the hospital was not just far away, it was another world, an alien world off of TV where everyone lived indoors and wore the same outfits and had strange systems of government and bizarre rivalries with other species. This was the real world: Yonge and Eglinton, the left lane turning onto Mount Pleasant, Gaul's Esso, Charlie's Sunoco, Cruikshank Flowers, Britton Drugs, Melanie's street by Sherwood Park, the Mt. Pleasant Bridge with the Bridge Slippery When Wet sign Glynnis still saw as a car on duck feet even though she'd recently figured out the feet were supposed to be skid marks.

They turned onto her street, where the big trees were all stripped bare, their rickety bones tossed and pummelled by the wind. Behind the cold and lonely-looking birch tree on their front lawn, the Riggses' house sat solid and bricky, confident and dormant with the lights off and dim bluish daylight visible through the windows. It had a smell when they'd been away that Glynnis loved, a cool smell like laundry hung out in winter that made her feel like the house was pretending indifference to them but was secretly excited they were home, like its furnace was churning a little faster down there in the heart of it.

Glynnis took a deep breath as she swung in the front door on her crutches, but the smell wasn't there. The other, regular lived-in smell was, but not the house-awaiting-the-return-of-its-people smell. Of course that made sense — life had gone on here as it had for all the strangers she'd seen in the street. No one had been away but her.

She felt cheated and detached, although she could tell that her mother was trying to make everything special for her. She had to drum up enthusiasm for the Welcome Home banner strung up on the living room wall — clearly Carol's handiwork, the *l* squished in as an afterthought — and for the cards and flowers from relatives on the mantel and stereo cabinet. It was easier with the little gifties people had got: puzzles and word-search magazines and stuffed animals and Encyclopedia Brown books. It was easier still when Mrs. Riggs said she'd got all of Glynnis' favourite foods and that Glynnis was allowed to watch TV all day if she wanted, though Mrs. Riggs hoped she wouldn't overdo it. Tomorrow she'd start catching up on her school-work, but today was hers. They'd brought the TV up from the basement just for her.

"When do I get to go back to school?"

Mrs. Riggs looked bemused for a moment, then shook her head as if to rid herself of whatever thought she was having. "You and Carol. What a pair." Glynnis waited for her to elaborate, but she didn't. "You need to keep that leg immobile and elevated at least until your next appointment with Dr. Fisher. Two weeks."

"Two weeks!"

"Minimum."

"Shall we set you up on the chesterfield?" Mrs. Riggs asked.

"I want to see my room," Glynnis said. Her mother had told her, in one of her serious we're-having-a-talk voices, that they had decided it would be better if the girls each had their own room. They had finished the attic for Jay and moved Carol into Jay's room. Glynnis was not to think they were separating her and her sister to keep them away from each other or out of fear that their quarrelling would escalate, but simply because it was the right time.

Her room hardly looked different at all. It still had two beds, the same bedspreads, the same furniture. She crutched around it, touching everything, thrilled with its particularity, its herness. There were fewer things on the dresser and one of the bookshelves had been cleared off. Carol's teddy bear and her other stuffed animals were gone. Her clock radio was now on … No. It was a new clock radio. Her own. She tried it out and lay on her bed listening. When she tired of that, she went to look at Carol's room. New paint job in Carol's favourite colour, yellow, new curtains with matching bedspread, yellow with a floral pattern, Reginald propped up on the pillow. Jay's old furniture, painted yellow. She was mildly jealous that Carol got new things while Glynnis kept the old. But she liked the old, too. She liked coming back to it.

She toured the bathroom, turning on the taps just to touch them, touching the towels, then toured her parents' room. She wanted to go see Jay's room in the attic, but her foot was throbbing. If she had to lose it as an attic, it was too bad Jay got to live there and not her, but it was also right since he was older.

Downstairs, she lay on the chesterfield, two pillows behind her back, another two under her leg in its splint and bandages, watching *The Friendly Giant*. Beside her, her mother had set up a TV table with a glass of milk for her bones, plus the books and games people had given her. Overtop of her was what her parents puzzlingly called "the car rug," actually not a rug at all, but a soft, red plaid blanket. Apart from the television and the distant sounds of her mother going about her business, the house was still. Bursts of wind and rain pebbled the windows. The house, naturally, stood firm against the elements, and lying there in the yellow light of the lamp in the otherwise dim room, Glynnis got the feeling she'd missed upon entering, that the house was like a reserved butler in an English novel who loved its inhabitants deeply without ever saying so and protected them without their ever knowing it. She tugged the car rug up to her nose, loving its woolly smell, loving it for having been around since before she could remember, for having a mended tear at one end, for being immediately identifiable as itself amongst all other blankets in the world.

Late in the morning, Mrs. Riggs asked as she passed through the living room on her way to the door if Glynnis would be all right on her own for five minutes while Mrs. Riggs went to pick up Carol for lunch. Glynnis said of course, but why did Carol need to be picked up;

Glynnis was the one with the broken leg. Mrs. Riggs came back with her coat on, holding her gloves in her hand, and perched on the edge of the chair next to the television.

She turned the volume down. "Odd as it may seem, my dear, you are not the only one who got hurt in this accident. Children can be very cruel." She almost shuddered saying this, and looked sharply at Glynnis for a time. "Carol is having a very hard time of it at school. She needs special consideration right now. You are not to lord anything over her, understand?"

"Yuh," she breathed, not taking her eyes off *Elwood Glover's Luncheon Date*. The world's most boring show. Everything on it was blue-grey, the desk, the chairs, the 3D wall in a pattern of alternating innie and outie brick-sized rectangles behind the desk, Elwood himself, his suits, his hair. It all blended in, kind of like watching the dots on the ceiling at the hospital. Elwood was talking to a lady in a grey-blue suit-dress about a craft fair to raise money for crippled children.

⌐

THE FRONT DOOR OPENED and Carol shouted hello before running into the living room and right up to her and giving her a hug. Glynnis pulled back. The only time she remembered getting hugged by Carol before was at Christmas or her birthday to say thanks for the present.

"Welcome home!"

"Yeah."

Mrs. Riggs stepped into the living room from the foyer and smiled at them.

"Did you see the banner I made you?"

Glynnis resisted the urge to bug her about the *l*. "Yeah. Thanks."

"What are you watching?" Carol asked.

"Elwood Glover."

"Give me a hand, Carol?" Mrs. Riggs said, and Carol followed her into the kitchen but was back quickly.

"May I get you a glass of ginger ale before your meal?"

"May I get you a glass of ginger ale before your meal?" Glynnis mimicked.

Carol's head went down and her face went pink.

"Fine," Glynnis said. "Get me a glass of ginger ale."

Carol skulked out and back with the ginger ale. Glynnis ignored her and she left again.

The next time she was back it was with grilled cheese and their mother, and Glynnis had to thank Carol nicely.

After Mrs. Riggs finished eating, she left the two of them watching *The Flintstones*, Glynnis on the couch, Carol slumped in one of the easy chairs. Glynnis didn't even want to look at her.

The episode was the one where a radio station does a promotion of a band called the Way-Outs by saying, "Bedrock is being invaded by creatures from way, way out" and everybody thinks it's Martians. Usually Carol and Glynnis sang along with the Flintstone songs — *Here we come on the run with a burger on a bun* and *Happy anniversary* and this one, *Gonna go way out, way out, that's where the fun is*. Right now Carol was singing under her breath and Glynnis said, "Do you mind?" and Carol stopped, didn't make a peep for the rest of the show.

Mrs. Riggs took Carol back to school. Glynnis watched game shows until Mrs. MacDonald brought Carol home after school with Sandy and Alison. She came in with her palms spread open at the ends of her outstretched arms, singing, *Well, well, hello, Glynnie, yes hello, Glynnie, it's so nice to have you back where you belong*, and then she clapped her palms on Glynnis' cheeks and kissed the top of her head. Glynnis felt shy. The MacDonalds had come to visit her at the hospital. Alison had been bored; Sandy had been afraid. They had that same how-do-we-talk-to-the-sick-person look about them as they advanced now. Sandy carried a present, which Alison went to take from her and Sandy yanked back.

"I'll give her the present."

"No, I'll give her the present, Alison. I picked it out."

"You did not, you wanted to —"

Ah. These were the people she knew.

"Why don't you both do it?" Glynnis said.

Carol faded into the background, head forward, back of hand over mouth, teeth nibbling at the cuticles of her fingers.

Jay was home next.

"It's not Jay," a falsetto voice said. A dirty white clown puppet appeared from the foyer. "It's ..." Jay paused as he made up the name. "... Uncle Tiggly ..." he paused again, "Wiggly ... Squiggly, that's right, Uncle Tiggly-Wiggly-Squiggly, here to say, Have you had your beans today?"

Uncle Tiggly-Wiggly-Squiggly suddenly jerked out of view as a huge farting noise came from around the corner. "Oh my!" Uncle Tiggly said, jerking and farting again. "Oh! I, well, excuse me ..." More jerks and farts. "Pardon me! Uncle Tiggly-Wiggly-Squiggly apologizes for his shocking rudeness."

Jay came around the corner and spoke to the puppet. "Uncle Tiggly, control yourself!"

Uncle Tiggly jerked backwards on Jay's hand as Jay pumped his puppet arm over the hand he had cupped in his armpit. He looked threateningly at the puppet.

"Ooops," said Uncle Tiggly in a small voice.

"That's better," Jay said. "Now we can have a civilized conversation. Tell me, Uncle Tiggly ..."

"Uh-oh," Uncle Tiggly said.

"What?"

"Nothing." The puppet looked up at the ceiling nonchalantly.

"So tell me, Uncle Tiggly ..."

"Oh, dear."

"Oh dear what?"

"Oh dear, oh dear, oh dear, oh … Ahhh."

"So tell me, Uncle Tiggly, how long have you been a …" Jay sniffed. "What's that?" Tiggly played innocent. Jay sniffed again and made a face. "Oh, Tiggly, you've really done it now. I'm afraid you leave me no choice."

"No choice?"

"No choice. It's the random fling for you, my man."

"Not the random fliiiiiiiiiiing." Jay flung the puppet off his hand and watched him sail right through the middle of the pull-screen into the fireplace. A big poof of ashes went up. "Hey, that was pretty good," Jay said.

"How do you do that?" Glynnis asked when she'd recovered herself.

"It's easy. Two fingers go in the head, the little finger in one arm, thumb in the other."

"Ha ha. No, the farting noise."

"Oh, thaaaat. Ancient Chinese secret."

Glynnis flapped her arm and got nothing and then a feeble little phhht. She kept practising.

"So how's the crip?"

Glynnis answered with a fart, her first one.

"Does it hurt?"

Glynnis farted twice.

"Glad to be home?"

Two more farts.

"We missed you."

Three farts.

"You don't say." He stuck his hand under his shirt under his armpit again and squeaked another sentence. Glynnis squeaked back a rapid sequence. He gave a long, slow one.

"What on earth," Mrs. Riggs said, coming into the living room.

"We're having a meaningful conversation," Jay said. "It just happens to be in the language of farts."

"Really, you two."

The front door opened again, sending a waft of chill air into the living room. So close to the outdoors again. She'd forgotten what it was like. "Hello, hello, hello," Mr. Riggs called. They could hear him hanging up his coat. He came into the living room with his arms open. "There she is, the prodigal daughter." He took her face in his chilly hands and kissed her. Then he took her nose between his second and third fingers, pulling it away and replacing it with his thumb. This had delighted Glynnis some years earlier.

He stood back and marvelled. "All plumped up like the Queen of Sheba, eh, Jay?"

Jay pretended to fan her.

"Great to have you home."

Mr. Riggs went off to change and then they all had dinner in the living room like it was a holiday or birthday. There were more presents. Carol gave her a new Enid Blyton book and paper flowers in a découpaged jam jar. Jay had made her a wooden box in shop and also gave her a penknife and a piece of cedar to carve. Mr. Riggs had a model airplane kit for her, plus airline cards, which they already had a billion of, and a cribbage board, which they already had three of, and colouring books. Mrs. Riggs had got her the whole Little House on the Prairie series, plus one of the small doodle art posters so she could work on it on the sick table, not the floor like you had to with the big ones.

Glynnis pretended, as far as she could, that Carol was not there.

"Isn't it great to have your sister home?" Mr. Riggs asked.

Carol wanted to answer, Glynnis could tell even without looking directly at her, but was too nervous that Glynnis would take whatever she said wrongly. She had the sick rabbit look again.

"Just hasn't been the same around here," Mrs. Riggs said with a big smile.

"Yeah. Not as smelly," Jay said. Mr. Riggs frowned and shook his head at him.

All of this delighted Glynnis. She had not known how much she liked being in her family. Carol, too. Hate her or not, without Carol their family was not their family.

⤶

FOR THE NEXT SEVERAL DAYS, Glynnis only talked to Carol when her mother was around. Otherwise she ignored her. Carol hovered, solicitous, bringing Glynnis things she hadn't asked for. Cinnamon toast. Juice. Cookies. Toys of Carol's that Glynnis liked.

Finally Carol said, "Please, Glynnis, I'll do anything."

Glynnis said nothing.

"You can ignore me forever, I don't care, I deserve it."

True.

THE FOLLOWING AFTERNOON, Carol whined by Glynnis' bedroom door, running her finger along the bookshelf attached to the wall there. "Why won't you talk to me?"

Glynnis didn't even look up from her reading. "Simple. I hate you."

"But I'm sorry."

"But I hate you." Now she looked up.

"You can't hate me."

"But I do."

"Everybody hates me, I might as well die."

And now Glynnis looked back at her book, all casual. "Fine. Go ahead. Die. Won't bother me."

Carol stood there, starting to blubber.

"Sayonara," Glynnis said. "Arrivederci. Go die. See ya."

"You're so mean."

"Oh, yeah. I'm the one who knocked a piano on somebody."

"Please, Glynnis, I'll be your slave forever, I'll do anything, please."

"Maybe I don't want you to be my slave. Maybe I don't even want to see your stupid fat face." Seeing that this made Carol's stupid fat face crumple, Glynnis kept going. "Stupid fat face, stupid fat face, stupid fat face." She put down her book.

"Shut up."

"What, are you going to make me? Eh? Eh? Gonna make me? Come on, make me. Make me. *Carol is a big fat cow, doo-dah, doo-dah, Carol is a big fat cow, oh da-doo-dah-day ...*"

"Shut up."

"*She's so big and fat —*"

"Shut up."

"*— She can squash a cat — or her sister — Carol is a big fat cow, oh da-doo-dah-day.*"

"Stop it."

"What's going on up there?" Mrs. Riggs voice asked. They didn't even act like they'd heard it.

"Make me. *She's a big fat blister, she can squash her sister —*"

"Stop it, I hate you."

"I knew you were faking, I knew it. 'Glynnis, would you like a ginger ale? Do you want to listen to my record player?' Faker."

Heel of hand on bottom of shelf, Carol shouted and shoved at the same time. "Shut up." Her end of the shelf whipped up and slammed back down, rapping her knuckles. Books toppled off the end and Aunt Helen's china flowers flew through the air and hit the lower half of the dresser. Carol's eyes went big and she sucked on her knuckles then fled to her room.

"Girls? What's going on?" Mrs. Riggs was at the top of the stairs. "Carol, come out here right now." No answer. No Carol. She'd be on her bed crying. Mrs. Riggs would give her a talking-to and then she'd come and quiz Glynnis. Who had nothing to fear as she was not at all at fault.

The front door slammed. Five minutes later Jay was in her doorway eating a piece of bread and peanut butter. "What's going on?" he asked Glynnis.

"Mom's chewing Carol out."

"What did she do?"

"What does it look like?" She nodded at the books on the floor.

"What did you say to her?"

"Nothing, why's it always my fault if Carol knocks something over?"

Mrs. Riggs came down the hall.

"Hi, Mom," Jay said.

"Can you give me a minute with Glynnis?" she asked.

"Sure." He went up to his room in the attic.

Mrs. Riggs sat on the bed. Glynnis found she couldn't look at her. Did Glynnis remember their talk about forgiveness? she asked. Nod. "You are not acting in a forgiving way."

"Yes, I am."

"Don't give me that."

"Why should I forgive her?"

"You're sisters. You're going to be sisters your whole life. You need to get along."

"Why?"

Mrs. Riggs sighed impatiently. "I know you think you're the injured party here — "

"I *am* the injured party here."

"You are not the *only* injured party. You must understand — you must — what it's like for Carol. She is in absolute torment. She feels responsible. If you keep blaming her, listen to me, Glynnis, if you keep blaming her she may never get over it. Never. Do you understand what I'm saying? Physical injuries are not the only kind."

"Why should she get all the sympathy?"

"Don't kid yourself, my dear, you get plenty of sympathy. She can have a little, too. Now I want to hear you say you forgive her and you are going to try to get along."

She couldn't say it. There was no way she could say it. It would cost her her TV privileges forever, but she couldn't say it.

"YOU KNOW WHAT you guys need?" Jay said, coming into Glynnis' room before dinner.

"What?"

"Peace talks."

"Peace talks?"

"Peace talks. You're at war. So if you want peace, you've got to have peace talks. Otherwise you'll be at war forever, you'll be like the Middle East, an eye for an eye, a tooth for a tooth, and it'll never stop."

"Sounds good to me."

"No, but seriously. Doughgirl wants to make peace. That's what she's been trying to do ever since you've been home. The important question is, do you want to make peace."

"I don't know. I guess."

"Okay. I'll go parlay with the other side. Meantime have we got a ceasefire?"

After supper, Jay made a Peace Talks sign and put it on the door to the rec room. Inside he had a card table set up with four chairs, one with a pillow on it for Glynnis' leg. Paper on the table.

"Okay. Will the representatives of Carolland and Glynnisland come to the table? We are here to negotiate peace between these two warring countries, to forge a new bond and a common future. Do both parties enter the negotiations in good faith? Yes? Good. All right. Now negotiations like these are based on a balance of demands and concessions. If you make a demand, you've got to make a concession. Now in front of you is a sheet of paper. I want you each to write down the demands that you feel would satisfy you and lead to lasting peace."

Glynnis wrote: Personalaty transplant. No freak outs. No tantrums. Carol has to lick my feet. She handed it over to Jay. Carol handed her sheet, too, but it was blank.

"I don't have any demands," Carol said. "I'll do whatever she wants."

"Good."

"No, it's not good. You don't make for lasting peace by conceding everything. Look at history, my friends, look at history, look at Germany after the first world war —"

"'My war'?" Glynnis joked in Miss Balls' voice.

"That's right. Treaty of Versailles. Okay, it's a little different 'cause they didn't concede and Germany had no choice, but the Allies made them give up too much. It was bound to cause resentment and look what happened. Double-u-double-u two. We don't want that. We definitely don't want that. So let's say The Piano Incident was World War One and we're negotiating peace. Okay? So Diplomat Carol, you write down the things that would prevent that from happening again."

He handed them both back their sheets and they both wrote until the page was filled.

Jay took the sheets. "Okay. Let's start by simply reading out the lists of demands. Only we're not going to be able to find a surgeon to perform the first two of Glynnis' demands."

"What?"

"She wants you to have a lobotomy and a brain transplant."

"Ha ha, very funny."

Jay continued. "Item three: control temper; don't be a suck; no hitting; no kicking; lick my feet; Complete Carol Improvement Course; Glynnis' slave for 30 days. Those are Glynnisland's demands. Now Carolland's: can't steal my friends; play fair; no calling me names; no hitting; no showing off in front of Alison. Sounds fair. Look, you've even got a few in common. Play fair, don't hit." He wrote these down on a new sheet. "Can we broaden that to no violence? Including pinching, throwing, kicking? Okay. Now. What's this Carol Improvement Course?"

"Me and Sandy were talking," said Glynnis, "and Sandy was saying, you know, Carol's not that bad, she's just gotta learn how to be, you know, more normal. Like not be a suck and stand up for herself. Without going bonkers. That kind of stuff."

"Carol? What do you think of that?"

"I'm not a suck."

"Well? Actually? Sometimes you are," Jay said.

"Glynnis is a suck, too. She's always, 'Mom, Carol's doing this. Mom, Carol's doing that.'"

"Fair enough. But the course. It's like rehabilitation?" Jay said to Glynnis. "Make her into a contributing member of society?"

"Yeah."

"Should there be a complete Glynnis Improvement Course, too?"

"Nothing to improve."

"Oh you're perfect, are you?"

"Of course."

"Pardon me if I beg to differ."

"Pardon me if I beg to differ."

"I'm not playing, Glynnis."

"I'm not playing, Glynnis."

"Watch it. Don't want these peace talks to break down, do you? Another millennium of war in the Middle East? I veto the Complete Carol Improvement Course. It'd be the blind leading the blind. Let's move on. Next: 'She's just jealous.' That's not a demand, it's a gripe. We'll cross it off."

"But — "

"Gonna make demands, gotta make concessions. 'Don't hit,' we've covered that. 'Slave for 30 days.'"

"I thought you said you didn't want me to be your slave," protested Carol.

"I changed my mind."

"Okay," said Jay. "Let's look at Carol's demands."

"It's for her own good," said Glynnis.

"What is?"

"The Complete Carol Improvement Course."

"Seriously, Glam, I don't think it's a good idea. Moving on. 'Can't steal my friends.'"

Glynnis rolled her eyes. "Like I'd even want to."

"She does it all the time. I meet someone, I like them, she steals them."

"I can't help it if people like me better." Glynnis turned to Jay. "That's why she needs the Complete Carol Improvement Course."

"Drop it, G."

"Who'm I going to steal, Daintry? You don't even have any friends."

"That's 'cause you stole them all."

"Girls, girls. Demands, concessions, demands, concessions. Right? So Glynnis, can you agree to not stealing Carol's friends or can't you?"

"I'm telling you, she doesn't have any."

"Shouldn't be hard then, should it?"

"Oh. Guess not."

"Okay, then, moving right along. God, this is taking forever. Now I know how Metternicht felt. 'Play fair.' Got that. 'Stop showing off in front of Alison.'"

"I don't."

"Yes, you do."

"No, I don't."

"Yes, you do."

Jay got up from his chair and made as if to walk out. Silence. "This is like the last demand. If you don't show-off, why would you have a problem agreeing not to?"

"Oh. Right. Okay. I still want the Complete Carol Improvement Course and I still want her to be my slave."

"Glynnis —"

But Carol cut in. "Okay."

"Really?" Jay asked.

"Yeah."

"You must really want peace. But hey, who am I to question. I still think thirty days is too long, though. How about ten, including the five she's already done?"

"Fifteen."

"Twelve."

"Okay."

"Hey, I'm good at this. Aren't I good?"

And so for another week Carol fetched and carried for Glynnis. She brought her breakfast in bed. She changed television channels for her. She responded to bi-minutely calls to turn the pages of Glynnis' book. She did homework (although that wasn't really worth much, since some of it needed correcting). She left the room backwards, bowing. She said, "Yes, master. No, master. Whatever you wish, master." She flushed the toilet for her. She brushed Glynnis' teeth. She cleaned Glynnis' room. She repeated after Glynnis, "I am the lowest of the low. Glynnis is the highest of the high."

At the end of the week, Glynnis said, "I release you from your enslavement," and Carol said, "Thank you, master."

"Now you just have to complete the CCIC and you're rehabilitated."

FOR THE Complete Carol Improvement Course, Glynnis recruited Sandy, of course, and also Melanie. Lesson One was Don't Be a Suck or a Wimp.

"What we are going to do," Glynnis said, "is we're going to call you a whole bunch of names and you're not going to cry or get mad or anything."

"It's easiest if you think of yourself as a piece of wood," Sandy said. "Or something."

"Ready?" Glynnis asked, and Carol nodded.

"I'll start," said Sandy. "Four eyes."

Then it was Glynnis' turn. "Cow."

Then Melanie's. "Killer."

Sandy: "Rat."

Glynnis: "Paleface."

Melanie: "Stupid."

"Dumbhead."

"Idiot."

"Porky porky pig pig."

"Stupidhead."

"Psycho-killer."

"Leg-breaker."

"Four eyes."

"You said that already."

"So?"

"Stupidhead."

"Freezerface."

Glynnis broke up. "What kind of an insult is that?"

"I don't know," said Melanie. "I just made it up. Freezerface, freezerface."

"Okay, okay. Back to insults." Glynnis composed herself, took a long breath in, out. "Freezerface."

They all laughed, even Carol.

"Okay, seriously, you guys," said Sandy. "Big bum."

"Greedy guts."

"Grizzly oats."

Peals of laughter.

"Is that enough?" Sandy asked. "Are we done yet?"

"Of course we're not done yet," said Glynnis. "Dumb-ears."

"Goof."

"Whiner."

"Goof."

Sandy blanked.

"Come on, Sandy," Glynnis said. "Pick it up."

"I can't think of anything."

"No-brain," said Glynnis.

"Empty head."

"Killer." Glynnis.

"Killer." Melanie.

"Killer." Glynnis. "Killer." Glynnis and Melanie. "Killer, killer, killer, killer, killer." They got louder and louder and faster and faster until they were just shouting *Aaaugh*.

Carol didn't flinch.

"Wow," Sandy said. "That's pretty good. I think she's got it."

"By George, I think she's got it," Glynnis shouted.

"It's easy," Carol said. "I can tell you don't mean it."

"But we do," Glynnis said. "We do."

"Do not."

"Oh no? Killer. Shit-for-brains. Lowlife. Scum-sucking lowlife piece of crap shit."

"Geez, Glynnis," said Melanie.

"Come on, how would you like it?" Sandy said.

"Oh yeah? Well, how'd you like a piano on you, eh? How'd you like that?"

There was an uncomfortable silence and a funny feeling in Glynnis' stomach.

"I have to go home," Sandy said.

"Me too."

"Go ahead," said Glynnis. "You're wimps, too. She's got to learn to take it when people do mean it and I mean it. Piece of crap shit."

"Look at her, Glynn."

It was like Sandy had said. Carol was a piece of wood.

"You don't even know what you're talking about," Sandy said to Glynnis. "If anybody knows how to take an insult, it's Carol."

"She's right, Glynn. She goes like this, I've seen it before."

"She's faking," Glynnis said.

Sandy waved a hand in front of Carol's face. Mel snapped her fingers. Nothing. Glynnis took two fingers and made as if to poke at her eyes in a way that made it impossible not to flinch. Nothing.

The knot in Glynnis' stomach turned to water. "How does she come out of it?"

"I don't know. I've only seen it once. Alison says she just goes blank for a while and then she picks up where she left off."

"Carol?" Glynnis said. "Carol?" No reaction. She didn't even blink. "Are you okay? It's over. I'm sorry." Blink. Blink, blink. She was back. They both relaxed, shoulders slumping.

LATER THAT NIGHT, Glynnis went into Carol's bedroom. "Carol? Where do you go when you do that thing?"

"Nowhere."

"What do you mean, nowhere?"

"That's where I go. It's like the same as here but it's like a place, too, where it looks all the same but it's not because nothing happens. It's nowhere."

"Do you like it there?"

"I don't mind." A pause. "Glynnis?"

"Yeah?"

"Will you read me the rest of *My Friend Flicka*?"

"You haven't finished it yet?"

"I was waiting for you."

There wasn't room for Glynnis and her foot and Carol in Carol's bed, so they went into Glynnis' room and with Carol in her old bed, Glynnis read to her from where they'd left off.

Miss Balls

HOW WONDERFUL TO BE BACK, to take out her uniform, iron it and put it on, warm and smooth. She looked best in a uniform, it was her natural state of being. In mufti she felt drab and angular and obliged to soften her angularity. In uniform she looked neat and smart, trim and happy. She buttoned her top and knotted her tie, humming.

"My dear, I am honoured," Beryl had said to Rowena when asked to fill in for the AWOL Tawny Owl, a warmth spreading through her chest like the warmth coming now from her freshly ironed top. "Don't give it another thought."

Judy. Chah.

When Judy had called Beryl into HQ in the spring, Beryl had assumed — quite naturally, as their last conversation had turned almost completely on the question — that she wanted to discuss Beryl's *History of the Guides in Canada*. Judy's greeting had been warm, effusive, and Beryl was encouraged. Previously Judy had agreed in principle to the project but disagreed about the timing. Judy thought that having missed the 50th anniversary, the book should wait for the 75th. She didn't seem to realize Beryl would be too old then. At seventy-five she had plenty of pep for an endeavour like this. At eighty-nine it was a good deal less likely.

After much idle chitchat, Judy wasn't seeming to come to the point, so Beryl came to the point for her. "Well, Judy, shall we get to business?"

"Oh, dear," Judy said. "This is very difficult."

Suddenly, Beryl knew the real reason she was there. "You've given the *History* to Irene!"

"What?"

"She's been angling after it this whole past year."

"I'm sorry, Beryl. Irene?"

"Don't be obtuse, Judy. You've given Irene the go-ahead to write the *History of the Guides in Canada*, haven't you?"

Judy seemed relieved. "No, no, no, no, that's not it at all."

"Then what am I here for?"

"What are you here for. Well." Judy looked at her clasped hands and looked up at Beryl, smiling uncertainly. Her tongue flicked over the faded pink of her lipstick. She looked as if she were about to ask Beryl a favour.

"You don't need to feel shy about asking my help, you know, dear. I have been stepping aside to let others try their hand, but I'm always happy to help out when I'm needed."

"Ah. Stepping aside."

"There are other things in the world."

"Yes, indeed, there are," Judy said quickly, then seemed to lapse again.

Beryl sat forward and waited.

"Your *History*, for instance."

Odd duck, Judy. If she'd wanted to talk about the *History* all along, why this beating about the bush? Beryl launched into her proposal. Massive mail-out, calling for records and recollections and so forth. Funding for the mail-out. Funding to travel across the country to delve into archives. One couldn't rely entirely on individuals to be forthcoming with documents and photographs. Since Guiding was a *movement* — look at how it had spread like wildfire from the very beginning — it was important that there be input from the ground level. But it would take a massive effort to send out the call to all former Guiders. And it would take the personal involvement of the project's overseer to fill in the big picture.

"You know what you should do, Beryl," Judy said, in a tone that suggested limited interest after all, "is work out a budget and we can discuss what's possible from there. Now, if you're going to be jaunting all over the country, are you thinking of stepping down from the 14th?"

"Never crossed my mind," Beryl said.

"Ah. Well, now that it is crossing your mind ... how is the crossing?"

"Always said I'd be with the 14th till I dropped."

"What if you *did* drop? Right in the middle of a meeting. How do you think that would be for the girls?"

"That's terribly morbid, don't you think?"

"I don't mean to be, but you are ... getting on, aren't you? It is seventy-five this year, isn't it?"

"We don't all drop dead at seventy-five. Look at Olave, over eighty, and still going strong."

"Beryl ..."

"You're not far from seventy-five yourself, distant though it may seem now."

Judy sighed and with deliberation placed her hands one on each thigh. She raised her eyes to Beryl's mouth and no higher. "Beryl, there have been complaints." The eyes flicked up and then down.

Too close together, Beryl thought of the eyes, before fully registering what had been said. "What sort of complaints?"

"You've been with the 14th a long time."

"Yes, yes." Get on. Get on.

"Times have changed."

"I may be old, Judy, but I am not an imbecile. Anyone can see that times have changed. Why, camping used to mean open skies and trench latrines; now it means tents and flush toilets."

"I mean Toronto has changed. The 14th has changed."

Beryl went rigid. "It's the Blacks."

"You called a Guide's little sisters pickaninnies, Beryl. You can't do that. I'm frankly surprised that you did, I would've thought even you would have —"

"I don't see what's wrong with 'pickaninnies.' All it means is little nigras. Check your dictionary."

"This is what I mean, Beryl. 'Nigras.' Times have changed. You can't say 'nigras' anymore. I'm not sure you could ever say pickaninnies."

"Of course you could. Everyone could. They said it themselves. You're taking the imagined hurts of one woman far too seriously, Judy. Claire Webb is, well, a great help on outings and so forth, but she is … *sensitive*. She sees slurs where none exist."

"Beryl, I know it's hard to understand. You've had one way of speaking your whole life, and suddenly it's not okay anymore. But trust me when I tell you, it's not just Claire Webb."

"Don't give me that. It's she and no other. She's come in here in her bossy-bossy way and made a demand and —"

"No, Beryl, that's not —"

"All right, Judy. I will never again use the words pickaninny or nigra. Are there other forbidden words? Perhaps you should give me a list."

"It's not about the words, Beryl, or at least it's not just about the words, it's —" She seemed to run out of steam here, as if she'd suddenly decided it wasn't worth bothering to explain. Her tone shifted. "I'd like you to step down."

"You think I'm a racist. Judy Prudhomme, I assure you, I am no racist. I've had a pen pal in Kenya for fifty years. Fifty years."

"I'd like you to step down."

"Claire Webb is an overprotective mother who blames her daughter's failures on the prejudices of others where no prejudice exists."

"Claire Webb was a district commissioner in Jamaica before she came here six years ago to do a PhD in education. I'd like you to step down."

"You're afraid. You're frightened of her. You're frightened of what she might do, how loud a noise she might make."

"No, Beryl."

"You are making me take the fall."

Judy sighed and pinched the bridge of her nose.

"I never pegged you for a coward, Judy." Beryl rose. "But I see. I see. No, no. I see. I won't trouble you further."

Afterwards she felt beaten. Beaten, and she hadn't even fought. At the time it had seemed as if in the face of such indignity, dignified retreat was the best option. Now she cursed herself. Battle was what she should have given.

Her dignity had not been so assaulted since she was eighteen and her father had ridiculed her plan of becoming a nurse. Then she had been resolute. Then she had made like she'd given in to his wishes, all the while planning her escape and the fulfillment of her dreams: brave service, service glorious in its mundane ingloriousness, its dogged going-on fulfillment of duty. Now she was too stunned to even think, and too old to have any plans but the ones just dashed — to command the 14th Toronto Company until her decline and demise and to devote her remaining time and energy and faculties to a history of the Girl Guides in Canada.

In the next few days she became outraged, reliving the encounter every ten minutes, revising and expanding her responses until they accorded with her sense of fairness and justice, until she could be proud of having given a good argument, an inarguable argument. Judy's weakness and fear had led to this pass. She, Beryl, was taking the fall for Judy's inability to challenge an angry, educated Black out of fear of seeming racist herself. A wrong was being done. A terrible wrong. She was not prejudiced. She was not a bigot. No one valued the worldwide nature of the Girl Guide movement as much as Beryl did. She incorporated more learning about other countries than most, she'd be willing to wager. What about Mafeking Day? Guides Around the World Day? Claire Webb would be gone in a year. Miss Balls would still be out on her ear. It was not only unfair, it was unbelievable. What a way to end sixty years of service.

But to whom could she protest? Judy was the provincial commissioner — it had already gone past division and area. She could lodge her disagreement with Judy, certainly, but that would not change anything. Olave? Could she write Judy and carbon-copy Lady B-P? If only she could be certain Olave would stand up for her. Olave did have a tremendous memory, but would she remember one lowly Toronto Guider? Yes. Yes. She must. How many times had she greeted her on her Toronto visits with a warm, two-handed handshake after her salute? How many times had they had their wonderful teas, when they talked of everything under the sun and Olave had called her a dear, dear friend? Did she not send a Christmas card every year?

Finally, after many drafts, Beryl rolled two sheets of paper and a piece of carbon paper into her typewriter and wrote to Judy a letter of protest. It covered five pages. She folded both copies and slipped them into envelopes, stamped and addressed them and put them with her bills to be mailed. The next day, running a little late, she scooped the whole lot up to mail on her way to Sunnybrook to visit the veterans. She heard a snick — a letter falling? — as she lifted the bundle from desk to purse and glanced quickly in the dark space behind the desk, pretending she didn't see the faint gleam of white down there before leaving.

She did not understand how, having written (and mailed, yes, she was quite sure she had mailed the letters, both of them) the letters, she did not feel better than she did. Everything seemed changed.

She saw the veterans differently — or saw them see her differently. Sneeringly. Had they always? Had she been blind all these years? It took her back to her training days, when men on the street saw her uniform and made comments, before she learned that they hardly ever meant it, they said things for their friends to hear, not for themselves. If joking about an unattractive nurse gave them a laugh, who was she to take offence? They only did it when they were whole and hearty, never when they were hurt. It didn't matter what you looked like if you were strong and firm and quick with their dressing. To most you were … not quite compadres, but closer to that than to the way they normally saw women approximately their age who weren't related to them.

BERYL WAS IN A blue funk for weeks, and would have been for longer if not for Elsie, who invited her up to her cabin for August, as usual. There was nothing like the outdoors to take you out of yourself. The loons calling, beavers slapping their tails. Perhaps she had a little too much time to herself — Elsie took the canoe out each day to sketch and paint. She was doing quite well these days as a painter. She had an annual gallery show that Beryl went to with Marion and Joan. When Beryl found herself stewing on the business with Judy, she went for a long swim. She kept to the shoreline for safety, and Elsie's little dog, Mortimer, ran along the shore to keep an eye on her.

And then home. Thud. For the first fall in forty-seven years that she would not be leader of the 14th Toronto Company. She pretended to be sick for a whole week, ate soup and watched television soap operas. One day she did not get out of bed at all. Then she told herself to snap out of it. There was more to life than Girl Guides.

One didn't want to thank God for little Glynnis Riggs' accident, but, well — now she was Snowy Owl of the 344th, wasn't she?

REFLEXIVELY, BERYL CHECKED her watch as she went to fix her beret in place in the front-hall mirror. Humming and adjusting the hat's angle, she felt a pull to check the watch again. One o'clock. It did say one o'clock. How could that be? When last checked it had said two. She held the watch to her ear. Yes, ticking. The kitchen clock also said one, as did her alarm. Well, then, it was one. She'd misread the face. What comes of having no numbers on a watch. But two whole hours. My. Still in disbelief, she checked the clocks in the living room and study.

Well. Diaries, then. If she meant to write memoirs, after all, she'd best go to the source. She had skimmed them in June in preparation for the meeting with Judy, surprised then at how much she had forgotten. She'd thought of her memories as clear as crystal and as full as lakes, solid and continuous, but evidently this was not so.

Now she found the same thing. There were people she referred to in her diary whom she could not remember at all. Jean Ferry, for example. A Guide, evidently, and a friend, but Beryl for the life of her could not remember which one. Jean Ferry was not in the photograph. And then there was someone she mysteriously referred to as E. *Invited to tea at E's!!!!!* Possibly E. was a friend of L.M., whom she did remember, Lydia May Foster, whose game was exclusion. Scrupulously polite and cold as a fish to Beryl, Lydia May was fervent and gossipy within her gaggle. How was it that she remembered her enemy and not her friend?

About anything important, the adolescent Beryl had been cryptic, which left her bemused now, and sad. The girl writing seemed a stranger, maddeningly vague about the stirrings of her heart. Of the weather and wind speed and barometric pressure she was unstinting. Of outings and occasions and anecdotes, similarly. Of her loves and hates, hurts and prides, only elliptical entries.

She put down the first book and took up the last. Out fluttered a small, browning envelope. Her chest seized.

Oh, time. Oh, heartbreak.

She bent down and retrieved the envelope then sat, looking at it, feeling the texture against her fingertips.

At last she turned the letter over and saw that the seal, finally, had broken. Dried, actually. A band of sepia-coloured gum bordered the envelope flap, now loose and easily flipped up to withdraw the letter, the letter that had lain fifty years unread.

It did not matter, sealed, unsealed, read, unread. The contents of the letter would bring nothing back. Time passed and was gone. Look at how she forgot. Who on earth was Jean Ferry?

Time passed. The diary today was not the same diary as when it had been freshly made paper, blank, ready to receive ink, nor was the letter the same as the one Beryl had received in 1918 and tucked unopened into the diary after the last entry when there was nothing more that was interesting to say.

Tears filled her eyes and rolled down the sides of her face.

Time passed. Oh, how time passed.

Then, letter in hand, she had the same feeling as when she first received it. No, not quite the same feeling, for now there was no surprise, no kick in the gut. But the same strange ghostly feeling as if she were lifting off the ground. The same sandy grass smell of the lawn outside the convalescent hospital, the same feel of warm canvas under her. The same conviction in the pit of her stomach that she should not open the letter, that to open it would be to have all come bursting out and fling itself to the skies and be lost forever.

Ah, recoverable after all, said a pocket of her mind. She quickly closed it off for fear of losing what she'd got.

The letter, tucked in the diary for fifty-three years. The writer, alive, writing board across her knee in a habitual posture, just as in Beryl's first sight of her on the train platform on the way to Southampton for embarkation, one of five Canadian Nursing Sisters uniformed in sky blue, as Beryl was, with two columns of big brass buttons on the chest.

Beryl had paused on the platform, shy of approaching, despite her desire to blend into a crowd again after making her very obvious way through London. Veteran nurses they must be, though a few were young.

"Ho! Canada over here!" One nurse was now up and waving, having recognized Beryl's blues. Miss Ross, that was, a tall, cheery girl from Vancouver. Beryl had to smile, return her wave and go straight over. Meantime the shout of Canada had sparked one of those spontaneous outbursts of song you heard oftener toward the beginning of the war than now, "The Maple Leaf Forever" echoing down the station tracks. The very song she and Tom had sung, determinedly homesick, as they explored their cousins' nook of Britain upon first being deported to England after their mother's death. (A part of her had been excited to come to England — the home she knew but had never seen — but she kept this part secret from Tom.) *In days of yore, from Britain's shore, Wolfe the dauntless hero came.* And now the nurses sang, too, in a patriotic fervour, turning their heads to acknowledge Beryl's arrival. A ready-made opportunity to prove herself Canadian — she was nervous about the claim after eight years in England — and the only one designed to make her weep. Abruptly, she had a moment of detachment, in which she saw the Canadians soldiers and nurses as an absurdly loyal little band. What had they in common, really? This song, whose crescendo came now … *The thistle, shamrock, rose entwine* … Ah, yes, that was the beauty of Canada, wasn't it, all hearts entwining. There it was, the love she had tended and fostered all these years, joining theirs. *The Ma-ple Leaf forever!* Oh, Canada! Oh, Toronto! Oh, home! Lake and maple, sturdy oak, fragrant pine. Skating parties. Sledges. Horrible roads. Brilliant autumns. Of course she was Canadian. No one could tell her she was not.

Desultory cheers flew up as they ended their song and Beryl took the moment of distraction to wipe her eyes. The soldiers introduced themselves — Princess Pats from Edmonton — on their way back to the front. The nurses were Miss Boothson, Miss Ross and Miss Flint, from Ottawa, Vancouver and Montreal, respectively. Beryl did not immediately catch the names and ports of call of the others.

Miss Ross wanted to know if Beryl knew the Macfarlanes in Toronto, and although she did not, Beryl was worried that one of the sisters would know someone who had known her in Toronto and that between them they would work it out that Beryl was too young to serve and she would be given a dishonourable discharge or whatever they did to underage nurses. In this nervous state, she stuttered, "I fear I hardly qualify as Canadian, having been away so long."

"Nonsense," said the first one, the one who had been writing a letter, Miss Boothson. "Once a Canadian, always a Canadian." She smiled, looking directly into Beryl's eyes so that Beryl felt almost hit by her warmth. Miss Boothson had a bright, round face with a nose like a little knob in the middle of it. Then, just as quickly, the warmth was gone, the face turned back to the letter.

Miss Ross was talkative, regaling Beryl with stories of their previous posting on the Isle of Lemnos, at which the whole gang began reminiscing about the horridness of the heat, the cold, the lack of water. She was happy to hear everything they told her and they were happy to tell it, and they passed their time very pleasantly in recollection and in the usual speculation about the war.

FINALLY TO FRANCE, Beryl thought, when the crossing was underway. The sea and sky were grey, befitting her *as to war* mood. Her eyes must be gleaming in keenness.

As the ferry surged along, she had a sudden sense of the mass of *things* streaming into France: sheets and blankets and stretchers and ambulances, morphine and saline and ether and mortars and pestles, horses and dogs, pigeons and veterinarians, socks and scarves and sweaters and mittens, grenades, machine guns, gas masks, truckloads of bullets, boatloads of mortar shells, miles and miles of canvas, tinned food, pots and pans, evaporated milk, cigarettes, chocolate, forks, plates ... But mostly *them*, she and Miss Boothson and Miss Flint, the troops who shared the ship, the men — mostly men, but women too — from all over the world right now steaming Franceward (and Serbiaward, and Italyward, and North Africaward), volunteers drawn forth from every land by the call of right action. Never before in history had there been such great traffic. And she, Beryl Balls, was a part of it, part of this great stream of human resolve. They could not fail.

Upon their arrival in Boulogne, her sense of the stream was only strengthened. The docks were lined with stores and the streets with troops: Canadians, Australians, Highlanders looking very splendid in their kilts; then, equally splendid but far more exotic, the Bengal Lancers, and not five minutes later, a company of perfectly brown Gurkhas. In turbans! Beryl felt as if their hearts were all knitting together, all the noble peoples of the Empire, uniting to defeat the foe, whether they fully understood their role or not.

The other nurses were feeling it, too, she could tell. It was as if they had all swelled upon arrival, brimming with the desire to fall in and get to work. Their personalities receded and their mechanical roles as part of the bigger effort took over. Still, Miss Ross could not help exclaiming over the age of everything. "The streets are so narrow!" "*Look* at that arch!" "How old do you think these stones are?"

"Oh, about seven hundred years, I'd say," said Miss Flint, with a twinkle you'd have not thought her capable of. She had been there at the start of the war and had the answer already.

As in England, Beryl remarked on the preponderance of old men, women and children among the civilian population, but it seemed especially eerie in this foreign city, as if it were a town bewitched. The women's costume, black skirts and tight bodices with stiff lace bonnets, emphasized the otherworldliness, the fairy-tale quality of the native town on which was superimposed the supremely modern stuff of this war, the tanks and heavy artillery and transport trucks and ambulance cars and trains and surveillance balloons hanging in the channel like cartoon clouds, the fit troops in their drab gear, the bayonetted, shelled, shell-shocked, gassed, wounded in their mud-soaked uniforms on their way home. It seemed crazy and noble and unreal all at the same time and Beryl dedicated her heart to the long fight ahead. *She* would stay strong. The war would knock down others but it would not knock down her. No, sir.

They hoped for orders at their hotel, but there were none, and they spent the remainder of the day and most of the next exploring the old city. This felt odd in contrast to Beryl's sense of purpose. They were like tourists, with Miss Flint as chaperone, and Beryl was reminded that she was to have toured the continent with her aunt and cousin in 1915. She was glad to have escaped that. She and Emily would never have agreed on what to see and do and she would have been rigid with embarrassment at the intimations of matchmaking when they ran into families touring with young men. If she had to be a tourist, she was glad it was with Miss Boothson. There was something about her — beyond the quick likability that attracted everyone — that Beryl was drawn to and a little in awe of. Warmth was the chief offshoot of it, but it was not the main thing. The main thing Beryl could not for the moment identify. She only knew she would always want to be close to it.

Miss Boothson, however, did not seem to care more than was polite about Miss Balls. You could see she was one of those people who was very bright and whose intelligence made them restless. Every once in a while she condescended to join the rest of them and that warmth flashed around before shutting off again. Her great friend from Lemnos was now posted to Amiens. She remained more occupied with her letter writing — and sketching — she dotted her letters with sketches, Beryl saw — than with anything else, though once, after tea in the hotel, she threw down her pen and said, "Oh, I hate this idleness." She stretched her hands to the ceiling, imploring, "Give us a posting. Please."

"Well, Bootsie," Miss Watson said the next morning, waving a sheet of paper at a group of them returning from a visit to local hospitals. "Your prayer's been answered."

They threw up a cheer before crowding round to see who went where.

"Flint and I for the McGill," Miss Watson said. "Ross to Le Tréport. And Bootsie and Ballsie to the No. 7 at Etaples."

Beryl flushed with pleasure.

Bootsie laughed, shaking her head. "Bootsie and Ballsie. Oh, dear."

⌐

WORK AND FRIENDSHIP *had* made her happy. Of course there'd been that dreadful time after the war when she trod the earth lost and bereft, but that was what life was, difficulties encountered and overcome. Postwar blues and then back to Canada and work and Guides, the14th, Doe Lake, new friends and dear friends, work and friendship. So it went. This business in the spring, now, it was no different. A passing thing she should never have given so much thought to. Terribly happy. Oh, indeed. Though never quite so happy again.

Looking back over the summer now, as she stepped out the door on her way to walk to Brownies on a clear, fresh day in early November, the business with Judy seemed a distant phase, an embarrassing hash of emotions. Not distant enough that she felt thoroughly safe — she could still be taken by a cloud of doubt, a fog of low murmurs. *Fool. Fool. All your life you've pretended.* But the clouds were farther and farther apart. The fall had revitalized her. Rowena's calling on her had revitalized her. Spending time with children again, with Carol and Glynnis and Jay, had revitalized her. They liked her. Clear as day. She did not *need* children to like her — you could not have that need and be an effective leader — but she liked them to like her. She very much liked them to like her. That was what she missed about the 14th: the girls, their smiles and laughter, their calling her Cap'n. Their liking her. She was a fun captain. A fuddy-duddy, no, not she. She had all sorts of ideas for making things fun. In some ways she was like a child herself — had never lost that sense of life as an adventure that children had, an adventure in which one could be a hero, ordinary as one might be.

She felt terrific and young and heroic all over again, walking down Bayview in the keen fall wind with the low angle of the sun on her face. The wind channelling behind her glasses stung her eyes in a pleasant fashion so they teared in pools at the corners. Then the wind hit the pools and cooled them. Her skin felt taut, her sorrow keen but overcome, distant and romantic. The narrow streets of France were the narrow streets of sorrow. Bayview Avenue, broad and modern, was the prospect of hope. Just walking was a great adventure. This was a lesson she wanted to impart to her girls, to everyone. If you had the right attitude, just walking could be an adventure. Wasn't that wonderful?

Glynnis

GLYNNIS' SCHOOLWORK took so little time she wondered what they did all day at school. Come Wednesday noon she had nothing left to do except her leaf project. Miss Hildebrandt suggested book reports.

She'd reread *Little House on the Prairie* and read *Little Town on the Prairie*, *Farmer Boy*, *Biggles at Sea* and *The Wizard of Oz*, which was not like the movie. She had watched *Uncle Bobby*, *The Electric Company*, *Mr. Dressup*, *Chez Hélène*, *The Flintstones*, *The Merv Griffin Show*, *The Price Is Right*, *Beat the Clock*, *Lost in Space*, *Gilligan's Island*, *Get Smart*, *The Brady Bunch* and of course *Elwood Glover's Luncheon Date*.

She had filled sheet after sheet of the pendulum drawing toy the MacDonalds had given her with brightly coloured patterns and had given them titles designed to make Jay laugh, like 'Vacuum Number 6,' 'Boy with Vase,' 'No, it goes the other way.' She had finished her book of word-find puzzles. She had built the airplane model. She'd covered the chesterfield with shavings as she attempted to make a paddle from the cedar block Jay had given her. It ended up looking like a spoon. She had tried to do magic tricks from a magic kit she'd got for her birthday and never used, but had failed and thrown the book across the room. She had worked on her doodle art poster. She had slept and dreamed and taken 222s. She had played with her mother's jewellery box, the one with the ballerina on the puffy cover and the song inside from *Swan Lake*. She looked forward to Jay coming home, and was disappointed when he had other things, rugby practice or fencing or debating. She even looked forward to Carol coming home.

Now she was poking around the den while Miss Balls did laundry in the basement. Her mother had taken Carol to the psychologist. The den housed two mahogany desks, a big one for her father and a smaller one for her mother. On a side table by her mother's was Mrs. Riggs' new electric typewriter that they weren't supposed to touch. Glynnis pulled the cover off the typewriter and flipped the on switch. She hit a key. Whap. The indent of *a* showed faintly on the rubber roller. Paper: second drawer.

She rolled a piece into the machine, leaned her crutches up against the side of the desk and sat. Like a concert pianist about to play a concerto, she held her fingers over the keys. She leaned forward as if into a song and then slightly back, letting her fingers fly. Super-secretary speed typist, fast and furious. Nonsense came out on the page, but for the time being that didn't matter. The sound of the keys, the sound of the ding at the end of the line — they were what mattered. Type-itty-type-type-type, ding! Whirr-lunk. Type-itty-type-type-type, ding! She paused and listened to the silence of the house, her heart tapping more quickly than usual in her chest. One had to keep on one's toes, as Miss Balls liked to say.

Wiggling her fingers elegantly over the keys, she leaned in to play again. The little arms of metal flung themselves pleasingly at the page.

How hard did they hit, she wondered, sticking her finger in front of the place on the page where they struck. Ow. Hard. On her finger, a little white *z* faded to red. It would be fun to type a word onto her fingertips. She tugged the ribbon gently to see if she could pull it out far enough to slip a finger behind it. "z. o. o. m.," she wrote, then held her hand up to look at it. "w. o. o. s.," it said. She hung her stinging fingers upside down. Zoom.

Standing on her good foot, she peered into the valley of the middle, all the metal arms nestled in their places. Each letter was actually backwards on the arm, so when it hit the ribbon it was frontwards, and there were two versions on each head, a small letter and a big one. How did you get the big ones? Glynnis systematically pushed all the keys that didn't have letters on them. Zzzzz-clunk, went the one that said 'tab.' K-chuh, k-chuh went the one with four lines and an arrow that automatically rolled the roller for you. Others didn't seem to have any purpose at all. Like 'shift,' which just went clunk when you hit it. She kept looking for what it did. It had to do something. But maybe only when you combined it with something else. Then she noticed the clunking moved — *shift*ed, aha — the metal heads. She held the key down and hit another key: *M.* There it was. A capital. She began typing.

Good morming Bbootsie.g

It was hard finding the letters. Why weren't they all just in alphabetical order?

Good morninf Ballsie.

How did you sleeep/?

Very well, thankyou.

How didyou sleep/?

Like the dead.

Oh, Ballsie, do not say that it gives me thw shivvers.

"Glynnis?"

Oh, no. Miss Balls.

"Lunch is ready." Miss Balls' head appeared in the doorway. Glynnis covered the typewriter, leaving the sheet in, and followed Miss Balls to the kitchen.

"Was that you on the typewriter?" Miss Balls asked, and when Glynnis assented, "Have we another scribe in the family?" In the '40s, Miss Balls had published a book, now out of print, *Judy Jones, Girl Guide*. Mrs. Riggs had an inscribed copy. Glynnis knew that Miss Balls had always meant to make a series out of it but had never got round to it. Now Miss Balls was thinking of writing her memoirs.

"I'm just typing my book reports," Glynnis said. She had to change the topic of conversation before her mother got home and she was revealed to have been working on the forbidden machine.

"Typing's a terrific skill," Miss Balls said.

"Did you have to type your nursing reports during the war?"

"Oh, heavens no. We hardly had time for that. It was all handwritten. You can see the importance of a clear hand, can't you. They'd come in, the cases, with a card pinned to them. Medical. Surgical. Head case. And their wound. Some were quite a puzzle. Thigh? Or liver? Well, you just looked at the thigh, didn't you." Success. Off typing and onto the war, and just in time. Mrs. Riggs could be heard coming in the front door.

After lunch, Mrs. Riggs took Carol back to school and then was going grocery shopping and Glynnis hurried to the typewriter, meaning simply to remove the evidence, but as she pulled off the cover and began rolling out the page, she couldn't help reading it, and reading it, she couldn't help admiring the beauty of it. Typed letters! Making up typed sentences! So immeasurably better than what was possible by hand. The gorgeous hooks on the stem of the d and on the bottom of the *m*! The pure *typed*ness of the *a*! She stopped rolling, listening again. Silence. Or rather steady-state house noises — ticking clock, hum of fridge. She sat down, rolled the page back in. Her mother would be gone at least an hour.

```
sorry, bBootsyI dont mesan to scare you.
    wWe are a round enouighdead ppeople withouty you
going around saying yoou sleeep lik e them . Its not
goodl luck to saythings liek tha.
    I said i"M sorry, all rifvght?
```

Slow work and her mistakes began to annoy Glynnis. The letters were still beautiful, of course, but the words, when misspelled, were not. Nonetheless, her heart was again beating quickly. Her fingers tingled.

```
You don't know what it is liek finding thos poor
sweaet boys dead in thier beds in thre morbing.
```

"Ordinary secretary, one two three," Miss Balls chanted like the skipping game.

Glynnis jumped.

Her instinct was to rip the page out of the typewriter and crumple it into a tiny ball. Instead, she very casually leaned forward and rolled the page out, turning it upside down on the desk beside her and inserting a new page.

"Are you using all your fingers, now, dear, or are you hunting and pecking?"

Hunting and pecking. What a perfect expression.

"Well, how about a typing lesson then, what do you say?"

"Sure. Great."

Miss Balls had taken a do-it-yourself typing course when writing *Judy Jones*.

GLYNNIS' CHANCES to use the typewriter were limited. Her mother did not go out enough, Miss Balls lurked too much, and while the thrill of illicit behaviour enlivened her days, she really did not want to be caught. Mrs. Riggs would show Miss Balls what she had written and they would not get it and Miss Balls would be hurt and Mrs. Riggs would be angry and embarrassed that a daughter of hers should be so callous as to make light of serious historical matters and Glynnis would be in huge trouble. Thing was, she did not mean to make fun of Miss Balls. It was just that, like Everest, Miss Balls was there. And it made Jay laugh.

After a couple of close calls, Glynnis asked her mother outright for use of the typewriter. "For book reports," she said, hoping she was not blushing too badly. Her mother was thrilled. "You can have your father's old one." You needed fingers of steel to type with it, but it made the same gorgeous letters, and that was enough for Glynnis.

Carol wanted to know what Glynnis was typing all the time. Glynnis wanted Jay to be first to see it, but Carol pestered and Jay would not be home until suppertime. "This is amazing," Carol said after Glynnis had finished reading her work aloud. "We should act it out." Carol was good at impressions. She did a perfect Miss Glory-of-the-British-Empiyah Balls. Once through the script, they kept going, making it up as they went, laughing until they were giddy. It brought back a naturalness, an easiness to who they were together that since the accident had been so precarious as to be dropping earthward, like a plate falling off a table. Remarkable. Glynnis had actually missed Carol.

When their game trailed off and they were just lying there on the bed, Carol said, "Miss Balls hates me," and she began to cry.

All Glynnis' annoyance flooded back. It's your own fault, she wanted to say. Instead, she sighed impatiently and rolled her eyes. Carol was lying within reach of her and she stuck her hand out and flicked Carol on the arm with her middle finger, waiting for her to say, "Ow, quit it," but she didn't. She stopped crying and lay there unmoving with Glynnis' fingernail whapping her upper arm until Mrs. Riggs called her to come set the table for dinner.

THE NEXT DAY, Mrs. Riggs brought Sandy and Melanie home with Carol to play with Glynnis. Before the accident, chances were that Carol would go off on her own or with her friends, or that she would play with Glynnis and her friends. Before, they might all — Glynnis and her friends, Carol and hers — have joined forces once in a while to play hide-and-seek, or road hockey in the drive-way, or SPUD in the backyard. Or they would have gone down the street to Cheltenham Park and played kick the can with the other neighbourhood kids. So it shouldn't have seemed strange that after they hung up their coats in the front hall, Carol didn't go off on her own but stuck around. But it did feel strange, possibly because Carol stood too close behind them as if worried they'd get away from her somehow, looking eagerly from Melanie to Sandy to Glynnis.

"Hi, you guys," Glynnis said. "What do you want to do?"

"I don't know, what do *you* want to do?" said Sandy.

"I don't know, what do you want to do?" said Glynnis to Melanie.

"I don't know, what do you want to do?" said Melanie.

"I don't know, what do you want to do?" said Carol.

"Let's go downstairs," Glynnis said unhappily, certain they would all have a bad time.

They played hands-down until Melanie said, "I *always* lose at this game, let's play something else," and then they played crazy eights until Melanie said, "I hate this game, let's play something else," and then they played battleship.

"Bad luck, Bootsie," Glynnis said as Carol's first battleship sank.

"Never mind, Ballsie," said Carol. "Stiff upper lip, what."

"Who're you guys?" Melanie asked.

"Bootsie and Ballsie," said Carol. "Hey!" She turned to Glynnis. "Melanie and Sandy can be Dr. Peanut and Batsy! They can all play Wartime Hospital!"

"No," said Glynnis.

"Come on," said Carol.

"What's Wartime Hospital?" asked Melanie.

"It's this play Glynnis wrote, it's hilarious. Come on, Glynn, it'll be perfect."

"No."

"I don't know. Sounds good to me," said Sandy.

Carol ran off and got the script, while Glynnis reluctantly told them what it was about and how they should act: Bootsie and Ballsie were nurses in the first world war, Batsy was their bossy matron. She was in love with the new doctor, Dr. Rex Gorgon, and the old doctor, Dr. Peanut, was in love with Batsy. Dr. Peanut was also deaf and going senile.

Melanie, it turned out, was a perfect Batsy.

They, too, left off following the script. "Smarten up," Melanie would say as Batsy. "Fart and sup?" Glynnis would say as Dr. Peanut. "Pip pip," said Carol-Bootsie. "Spit spot," said Sandy-Ballsie, throwing in a little Mary Poppins. This kept them occupied until Mrs. Riggs called down the stairs that it was five o'clock and time for Sandy and Melanie to go.

They played it again two days later. And the day after that. They told everyone at school about it. They played it at school. They played it at home. They used ketchup and mustard for blood and pus. The beefeater doll got a recurring role as the man whose head Dr. Peanut amputated by mistake. Wartime Hospital was a smashing success.

GLYNNIS' CRUTCHES punched circles into the frost-laden grass either side of the narrow walk to the driveway. Her mother yelled at Carol to hurry up.

"Boy!" she said. "You're sure eager, aren't you?"

Naturally Glynnis was eager. She was going back to school. Mrs. Riggs started the car, then got out to scrape the windshield. Mrs. Riggs yelled for Carol again before she ran out with her coat undone, slamming the door behind her.

"It's about time," Glynnis said.

"Sorry."

The first few blocks the streets were quiet and still, just a cleaning lady bundled up in scarf and overcoat, her flowered housedress peeking out underneath, plodding her way to someone's house.

A block farther on they began passing pairs and clumps of children, skinny, red-haired Robbie Ross running after his older sister. Alison, Sandy and Muffy Newman, who was in the other grade two class. Jeff MacDonald looking wiry and tough. Tony Briscott on his bike as usual, bare-handed, bare-headed, open jacket, no socks. Little Kevin Money pulling up his pants every six steps.

This was what school did, drew everyone in like gravity, this was proof of its greatness, all these living creatures congregating from their spread-out dwellings to this hub where real life happened. For a minute Glynnis pictured the scene as if looking down on an electronic map, with each child a white ball of light travelling toward the centre. You could picture the hospital and its ambulances that way, too, but the hospital version was corrupted by having sickness and brokenness at its core, whereas school — school was pure, beautiful energy.

As soon as the car came to a halt, Glynnis hopped out, Carol hurrying after her. "Straight inside now, girls," Mrs. Riggs said. Glynnis was not supposed to have her leg down for more than a few minutes at a time or she'd get phlebitis.

"Incoming wounded," Melanie shouted in her Batsy voice.

"Shortcoming spoon-dip?" said Toby Wein. Oh. Dr. Peanut.

Everyone wanted to operate on Glynnis. They had made up more characters. In addition to Bootsie and Ballsie, there were now Boopsy and Bitsy and Flopsy and Mopsy. Glynnis was peripheral to her own game, but she didn't realize it fully until later, when she was lining up after the bell with Sandy for her partner, Hilary Fehlings and Yolanda behind them and Melanie and Janet behind them. Out of the corner of her ear, Glynnis heard Janet say something to Mel about wanting to go roller skating at the Terrace for her birthday, too. And she heard Mel hush Janet and saw Sandy eye her nervously. And so they said nothing. Mel avoided her the rest of the day, and the next day she brought an invitation, just like Alison had brought to Carol, saying she'd given them out last week at school and that was why she hadn't given one to Glynnis. Patently untrue. She'd been over to her house twice that week. She'd had lots of opportunity. "It's a roller-skating party, though, so you might not want to come. Or you could come for, like, cake." Melanie saw her face. "It's not like that, I swear. All it was is I forgot. Glynnis."

Sandy said it was because Melanie hadn't wanted to make Glynnis feel bad having to watch everybody else having fun roller skating while she sat on the sidelines.

"Yeah, it's a whole lot better not inviting me at all." She was glad of Sandy, but she thought of other small references her friends had made over the past few weeks to things they had done together without her and that they had tried to keep from her and she saw that they had all moved on, they had made a life without her and did not particularly want to bring her back in. She had a sudden vision of the future. People would not ask her to do the things they used to ask her to do — tobogganing, skiing, skating, dodge ball, kick the can, nicky-nicky-nine-door. They would think, Glynnis: nope, can't do that. Nope, can't do that. They would take from her all her ideas and turn them into something she could not play.

Then she wiped that vision away. When her foot was better, all that would change.

⌣

CAROL HAD CONFESSED to Glynnis her hope that Brownies would be cancelled after the accident, but Glynnis knew her mother would never give in like that, not a chance. Glynnis didn't think it was fair, now that she'd seen Carol go catatonic. If Tawny Owl had been allowed to quit, Carol should be allowed to quit. Mrs. Riggs, however, thought it important that Carol keep going to Brownies. She had to own up and move on, and not going would only allow her and other people to think she needed to be banished.

Miss Balls had replaced Tawny Owl. They were supposed to call her Snowy Owl.

Alison flounced over to where Glynnis and Cathy were playing see-see-my-playmate and said, "Glynnis, darling, how *are* you, it's been an age," though in fact it hadn't been, she'd been at their house two days before when she'd been a head case for Wartime Hospital. "Tell me *everything*!"

"Where to *begin*!" Glynnis said. Other girls she hadn't seen since the accident were drawing round. "The hospital was *dreadful*, darling, dreadful. Not a bit of colour anywhere, just white, white, white. And the *food*!"

"Can I sign your cast?" Susie Marks asked.

"Does it look like I have a cast?"

"Casts are *so* passé," Alison said. "*Splints* are all the rage this season."

"Well, how was I supposed to know?" Susie said in a huff.

"They're kidding, Susie," Julie Rice said.

"I know that," Susie said.

Carol, meantime, stuck by their mother, asking if there was anything she could help with.

The previous week they had learned Indian tracking signs and this week they were going to put them to use. In fact, Miss Balls was outside right now setting trails for them to follow. After they'd done that, each Six would have fifteen minutes to set their own trail, and the rest of the time they would follow the others' trails. This was Glynnis' favourite part of Brownies, tracking and orienteering, and she was supposed to stay inside with Miss Balls and keep her foot up. However, it was never difficult to convince Miss Balls to go outside, she believed so deeply in the power of fresh air. Baden-Powell, she said, loved fresh air so much, he slept out on his porch, summer and winter.

Across the street from the church was a little wood about the size of two city lots, and it was through this that the trail led. Some of the trail markings were obvious, like broken sticks laid into arrows pointing the direction you were supposed to go, but others were less so. One rock set on top of another meant go straight on. The same with a rock on one side meant go in the direction of the third rock. Long grasses tied together meant go in the direction they're pointing.

Along the route were stations with different patterns of dots on pieces of paper kept dry in plastic bags that they were to copy into their Brownie notebooks with their Brownie pencils kept in their Brownie pouches.

The other groups were well ahead, and though you could see them through the trees and undergrowth, it didn't mean you could just follow them because you might miss something. Glynnis led the way from the starting place, spotted the markers and made her turns. She could feel Miss Balls' approval at her swiftness. If she hadn't been on crutches, she might have impressed her with her stealth and silence as well, since several years back Miss Balls had told her the secret to walking quietly in the woods was to roll your weight from heel to toe instead of planting the whole foot at once. It worked even better if you wore moccasins.

Half a dozen turns into the course, they could hear another group ahead of them.

— I say, Bootsie.

—Yes, Ballsie?

— I say, Bootsie.

— What do you say, Ballsie?

— I say we go right, Bootsie, what do you say?

— Pip pip, Ballsie.

— Aye aye, Bootsie.

— Chip chip, Ballsie.

— Pie pie, Bootsie.

— Poo poo, Ballsie.

Glynnis had seen the next marker already, tied-down grass this time, but she pretended she had not. She pitched her voice loud. "MISS BALLS, MY LEG'S REALLY SORE. Do you think we should go back inside, MISS BALLS?"

The voices shut up. Brush parting and twigs breaking barely covered snatches of smothered laughter receding in the bush. Miss Balls did not answer right away. She stood stock still in her green rubber raincoat, sou'wester hat and rubber boots, her long face stiff and pale. She looked as Carol had when Glynnis had come to her defence at Alison's birthday or when Glynnis had made fun of her and Daintry playing house. She had the same open-mouthed pause. And then same clamped lip and hard eye. And then something different, a face trying to soften, a smile forced on unwilling cheeks.

"If you like, dearie."

Miss Balls

WHAT A STRANGE, ghostly feeling. Suspended in time, like a bubble in glass, but no, something that then moved on, ash rising up from a fire, something airy and at the whim of other forces. How easy and strange it was to float this way, back inside with Glynnis, through the rest of Brownies. Her voice spoke, her body went through motions, she covered up quite well, but inside she floated. She wondered, briefly, if she was having a heart attack.

❧

SHE AND BOOTSIE had shared a hut at Etaples, another bit of luck. The camp was enormous, bigger than the town and much more populous. Eight hospitals. Transit camps for troops. Trains and trucks running through the middle. Practically a city, weirdly uniform and temporary. Buildings all the same height. Canvas, wood and tin.

Beryl felt Bootsie was rather above her, at first. She was older, for one. Everyone was older than Beryl, of course. Unless someone else had lied about her age, Beryl was the youngest nursing sister on the Western Front. But she somehow felt her youth more with Bootsie, as if Bootsie were a marvellous upper-school prefect and Beryl a lowly first former. Twenty-eight! An operating room nurse!

But how natural, that first day after they'd unpacked their few things, to have Bootsie invite her for a walk, and how foolishly glad Beryl was for such an ordinary invitation.

"We must get our bearings," Bootsie said. "Not least how to get in and out of this maze." They located the wards and mess tent, latrines and bathing tent of their hospital, then threaded their way down dusty rows of wood and canvas where here and there someone tried to cultivate a garden plot or a pot of pansies for colour. They walked down to the town, talking of this and that, where they had trained, what they might expect here. So far, said Miss Boothson, it seemed very civilized, compared to Lemnos. "Running water! Heaven. Why, the huts here even have floors."

"I suppose I've been spoiled, being at the London," said Beryl.

"I don't suppose any of us has been exactly spoiled."

"Compared to the men, we have."

"Very true, Miss Balls. Very true."

Miss Boothson was pleased she would be closer to her brothers. They were twins, Neil and Warren, in the 38th Battalion. She'd just seen Warren in London, on leave. Neil ought to have been there, too, but at the last minute his leave was cancelled. Red tape for you. Terrifically strange to see Warren alone. They were the finishing each other's sentences kind of twins. Warren kept glancing sideways and then looking lost to find no one at his shoulder. Bootsie had found herself crossing her eyes to pretend there were two of them.

Back home there were younger brothers chomping at the bit to grow up and get over here. She shook her head. She spoke of all her brothers with such affection that Beryl wondered at the secret of it — a family that got on. She and Tom had been a special case in her own family.

"Have you any brothers, Miss Balls?" Miss Boothson asked.

Beryl's eyes teared up. She nodded. "One. Monty. Italy," she managed to say. "But —" She bit her lip.

"But there was another," Miss Boothson said, looping her hand round Beryl's forearm.

"Tom," Beryl nodded.

"How did you lose him?"

"Ypres. First day in the trenches. First casualty in his battalion. Sniper." She remembered getting the telegram, thinking it couldn't possibly be that, it was far too soon, he'd barely embarked.

They came out onto the dunes by the sea on the Paris-Plage trail (they'd had directions of a passing padre), which they'd save for another day. It was a bright May day and the wind blew off the sea, bringing the fishy, clayey smell of tidal flats. The observation balloon hung over the channel like a bloated angel.

"Oh, dear," said Ballsie, using her handkerchief, acutely embarrassed. "What's come over me." She cried badly, of this she was aware. Some did it prettily. Not she. She did not do anything well, except, perhaps, nurse. While nursing she thought of nothing but the work in front of her. She did it and was pleased to be doing it. It was all of her until she was off shift, when she had to cope with being Beryl again.

Miss Boothson still had hold of Beryl's arm. "Don't give it another thought," she said with that great warmth of hers. A general warmth, not a particular warmth grown of real liking, Beryl sensed, but it suffused her nonetheless, and she felt not quite so gormless as the moment prior when she'd been boo-hooing.

Later that first day, the Sisters in the mess were aroar with tales of their own first days in camp. Horrendous convoys, torrents of rain, no orderlies. The second day they experienced it for themselves, the rush to discharge enough men to free up beds, the wait, wait, wait into the late evening on an empty ward until in they streamed, walking cases, stretcher cases, hundreds of them. Two hundred and seventy-four, to be exact. The orderlies and ambulance teams lined up stretcher cases on the ground until they could be directed to the appropriate ward, the mud and blood and who knows what other foul detritus of battle washed off of them. Beryl was on the medical ward, though she preferred the surgical, and spent the night stripping and washing and getting food and the appropriate medicine into feverish men. It seemed impossible that they should be able to get to every last single man before morning, but in fact, they did. She emerged, stretching and yawning, just past eight in the morning at the same time as Miss Boothson. They caught each other in the very same posture, a squaring of the shoulders, a rolling of the neck, and laughed. Her mind felt keen as a scalpel edge. "I ought to be tired, but I'm not ready for bed at all, are you?" she said to Miss Boothson.

"Not at all."

"Let's go for a walk."

"Down to the sea?"

They stood by the sea and breathed in the funny, fishy air, bought coffee in town and drank it from big bowls until they were sleepy enough and returned to their hut. They walked back in the most companionable silence Beryl had ever experienced. Dropped into sleep.

THE NO. 7 CANADIAN GENERAL was busier even than the London, the state of the patients worse. They either died or got better between here and Blighty.

The shell shock cases were new to her, and disturbing. There was nothing — nothing! — physically wrong with them. And yet they shook and gibbered and wept like head cases with the brains falling out. Or were silent — mute — deaf — catatonic. One fellow had hysterical blindness along with a rather nasty gash in his forearm.

The wound was what kept him here. He did really seem to be blind — at least, he did not flinch at tests flung at him that no seeing person could fail to flinch at. But he alternated between pestering the M.O. with possible causes — a tumour was the strongest contender — and apologizing for his condition and pretending bafflement. Beryl alternated between utter conviction he was a fraud — the arm would heal and he'd be sent back unless he could call on some other ailment — and the unbelievable yet seemingly inescapable conclusion he genuinely could not see. He was not someone you would have otherwise thought weak-minded. And yet ... Well, obviously, you did not know a mind until the mind was tested.

Amongst the hospital staff was a camaraderie Beryl had never known. Guides had offered something like it. Child's play compared to this. Several times a week, they did the impossible — received 380 patients in a night and sent 360 of them on thirty-six hours later, only to receive the next 300 — and there was nothing like doing the impossible to bring the people who had done it together. How they *roared* with laughter! How infectious was pep and pluck!

Bootsie acquired a stove, and they began to have small parties in their hut, informal gatherings for tea and toast, the talk everyone likes to exchange at the end of a day, patients who were a particular worry, the sorry state of supply cupboards and how they'd improvised with what they had. Gradually, Beryl came to notice that Bootsie sought her out. She sought her out in the mess tent. She sought her out when she received a parcel and wanted to share. "Ballsie," she'd whisper. And Beryl would hurry back to their hut.

"Here," said Bootsie, once. "Honeycomb." She held out a dripping teaspoon.

"Manna!" crooned Beryl.

Mostly, they walked. Bootsie liked to get out of the camp at least once a day. They walked north to Hardelot. They walked south to Berck. They walked east to Montreuil. Rain or shine, they walked.

Quite soon and without any fanfare, Bootsie had begun reading her brothers' letters aloud to Beryl, as if sharing brothers. On fine days they did this outside, letting their hair dry in the sun or as they sat out after a picnic lunch.

June 11, 1917

Dear Helen, Thanks for yours of the 5th. Feel a bump a few days ago? Messines Ridge being removed from the face of the earth. We saw nothing, but felt the ground shake like anything. News came hard on its heels where and what. Largest single explosion ever, something like 19 separate points of detonation. So that's what the moley engineers have been up to all this time. Quite a feat. Apparently the army occasionally can do things right. Or perhaps it's a case of doing the complex well and the simple badly. Three marches in five days. They can't seem to decide where they want us. Looks like we go up tomorrow, though.

Managed to bathe in a muddy stream yesterday and felt like a newborn babe.

No word on leave yet. C.O. says another month, likely.

P.T. sends his love. Oh, yes, Warren, too.

Your devoted brother,

Neil

"Which was born first?" Beryl asked Bootsie one afternoon. Then wrote, "Dear Mr. Boothson the Younger. I hope you do not mind that your sister shares your letters with her 'roomie.' Mail of any description is a great boon, as you know. When your letters arrive, we find a time to retire to a quiet spot, and Bootsie — Helen, I should say — reads them aloud. I feel I am coming to know you two. Although you are already quite possibly the world's most written to pair of soldiers, I hope an occasional addition to your bulging mail sack from me will not go amiss. We have had a few of your crew through here. Corporal Lindsay sends his regards ..."

"Dear Mr. Boothson, the Elder ..."

"Dear Miss Balls, Any friend of Helen's is a friend of ours. They've got us building roads now. We shovel gravel and sing spirituals all day long ... Virtually all plant life here has been obliterated. No crops, no weeds, no flowers. I don't know why dead plants should affect me so when dead *homo sapiens* and *equus caballus* are so regularly planted throughout the landscape."

Out for an afternoon walk helping Bootsie pick flowers for botanist Warren, Ballsie had the most curious feeling. Happiness. She was happy. Tremendously happy. Happier than she'd ever been. She had work she liked, a sense of place. She was mistress of her own fate. And she had Bootsie, a friend who every day became dearer. What had seemed her heart's greatest desire in Boulogne — to be Miss Boothson's bosom companion — had happened. What was wonderful — perhaps even what made it happen — was that she had not really been paying attention.

Dreadful that this work — this war, which was taking so many lives, which was destroying a generation — should make her happy. Others spoke of what they had to go home to, what they missed. She missed nothing. Not her bed, which had never felt like hers in any case, not her aunt or her cousins. Tom, of course, but he was no longer there to go home to. She could not permit herself to think of her father or she would feel twisted inside. Sometimes she worked a scenario in her head in which he entered the hospital on his deathbed, having been hit by a piece of shrapnel in the line of duty. She would tend to him, and he would confess to being proud even of her defying him. Other times she shivered to think she might barely cross his mind, even as a nuisance. He had not roared into London from Chatham as she had half-expected, he had not even sent someone after her. He had merely let her go and sent a note via his sister: his daughter, Beryl Balls, was to expect nothing further of him. Period.

Now the baby had been born, his new wife's baby. A new wife and child, a new home to live for.

As they walked back to camp, Bootsie took her arm, as she so often did, a simple, natural gesture, now a covenant of friendship. How it buoyed Beryl. If this were all she had in the rest of her life, she thought, she would be happy. Work and friendship were what she wanted. An ache there might be where her father ought to have been, but work and friendship were all she needed.

⌇

NOW, HOME FROM BROWNIES (how *had* the children known what she and Bootsie called each other), she held the letter in her hand and felt again the lifting sensation when it had arrived all those years ago.

Ten days before the letter's arrival, she had been taking her first walk out from the hospital after diphtheria had confined her to bed a month. Her companion, another convalescent sister, walked slowly and did not want to go far, which you could hardly grudge her, but it showed how much she was not Bootsie, and Beryl held that against her. The day was warm, full summer once again. It did not seem possible that only last summer she had arrived in France for the first time. The pine woods she walked in did not seem possible, the sand under her feet did not seem possible. The trees had branches and needles and rustled in the wind, making that pleasant universal sound. Everywhere in the world are trees making this sound, except the poor blasted trunks of no man's land. There would be no sounds except those of the guns and of crows.

She needed to get back to work. She had been too long a patient. Being a patient was a sort of torture. Bootsie was posted now on the hospital ship, *Llandovery Castle*. Beryl could hardly hope once again to be posted with her friend — three postings together was already remarkable — but she had requested it anyway. Bootsie had written with her usual quick, funny sketch of the crew — too large on the ship to write about in detail — and Beryl wished to be a part of it.

When they got back to the hospital, a nurse rushed up to them. "Have you heard the news?"

"What news?" Beryl could not tell if the news was good or bad, only that it was extreme.

"I never thought they could go so low."

Bad news. The nurse clutched a handkerchief to her chin.

"Oh! It's a crime! It's dastardly! It's beyond all —" The nurse finally broke into a brief sob.

Beryl waited still, dread crawling inside her chest wall.

"The Germans have sunk the *Llandovery Castle*."

Two hundred and fifty-eight had died, including all fifteen nursing sisters.

Cheeks clasped between her hands, her breathing shallow, Miss Balls walked stiffly out of the hospital and then ran to the back, where in the shadow of a bush she let herself collapse with her knees bent beneath her. She would not join Bootsie. She would not join Bootsie ever again.

A week later she received the letter she now held in her hand. Bootsie's last letter. It would be quite ordinary, full of Bootsie's spelling mistakes and sketches of her immediate surroundings, and she could not bear that Bootsie's last letter be nothing special. She could not open it. Unopened, it was a goodbye note, a love letter, a thank-you.

Beryl realized she was crying now, immersed in her memories. She wiped her eyes, blew her nose and went to slip the letter in the back paper-pocket of the diary. The envelope — sealed by Bootsie's tongue fifty-three years earlier — had come unsealed. The old glue was a dry brown on the paper. Her hands flipped back the flap on the envelope and withdrew the thin sheets of paper. Without thinking, she restored her glasses to her nose and opened the fold.

My darling Ballsie, she read.

She bit her lip, refolded the paper, slipped it back in the envelope and let the tears slide down her face.

Carol

WHEN HER MOTHER dropped her off at the new school on the second day, Carol was surprised to find that it actually looked a lot like the old school, where they'd just left Glynnis. Three storeys high, deep red brick, with a sort of churchy, old-fashioned main door that probably nobody but parents and teachers used, and the very same head-high evergreen bushes on either side of the steps leading up to it.

None of this had she noticed yesterday. Yesterday she'd been looking at her new Christmas mukluks and humming the mukluk song in her head to distract her throat from her stomach, which felt like it could upchuck any second. Her feet in her mukluks, on the other hand, felt perfect, all cushy and enclosed. The rest of her was hot and bulky inside her duffle coat, except for her legs, cool in their scratchy leotards. *In the land of the pale blue snow, where it's ninety-nine below, and the hm-hm-hm hm-hm-hm hm-hm-hmmm,* her head went as her mother pulled on her mitted hand. Her mukluks, sleek animals, nosed up steps, through a door, down a hall, up steps, through a door, then stopped. Her mother's hands appeared below her chin, tugging on the lapels of her coat. "A brand-new start, Carol, just think of it. A brand new start. Chin up, now." The mukluks were sealskin. Not real sealskin, Jay said, but Carol liked to think of them as real seals.

Adult shoes stepped into her circle of vision, lady adult shoes. Adult conversation occupied the air above her.

"What did I say, Carol? Chin up. You can't live your life looking at your shoes." Low quarter-chuckles, more adult exchange. Carol lifted her head but kept her eyes on the boots. Puddles were forming beneath them from the snow. If they really were seals, they'd go diving away in the sea, and she'd go with them to the land of the pale blue snow. A brand-new start.

"Carol? Remember Miss Boskovich? Remember we met her before Christmas?"

"It's *Mizz* Boskovich," the other voice said, "but never mind. Good morning, Carol. Welcome to John Fisher. We're very glad to have you." Screams and shouts of children gathering outside filtered through to the morning-grey hallway. Carol swallowed to keep her stomach in check.

Where it's ninety-nine below, and the polar bears hm-hm-hm-hm-hm-hmm. The seals dove into the puddle, Carol diving after them. They were very fast, and so was she, very graceful, and so was she. They could zoom up as easily as they could dive down, they could veer and spiral in any direction at all. They were taking her to their igloo at the bottom of the ocean.

Up above the water, her mother talked to the teacher some more and then talked to her some more and then left. The teacher, a blob with *That Girl* hair and Nana Mouskouri glasses, took her hand and led her into the classroom. Even then Carol didn't notice right away it was different. The teacher-blob was showing her a row of cupboards and saying something about hats and coats and boots. She held out her hand for Carol's mittens and hat, tucking them beneath her arm, reaching next for her coat. She slipped mittens and hat into Carol's coat sleeve and hung the duffle up on a hook inside the cupboard. Then she held up a big clothespin, with 'Carol R.' printed on it in magic marker. "This is to keep your boots together," the teacher said. "We don't just throw them into the cupboard willy-nilly." She stuck out her arm for the boots.

Carol looked down at her mukluks. Her seals, her friends. If she took them off her feet, she wouldn't be able to dive into the dark green sea.

Arms hugged chest. Head shook no.

"You don't want to take off your boots?"

Head shook more decisively.

"Uh-oh," said the teacher. "This poses a bit of a problem. You see, we have carpet in our classroom, and we can't get it all mucked up with mud and snow."

Carol looked up and saw, instead of a classroom, a gigantic, colourful rec room. The carpet was orange, with clusters of tables on it and big floor plants like the one the German on *Laugh-In* who said "verrry interestink" hid behind. Huge painted flowers and blue sky covered the wall opposite the window. Billowing between the rows of lights on the ceiling were big swaths of red, yellow and orange cloth with patterns on them. One back corner held a floor lamp and bean-bag chairs, the other a table with fish tank and fancy hamster cage.

"If you take off your boots, I'll introduce you to Napoleon, our guinea pig."

Carol took off her boots.

Today, though, she couldn't go straight in and play with Napoleon, today she wouldn't get to lose herself in the feel of cool footpads and little tickling claws. Today she had to go to the schoolyard with every-body else. Sometimes her body just did what it wanted, froze in place, or bent away from things, or ran, so she wasn't sure she actually could go into the schoolyard, even with her mother watching from the car, waiting to see her go up the steps, into the trampled white expanse with its roving hordes of screamers, snow-flingers and face-washers.

She lifted a leg. *Here I go*, she thought, lifting the other, *here I go, here I go*, more for the rhythm of the words than their meaning.

One seal, one step, two seal, two step, three seal, three step. Mukluk, mukluk, mukluk, top. She turned and waved, watched her mother drive off.

Looking into the schoolyard, she didn't recognize a single shape, a single coat or hat or way of running or throwing or playing. Flocks of kids tore around like starlings and she didn't know any of them. Tammy, that was the girl from yesterday, she had a red tam so it was easy to remember and matching scarf and a navy blue coat, but none of the shapes Carol saw fit her. Carol didn't really know her, anyway, she'd just recognize her hat and scarf if she saw them. Knowing people meant being able to tell them at a distance by the way they held themselves or the way they moved. Like knowing Glynnis for her bony, coltish walk and her square shoulders, or Sandy for her sandiness and for the way she tucked the hair behind her ear from where it hung down either side of her eyes or else sucked its tips into points, and for the way her toes pointed in a little. Or Daintry for her glasses and how small and tight she was in her movements, like a mouse, Alison for hands in pockets or folded across her chest, weight on one jutting-out hip and the other foot resting nonchalantly. Carol scanned the landscape of hurtling bodies ahead of her and didn't know a single one.

To her right was a spiky iron fence setting off the teachers' parking lot, to her left a railing of horizontal iron bars. A quick duck between them and she was on the snowy lawn of the school, bounded in front by a hedge and another stretch of spike fence. Here the snow was untrampled, only a few sets of prints on it. Poof. Poof. She made her own meandering set of tracks, mukluks kicking up geysers of snow. No children, no nothing, just seals and snow, except, uh-oh, a heavy man in overcoat and tuque, keys jingling as he jogged along the sidewalk and upstairs to the fancy main doors, teacher in a hurry sliding his swift glance over her, slowing as if to ask what she was doing. And then, breathe out, going on.

Quick. Behind the evergreens guarding the stairs. An odd combination of soft and prickly, they brushed against her face as the back of her coat rasped on brick. Cool cave of green and white. Until the noise and colour and surprise were unavoidable, she had this cool refuge, this green smell and the silver smell of snow.

At her old school, there were two bells. The best moment came between them. When the first rang, everyone had to freeze and be quiet. The bell would echo and fade, just as it was doing now, all clangour ceasing, leaving a wonderful silence that if you listened carefully was actually not silent, but filled with regular sounds of the world — birds crying, wind in the trees, cars driving by.

She heard a man whistling somewhere down the street, wind brushing over snow, a car horn from one street over, a rumbling inside the school like hundreds of feet on stone floors or a janitor rolling a big bin, children's voices filling the classroom above her. Children's voices filling the classroom above her. Oh no. What had happened to the second bell? Branches whapped her face as she dashed from her silver-green cave.

MS. BOSKOVICH believed in everyone learning from one another. That was why all her pupils worked in groups and why she invited visitors to the class every second Friday. "There's something to learn from everybody in the whole wide world. You can't possibly learn enough from just one teacher," she had said the day before as Napoleon crawled over one then the other of Carol's hands. "We're all teachers. We're all pupils. We're all students of life." People, she went on, had different strengths and working in groups allowed them to benefit from one another's strengths. Carol's throat constricted and her eyes stung.

Ms. Boskovich brought her face close to Carol's. "*Everyone* has strengths," she said firmly, meaning *even you*. "It's a matter of finding out what they are."

She was nice, but she was wrong. Carol had no trouble cataloguing her weaknesses. She was bad at reading, at spelling and at math.

Her printing was okay, but her writing always went wrong after three letters. She couldn't throw a ball or catch one or dodge one. She'd come last in her division in figure skating and failed her Red Cross Juniors badge and had only just got her C badge in skiing the week before, when Glynnis had got hers a whole year earlier and was a year younger. She couldn't draw or paint. She'd passed her grade two piano, but she didn't want to go near a piano any more. (Piano lessons were one thing her mother had let her quit after the accident.)

Her parents said she was cowardly and had to learn to control her temper, and they were probably right. Glynnis and Melanie and Sandy said she was too weak and push-aroundable and had to learn to stand up for herself, only without being mean back. They were making her practise after school.

Carol have strengths? Ms. Boskovich didn't know the half of it. She didn't know that most of the time, Carol was just somebody who wanted to disappear and who occasionally succeeded.

Although, maybe you could count her singing. She could keep a tune. And her printing. It wasn't teacher printing like the perfect kind on the Bristol board signs that hung above each pair of pushed-together trapezoidal tables Ms. Boskovich was calling group work stations. But it wasn't bad printing.

Perfect though it was, she didn't understand what the printing on the Bristol board signs said, even when Ms. Boskovich said it was French, that each group had chosen their own French name. Carol's was Le groupe de la grenouille, did Carol know what that meant? At Carol's old school, French didn't start until grade four. She knew *porte* and *fenêtre, jupe* and *chemise, chien* and *chat, bonjour* and *au revoir.* She knew *Napoléon avait cinq cents soldats.* She shook her head.

Ms. Boskovich snagged one of several paper cut-out frogs hanging like the sign on fishing line from the ceiling. "Any idea now?" the teacher asked. Frog, Carol wanted to say, but it wasn't happening, her mouth wasn't saying it.

"What do you think *groupe* means?" Ms. Boskovich waited. "Maybe group possibly?" No reaction from Carol.

"And *grenouille*?" Carol shook her head again and Ms. Boskovich grabbed the frog a second time, mouthing the word frog really slowly until Carol said it.

"Whew, Carol, you're really making me work here. It was Burt's idea." She picked up a folded-over piece of cardboard from the Groupe de la grenouille work station. Burt L., the perfect printing on it said. "Frog. He thinks he's pulling one over on me. But *grenouille* just means frog." She put it back down again. "*Frog* can mean French person, not that you should ever use it that way, but *grenouille* just means frog. Well, sometimes piggy bank, too, but never French person. Personally, I love that, how some things just don't translate, but I've noticed it makes a lot of kids mad." Carol's heart slowed reassuringly as the teacher rambled on. "Kids want everything to be clear and literal, this means that, no ifs, ands or buts.

"Look, I've made you a nameplate. You take this crayon tin and sit at my desk and decorate it until the others come in, all right?"

Carol concentrated on drawing a frog beside 'Carol R.' as a wave of noise washed down the hall ahead of the kids coming in, crashing into the back wall of the classroom before separating into individual voices. It looked more like a leafy plant than a frog. Carol drew a flower growing out of its head.

Once all the kids were in their seats, Ms. Boskovich introduced Carol and told them she'd be in Le groupe de la grenouille and that it wasn't easy coming to a school partway through the year, so everybody should be extra thoughtful and help Carol adjust, which Carol heard with a tightening of the throat. She might as well have said, Be extra mean. She might as well have said, Crowd around and chant *New Kid, New Kid, New Kid*. The buzzing that followed seemed to confirm it. Then Ms. Boskovich had everybody in the class introduce themselves. When she took her seat after "O Canada," the girl in her group leaned over and said, "Finally, another girl in my group." *Tammy H.*, her nameplate decorated with tulips said. She was Japanese. The collar of her white shirt made an oval beneath her chin and across her shoulders. Her pigtails were perfect, her posture good. She looked like an illustration in a book of a good girl.

Tammy H. showed Carol around at recess, the water fountains, the washroom, the playground, the cootie corner, portable, pleasure rink, hockey rink, teacher on duty who Tammy had had in grade one. With each thing pointed out, Tammy would turn to look at Carol, and Carol's head and shoulders would twist away on their own, creeping ever more away from the look until it ended or they could twist no farther. Still, she noticed things about Tammy, that her cheeks turned pink in the cold and her clothes all seemed just the right size and she had a bright red tam and matching scarf and mittens.

In motion, things were fine, but when the tour was done and Tammy-with-a-tam introduced Carol to her best friend, a girl with long, wheat-blonde hair and spaces between her teeth and a white tam, other kids began to gather around, too.

"Was your father transferred?" Tammy asked. "Is that why you moved? Anita's father was transferred here last year. She's from Montreal. Where are you from?"

"Nowhere."

"Your father wasn't transferred?" the friend asked.

She shook her head.

"Was your mother?" Tammy asked.

"No." Carol's head was down. She scuffed her mukluk back and forth in the snow.

"O-o-oh," the friend said, whispering behind her hand to Tammy.

"Anita says maybe your parents split up and that's why you had to move and you don't want to say."

Carol shook her head again. "I'm just from Blythwood."

— Is this the new girl? someone asked.

— Are her eyes pink? I heard her eyes were pink like a rabbit's.

— I can't see them, can you?

—Where're you from, new girl?

"Blythwood," she said.

— Doesn't she look like the Man from Glad? Maybe he's her father. Hey, is your dad the Man from Glad?

—That'd make her, like, the Girl from Glad.

— Girl from Glad. Girl from Glad.

Carol felt her chin digging into her shoulder.

"She's shy," Tammy's voice came through. "We have to show her extra consideration and I don't think you're doing that, so I think you should all just leave now because there's too many people around."

— Oo-oo, listen to Two Shoes.

— How come you get to stay?

—Teacher's pet.

—Teacher's dog more like. Arf, arf.

NOW, CAROL BANGED her knee ducking back through the iron railings as she raced from her evergreen sanctuary. She stopped a few feet on. The scene in front of her was so still. Everyone had gone in. They'd left bootprints trapped in the half-slush, peaks of off-white thrust up between the valleys. The peaks looked timeless. The doors looked locked. They wouldn't be, but they looked that way, like doors in a nightmare when someone is chasing you and these doors are your only hope. She stood until her breath slowed, then moved forward, watched her mitt grasp door handle, felt her arm pull it open and her feet step through, in and up the slushy, brown-puddled stairs.

Noise billowed out of her classroom. The others were still taking off their outdoor clothes. No one noticed she was late. No one noticed her at all until she got to her table and a skinny boy with buck teeth asked, "Are you an albino?"

"Roddy," Tammy said. "You don't have to answer, Carol."

Her mother said she had to be ready for that question, to be prepared and to be patient with people. *Yes, I have a genetic disorder,* she was supposed to say, *my body cannot make pigment, and so I have white hair and very pale eyes and am near-sighted, but otherwise I am completely normal.* She'd been made to practise this, but she'd never used it. Her mother had, but not her. Instead she nodded slowly.

"Are you from Blythwood?"

Carol drew in a long, silent breath, eyes widening and sight blurring. She felt sick. He knew. The whole point of a new school was that nobody would know about her and the accident. Nobody would know that something was wrong with her. There *was* something wrong with her, she knew it because that was just something you knew and plus, who got sent to a psychologist except people who had something wrong with them?

"Yeah," Tammy answered for her. "What about it?"

"Are there any other albinos at Blythwood?" the boy asked, sounding puzzled.

If Carol hadn't been half-frozen with anxiety, she would have shaken her head and given herself away. Instead it dawned on her to nod. "There's three," she said.

"Oh," he said. "That explains it."

"Explains what?" Tammy asked, but there was no time to get an answer because Ms. Boskovich was calling them to order.

A FEW DAYS LATER, Roddy said, "You lied. There's not three albinos at Blythwood."

Carol's mouth went dry.

"So what?" Tammy said.

"So that means she's the one that did it, she's the one that pushed a piano on her sister."

"What?"

"You don't look that strong."

"Roddy," Tammy said in a scolding voice. "It's not true is it?" she asked Carol.

Carol said nothing. She neither confirmed nor denied. But by the end of the week everybody knew. She waited for them to start up again, the jeers and the taunts. But no one taunted her. Everyone just kept their distance

HER GROUP DID a project on Vikings. Ms. Boskovich had written the five senses on scraps of paper and had the students draw them out of a straw hat. Warren French got sight. Roddy Kirsch got sound. Burt Lafayette got smell. Tammy got touch. And Carol got taste.

"How come I get smell?" Burt asked. "Warren should do smell. Warren makes a smell."

"Ha, ha," said Warren.

"I love doing smell," Roddy said. "Smell is the greatest."

"You would, Roddy," said Tammy.

In the library, Tammy told Carol to go look up Vikings in the encyclopedia while she and Roddy and Burt looked for books to divvy up between them. The encyclopedia entry wasn't long. It had pictures of big blond men in metal helmets with shields and swords, also of the same men in boats. Each person could just read it for him or herself almost as fast as she could say what was in it.

For a while they all sat together on the low, orange-padded benches, reading to themselves, Carol with her fingers to her eyes as the Special Reading teacher had showed her, Roddy moving his lips. Then Burt said to Carol, "You're perfect for this! Look at these pictures!" The Vikings did look like her. None of them had glasses and they all looked very strong, like superheroes, including the women, but they did have white hair, and even white eyelashes, some of them. Tammy said she could braid Carol's hair like in the pictures.

Carol read about how the Vikings were pirates and warriors who raided other people's villages so everyone was afraid of them. They travelled long distances in the ships they built and even reached America almost five hundred years before Columbus. It didn't say anything about Canada.

She read about how they admired warriors and preferred to die in battle instead of at home in their beds. If they died at home, they would not go to Valhalla, the heaven for warriors, where Odin, the head god, lived.

"Hey, listen to this," Roddy said. "'The most feared Vikings were the berserkers — warriors who fought furiously in battle. It is thought that they chewed fly agaric, a poisonous toadstool, and that this caused a kind of hype ... hype —'"

Tammy leaned over to see the word. "Hypnotic."

"'Hypnotic rage.'" Carol flushed. "'When the berserkers were battle-crazed in this way, they believed they could not be harmed. Although berserkers were respected in Viking society, they were dangerous. A writer of the time described them as "not bad people to talk to as long as you don't upset them."'"

Roddy put the book down. Carol's heart thumped wildly. "Hey," he said. "This is you."

She examined her mother's face in the car that afternoon, unable to ask again about being adopted, since Mrs. Riggs looked like she was ticking off a mental list and convincing Carol she wasn't adopted wouldn't be on it. The first time she'd asked her mother if she was adopted, Mrs. Riggs had said no one knew better than she exactly where Carol had come from and it wasn't the Children's Aid, it was her own womb. Jay had been three at the time, and they'd just moved into the house. Mr. Riggs was flying the Toronto-Vancouver route. Carol was ten days early, but luckily Mr. Riggs was off rotation and took her to the hospital and Jay to Aunt Helen and Uncle Bob's house. That was right around dinnertime on June 18, and at exactly 1:08 in the morning of June 19, Carol was born. Then she'd got out the photo album and shown Carol her baby pictures to prove it. There was one picture of her the day she'd come home from the hospital, four days old, with her tiny fists up around her round face, her skin just as pale as ever, her pale eyes peering through slitted newborn lids.

Jay said he remembered it. He explained how babies were made and how they were born and said he'd been there, he'd seen their mother get bigger and bigger and go to the hospital and then come back with Carol. Of course, he'd say, I wasn't watching the whole time. They could have switched you in the baby ward and I'd never know. Mrs. Riggs had pooh-poohed this, too. "They put you in my arms the minute after you were born. Don't you think I'd know you forever after that?"

Carol still wasn't completely satisfied, though, and couldn't stop herself from asking repeatedly or alluding to her real parents. Mrs. Riggs got impatient. "You're ours, you always have been and you always will be. Do not ask me again."

Mr. Riggs, for his part, never seemed to tire of explaining Mendelian genetics.

She wanted to be related to all of them, her stern, practical mother, her bluff, hearty father, her wry, clever brother, her smartypants sister, but where they were colourful, capable and smart, she was colourless and dull, a nonentity.

At home she looked at the family picture in the downstairs hall-way, the colour one taken the year before by the birch tree in the front yard. In it, she stood with her right hand on her father's shoulder as he was crouched on his heels. His right arm was across their kneeling mother's shoulders. Jay stood behind them, and Glynnis just behind and beside their mother. Carol liked how happy they all looked in this picture. If she strained, she could almost make out in herself and her father the same broad face, the same ample cheeks, the same pulled-straight upper lip above a bow-shaped lower one. Come to think of it, he looked like he could be a Viking if he grew his hair and beard.

He was home at dinner.

"Do we have any Viking blood in us?"

"You're Scots and Welsh on the Morgan side and English-Irish on the Riggs," Mrs. Riggs said.

"The Vikings founded Dublin," Jay said.

"Did they now?" Mr. Riggs said. "When would that have been?"

"Few years ago. Eight hundreds maybe?"

"There you have it then, Carol. More than one thousand years ago, we might have had a Viking ancestor. Think of it. One thousand years ago. Wow." He shook his head. "What's got you thinking about Vikings?"

"Carol's doing a project on them," Mrs. Riggs said. "She has to find out what they eat and drink."

"Tastes of the Vikings, by Carol Riggs," said Jay.

"She thinks she's a throwback," said Glynnis.

"And so she is. Who knows how long those recessive genes have lurked around in us, eh, Rowena? You," he reached out a broad paw and chucked Carol on the nose with a finger almost as broad, "are one in seventeen thousand." It was an old joke, but Carol still liked it. Those were the odds of being an albino, one in seventeen thousand. She'd only seen one other true albino in her life, a clerk at a grocery store in Parry Sound on the way to the cottage. His glasses had been even thicker than hers, and his face was scrunched up the whole time as he squinted to see better. She had stared and stared and stared, waiting for him to notice her and smile, but he never did.

Part Two

A NINE-INCH SQUARE gives you half the city and all of the places he's ever lived. More city than he knows. More city than he'll ever know. With leisure and a slightly more obsessive personality, he'd make a point of walking every single street.

Grid city, you think on the ground as you dodge Bloor with Dupont, Yonge with Duplex. From the air you see it has a diagonal streak — the ravines, most prominently, running NW to SE here down to the Don. Roads, too, next to the ravines, or following streams that no longer exist. Vaughan Road. Chaplin Crescent. Davenport, which, a cousin has told him, was an Indian trail long before a city got itself tossed up. Lady Simcoe mentioned it in her diaries.

Only the thinnest of thin strips remain of the land that was here before, one hundred or two hundred or fifty yards of tree and bush on the steep ravine walls. Ravine bottoms are groomed strolls for Sunday walkers. The streams run in concrete streambeds.

Centre left, the 401 and the Allen make a *T* with the *T*'s east arm tipped up like it's waving to Pickering. The lower half of the Allen is white with new, undriven-on pavement. One last middle section awaits the laying down of concrete. Diagonalling off Donwards from the bottom of the Allen is the Cedarvale ravine, white, too, with sub-way construction.

Between this line and the rail line almost parallel to the east is a broad-angled band of light grey pocked with white. White means pavement. White means industry. White means new construction. White means many houses packed close together. Working-class neighbourhoods.

The next band east, between the Allen-Cedarvale-Spadina diag-onal and the diagonal of the West Don, is a darker grey area, less to no industry (but for a white splash at page's edge near Laird in East York), darkest of all in that inner city suburb (rounded streets with the meandering layout of cemeteries), Rosedale. And Cabbagetown, too, indistinct, slightly out of focus at the bottom right so far from the picture's centre, with its old, old trees (and except for the hor-ror of Regent Park, some pattern-maker's blot, which might have been designed by the designers of linoleum). Cabbagetown, where his grandfather was born. St. James' cemetery, where his grandfa-ther lies. Rosedale, where his mother was born. A strip of Riverdale, where his father grew up. Bottom left corner is another dark grey bit, the northern edge of High Park. Cabbagetown's on the rise now, in 1976. Parkdale's on the decline.

Bottom right, black and white squarelets spell commerce. Downtown. Tall buildings, square shadows. Such a small area for such a wide influence. Right next to it, Rosedale.

On one of these downtown roofs in a year and a bit, a boy will be stashed in a bag.

For now, the city muddles on, pleased with the turn it is taking, flush in a new age of made-at-home, here-is-good civics — a think-ing city, a forward-looking city, a greening city. A Canadian city.

1977

Glynnis

ALMOST HALF THE CLASS packed up their stuff and headed off for the first cross-country meet of the year. Out the door before they were even out the door, they talked high and loud and fast. Their calves, you could see, were springy, their hearts nervous. They'd already — except Hilda — forgotten the rest of them, erased them from their minds. Hilda was too conscious of the slender leaf of fortune separating her from those remaining. "So long, suckers," she said to the portion of the class stuck in school. Glynnis kept her head down and toyed with her pencil. Hilda was embarrassing. Last week, Glynnis had invited her to spend the coming Thanksgiving weekend at her family's cottage.

"Aren't you going to invite a friend to the cottage for Thanksgiving?" her mother had pestered daily. "You have to go out of your way a little to make new friends, you know, dear." Thanks, Mom. I'd been wondering: How *do* you make new friends?

Finally, just to get her mother off her case, she'd said, "Well, Hilda, I guess." Sandy, she knew, would be going to her own cottage. Mrs. MacDonald always wanted the whole family there for holidays.

Then it was, "Now, you're going to invite Hilda for Thanksgiving today, right?" until she had no choice and Hilda breathlessly and immediately said yes, and here they were, Hilda being Hilda and asking Glynnis publicly and regularly what she should bring and where her cottage was and whether there was electricity, Glynnis' cheeks burning and her eyes cast down. Glynnis Riggs, friend of Hilda. Christ.

Thing was, Hilda was really okay. Just: Hilda was guileless. This was a fault.

Not that anyone had a right to look down on Hilda.

Just because people could run did not make them better people. Except that it did.

That was the inescapable fact.

Glynnis inked the pen well on her desk as the last of the cross-country runners filed out.

"So long, evil jock Nazis," she heard a voice with a slight lisp mutter. Glynnis looked up and into the deadpan eyes of a thin, sallow girl who played flute. Tamara. The two rows between them were empty. The boy in front of Tamara bent his head and snickered.

How could Glynnis not have known Tamara was funny? They'd been in the same class for a whole month.

Glynnis watched more closely and saw that every so often, Tamara did this, muttered things out the corner of her mouth. Then Stephen would laugh a sort of silent Ernie laugh, mouth open in a Muppety wedge, head and shoulders bobbing up and down. And Tamara would look quietly satisfied. She didn't seem to care if anyone but Stephen heard her. She was playing to an audience of one. You could do that. Play to an audience of one. Wow.

The science teacher was saying they had a golden opportunity to get a jump on the rest of the class on their science fair projects. The science fair wasn't until March, but some experiments might take months. You didn't do science overnight, she said.

Psh, Glynnis scoffed, and looked around for other rolled eyes. You could do anything overnight. But the rest of the class was attentive, except for Tamara and Stephen, engaged in their continuous private game.

The teacher went on about the scientific method and how it could sometimes take a long time just to formulate your hypothesis, golly gee whiz, and testing it, boy! took even longer.

They should all be let out of school. If the cross-country team got off, everyone should get off. Then she could go to her spot in the ravine and lie down and smell the leaves and be zen.

Now the teacher was saying that since they'd have to live with their project a long time, they should pick something they were interested in. "Only please, please, please, please," she said, "don't do volcanoes." On the board she wrote, "NO VOLCANOES" and underlined it three times. Then she asked them what they were interested in.

"Volcanoes," Glynnis and Stephen said at the same time.

"Ha ha," said the teacher. "Very funny. Please. I beg of you. Anything but volcanoes."

"Drugs," said a paunchy buck-toothed boy. Joke.

The teacher wrote it down.

"Black holes."

"Dinosaurs."

The teacher turned to the board. NO DINOSAURS, she wrote underneath NO VOLCANOES.

"TV," said Tamara. Also a joke but again the teacher wrote it down. Tamara looked at Stephen and shrugged.

And so it went on. Serious answers, dumb answers, the teacher wrote them all down. Optics. Astronomy. Airplanes. Plants. Alternative Energy. Jiffy Pop, et cetera, et cetera until everybody had said something except Glynnis and two others. Glynnis couldn't, for the moment, think of a single thing she was interested in. Revenge? Books? The teacher asked the drabbest girl in the class, so drab she almost failed to exist. "Arlene?"

"I don't know," said Arlene in a whisper. Glynnis' cheeks felt hot for Arlene's sake. This was new, sympathizing. She did not like it.

"Oh, come on, you must be interested in something. What do you like to do?"

"I don't know."

"There must be something."

"Fishing?" Arlene said.

"All right," said the teacher triumphantly, putting it on the board with the others.

Wow. Arlene liked to fish. How about that.

"Glynnis?"

She was still trying to picture Arlene fishing. "Albinos," she said. Damn. *Sleeping*. She should have said *sleeping*.

Next they had to put the thing they'd said in the middle of a page and brainstorm around it all the questions they had about that thing.

Glynnis doodled. Her mind was on the runners. On Hilda, who was on the team and shouldn't be. On herself, who wasn't and should. On injustice, on the blindness and ignorance of her classmates, who treated her like there was something wrong with her, like she'd been crippled from birth, when really she was one of them and only an accident separated them.

Sometimes she could walk in a new place among new people and imagine that people saw her limping and thought, *There is a girl with a tragic accident in her past. What fortitude she has. How cheery and uncomplaining she is.*

And then she'd walk up to a counter, say, in a mall, and ask for an Orange Julius and the person behind the counter would talk really loudly and slowly, "Would you like a large or a small?" and she'd know they thought she was retarded. Sometimes she'd say, "I'm not retarded, you know," and they'd act embarrassed. And sometimes she would act retarded, fold the back of her tongue over her bottom teeth and pretend to have a fit. Sandy hated when she did that. Alison thought it was hilarious. Then Glynnis would remember

Delilah and feel strange because she had made fun of Delilah and because Delilah had died. Her mother still saw Delilah's mother for lunch once a month. She had a new husband now and a new two-year-old and cried each time, remembering Delilah.

If the accident that had smashed Glynnis' distal growth plate and partly fused her ankle had been neutral, nobody's fault, or the fault of a driver of another car, say, she thought she would have been perfectly well adjusted about it. Accidents happen, there's no reason they shouldn't happen to her as much as to anyone else, no use crying over it. But it hadn't been nobody's fault, and there were times when hatred for Carol crackled in a small fiery ball in her gut. Then she would do something small and mean, like dip Carol's toothbrush in the toilet she'd just peed in and put it back in the holder. The fiery ball would dissolve. Later she'd feel secretive and dirty about it. Later still, a surging conviction would come over her that there was no such thing as fault, or rather that fault didn't ultimately matter, fault was a tangled thread that could never be unknotted and didn't need to be anyway if everyone just accepted the outcome. As she had done. She was a person with a bum leg and she was moving on.

⌐

THE FIRST two weeks of school, everybody had been asking one another:

— Are you going out for cross-country?

— Are you?

No one had asked Glynnis.

Nor had she been able to ask them, because what if they out of politeness or malice said, Are you? She would not be able to say yes. She didn't want to say no. She seemed to have lost the knack of knowing how to talk to people, of knowing what their intent was.

She had been thinking of going out for cross-country. She had recently watched a movie about a skier who was paralyzed in an accident and then did physiotherapy and was able to do things nobody thought she could do. Glynnis' own physiotherapy happened only every six months these days and consisted of them measuring her angle of rotation and asking if she did her exercises and stretches and then doing the exercises and stretches again. It would not effect a miracle. The miracle would have to come from Glynnis. Walking through the ravine on her way to school, Glynnis began to entertain fantasies of training secretly every day, making miraculous progress at her two-steps-on-good-leg-one-step-on-bad-leg run-hop, and then coming out and surprising everybody by her amazing come-from-behind first- or second- or third-place finish. With this in mind, she changed her route slightly to take in more ravine and left earlier in the mornings so she could run-hop the trails and attack the hills.

She was now, actually, a little glad for the shoes that had so destroyed her a few weeks earlier, a pair of Adidas ROMs with the left sole built up. Her mother had bought them to compensate for the Frankenshoes, brown orthopedic horrors she'd forced upon Glynnis and made her promise to wear for the sake of proper hip alignment and the future of her back. Again Glynnis sensed the weakness in her mother. Mrs. Riggs thought that Glynnis would be bug-eyed with excitement over the Adidas. In fact, they were almost worse than Frankenshoes. Adidas ROMs were the perfect shoe, showing up their rival North Stars in all regards, navy being a more satisfying stripe colour than turquoise, three being a more aesthetic stripe number than two, and the spacing of stripes, the ratio of stripe to white, being in ideal balance. To be given the perfect pair of shoes — but adulterated by two and a half inches of built-up sole — was like shouting, "NEVER!" in Glynnis' ear. And there was her mother, all smiley and pleased with herself while Glynnis' gut crawled with ruination. She tried desperately to call up calm and gratitude, but got only banks of tears in her eyes. "Thanks, Mom. Really," she managed to squeak out, then went to her room and closed the door.

Now, seeing the shoes in action, she began to think of them not as adulterated but as tools specialized for allowing her unique physiology to triumph, she saw them not as enemies but friends, flawed and particular as individuals.

Jogging a little, on her way to and from school, in her regular clothes, was not enough.

On the weekend, Glynnis told her mother she was going to Sandy's and then took her bike down past Sunnybrook to Serena Gundy Park, where there was a vita par coeur course. You ran the course, which went around a big field and through the woods, and along the way stopped at the stations and did what it said on the sign — chin-ups or step-ups or arm circles.

When she was running through the woods at one point, she spotted a young maple whose trunk diverged in a V just above the ground. Checking to see if anyone was around, she ducked off the path to the tree, sat down, wedged her left ankle in the V, then put her other foot on the tree trunk and pushed. She was her own physiotherapist, training the leg to stretch and grow in the right way. The woods were her clinic.

And this was a childish game. As if to confirm this feeling, a lady and a man jogged by and asked if she was all right.

"I'm fine," she said. "Just stretching."

But if it worked?

That night, her ankle ached.

She made it to the park again on Monday, but Tuesday she had swimming — which was fine, it would build up her cardio — and then Wednesday it was her turn to walk Miss Balls' dog. Fortunately, Carol really *really* wanted to walk Miss Balls' dog, so fine, no problem, she could go walk him. Glynnis trained. Thursday she had trumpet and Friday she went to Sandy's house.

They didn't talk about school, they didn't talk about anything, they just watched TV. It was about the third time that they'd done that, just watched TV, not said much, and on the way home Glynnis was thinking about how they were best friends and best friends can do that, they don't have to do anything else, but she wondered, too, if maybe she was just really boring. Or if it was Sandy, if Sandy was really boring. Or if Sandy wanted to ditch her but was too chicken to actually ditch her and instead was trying to bore her into not being friends.

Glynnis got in another three training sessions before the tryouts on Monday morning.

On Monday she put her track shorts on under her pants, told her mother she was practising a trumpet duet with Gord, and rode to school in a light September chill. At the top of the ramp down into the playing field, she stopped her bike. Already fifty kids milled around down there, stretching, jogging in place, taking off their track pants.

She rode down the hill and across the flat and up the other side. Locked her bike. Walked back down the hill. Over to the crowd. She put down her knapsack and pulled off her left shoe, the built-up Adidas, about to take off her pants.

"What are you doing here?" asked Sandy with perfect innocence.

Hilda trotted up. "Hi, Glynnis. You trying out? Wow, that's really great. I mean, you have as much of a chance as I do."

"I've just got a stone in my shoe," Glynnis said, upturning the shoe. "Besides. You don't *try* out for cross-country. You *go* out for it. They take everybody."

"Oh. Sorry. I thought … Sorry. I just … Sorry."

Shut up, Hilda. "I have to go to the can," Glynnis said. She put her head down and made for the closest doors, the ones that led to the pool dressing rooms and the stairs to the gym change rooms.

"Wish us luck," Hilda said.

"Luck," said Glynnis.

In the school was a terrific stillness, as if time had stopped within its walls — outside you could hear the usual tumble of voices. She fetched her trumpet from her locker, stopping en route to the music room to look out the window in the stairwell. All the kids stretched together now, legs wide, bend forward forward forward, release. Left leg, bend head to knee, hold toes, hold it hold it hold it, release. Right leg. Then they ran the hill, sprinted it, half at a time. Her track shorts bunched uncomfortably under the waistband of her pants. They ran the hill again.

She found it difficult to take herself away from the window. She picked Sandy out with her slightly pigeon-toed gait. Hilda, with her knock-kneed one. Little Kevin Money, Toby with a rolled bandana round his head, Brenda stick-legs, Mish Cohen shaking out her arms and legs. Tracy Novak on her back pretending to sleep.

Now they were stretching again and lining up, the boys were, at the edge of the grass on the playing field, facing the ravine. Same run they did in gym class, when Glynnis had almost caught up to Hilda in the last stretch but then her good foot had slipped on a clump of wet leaves in the gutter. Hilda was going to be on the cross-country team. Hilda.

She watched the boys take off, the long, narrow line of the start turning into a sharply pointed arrowhead as the leaders sprinted for the ravine. Then the girls, Brenda way out in front, then Mish and Tracy, then Sandy, then the pack, at the end of which trailed Janet Pons and Hilda. Finally they disappeared from view and Glynnis continued up the stairs to the music room.

When she got there, she took out her trumpet, blew air through it to warm it up for a long time. Buzzed her lips in a low, farty drone, bending the note up and down. Stopped. Leaned forward with her elbows on her knees, brought the trumpet to her lips. Sat up straight and blew the opening fanfare of the racetrack. On the last note she did a fall. She had a flash of lifting her trumpet up in her right hand, bringing her hand down and ramming the bell against the floor. Instead she put it back in its case and took it with her outside across the field to the top of the hill the team had been running up earlier. She sat, picking apart burrs until the runners started to appear.

They had to come down the street toward her and then cut down the hill back onto school property and the finish line, which was the same as the start line. She took her trumpet out of its case. She meant to bugle them into the finish.

By the time the runners came into sight they were giving it everything they had, especially the ones who were just behind someone else and trying to overtake them. She put the trumpet to her lips, watching. Even the first guy, who was all alone. He had no idea she was there. Neither did the two teachers who were coaches, down on the field with stopwatches and clipboards. Now was the time for the fanfare. Dunh-da-nunh-da-nunh-da-nunh-da-naaaa. But she merely kept the trumpet to her lips and blew air through it.

The next runner had a decent lead on the runner after him and didn't seem to know that the guy behind was going all out until he heard the steps behind him and he turned to see himself being overtaken.

Then began a footrace between them. As she watched, she tongued the crisp notes of the fanfare into the mouthpiece without buzzing her lips. They dropped down the hill in long strides, the one who'd come from behind coming even with the other, then passing him definitively. Would he stay that way? She wanted to know, and in that desire to know she felt the beauty of competition, how it compelled you every time. You felt for the person passing, you felt for the person being passed. You felt a great wash of emotion for how hard people tried at things, how stupid it was, how trivial — a running race — a nothing. But a nothing from which you were excluded. From the joy of which you were excluded. From the status of participating.

From the status of your rightful rank at the finish.

Over and over again as she watched was this drama played out. One person who made the move to come from behind would do it too early and exhaust him or herself before even catching up, and the front-runner would sprint away, heels nipped, while the would-be passer suddenly lost the will to keep the legs moving, and maybe even fell behind the person behind them, now making *their* move. Some of the pairs battling it out were jokey and jovial with each other, and you got the feeling that they'd be happy with either outcome. Other pairs seemed to demonstrate genuine enmity, and you got the sense that each would accuse the other of cheating or that they would come up with excuses for themselves, that they had not been feeling well or had had a cramp or a stitch or bad running shoes. She saw, suddenly, that she herself did this sometimes. Regularly, even.

There was also the moment of giving up that she watched once, twice, three times, hating it as much each time. This, too, she recognized. She was, she saw for the first time in her life, a bad sport.

With simultaneous detachment and engagement, she saw herself as small and ridiculous — saw not just herself, her body, as small and ridiculous, but her thoughts and feelings, too, as small and ridiculous. It was sort of like a Möbius strip of the mind. The feelings continued, like that billowing ribbon folding on itself, while the mind detached and saw the feelings like a bug crawling on the ribbon.

And then the race was over, they'd all gone inside to change and get ready for school. Glynnis stayed where she was. She had never not wanted to go to school before. It was quarter to nine. Other kids were arriving.

This is what it's like for Carol, she thought. She determined to be nicer to Carol again.

Now she lay back and looked at the sky scratched by the stretchy kind of clouds. Geese flew overhead, not going south but west.

How did they know, how did they decide where they were going? Did a goose actually decide anything at all? Or did it just do what felt right in its goose-being? Hey. *That's* what zen was. It was trying to be a human being like a goose was a goose being. Although of course she could be dead wrong. She would have to remember to ask Jay. "Be zen about the shoes, Little Sister, be zen about the shoes," he'd said.

The bell rang. She lay there a while longer, noting that every second after a bell you had not responded to felt very long. Now she put her trumpet to her lips and blew her fanfare into the unpeopled expanse, into the still air around this patch of land (that seemed a no-man's-land, not Glenview, not Lawrence, not alleyway to apartment buildings, not street, not Havergal, but in between all these things), certain that in all important senses of the word, no one heard. After a minute or so she got up and went inside.

"How good of you to join us, Miss Riggs," Mr. Duckworth said.

"Yes, I know," said Glynnis. "I am the soul of generosity." Some people laughed. Others rolled their eyes and whispered. Ducky gave her an odd look with his cocked head as if to say, *Oh. Now I know you. Now I know who you are.* Did he also say, *Welcome?*

⌒

IN SCIENCE CLASS, after they wrote out the questions that they had about their science fair subject — for which Glynnis had written nothing; she already knew about recessive genes and pigment and vision and nystagmus — they had to trade pages with someone else and write down questions about *their* subject. Glynnis got Tamara because Mrs. Capp wouldn't let Tamara and Stephen trade with each other.

Tamara's sheet said about TV, "How does it work?" "Does it really rot your brain?" and "Is Bob Barker's hair real?"

Glynnis wrote, "How come on *Gilligan's Island* they can build huts and bunks and tables and chairs but they can't build a boat or fix the *Minnow*?" "Is *The Edge of Night* really a form of brainwashing?" "Mrs. Sarnicki: cleaning lady or spy?"

They traded back.

While she scanned what Tamara had written, most of Glynnis' attention was on Tamara's response to what she'd written. At first nothing. Then a tiny snort. Another snort. Glynnis smiled more widely. She read: "Where do albinos come from?" "If two albinos mate, do they always produce albinos?" A laugh from Tamara. The Mrs. Sarnicki one? Had to be. Glynnis read on, snickering herself now: "Are albinos better at music than regular people?"

Glynnis read the last question: "Is it true albinos die young?"

A question-mark-shaped snippet of panic fluttered in her chest even as she fell into giddiness. Is it true albinos die young? No. No. Of course it's not true.

Is it?

GLYNNIS STOPPED at George Locke Library on the way home. The librarian found her a textbook, *Congenital Diseases and Conditions*. Club foot, cleft palate, dwarfism, hermaphroditism, hemophilia, a heap of other conditions. And albinism.

In some pictures people were naked and their eyes barred or their heads cut out of the picture. One of these was a hermaphrodite, with breasts and a small protuberance, a penis, apparently, though it looked nothing like the arrow-shaped penis graffiti boys put on walls.

The entry on albinism was not long, less than three pages. It began by talking about recessive genes and how if both parents had the recessive gene, there was a one in four chance that the offspring would exhibit albinism. It talked about melatonin and its lack, about poor vision and the eye-shaking that was nystagmus, and sensitivity to light, and so on. And then Glynnis' reading slowed. There it was in black and white. "Because heart conditions and other health problems often accompany albinism, albinos tend to have a shorter life expectancy than average and many die young, 20-23."

Did Mom and Dad know this?

Did Carol?

AT HOME, Carol watched TV.

"Hi, Crull."

"Hi."

"What are you watching?"

"I got here first. I'm not changing it."

"Who said they wanted you to?" She was watching *The Edge of Night*.

"How ya feeling?"

"Fine."

"Does your heart ever feel funny?"

"What do you mean, funny?"

"I don't know, like it's skipping a beat or something."

"I don't know. If I'm scared, maybe. What do you keep looking at me for?"

"No reason."

"Well quit it, then."

"Okay. Who's that?"

"District Attorney Mike Karr."

"Where's Mom?"

"Class. Your turn for dinner."

"KD?"

"Sure."

"What's he doing?"

"Glynnis, I'm trying to watch TV here."

"Oh, like you're really missing anything." And then she remembered. "Sorry."

"What's with you today? You're acting weird."

"Thank you."

They ate their Kraft Dinner in front of the TV the way they generally did when their parents were out. When one person made dinner, the other was supposed to do the dishes, but Glynnis helped Carol anyway. She asked if Carol wanted to make cookies. They had not made cookies together for a long time. They had not done anything together for a long time.

"Is there something you want?" Carol said. "'Cause if there's something you want, you can just ask for it."

"No, I want cookies. Why are you so suspicious?"

They ate a quarter of the dough and reminisced about the time they'd eaten half of it and had both had terrible stomachaches. Their mother got home just as the cookies were coming out of the oven. Carol went to practise her guitar. Glynnis stayed in the kitchen while her mother made herself a cup of tea.

"Mom."

"Yes?"

"What did they tell you about albinos when Carol was born?"

"I've told you both before."

"I know, but tell me again."

"Well, they explained about the recessive genes and the lack of pigment and so forth and that Carol would likely have poor vision and that her skin and eyes both would be very susceptible to sun and we'd have to be extremely careful to protect them or she might burn badly, but that otherwise she'd be perfectly normal."

"That's it? Nothing else?"

"That's it. Why?"

"No reason."

Carol

MRS. RIGGS SMACKED her hands together as if to dust them off and took off her apron. "All right. Ready? Let's go."

"Go?"

"Really, Carol, you have a mind like a sieve. I'm dropping you off at Miss Balls' to walk the dog. Come on, boop-boop."

"Do I have to?"

"Yes, you have to, you said you would. You were full of enthusiasm about it last night."

That had been fake, the enthusiasm. Carol had not wanted to walk Miss Balls' dog then, either, but had been playing the part of happy, helpful daughter. What she had liked was the idea of herself as a helper of the helpless. *Oh, yes, there is this old lady I visit, poor thing, all she has is her dog for company and now she has diabetic foot ulcers and can't walk the dog and if she can't walk it, she can't keep it,* she said to a filmy, interested person.

But Miss Balls was not really a poor thing, and though Mrs. Riggs said Miss Balls adored this dog (it was hard to imagine Miss Balls adoring anything), she could not possibly be so reliant as that on the dog, as she had only had it for a short time and had never planned to have it for good.

Mortimer belonged to her friend, Elsie, the one who painted and had a cabin in Algonquin Park. Elsie had had a stroke and Miss Balls had looked after Mortimer while she recuperated. (Elsie had been living at the cabin since retirement, painting, like Tom Thomson, Miss Balls always said, claiming that Elsie would go missing one day and they would just find her canoe. But Elsie had had a stroke instead.) Then Elsie had a second stroke and died.

Ever since the accident, Carol had felt like Miss Balls disapproved of her. She was a cowardly deserter. She was soft and weak and wanted toughening up. Miss Balls did not seem to have different expectations of children and adults, and this had been part of her appeal when they were younger. She assumed competency until proven otherwise. Patient with a girl trying to learn a skill like semaphore or knots, after a certain point she assumed one just knew certain things. She did not think, she often said, as the early Guide leaders had thought, that Guiding was a way to train girls to be good wives and mothers, although she saw it as a corollary. If women were strong and sensible, they would exert a good influence on their husbands and their children, and continue a race of strong, sensible people who knew how things must be done in any position they found themselves in. She did not like slatternliness. She was frugal. She rose early, did her calisthenics, ate breakfast and did her dishes right away. She liked always to be busy and doing something productive and she liked to tell you so. Her garden was ferociously neat, as was her house. She liked to burn her leaves in the fall. She went to committee meetings, organized marches and drives for food and clothing.

Carol liked things to be neat and orderly, too, but she also liked to be idle, and these desires were sometimes in conflict. She liked to watch TV and to listen to music and sing along. She liked to reorganize her drawers, to fold her clothes just so, to do hospital corners on her bedsheets. She liked to edge the garden, but not mow the lawn. She liked to sit by a campfire and sing songs in the dark with a blanket wrapped round her. She liked to be read to by Glynnis and fall asleep that way. Those were the times she felt peace, when she was organizing something, making it just so, listening to her sister's voice, and singing. The rest of the time she felt uneasy and self-conscious. She also liked to endure pain, to test the threshold of her tolerance for pain. She almost liked pain. She might have a weak will and weak eyes, but she had the strength to endure pain. Enduring pain let her endure other things as well.

CAROL KNOCKED AND WAITED. Through the bottom diamond window in Miss Balls' door she saw a short, thick yellow dog with large, sticking-up ears throw his head back and bark. His little feet came up with each renewed bout of barking. And then upon some command from Miss Balls he stopped and sat, looking through the door at Carol, panting. Pink pink tongue, little white teeth.

Miss Balls was taking a long time to come to the door. Carol opened the screen to knock again, and just before she did saw the shape of Miss Balls emerge slowly from the living room, and was embarrassed to remember why she was there. Miss Balls had something wrong with her feet that meant she couldn't walk, and here Carol had made her walk.

Through the door she beckoned, and hot-faced, Carol let herself in. Miss Balls had already turned back through the door to the living room and spoke over her shoulder. "Did you not hear me tell you to enter?" She was using two canes. Something smelled bad. The dog galloped back and forth between the two of them.

Carol shook her head and then realized Miss Balls couldn't see her. "Sorry," she said. "Sorry. Sorry."

"Mortimer is a very talented dog," Miss Balls said sharply, "but he has yet to master the opening of doors."

Carol apologized again.

Mortimer trotted after Miss Balls, looking attentively at her as she turned and let herself down into an armchair. How could he like her so much?

Then Miss Balls surprised her. "Has he? Has he?" she said to Mortimer in a voice Carol had never heard her use before. HAZ*ee*, it sounded like. HAZ*ee*. Mortimer wagged his tail.

"He's so cute," Carol said.

"What an atrocious word. Never fear, Mortimer. She means it in the best way possible. Now fetch your leash."

Mortimer trotted past Carol's feet where she stood in the living room doorway, down the hall to the back door, snagging an end of his leash off the boot-mat there and trotting back to Miss Balls with the leash trailing behind him.

"Fetch your ball." Off he trotted again to the back door, returning this time with a rubber ball. Carol adored his trot, the bounce of it, the spring, the quick left-right-left-right-left-right-left-right, the waggle of his hips.

"What kind of dog is he?"

"What kind of a dog is he?" Miss Balls repeated in a shocked voice. "He's a Corgi."

Mortimer was dropping the ball and picking it up, dropping the ball and picking it up, looking expectantly at Miss Balls in between.

"Patience, Mortimer," she said. "Sit." He promptly did.

"He's amazing."

"Do not get a swell head," Miss Balls said to the dog.

Despite the short time of their acquaintance, it seemed as if Miss Balls and Mortimer understood each other perfectly.

Miss Balls told Carol where she usually took Mortimer for his walk, to a little park where they played fetch. She snapped on the leash and then held it out for Carol. She told her how to say, "Heel," stepping forward with the left foot, and how Mortimer was supposed to sit each time they came to cross a street. She got Carol to try it through the house.

"Heel," Carol said.

"Left foot, left foot."

"Sorry."

"And you don't need to shout, he's not deaf, just a good, firm 'Heel,' and off you go."

"Heel," she tried again, and Mortimer trotted next to her into the kitchen and back. When she stopped, he sat beside her.

Satisfied, Miss Balls sent them on their way, saying she felt like a bloody great invalid not being able to take him herself, but doctor's orders were doctor's orders and she was not, truthfully, up to her usual pace.

Outside, Mortimer tore down the stairs and peed on the lawn, then dragged Carol out to the street. He was surprisingly strong for such a little dog.

"Hey," Carol shouted. And then, "Heel!" Mortimer ignored her. "Heel," she cried again, stopping. This time Mortimer trotted back next to her and sat. Left foot first, she thought, following through as she said "Heel," and he did. Amazing. Fantastic. She stopped before crossing a side street and Mortimer sat. She said, "Heel," and he heeled. Mortimer was a genius. She liked that people passing by might think he was hers. A girl and her dog. Carol and Mortimer. If Mortimer were her dog, he would love her as much as he loved Miss Balls. He would love her devotedly. He would listen and do what she said. He would go for help if she were hurt and sit by her side and howl if she were dead.

She stopped suddenly. Mortimer stopped, too. The dead boy had wanted a dog. And then the boy had been killed. He had died dog-less. There was no one to sit beside him and howl.

If he had had a dog, he would have been found sooner. If he'd had a dog, the dog would have protected him, he wouldn't have died. He wouldn't have needed the man and his offer of money, which the boy only took because he wanted a dog. He wouldn't be dead and Carol would never have heard of him. She'd never have known that she'd noticed him that day downtown, flicking his shoeshine cloth in the thick heat.

"Come on, Mortimer," she said, running down the street, and he obliged her by running right alongside. Carol had the odd feeling again, the feeling of taking flight, as if there were an alternate her, a paper her that flew up in the air like a kite in a big wind. While the earthbound her ran along the street, the kite her, taut and whipped, rode the wind.

Gradually the imaginary wind dropped. The kite her did not fall so much as fade away to nothing as she approached a schoolyard with a swing set and playground set in sand in the back corner behind a strip of grass at one end of which four or five children played soccer. She remained conscious of the dead boy and his wanting a dog. Snapping the leash off Mortimer felt like being the boy for a little while, letting him into her to know what it was like to unsnap the leash of your dog and see him dart back and forth, eyes on the ball in your hand. Ruff. Ruff. Pant pant pant. Dog happy, you happy. She drew back her hand (the boy's hand, slimmer, browner). Mortimer tore off in the direction it looked like she'd throw (he'd throw). She threw (he threw). The ball flopped to the ground a bare ten feet in front of her. The boy was gone. There was just her, pathetic her. Loser. Bad throw. She didn't deserve a dog. The boy did.

"Sorry," she whispered. "Sorry."

Mortimer didn't know where the ball was. Carol pointed. Mortimer cocked his head. She pointed again, moving toward the ball, but his eyes were farther down the field, and suddenly he was off in his little Corgi gallop toward the soccer players.

"Mortimer, come," Carol yelled, jogging after him. "Mortimer, no. Mortimer, come."

Mortimer ran into the middle of the soccer game. There was one kid in goal and four kids out, and Mortimer intercepted a pass, at first trying to bite the ball, but discovering it bounced off his nose. He ran after it and this time bonked it with his nose, giving chase again as he saw it roll off. Carol yelled, but he paid no attention.

"Dog's on my team," one kid said.

Mortimer was now pushing the ball ahead of him with his head toward the far end of the field.

"Hey! Hey! The dog's stealing our ball." One kid checked it off him, sending it to another kid in red jeans, who passed it back over Mortimer's head.

"I know that dog," another kid said. "He belongs to the neighbour lady."

"Mortimer, come," Carol wailed.

"He wants to play soccer," the kid in the red jeans said.

"Pass it to him, see what he does," said one of the others.

The kid passed Mortimer the ball, and Mortimer again put his head down and rolled the ball ahead of him. This time he was headed toward the goal.

"And Mortimer has the ball," said the first kid, who wore red, white and blue sweatbands on his wrists. "He's dribbling up the field, he's coming in on goal, and Gowdy comes out to make the save. This dog is incredible, ladies and gentlemen, incredible. He's got the moves, the talent, the drive, but he's no match for the stupendous goaltending of superstar Gowdy. Now Mortimer waits for the kick ..."

They played with him until Mortimer slowed and finally flopped down in the grass, panting. The kids followed suit.

"Your dog should be on *That's Incredible*," the kid in the red jeans said.

"He should," said Carol.

"He's not your dog," said the shortest of them, a kid in a blue turtleneck. "He's the neighbour lady's dog."

"Is too my dog. She's my grandma, and he's her dog, and I live with her, so that makes him my dog, too."

"I saw it once, *That's Incredible*, where they had this dog who caught sharks."

The kid in the Hawaiian shirt did the soundtrack from *Jaws*.

"What do you mean, a dog who caught sharks? Wouldn't the dog be just, like, shark meat?"

"Little sharks. On this big sandbar. Dog stands in the water like this, and then, pshhh, pounces, comes up with a shark, whop-whop-whop-whop-whop in his mouth, takes it to his master, master puts it in a bucket. Actually, I think they're called dog sharks. About this long."

"Because dogs can catch them?"

"I don't know. I guess."

"How come I never seen you before if you live with your grandma?"

"I don't live with her all the time. Just sometimes, when my parents are fighting." Where did this stuff come from? It came out so easily. Carol didn't even have to think.

"Oh."

THE KIDS HAD to go home at five. The one who'd asked why he'd never seen her before walked with her and told her how he was going to get a dog when he was ten. Maybe he'd get one like Mortimer. What kind was he again? A Corgi. And how old? Carol didn't actually know this. "Four and a half," she said.

The dead boy had wanted a dog. It was a refrain in her head now. *He was dead because he wanted the money for a dog.*

Mortimer heeled perfectly. The kid said goodbye to him when they reached Miss Balls' house and though she didn't know if the kid was actually watching, Carol didn't feel she could give a warning knock before walking in. Why would she have to knock if it was her house? She opened the door and was greeted by a noise like a tractor idling. She leaned down to Mortimer, who seemed unperturbed. The noise stopped. Silence. Carol jumped when it started again.

"What is it, Mortimer?" she whispered. Silence. Giant tractor snort. Finally, she recognized the rhythm. Breathing. Snoring. Miss Balls was snoring. It did not sound like any snoring she'd ever heard before, not like snoring on cartoons, not like her sister's light snorts, but there was nothing else it could be. It was as loud as a tuba. Carol snapped off Mortimer's leash and he trotted down the hall to the kitchen to drink.

Carol peeked into the living room, almost frightened of what she might see. But Miss Balls was just asleep in her chair with her head thrown back and her feet up on the little rocking footstool she had. Mortimer's toenails clattered over the kitchen floor. He trotted into the living room and lay down beside Miss Balls, who did not wake. She snored again. The television was on but the sound was off. That smell was still in the air.

Carol didn't want to just sit there in the same room, waiting for Miss Balls to wake, but she didn't want to wake her, either. She backed up a few steps and stood indecisively inside the front door. On her right was the hall closet, on her left a mirror with a narrow shelf below it. Her face in it was a shadowy oval with sheens of reflective glass over the eyes. She always wanted to see herself more clearly, but it was impossible. You had to go so close that you couldn't see, anyway, not the whole face, only one part at a time, nose, lips, teeth, eyes. Nonetheless, she did this, put her face up close to the mirror and looked at her nose (too fleshy), lips (chapped, but over- all not bad), teeth (good shape, a little small). An oddly timed snort from Miss Balls made her jump away from the mirror. The breath patterns settled back into sleeping rhythm. Carol stood nervously a few minutes longer, then when nothing else changed tiptoed into what Miss Balls called the study, the small front room opposite the living room, where there was an old-fashioned desk with wooden cubbyholes, a green filing cabinet, a bank of shelves across the narrow end wall and, opposite it under the window, a sewing machine on its own table. She was taking sewing in home ec and did not like it. On top of the filing cabinet were two pictures of soldiers and a picture of two nurses in weird sort of nunnish uniforms — long skirts, long aprons, white wimples. Carol picked this one up and studied it closely. The woman on the left was only recognizable as Miss Balls if you knew it was she. Long and thin and happy, a nicer smile than you'd think. Both women smiled. They had their arms around one another. This was Miss Balls' friend Bootsie, who had died. Carol put the picture down and went back to the desk, opening the left drawer, expecting nothing much, paper, pens, paper clips, but there was a stack of Jersey Milks in there. Had to be ten, easily. More. Would she miss one?

Snore.

Carol shut the drawer and stood still.

Snore.

She relaxed, meandered into the living room, where it felt like Miss Balls would sleep forever.

In the living room was a love seat, flanked by end tables under the front window, stuffed rocker covered with nubbly, scratchy, dull pink upholstery, a table with an oldish radio on it. An upright piano with more photos on it, men in uniforms, Miss Balls with her African friend, Ballsie and Bootsie in uniform, a whole team of nurses in front of a hospital in France. In this one, the nurses had their arms hooked through one another's and Miss Balls looked like she was laughing, many of them did, and it made her look like a different person, a person with a private life.

Miss Balls moved and Carol panicked, not wanting her to wake and find her there, snooping. For the second time she backed up to the front door, opened it and closed it again, and said, "We're home," and then came into the living room. Miss Balls' head bolted up and she made a sharp noise. She breathed out a long, voiced breath and then recovered from her dream or nightmare. "Oh, dear, excuse me, terrible, sleeping in the middle of the day." Mortimer hopped up and faced her, wagging his tail. "Well, there you are, my little button. Yes, my little wittle button."

Wittle. Miss Balls had said *wittle*. Now she looked up at Carol. "Thank you, my dear, he looks very happy. You like your walk, don't you, Mortimer, yes. Did you miss me?"

"He was incredible, he was playing soccer like he knew what he was doing, he goes ..." Carol bobbed her head to show how Mortimer butted the ball around. "Everybody was saying he should be on *That's Incredible*."

"Well, Mortimer, you've made a fan."

"Not just a fan, a whole fan club!" Carol said, and Miss Balls laughed delightedly. Carol couldn't remember ever making Miss Balls laugh.

"Would you like some tea and biscuits, dearie?" Miss Balls asked. "And maybe just the tiniest little square of chocolate. Check my desk drawer."

Carol put the kettle on, got cookies and a Jersey Milk for them and Milk Bones for Mortimer, and they sat together and elucidated Mortimer's fine points until Mrs. Riggs arrived.

AFTER DINNER, Carol went to her room. For the moment she was wrapped up in her own world, where children were happy and played with dogs and laughed with their happy, wise grandparents and ate snacks together. What if she lived with Miss Balls, and made dinner for her so she didn't have to get out of her chair? Afterwards the three of them would listen to the radio, and then they would go to bed and Mortimer would hop up and lick her face and curl into her side. They could be a good little family. A family of oddballs.

She put on Barbra Streisand, but Barbra seemed wrong, too modern and silky and polished. The music to her daydream should be something older, something Miss Balls would listen to on the radio, something they could sing together. But she left Barbra on and gradually let herself be swayed into the teary melancholy, oddly pleasing to inhabit, brought on by "People Who Need People," a song she was wont to cry to bitterly, thinking how she needed people but did not have them. Now, it felt, she did have them. She had Miss Balls, whom she'd made laugh, and Mortimer, who was not officially a person but might as well be. They would all mourn her deeply when she died. She drifted into the comfort of imagining her funeral: the weeping, the eulogizing, the self-recriminations. How she died was not really part of the picture. A car accident, leukemia, strangled.

She pulled out the clippings with the picture of the boy with the light brown hair, so soft-looking, the understanding eyes, the little smile. She read the first article, the one that said he was missing. The second article, that said he had been found on a rooftop, drowned and wrapped in plastic. A photograph from above, like her father's aerial photographs, showed the rooftop.

Then she turned to the other articles, the ones that filled in the gaps: the man had taken him and his brother and his friend for a hamburger and then said he needed one of them to help him move cameras. "Give me the money, give me the money," the boy had said. He needed the money for a dog he'd picked out from a neighbour's litter. The dog was free but his family couldn't afford dog food, he'd have to pay for that on his own. She had kept every article, though there was less of the boy each time and more and more of the men, in whom she was not interested, except to foster a deep hatred. The last article was about the boy's funeral, which was jam-packed —

every Portuguese person in the city — and hundreds of others who stood outside the church. His mother and sister fainted. For his family, she imagined the family of the girl in Glynnis' hospital room after the accident, with the father who always looked angry and the mother who looked sad. They ate strong-smelling foods out of tinfoil packages. The girl was embarrassed of them. But the boy wasn't, or only a little, and only because he wanted to be Canadian like her.

She re-created again emerging from the shoe store that Thursday, walking down the street to the Eaton Centre. There he was in his yellow shirt and blue pants, his North Star running shoes, wielding his cloth with the flair of a carnival worker, eyes twinkling at the grown-ups. *Shine your shoes, ma'am? Shine your shoes, sir?* She stared at him and he flashed her a smile.

She made a sort of promise to herself — to him? — to live with Mortimer what he might have lived with his dog. This made her wonder what had happened to the puppy he had picked out. She imagined it, lonely, in the SPCA. If there was any way she could have found out which puppy it was, she would have gone down there and picked it out herself. But she had Mortimer. And she would share.

Rowena

CAROL CHATTERED AWAY like a six-year-old, Mortimer this, Mortimer that. He *actually* played soccer, Miss Balls was *actually* funny, she was cracking jokes, she was saying wittle. "Wittle Mortimer." Rowena learned more about Carol's inner life in a ten-minute car ride than she'd learned in the last two years.

"I gotta tell you," said this new, communicative Carol, "I've been scared of her ever since, ever since, you know, that time I had to go over and apologize, after the, you know. What she said was, in her war, they shot deserters. Like that made me feel really good. Oh, I'm a deserter, I should be shot."

Oh, dear. Tact had never been Beryl's strong suit.

"God, I thought, she must totally hate me —"

"Please don't swear, Carol."

"It's not swearing, Mom —"

"It is to me."

"But maybe she didn't hate me, maybe she was just, I don't know, just like weird or, you know, in her own world. I came back from the walk today? And she was snoring, I didn't even know what it was at first, it sounded like, I don't know, a truck or something. It was creepy. But then she woke up and it was all right, it was really actually kind of nice, I made her tea and she said she wants to teach me to play cribbage. Mom, you wouldn't believe Mortimer, he's the best dog."

And so it went, the whole way home. Rowena was a little taken aback after practically having to drag Carol over there and watching her trudge up the steps as if to jail. Now here she was Beryl's best friend. Maybe they ought to have got a dog when the girls had pestered her for one all those years ago. Maybe Carol would be better adjusted.

This dog-walking could be just the thing Carol needed, to pep her up and get her thinking about life and hope and the future that lay before her. Get her outdoors, away from the television. That alone would be wonderful.

Ever since Hillyard Brown had discovered a body in the melting snow last March while jogging through Alexander Muir Park, on Carol's route to school, Carol had been on a morbid streak. At first it seemed harmless enough. A group of children had played detective, they'd gone to comb the site for evidence. This had come to Rowena's attention because having found candy wrappers and cigarette butts, the children had called the police, who had spoken to the mother of the caller, who had called the rest of the mothers.

But then Carol had become convinced that she would be the next to come upon a body. Having come as close as she had to this one, Rowena argued — she might, indeed, have walked right past it day after day as it lay under the snow, a thought that made Rowena shudder; what if it *had* been Carol who found the body? — she was unlikely to find another, but Carol would not listen to reason. She would not go to the garage by herself to get anything from the freezer, she would only go for walks with a stick to beat out the grass in front of her.

And then the shoeshine boy.

Found in a plastic bag.

On the roof of that building. The thought just about made Rowena throw up. Carol's age exactly.

Carol thought she had seen him, she claimed he had smiled at her. Glynnis and Rowena didn't remember a shoeshine boy at all. Glynnis said when they heard the news (they were at the cottage), "Shoeshine boy. I didn't know there were shoeshine boys anymore." Carol didn't say then, *Yes there are, one smiled at me the other day*. She didn't say anything. Then Glynnis called out excitedly, "Hey, we were there. We were right there." Carol went still. She bit her lip. But she still didn't say anything about having seen him until Glenn brought up the paper with the boy's picture. It was possible, Rowena supposed. But not very likely. They'd gone to get a mould of Glynnis' foot made for her orthopedic shoes in a tiny, dingy little store just off Yonge Street at Alexander, and the girls had insisted on a side trip to the new shopping mall at Dundas.

Carol said Rowena and Glynnis had not seen the boy because they were arguing about the shoes. Possible. But what Rowena really thought was that Carol was fantasizing a connection with the boy to put herself in a central position with respect to the incident. To make his death real. Or less unreal. Or less terrifying. To keep him alive somehow. To make it *matter* as it did not seem to matter to Glynnis (who was a snob, anyway — she would think a shoeshine boy's life a trifle. A poor boy's life a trifle. An immigrant boy's life a trifle. With Glynnis, the trouble was entirely different than with Carol.)

"I saw him, I saw him, I saw him," Carol cried when Rowena had put these theories to her. "You never trust anything I say."

Rowena sighed. "That's not true, Carol. I trust you. But this ... no, listen to me, maybe you did see him, maybe you did, I'm not saying you didn't. But ... It's awful that he died. It's despicable the way he was killed. It's unfortunate, too, that someone else died publicly in our neighbourhood. But people do die all the time. It's not specially related to you. It's not related to you at all. You should be thinking about life and living, not death and dying." Though maybe that was the answer. Maybe she needed to read *On Death and Dying* to move through it. Just in case, just to feel she was taking some action, Rowena got a special large-print edition out of the library and put it in Carol's room, but when Rowena asked if she'd read it Carol said no, she didn't need to.

"Do you think we need to send her to a psychologist again?" she asked Glenn.

"Maybe she saw the kid."

"That's not the point."

"Take her to U of T's anatomy open house. Show her the real thing."

"Honestly."

"Why not? It might be just the ticket."

"To nightmares."

"She already has 'em."

"She does."

They decided against the psychologist.

The things Rowena had to deal with as a parent were things she had never expected. An eighteen year-old on drugs. A thirteen-year-old obsessed with death.

You never did know what you could expect, she should have learned that by now. But she went right on thinking things would be as expected, her children would bump along through minor ups and downs to responsible adulthood, she and her husband would bump along similarly. She was not so far off, really. The bumps were just bigger than she'd anticipated.

After dinner, Rowena headed downtown to the workshop she had told no one about. Considering Ministry. Until seeing the poster on notice boards about campus she had not known she was considering ministry. Since, her considering had been distant and amused. Who'd have thunk it. She more than half expected to come out of the workshop realizing it had been a silly whim.

Who would be there? Who did consider ministry these days?

Not young people, surely. Hadn't it fallen rather out of fashion? But here was bright chatter spilling out into the hall from a room full of ... middle-aged women! No, not only of them, there were young people, too, and middle-aged men, in fact, quite the mix. But the women. There was Sue, from her History of Christianity class, and Joan, from Philosophy and Religion, and several more she didn't know. It made perfect sense, of course. It had not been a career that women could consider when Rowena had been at the stage of life to consider, failing marriage, a career for herself. Now it was, and here they were. But she had been expecting to be the only one and felt now the others must be much more certain than she. They greeted one another like the veterans of coffee hours they were. Lovely, warm people. See how they approached the solitary-looking black man, see how his solemn face broke into a wonderful smile.

A casually dressed man with a fringe of grey hair and a good-looking face called out, "Good evening," and had them draw their chairs into a circle, though two young people chose the floor (why couldn't Jay be like them?).

"Now I know you're all here for the money," the leader began. "So I'll get right down to it." Bright, smiling faces. "There is none." Chuckles. Shifting in their seats. Settling in.

They had to introduce themselves and say why they had come. Most had a similar story — had always been involved in the church, had felt a call, had other careers but felt unfulfilled, their true place was in the church. "My gosh," Rowena said when her turn came. "To tell the truth, I just saw the sign and thought, 'That might suit me.' I don't know about a call."

"A call of some kind brought you here," said a frank-faced woman who leaned forward, elbows on the knees of her corduroy skirt.

"I suppose that's true," granted Rowena, and later in their small group discussion trying to describe *call,* she found herself saying, "It's a feeling of gratitude, isn't it, a tremendous gratitude, and out of that gratitude, a knowing that it's within oneself to give, a knowing that giving is the, the balancer in life, the thing that makes things come into balance ..." She was thinking of seeing Glynnis' face after her first operation, of the great rush of gratitude that broke her open to a new emotional and spiritual awareness, one that let her comfort Libby and counsel Glynnis and shepherd the girls through their reconciliation and confess to Glenn her own weakness — and it all came from God.

"Selflessness," said the girl with the big hips, nodding.

"Oh no, I don't mean that, I don't mean just the spirit of volunteerism, I mean the desire to give that comes from God, that is about faith. Not just the desire to emulate Jesus, but the desire to live life for the big questions, to *give* one's life to the big questions, even when the big questions are represented by small, ordinary things, like making a meal or visiting a friend."

"You have felt the call, my dear," said the corduroyed woman.

Rowena felt uncomfortably in the spotlight, even in the warm regard of the small circle, but she glowed within. She had become passionate in the telling. Passion had risen in her like the flush of a hot-burning woodstove, as if she were feeling a call right then, right there.

A hundred other instances of that feeling swept through her, rather as people described their life rushing before their eyes — a spontaneous carol-sing as she and the food bank volunteers stacked and sorted before Christmas; watching the sun rise Easter Sunday in Sherwood Park; singing in the junior choir; sailing with her daughters in a good stiff wind, all of them hiking out over the edge of the boat; taking her first solo flight; paddling in the early morning; battling a fish, every fish that gave a fight and later nourished them.

By the end of the evening, Rowena was on a high. What had been a remote and inexplicable whim had become a real possibility, and she had twelve new firm and fast friends. Now it just remained to tell Glenn.

As she came in the house, she could hear Glenn's tread on the basement stairs. He would have snapped off the TV upon hearing her pull up. He liked to pretend he watched no television. The children he made get up to change the channel even though they had a cable converter that let them change it from the couch, but when he thought no one would know, he lay on the couch like any of them, converter on his chest, popping buttons one after another. It annoyed her suddenly, the things they pretended.

"Good class?" he said, kissing her on the cheek and drifting into the kitchen to get a glass of water.

"It was a workshop," she said. "Considering Ministry."

"Were there many considering it?"

"Everybody," she said. "That's why we were there."

"It wasn't a part of your class?"

"Completely separate."

He swallowed the last of his water and put the glass down. He had grasped the meaning. His eyes bulged.

"What surprised me," she said quickly, flipping down the dishwasher door to load it (whose turn? she mentally questioned at the same time, and how hard was it to load a *dishwasher*, for goodness' sake?), "was how many women there were. My age, I mean. It makes perfect sense if you think of it, but —"

"You're considering the ministry?"

"Yes."

"You're thinking of becoming a minister."

"Is that so strange?"

"Well ... yes." That he even felt entitled to say it, whether it was true or not! With it came the smirk he wore when speaking of women doing things he thought they had no business doing, like flying jets.

What she hated most about this was that he was not even being true to himself, he was giving over to male chauvinism, he was putting his membership in the group 'men' over what he really felt about her. He *liked* that she knew how to do things like change a tire and have a debate. They had met when she was taking her pilot's licence, for goodness' sake. Mind you, she had never planned to be a commercial pilot, and that made her different; he could admire her spirit and determination in its small package without having to worry she'd take his job. (Her compactness appealed to him, she knew, just as his size appealed to her.)

"It never occurred to you, with all the religion courses I've been taking?" This was not fair. It had not occurred to *her*, with all the religion courses she'd been taking.

"No."

"I'm considering ministry, Glenn," she said.

"Really, Rowena. Well, how about that."

There was an uncomfortable pause as they stared one another down and then simultaneously looked away. A hardness to their interactions these days. Neither wanted to back down. Neither would admit there was anything wrong. They passed through the same house, pursuing their own goals, pretending to be happily engaged in individual pursuits and not to be avoiding one another. Then Glenn went on block and Rowena would feel a sense of relief, and a strange, for her, pricking sensation at the back of her eyes, as if she might weep.

He put the glass in the dishwasher as she bent to rummage for detergent under the sink. She poured the detergent and kneed the door up.

"Well," Rowena said, brushing off her hands. "I'm off to bed."

"I'll be there soon," said Glenn, but Rowena knew he would not. Perhaps she would not be a good minister, after all. Wouldn't a good minister be able to communicate with her husband? Wouldn't a good minister *want* to communicate with her husband? She thought of Lorraine's boast, "Oh, my husband's behind me one hundred percent!" and Celia — oh, how she liked Celia — saying, "Lucky you. Mine's only up to fifty-one." Rowena had said nothing, but had caught Celia's eye with a knowing smile.

In her dressing gown, perched, legs crossed, on the edge of her dressing chair, Rowena began her Considering Ministry diary, as recommended by the workshop leader. *Glenn can burst a bubble quicker than anyone I know*, she wrote. *Was all fired up. Now am riddled with doubt.* She put the little notebook in the drawer of her bedside table, picked up her book and lay with it across her chest as she recalled the evening and its personalities — the rather lovely, actually, mannishness of Brenda, in corduroy, the soft-spoken forcefulness of Joan, the wry forthrightness of Celia, quiet Sue. No, she had not been wrong to come away thinking what she thought and feeling what she felt. But there was a great deal more to consider, even apart from Glenn. Her decision would affect the whole family. They might have to move house. Weekends away? No more. And there were expectations of the family of a minister: that they show up to church once in a while, for example. Carol went happily enough now, but Glynnis and Jay chafed. So little to ask, one short hour out of your week to devote to reflection and contemplation, even if you do not pray or thank God directly for the gifts given you. Jay said he did not believe and Glynnis said she worshipped in her own private way, that church had nothing to do with God. Had they not been with her own children, Rowena might have enjoyed these philosophical debates. As it was, they worried her. She wanted faith for her children, and the principles of religion. They needed them. They were prone to self-interest and vanity, Jay and Glynnis. Carol, on the other hand, needed self-interest and vanity. She needed to know that she was loved by God, that she was worth something.

Oh, dear. If Rowena could not succeed with her family, how would she succeed with a whole congregation?

But how silly, churchgoing was not the issue with the whole congregation. She must care for the people that came, whenever they came, and understand they had their own way to God.

She took out the notebook again and wrote, *Somehow I feel I am beginning the biggest journey of my life.*

Glenn came to bed just after she'd turned off the light. He kissed her shoulder and she turned to him and they made love without speaking. This, too, was part of their passage through the house, this meeting occasionally in the dark, in speechlessness. At times it served only to emphasize their apartness and she would lie there afterwards burning with shame that she had feigned interest, remembering him young and the two of them ardent in order to feel less indifferent. But she did it for him — he always seemed to feel some rift repaired afterwards and that was reason enough. For him it was a way of talking without talking.

At times — tonight — her body surprised her by wanting it.

Glenn would come around. She wished he didn't have to, she wished he were already there. But he would come around.

Miss Balls

EACH TIME SHE dozed off it was into the surgical tent at the Casualty Clearing Station, and when she woke the tent was what lingered, no matter where the dream had taken her. The cold on her ankles, the dampness, the smells: gas gangrene, iodine, saline, blood, wet wool warming. The beds with their absurdly grateful men, even the thirsty abdominal cases grateful for a bed, for something like warmth, for a girl's face above them, blessed substitute.

All of it was there, the enamel supply cupboard behind her, the small folding desk by the stove, the sound of the guns, the shaking of the ground. And in it her own activity, bed to bed, dressing to dressing, drip, blood pressure, pulse, temperature. Good morning, Mr. Cameron, how are you holding up? Good morning, Mr. Simms. Mr. Flynn. Corporal Jones. Findley. MacCullough. Stanley. And their answers, Oh, pretty right, Sister. Brilliant. Thumbs up. "I'm just going to change your dressing now." The drawing forward of the stool. The long, delicate process of getting the bandage off, picking out the newly surfaced bits of shrapnel, irrigating, rebandaging, refixing the Dakin's.

Hundreds of men passed through whom she would never recall. And dozens that she would, by their faces, their wounds, by the things they said. The freckled one with the sucking chest wound who was happiest about getting his boots off. The handsome one who opened his eyes blearily as she took his pulse, then opened them wide, wide, smiled broadly and said, "Emily! You came after all," and then died.

Her memories were never in order. She would have one memory then another from years later and think she ought to put them in order after all; there was something dastardly in the way they ran all over, tiny, incomplete, inconsequential moments repeating, taking up more mind space than they were worth, while certain important scenes had slipped permanently from memory so that she knew them now only by the report she could give of what had happened, not out of memory itself. For a long time she had not begun the memoir after all, though she wrote it in her head daily, slotting in memories as they came, writing the first paragraph mentally before meandering off to muse on the whole, on where she would begin (birth? the birth of her parents?), flip-flopping back and forth until she got lost and practical matters took over anyway, walking the dog, getting dressed, cashing her cheque.

When she had begun to write, less ended on paper than went through her mind. Then the next time she made a start, she would fiddle with what had come before. A dozen starts shared a file drawer. None got further than the first few days at Etaples.

She'd left off for a time, in the hopes that inattention would bring clarity that close attention did not: a sudden falling into place when she would sit down at the typewriter and out the whole story would come.

This did not happen. The cycle continued. Memory, placement in life's context, reconstruction of surrounding events, composition of two or three sentences, then mind straying back to flashes of certain moments, certain feelings. And then she'd re-feel the feeling before eventually coming to and having to get on with the practical things of life. So nothing got written.

The plan of the book was this: 1. A foreword dedicating the book to the Guides of tomorrow; 2. Quick summary of childhood — birth, Toronto, 1896, hot August day. Happy early days in Toronto with Papa, a former Royal Engineer with service in Burma, Mama, brothers Monty and Tom, and later, baby sister Lizzie. Beryl almost sick with excitement when Papa visited the nursery, she and Monty competing for his attention while Tom went off in a corner. Papa preferring Monty, calling Tom a weakling and a coward. Beryl harbouring secret feelings along same lines, while loving Tom best.

3. Sorrow. Mother and Lizzie die of scarlet fever. Tom's survival. Household dissolved, Tom and Beryl delivered into the arms of strangers, Aunt Charlotte, in England. Very unhappy (although terribly excited to be in the midst of so much history! Stonehenge, for heaven's sake!). Adversity draws them together, constant companions until the tearful day Tom sent to boarding school.

4. Guides: formation of troop, character of Captain, reception by town (bad), weekly doings (good), incidents of note (poacher, flood at campout, etc.).

5. Pre-War Period: Beryl reunited with Tom at holidays and half-terms, lovely time, tramps galore, as when they had been fresh new arrivals pretending with the discovery of each new town the discovery of savage tribes. Colonials exploring in England.

Father's visits, one per year, uncomfortable affairs wherein Papa tried to curb every activity that gave her meaning — Scouts, bicycle riding, golf — Tom taking her part and almost struck a blow. No cowardice now, none whatsoever.

Plans, in 1914, for a continental tour, and then for Beryl to return with Papa to Toronto, to 'come out' under the guidance of his new wife. Beryl's preference to train as a nurse. Ire of Papa.

6. War declared on eighteenth birthday. Monty, Tom and Papa all join up in first week, Monty with Canadian contingent, Tom with Lancaster Rifles, Papa with his old regiment. Tom dies at Ypres.

Beryl presents self to Matron Luckes at the London hospital, as a nurse probationer. Age? Twenty-one, stated confidently, chin steady. Age in fact? Eighteen and four months.

7. Training tales, ending with the episode where she takes herself boldy into the office of Major Margaret MacDonald of the Canadian Army Medical Corps and makes her case for recruitment as Staff Nurse. "You may be in luck, Miss Balls."

8. France. The writing Sister, the Boulogne crossing, the posting to Etaples.

This was as far as she had been able to get in any writing of the memoir. Wartime, which ought to have been easiest, was somehow impossible to get down. She could not make things lie still enough to write about. They danced and fractured, there was an infinitude to them. They splintered. The splinters splintered.

But it was here that things began to get important. It was here that her life seemed to begin.

In the ward, bleary-eyed, four days into the push on Passchendaele, four days with one day's sleep. Incessant drumming rain on the canvas roof like to drive you mad should you listen, a marquee full of men waiting, listening to the rain themselves, half-dead with relief, or just half-dead. Light-rail ambulance clanking up with more. And here, under your nose, the gangrenous flesh on the thigh of a curly-haired boy who's lain in mud a day and a half waiting for help.

Stay awake. Clean up around the wound, try to get him partly clean, a little comfortable before the surgeon cuts away the diseased flesh. Stay awake. Swab the bubbled hydrogen peroxide. There. There now. Don't ... nod ... off ...

Wake up! Wake up!

The boy, where's the —

Oh. Home. Toronto. The smell arose from her own foot. Rowena's older girl was here — Ah. To walk Mortimer.

What a terrible nuisance this foot of hers was.

Mortimer wagged his tail and smiled up at her. Stupid not to get a dog all these years. Could have erased the image of poor Blackie long ago. Carol liked Mortimer. Good. Beryl had feared the Riggs girls might be sullen and resentful about dog-walking for their mother's old friend. They were getting to that age. Golly, wasn't Carol smitten, though. Grand. Perhaps she'd like to give The Amazing Mortimer his Milk Bone. And while she was at it, Beryl wouldn't mind a biscuit herself.

Carol sped off. Cupboards banged, the tap went on, the kettle began its low, steamy hum. Rather nice to have someone in the house. Rather nice indeed.

A cup of tea and a corner of chocolate, a steamy hut filled with laughing voices, cribbage on the bed. What a terrific gang they were, she and Bootsie and Stewie and Jane, Sally Mac and all of them, Vera, Vera Lang, no, Vera was a character she did in skits, *Vera, I fear-a he'll never come-a near ya*, she could still remember the tune. Olivia Lang? Lang, at any rate, who put on buck teeth and the most dreadful hats. Oh, how they roared.

Perhaps she could teach Carol to play cribbage.

IN THE MORNING when Beryl let Mortimer out to do his business, the new little neighbour boy was in his backyard doing something with a hockey stick and tennis ball. Balancing the ball on the blade of the stick. He spoke in a stream as always.

"Do you have a MedicAlert? You should have one, I do, then if you pass out they know what it is. Where's your granddaughter? If we get a dog, Mom says I have to walk him, she's not going to on top of everything else she has to do. Mortimer, Mortimer." With the stick he flipped the ball over the fence. He was really quite adept. "Here, Mortimer, good dog, good boy. If we get a dog I want to get a Mortimer dog. Good dog, Mortimer, drop it."

Mortimer, who had retrieved the ball, obeyed the boy and released the ball. The boy scooped it under the fence with the blade of his hockey stick then flicked it over again.

"Is it okay that I'm playing with Mortimer? Can I come play in your yard?"

Beryl didn't want to start a trend with the boy, but Mortimer needed the exercise and she could not provide it. She told the boy yes and stepped back inside the house. The kettle was boiling, ready for coffee. That one should have a sibling. Its parents can't possibly talk to it enough.

Granddaughter? He must mean Carol. He'd seen Carol and not having lived there long, assumed she was her granddaughter.

Imagine. She having grandchildren.

Then she remembered she had imagined it once. In that thicket of time after Neil's death. Now it seemed quite impossible, exactly as impossible as when she was eighteen and decided she was not made for a wife and mother, she did not have the secret of it as other girls did.

But for a while when they had been on leave, when Bootsie had seemed to prize her grief above all else, when Beryl and Warren talked amongst themselves and shared shy smiles, she had been able to see it in her mind, she and Warren with a brood of sturdy, handsome lads and lasses. They, the children, favoured their Aunt Helen, who was loads of fun, a real panic. In their two large yards, hers and Warren's, Helen's and her husband's, their children tumbled over one another playing wholesome games in the fresh air.

One of those long-ago imagined children might easily have had Carol. In her eyebrows was something of Warren, how they shot up into a natural knit in the middle of the brow.

Now there was a knot in Beryl's stomach. Perhaps she needed to eat. It was terribly hard to keep track. She checked her watch, checked her schedule, thumbnailed off a Lifesaver. But the knot did not go away.

Bootsie, sliding it into conversation at the British Museum as if warning her off: Warren had a fiancée. Her eyes flashing. Beryl's face flamed at the memory. Had she really been so transparent? Was it such a far-fetched fantasy? Warren enjoyed her company, he honestly did.

And a day or two later, even more inexplicable, learning there was no fiancée. Beryl had realized by then that Bootsie was, in essence, right — Warren might settle for her, for companionship, if in ten years no one else was available. But why was Bootsie being unkind? Later still, that afternoon as they strolled the greenhouse at Kew, she realized with a stab of pleasure that Bootsie was jealous. Bootsie did not want either of them, Beryl or Warren, to like anyone more than they liked her. *Well, don't worry, Bootsie,* said her heart. *We never will.*

⌐

HARDLY A LARK, the first two months, but they're the summer of her memory as well as summer in fact. Sunny. Full of fun. She, privileged to be in the thick of war work, heartsick though it made her each day. People a marvel. One simply fell in love with all of them. Hardworking, bright-hearted crew. If not quite so many people had died it would have been exhilarating. Indeed, when they saved someone who absolutely seemed past saving, it was exhilarating.

They had very little leisure time, but it was the leisure time she chiefly remembered — the impromptu gatherings in huts, golf, their walks. She and Bootsie tramped at a satisfying clip, and they talked about everything under the sun, conscientious objectors, Canadian conscription, the election, women's suffrage, their own small lives.

"Does your father never write you?" Bootsie asked one day early on. A light rain was falling.

"No. No, he doesn't," Beryl answered quickly, then said nothing for a long time. She listened to her breathing. "He's disowned me, in fact," she said finally. "I think. I'm not quite certain."

Bootsie nodded. "I thought it must be something like that. What for?"

"No daughter of his would be a lowly trained nurse." Awful tone. Quickly, she tried to explain her father, how much she loved him, how he utterly could not see that she had to work, that she had no choice.

Helen's father, she returned, was a surgeon, or had been. She'd first assisted him at age thirteen, when they'd had to perform an emergency appendectomy at a cousin's farmhouse at Christmastime. A palsy made him unable to work now. Drove him mad.

They exchanged family information like this, back and forth — Ballsie's father's second marriage, the character of Bootsie's five younger siblings, Ballsie's memories of her pretty, gentle mother, Bootsie's youngest sibling's polio — until they knew all there was to know about one another.

Bootsie liked to get out of the camp at least once a day. A quick breather in the morning, a jaunt into town or past the dunes in the evening.

It was too strange to be so close to the holiday towns — in peacetime the area was popular with holidaying Parisians — on something so far from a holiday. And strange, too, that you could not help sometimes treating it like a holiday. Renting bicycles. Playing at golf. Bootsie preferred not to. She liked least of all the seaside holiday antics of nurses sneaking out of camp for beach assignations with officers. One or two you could not blame, you saw there was something there. But others.

August was a month of convoy after convoy, the regular two hundred per day or two hundred and fifty, and then the huge ones of more than six hundred. More work than it ever seemed they could handle. More awful wounds. Terrible sepsis. The wounded left days in shell holes, surviving on the same water their dead companions decomposed into. As August wore away, so too the holiday feel.

A giant storm toward the end of the month battered the camp and flattened half the hospital, signalling an end to her summer. Bootsie grew more angry with revellers. Partly to get away from Etaples, but more to be close to her brothers, Bootsie wanted to apply for a transfer to a Casualty Clearing Station. Beryl was in like a dirty shirt. They put their applications in just before month's end.

Meanwhile, new troops arrived (seeming smaller and younger all the time), did a week of field exercises and got sent off, arriving back by ambulance train a week or three later, minus a finger or leg or all measure of sense.

There was not much mixing between the hospitals and the camps, but rumours of unrest in the camps, especially amongst the obstreperous Australians, came and went. One evening in September, Bootsie went to take her evening walk and found she was not allowed to leave the area of their hospital. Nobody knew precisely what had happened and rumours flew. But somebody had shot somebody or fired shots in a crowd, and a group of men — some said a few hundred, some said a thousand — took up bayonets and cudgels and — nobody knew, exactly — made demands of some kind. A mutiny. When the military police tried to clamp down, there were skirmishes. The mutineers had tried to cross the Canche, the river that lay between the camps and Etaples, but had been stopped there.

At any rate, Bootsie did not get her evening walk. Nor her morning one. Nor one the next evening. Ballsie very often found her outside the hut, arms folded across her chest, as she looked up at the sky, as if the force of her longing could lift her up.

One evening, about ten days into their confinement, Ballsie came back from Stewie's hut around nine-thirty or ten to find Bootsie not home. At the latrine, maybe, or getting water from the wash hut, though when she did not return after fifteen minutes, Beryl began to wonder. After half an hour, she put her coat on over her nightgown and searched the wards, the mess, the chapel, the spots she'd found her standing before to look at the sky. She returned to the hut, checked inside, stepped outside again, uncertain.

"I'm up here," came a cool voice.

"How did you get up there?"

"Swing the door open, grab the door top, step up on the handle."

Beryl tried this and gave a little shriek as the door swung on its hinges. Her hands gripped the roof. She threw her weight onto her hands and pulled herself up. Bootsie was not even wearing her cape. Her arms were over her knees. Her perch gave her no advantage. There was nothing to see but huts and more huts, tents and more tents, stars peeking out behind the mist.

"I'll go mad if this keeps up," Bootsie said. "It's bad enough, this tremendous camp where nothing should be but sand and grass and fields. But to be kept here!"

Her shoulder was almost wet through with cold dew. She'd get a chill, which mattered less than their discovery by the night patrol. How to explain two nurses sitting on a roof in a shifting grey mist? Bootsie was so calm and cheerful through the day, so quick with a joke, you would never know that any of it got to her. So it was with most of them. Only rarely did they betray what their daily sights cost them.

"Ballsie, dear. I've worried you. I've made you climb up here —"

"You know I'm always game for an adventure."

"What is wrong with me?"

"You hate to feel confined," Ballsie answered simply.

"That can't be all." She was quiet for a time. "What makes you so steady?"

"I don't know. A lack of imagination, I think."

"We *must* get out of here," she said, just before rising and dropping down, and Beryl could only agree.

Every time Bootsie said *we*, Beryl thrilled. She had not realized how deeply alone she had been until now. And if the posting came for Bootsie only? She would not be steady then. She would crack open like dropped egg.

Word came two days later. Bootsie wrote to her brothers, *You must now address all correspondence to Lieutenant Boothson and Lieutenant Balls, 2nd Canadian Casualty Clearing Station!!!!!!!*

Contrary to all rules of army life, their little team was not to be parted.

~

SHE EXPECTED GLYNNIS that afternoon, but it was Carol again, clattering into the hallway as if she owned the place, which was both presumptuous and oddly pleasing. Beryl felt a little as if she were playing a game. Familial Ease, the game was called. She had played it, too, with Elsie, and as with Elsie, it gave her a stab, a pleasure so acute it was painful. If she ever dwelled on the thought that some people had this all the time, it would have killed her. Bootsie. Oh, Bootsie. They had had plans after the war. A little house. A garden. A Girl Guide troop. A summer camp.

"Hallo, dear," she said warmly to Carol. "Mortimer's all ready for you." In her head the dialogue continued. *And I shall put the kettle on for your return.*

~

THIS MEMORY: They've packed up their little hut. Beryl scans its whitewashed interior. She wishes she'd thought to wash the chintz curtains she made so they're as bright and cheery for the next girls as they were when she put them up. They've left, too, Bootsie's water-colour of the fishing boats plying the estuary. She's not sorry to leave, though it's the first place that's been truly hers and she has an enormous affection for it. Something has shifted. Their habit of doing things together has turned into an assumption they'll do all together. Now they are off on their first big adventure. Bootsie peers in from the threshold. "Is that it, then?" "That's it." On impulse, Beryl races to take the picture after all. But no. It belongs there. The next pair needs some reminder that they came before.

THIS MEMORY: Packing her trunks in Toronto, 1909. Looking round the nursery, deciding to take nothing. All the stuff of childhood — bears and bats and balls and dolls — all behind her now. The slow trickle of tears as she turns in the trap to watch the house out of sight. Old Mrs. Murphy waving.

THIS MEMORY: Entrained for the CCS, train still stationary, Bootsie fiddling with a bag up top, and there he is, out the window. Smaller moustaches, same man. Ramrod pose, ice-blue eyes. From forty feet away she sees the bite of those eyes. He's standing with another officer, pointing, consulting. The other man nods, asks a question.

Bootsie: "You look like you've seen a ghost."

Ballsie: "I have."

Bootsie follows Ballsie's gaze. Train has not started. Bootsie darts off the train.

"Major Balls! Major Balls!"

The men stop their conversation. He's irritated, does not like to be interrupted. But, oh, here he comes. Oh. Oh. Up the carriage steps, into the compartment. Under what pretence Bootsie has drawn him into the carriage, Beryl will never know.

"Papa," she says, standing.

His jaw tenses and un-tenses. "Beryl."

Her throat aches. Her chin juts.

Bootsie, stepping in. "You do us wrong, sir, to deny us the chance to do our bit."

"Please, Papa. I had to. For Tom."

"I want you safe at home. I want our women safe at home. Or what use is it fighting?" His voice is tight as he says this.

"There are greater things than individual lives."

"How unlike your mother you are," he says. Her heart makes a sound like rubber breaking. In a second he'll turn, step away. "You're too much like me." The blue eyes are glassy. He does turn, now, does step away, but turns back, asking, "What hospital are you with?"

She calls out the particulars.

Gone. She can breathe again. Enough to weep against Bootsie's shoulder, unsteady at last. "There, there," says Bootsie. "There, there, my darling. There there."

THIS ONE: Shivering in her bed, the second May at Etaples. Ears ringing. Oh, dear. Was she sicker than she thought? No. Airplanes. Droooone. Roar. Whiiine-crash-bam. Bam. Bam bam. Wood breaking. Shouts. Droooone. Roar. Ack-ack-ack-ack. Boom. Ground rocks. She's out of bed, on the floor. Curls up into a tiny ball. Bootsie. Bootsie. On shift in the O.T. Off floor. Out door. Race race race to O.T. Burst through door. Lights on only over operating tables. Orderly blanketing windows. "Bootsie!" Surgeons look up. Bootsie looks up. Oh, she's a fool. Bootsie, firmly, "Sister Balls, you're feverish." She addresses an orderly, tells him to look after Miss Balls until the all-clear. Fraser, dear man, makes up a bed for her. She shivers in a post-op bed. Later, Bootsie visits the infirmary. Darling, how foolish. I was worried. Bombing a hospital! One sister killed outright at No. 1 Canadian General. Three more injured.

And how many men? A hundred? More? Men whom they'd just saved. Oh, this war.

～

CAROL AND Mortimer returned — what a lovely little doggie he was! — and they sat down for tea as they had the day before. A period of awkwardness fell on them. Interaction that yesterday had felt meaningful today felt hollow. Familial Ease! How she deceived herself. What an awful fool she was, really. Well. Perhaps not entirely. She'd forgot how to talk to children, though, that much was certain. Then Carol asked if she'd ever had a dog before and she found herself telling the story of Blackie.

"There was a dog my friend Bootsie had during the war. Blackie. We called it Blackie. Neil called it P.T. I suppose it might have had a Flemish name before that. Or no name at all, more likely. Bastard offspring of a randy message dog." No. Not appropriate. Oh dear. "They used dogs to send messages in the war, not a lot of people know that anymore. I can't think now how anyone supposed they mightn't be caught just as easily as a telegram. Pigeons, now, pigeons made more sense. They used flocks of 'em. One even won a medal. Imagine pinning a medal on its tiny chest!"

There, she was getting it back, her touch.

"At any rate, Blackie. We called the dog Blackie, Bootsie and me. He was a little black dog about twice as tall as Mortimer. Skinny as a stick. Bootsie's brother Neil found him as a stray and called him P.T., for P.T. Barnum, the circus man — "

"Oh," said Carol. "I thought you were saying 'Petey.'"

"No, no, P.T., P.T. Barnum, because, Neil said, there's a sucker born every minute, as P.T. Barnum had put it, and that was Neil, saying 'hullo' to that pathetic little dog. 'Hullo.' Nothing more than 'Hullo, little fella,' and that was that. Neil was stuck with him.

But loyal? Little dog stayed with him all through Vimy. Went over the top, like any of them. Warren and Neil had just moved into our sector after Lens and they surprised us at the Casualty Clearing Station with a visit."

Bicycled up the road, Blackie loping beside them. Ballsie was outside dumping a wash basin. She knew them right away. Twins. "Bootsie," she hooted. "Bootsie! They're here! They're here!"

"Bootsie had been trying to see Neil for eight months, you see, only it had never worked out. Neil and Warren. Oh, they were lovely. Gangly boys, with dirty blond hair and a bounce in their steps. The clearest, merriest eyes you could imagine. One loved plants, the other loved animals. Bootsie was very happy and we had a marvellous day despite everything going on around us — "

The walk into Poperinghe, the town positively gay that day. The prostitutes waved and they waved back — why not? they were people, too — the flag flew at the little estaminet where they ate — everyone was cheery because they were not in the line. Beryl fell in love that day. With all of them. Even herself.

" — and then very soon afterwards the boys went into the line. The little dog with them. And then over the top for the last time."

She stopped. Swallowed. Had the queer feeling round her heart.

"Well, the next we saw P.T. was back at Rémy all of three weeks later."

She stopped again.

"How'd he get there?" Carol asked.

How good to have an audience. "He'd come in the ambulance with his master."

"Neil?"

"His master, Neil." An audience kept one going, didn't it. "I was working in the resuss tent. We had sort of a warming tray for them, a tobaggan-like dish that went into an oven. It was amazing what a difference warmth could make." Perhaps an audience was what she needed: Carol. And a tape recorder. "A fellow would look at death's door and then come all pink and healthy-looking once warmed. Anyway, Neil stayed pale, even after being warmed. He was conscious, he recognized me. Said something wry about how lovely to see me again, he trusted I was well. He himself was a wreck. His leg — a femoral fracture — had been splinted with a bayonet. The thing that broke it was a small matter of someone else's head in a tin hat. Would rather not have known that, actually, but it was one of the things he said over and over. 'Lindsay's bloody head!' And laughed. Bit delirious.

"Well, anyway, you could tell he was not long for it, poor boy. I thought my heart would break. He was just so — lovely. Even then. Sweating like mad after being heated. Hair plastered to head. Those bright, clear eyes. Blackie there, head on Neil's shoulder.

"I sent an orderly for Bootsie, but she was operating, they couldn't spare her until it was done, and then I'd have to substitute. I'd had only a very little operating-room experience and was terribly nervous but by golly I was going to do my best so Bootsie could be by Neil's side. I must have done all right, because they kept me on until morning. We did another three operations.

"First thing I did was check the ward. He was gone.

"In our tent, Bootsie lay curled up on her biscuit, Blackie licking her face."

Beryl fell silent, remembering. Helen had risen after that, and fallen on Beryl's chest in grief. "I knew it, I knew it, I knew it," she'd repeated. Clenched in her hand was a handkerchief, which she beat against Beryl's chest. "I knew I would lose him. Oh, I shouldn't have come." As if her need to see Neil had killed him. The dog whined at their feet. Helen wept, shoulders heaving. Finally Beryl got her lying down, and covered up. She piled on the blankets and still Helen shook. Her teeth chattered as her breath hiccoughed and the rain drummed on the roof and the ground shook from shell bursts.

"Don't go," Bootsie said, lying on her side, clutching the hand Beryl used to pull up her blankets. So Beryl lay down beside her and put the blankets over both of them and held Helen as her shaking slowed and stilled and her breathing became steady. Behind Beryl's legs, Blackie curled.

That afternoon when she woke, her arms were still around Helen. Helen shifted. Wept again. Beryl held her tight. Helen turned. She stroked Beryl's cheek lightly. "You're very kind, do you know that?" Beryl stayed very, very still. A rabbit. Heart racing. Nose sniffing. Ready to bolt. The dog hopped between them and lay down with his nose by their chins. No doubt he was thick with fleas.

"We became very attached to Blackie, Bootsie and I," Beryl resumed. "There is something very … innocent … about a dog in wartime. He doesn't know anything about it but he knows he loves you. You've had a horrid, exhausting day, and there he is, scampering about and rolling on his back for a tummy rub. He was like a … reminder … of better times, better things.

"Well. We had an M.O. who'd come unhinged, only we didn't know it at the time. Blackie often went missing during the day. Out foraging, I don't know, we never questioned where he went. One day we were working, as usual, and we heard a shot, a pistol shot, right in our yard. Gunfire we were used to — the snap of the sniper's rifle in the distance — and artillery at night, mortar fire, shelling, whizbangs, what have you. But a pistol shot! Right behind our tents! How we tore out to see what it was. Captain MacKenzie, pistol still in hand, still pointing at Blackie. Good shot, Captain MacKenzie. Blackie was dead.

"We didn't understand at first. Why had he done it? Why had he shot our dog? And then we saw. Blackie's teeth were around a familiar-looking object, a large stick-like thing.

"The incinerator, you see, had broken down, and the orderlies were storing the amputated limbs in the shed until they could get it going again. Blackie had got in somehow and dragged it out and was chewing on it. An arm. A human arm. You couldn't blame the dog, of course. It didn't know. It was simply hungry. But you couldn't not blame it either, or rather you … Well, it was the dog or ourselves we had to blame, wasn't it? All of us. Man.

"It's true he was mad, Captain MacKenzie, but we all knew exactly why he'd done it. Any one of us might have done the same, who can say? Even Bootsie.

"He walked off after that. I can see it plain as day. Holstered the pistol, turned his back and walked down the road toward Abeele, that was toward the border, the French border. I believe he fully meant to desert right then and there. Captain James went after him. Walked miles and miles until he could make him see sense, come back long enough to get a diagnosis of neurasthenia, get shipped out on the next A.T.

"I thought he was terribly brave just then. Captain MacKenzie. When he walked. Not what I would have called brave before the war. But I didn't know then what bravery was. How many different forms it can take. He held himself quite upright. Walked like a hiker setting off on a day's tramp. He knew he might be shot tomorrow. Today he was going to *walk*. Perhaps he thought being shot was better than the shame of breaking down."

Carol did not say anything.

Miss Balls realized Carol did not know she was finished. "And that's it. That's the story of Blackie."

"That's *awful*," Carol said.

"Yes. It is," said Miss Balls.

Glynnis

SATURDAY WAS A COLD, clear day, perfect Thanksgiving weather. The trees were half changed and the sunshine was bright and pale at the same time. Carol wore her tinted glasses. She sat in the front between Mrs. Riggs and the 'friend' she had invited, Miss Balls, who would have been invited anyway. "Invite another friend," Mrs. Riggs had said.

"Okay. Mortimer," said Carol, and Mrs. Riggs hadn't pushed it.

Glynnis was in the back between Hilda and Jay.

Carol was going to die young. Being embarrassed by Hilda seemed petty by comparison.

They played the alphabet game, where you have to spot the letters in order. They always tried to get through to Z by the time they passed the Ziebart sign on the highway, because otherwise it might be a long wait for the end of the game. Next they played buzz and then ink-pink. Carol seemed painfully happy, with her mother on one side and Miss Balls on the other and her long-haired, grown-up brother in the back seat, and Mortimer in the very back. All of them seemed happy, and Glynnis felt the weight of her knowledge. They were happy now, but soon they'd look back on this time and weep for the happiness that no longer was.

"Ink Pink," said Carol. She giggled. "Uhhhh, large, um, hair substitute."

Normally Glynnis would have been the one to sarcastically say, "Hmm, wonder what that could be."

"Ooo, tough one, Crull," said Jay.

"Big wig," said Hilda. She'd never played the game before. "Ink-pink. Uhh, mongrel stomach."

"Mutt gut," said Jay. "Inky-pinky." He thought for a moment. "Someone who spouts Shakespeare while aboard a vessel."

Mrs. Riggs got this one, boater quoter, and gave 'seafood entrée.'

"Fish dish," Hilda and Carol said at the same time. Carol was always so happy when she got one. Glynnis felt, as she sometimes did, much older than her sister. Her eyes filled.

Jay seemed diffident. He hadn't wanted to come. Glynnis had overheard the argument on the phone. Mrs. Riggs had told him to think of his sisters and how much they looked forward to seeing him. It wasn't fair that she had used them but it was true. They missed him. Now he seemed to have stopped playing the game and was looking out the window. She wondered if he knew about Carol dying young.

As they drove, the trees changed more and more. Past Barrie they were whole blazing yellow and orange and red trees. It was colder than in the city, and getting out of the warm, sleepy car, they shivered, but they warmed up unloading the car and getting everything down to the boat. They had to lend Hilda an extra sweater and windbreaker for the boat ride because she had only a sweatshirt and corduroy jacket.

Glynnis loved the boat ride, the bite of the wind, her mother standing up there at the wheel like a captain. She loved the channel markers, the islands, the familiarity of each cottage on the way, the YWCA camp, the narrows, the camping spots and picnic spots they sailed or paddled to in the summer. The year before, she had read *Swallows and Amazons* and had wanted to go on sailing adventures every day. She loved seeing her father's Cessna at the dock and seeing the boathouse and the cottage itself, perched on the granite, getting nearer and nearer. The flag was up and flapping crisply in the wind. Mr. Riggs and the MacDonald girls were on the dock to meet them and help them unload. Their eyes shone when Mrs. Riggs asked how the flight was.

"Fuckin A," Alison said and Sandy said, "Alison!" The adults just exchanged a look like they'd excuse it because she was going through a hard time.

Thanksgiving was the best time to fly up to the cottage. Sandy said it was like the movie they showed at Ontario Place, the one that made Glynnis almost cry with the song. *Superior country, your mystery calls me. Men cannot tame you, men cannot own.* She always wanted Carol to play it on the guitar.

When the MacDonalds had taken a load up to the cottage, Mrs. Riggs reminded Carol and Glynnis and Hilda to be sensitive toward them and suggested they try to keep them occupied as much as possible. Glynnis had told Hilda on the way up approximately what was going on: Dr. MacDonald had left; Mrs. MacDonald was "not taking it well." Drinking, this meant, though Glynnis did not tell Hilda that.

The problem was there wasn't as much to do as in the summer. They couldn't swim, it was too windy to canoe, the fishing season was over, and both the *Albacore* and the *Laser* had had their hulls scrubbed and their rigging packed away safe from mice and were put away in the boathouse for the winter. When it was just the family there on Thanksgiving, they usually did chores and then read or played games before meals. Now they stacked the wood that Mr. Riggs cut and Jay split, but there were so many of them, they mostly just stood there waiting, and Mr. Riggs said they should go do something else and come back when there was more to do.

Glynnis felt responsible for all of them. Hilda she'd invited, Carol was going to die young, Sandy and Alison were going through a family crisis. "You want to play horseshoes?" she asked.

"Horseshoes," Alison snorted.

"What's wrong with horseshoes?" said Sandy.

"Nothing wrong with horseshoes, sonny," she said in an old-person's voice, hand wobbling on her imaginary cane.

"Well, what do you want to do?"

"Nothing, let's play horseshoes."

When it became apparent Sandy was going to win, Alison got stupid. "Hey, let's play horseshoe chipmunk death," and she made like she was going to chuck the horseshoe at Chippie, the chipmunk that the Riggses had trained to eat out of their hands.

"Leave Chippie alone," Carol said.

"You are such a sore loser," Sandy said.

Now Alison did throw the horseshoe at the chipmunk, which easily evaded it and fled.

"That's our pet chipmunk," Carol said. "I don't care if you're a guest, you leave him alone. It took us the whole summer to tame him." She stormed off into the cottage.

"I'm not a guest, I'm a prisoner."

"Shut up, Alison," Sandy said.

"Wasn't my idea to call them."

"Shut. Up."

"Okay, okay, I'm shutting."

Hilda said, "You're upset because your dad left. I know how you feel. My dad left when I was nine."

"Can it, Hilda," Glynnis said.

"Oh, Christ." Alison turned and walked down to the water.

"Sorry, Hilda. It's just, that was kind of tactless, you know?"

Glynnis suggested she and Sandy and Hilda take the old trail down to the point. They walked in silence. After a few minutes, Hilda apologized to Sandy and Sandy said it was all right. "It's not just that she's upset," Sandy said about Alison. "She mighta done that anyway. But she'd be insulted that anyone thought she was that … transparent."

Sun still fell on the point and they went and sat in the sun by the water.

"How's your mom?" Glynnis asked.

"Don't know. She was passed out when we found her. Alison didn't want to call an ambulance. She's been passed out before, but I don't know, this seemed worse. So I called your mother. She called the ambulance."

"Aw, Sandy."

Sandy tried to shrug away Glynnis' sympathy but tears ran down her cheeks. Glynnis put her arm around her. Hilda, mercifully, was quiet, picking at the lichen.

"Ah, fuck," Sandy said finally, wiping her eyes.

"It'll be okay," Glynnis said. "Your mom's great."

"Oh, yeah. She's the greatest."

"No, she is. I love your mom."

"Oh, God." Sandy wiped her eyes again. "So. What's the price of tea in China?"

Glynnis considered. She wanted to tell someone about Carol dying young and she wanted to confide in Sandy so Sandy would feel they were equal, because they were, but something held her back. And then she meandered into it, still unsure. "You know, I was thinking I'd do my science fair project on albinos, I didn't know what else to do and Whatshername says we can get a headstart on it. Anyway, so I'm at the library, and I'm reading this book, and it says … it says … you can't tell anybody this, I don't even know if Mom and Dad know … I'm pretty sure Carol doesn't …"

"What?"

"I don't know if I should say."

"Oh, come on, you have to now."

"The book says albinos die young. They have weak hearts and they just sort of, I don't know, wear out or something."

"Oh, my God."

AFTER DINNER, Jay took the boat out to meet some friends and the adults stayed in the cottage and read. The girls went to the sleeping cabin. Sandy had got Alison to apologize to Carol about throwing the horseshoe at her chipmunk. "If I'd thought I'd actually hit it, do you think I would have thrown it? No way." There was a small woodstove in the cabin, in which Glynnis lit a fire. They had marshmallows to toast.

Hilda suggested they have a séance. "No," Carol, Sandy and Alison said at the same time.

"Okay. No séance. Truth or dare?"

"Why do we have to *do* anything? Why can't we just hang out?" Alison said. Glynnis liked that 'we.' Maybe Alison had got out what she needed to get out and now could be normal.

"Who's going to start?" said Sandy.

"Hilda should start. She suggested it."

"Okay, Hilda, truth or dare?" Sandy asked.

"Truth."

"Truth. Okay, uuum …"

"Wait, who gets to ask the question?"

"Isn't it usually the person who just did it?"

"Yeah."

"But nobody's done it."

"Wait, okay, so maybe Hilda should ask somebody else."

"Okay," Hilda said. "Glynnis. Truth, dare, double-dare, promise to repeat."

"Dare."

"I dare you to …" Hilda's eyes flitted around while she thought.

"Pass your hand through the candle flame."

"Easy." Glynnis did it. "Alison. Truth, dare, double-dare, promise to repeat."

"Dare."

"She always picks dare," Sandy said.

"Let's make it so you can't repeat yourself until you've done all of them."

"That ruins it. The whole point is you get to choose."

Glynnis dared Alison to jump from one top bunk to the other.

"Easy."

Alison asked Sandy. Truth. "What's a big thing you lied about?"

"Remember that lamp in the rec room? Me."

"I knew it."

Sandy dared Hilda to pick nose and eat it, right in front of them. She did. "Ew, ew, she's doing it, she's doing it," Sandy said, bringing her fists up underneath her nose in squeamishness.

"Well you dared me."

"I know but ... "

"Tell me you've never picked your nose and eaten it."

"Maybe when I was, like, six."

"Everybody's doin' it, doin' it, pickin' their nose and chewin' it, chewin' it," Carol sang.

Hilda asked Glynnis what the furthest was she ever went with a boy.

"Second," said Glynnis.

"Who with?" asked Hilda.

"That's another turn."

"We all know who with," Alison said. "Petie," she and Sandy said together.

Glynnis dared Alison to go steal a beer.

"No, they'll notice."

"There's a whole case there, they won't notice."

"Hilda, give me your sweatshirt." They followed her out the cabin door to the back door of the cottage and listened while Alison went in. Mr. Riggs asked Alison what they could do for her. She asked for something to drink. Mrs. Riggs answered that there was juice and pop in the fridge. She came out looking cool as a cucumber and holding a can of pop.

"Did you get it? Did you get it?"

She pulled a Carlsberg out of the pouch of Hilda's sweatshirt.

When they got back to the cabin she swore. They didn't have an opener.

"No problem," Hilda said. "Give it to me." She took the beer and put the lid between her molars. "Ow. Shit."

"Give it to me," Alison said. She took the beer out to the porch and rested the cap bottom against the railing, then hit the beer with her hand. The top came off.

She took a slug. "Ugh, it's warm."

Glynnis took a sip. Bitter. She passed it to Sandy, who passed it on without drinking.

"Truth, dare, double dare, promise to repeat," Alison said to Hilda.

"Do promise to repeat," Sandy said. "Nobody's done that yet."

"Okay. Promise to repeat."

Alison started laughing. "Oh, this is so good."

"What? What?"

"Go up to Miss Balls and say, 'Excuse me, Miss Balls, but do you have balls?'"

Everyone but Carol laughed. Hilda got up.

"Wait, you're not going to do it, are you?" Glynnis said.

"Sure, I am."

"No," Carol said, jumping up to block the door. "She's my friend."

Uncomfortable silence.

"O-kay," said Alison.

"It's not just that," said Glynnis. "It's too obvious. Mom'd know for sure we're playing truth or dare and she'd kill us."

Alison had to come up with another promise-to-repeat for Hilda. "Okay. You have to say, um, 'I eat snot-balls every day.'"

Hilda did it. "See," Glynnis said, "that's why nobody does promise-to-repeat, it's too tame."

"Unless you've got a phone, then you can make people call people up and say things."

"Nobody's done double-dare, either."

Hilda asked Carol next.

"She always picks truth," Sandy said.

"I like truth best," said Carol. "I'd like to just play truth."

"Okay." Hilda took a big breath. Her eyes sparkled. "Do you masturbate?"

Ew, ew, Oh, my God.

"You said you wanted to play truth," Hilda said.

Carol went completely pink and said no.

"You're lying. Everybody masturbates." Alison looked round at them.

"You mean you do?" Hilda asked.

"Well … Okay. Yeah. I do."

"Me, too."

"Oh, my God, I do not want to know this," Sandy said, covering her ears and going *la-la-la*.

"Glynnis?"

"It was Carol's question."

"So? We've told the truth."

"Okay. Yes."

Sandy squealed.

"All right, Carol. One more chance to come clean, now that everyone but Miss Squeamish here has."

Carol nodded.

"Aha. So you *admit* you lied. That means you have to do a dare instead. Everybody agree?" They all agreed. "Okay. I dare you to go jump naked in the lake and yell Ooga-Booga."

They all laughed at this just because they were at that point where you laugh at everything. Carol stood up.

"You're not doing it?" Glynnis said.

"I am." Sometimes there was a resolve in Carol that was as sudden as it was certain. It was as if by this one action, she could redeem herself in Alison's eyes forever. Glynnis knew that was what she was thinking. But her heart. Her heart might not be able to stand it.

"You can't."

"What do you mean?"

"It's too cold. It's dangerous."

"It's not that cold. Just in and out," said Alison. "I'll do it with you if you like."

"No. I'll do it on my own."

"We should all do it," Hilda said excitedly.

"No. Nobody should do it. Give her another dare, Al."

"What's the matter, Glynnis? Chicken. 'Fraid of a little cold water?"

Sandy seemed to catch on. "She's right, Al. It's too cold."

"Come on. We've been swimming in colder water than this before." She got up, too, and went to look for towels. She came back and tossed one to Carol. Glynnis had to jump up and grab Carol's hand.

"I'm serious, you guys. You can't do it. Well, you can do it, but Carol can't."

"Why not?"

"She's got a bad heart, Al," Sandy said. "The shock could kill her."

"No, I don't," said Carol.

Sandy and Glynnis looked at each other. "Yes, you do," Glynnis said. "I read it in a book, a medical textbook. It said albinos have weak hearts and ..."

"And what?"

"Nothing. That's it. Just they have weak hearts."

"No. You were going to say something else. I know you, Glynnis Riggs."

What had she got herself into? "They have weak hearts and they shouldn't have any big shocks like jumping into freezing cold water."

"That's not what it said. You were going to say 'die young,' weren't you? I could hear it, it's almost like you did say it. I could hear it in my head. Oh, my God." Carol sat down. They all sat down. "I wonder how long I have."

"It could be wrong," Glynnis said. "I just read it in a book, doesn't mean it's true. And, and, it didn't say every albino, it only said 'they tend to.'"

"I knew it," Carol said with a kind of awed satisfaction in her own predictive powers. "I knew it. I've always had this feeling I'd die young."

"You never told me that before."

"I didn't want to worry anyone."

Sandy began crying, then Hilda too, and Carol and Glynnis and Alison. Alison said she was sorry for all the mean things she'd ever said and done to Carol. "You know I didn't mean them, don't you?"

Carol nodded tearfully.

Finally their tears subsided. They sat in a circle on the floor with their arms around one another. "It won't be for a long time, still," Glynnis said. "You've got ten years at least. Probably more."

"What are you going to do?" Sandy asked.

"I don't know. Live life to the fullest, I guess."

WHEN THE TURKEY was finally ready the next night, all nine of them squeezed in around the long table on the cottage's enclosed porch, Mr. Riggs at one end carving and asking, in order of protocol — guests first, oldest to youngest — what meat each preferred and then passing the plate to his wife down at the other end to serve up vegetables. Hilda got hers third and had a forkful of turkey halfway to her mouth when apparently she noticed Miss Balls to her right and Alison across from her sat waiting with their food untouched. She put the fork back down. Big dinners were one time Glynnis didn't mind being the youngest, since it meant she got her food still hot. Once everyone was served, Mr. Riggs asked Miss Balls to say grace. She did the traditional kind, "For what we are about to receive," rather than the new, spontaneous and meaningful ones they were supposed to do now that Mrs. Riggs was at God school.

"Dig in," Mr. Riggs said. There was a brief stretch where the only talk was of passing gravy and salt and cranberry sauce and how good it all was. And then he swallowed and spoke again. "In the Riggs family, we have a tradition, a very simple tradition that we follow each year at Thanks —"

"Aw, Dad," Glynnis said. She had hoped, given Alison and Sandy's situation, of which he had to be fully aware, and Carol's, of which he wasn't, that he would skip the tradition this year. "Do we have to?"

"I'll thank you not to interrupt," he said. "And no, of course no one has to, I'm not going to force anyone to give thanks, but I would hope that we're all eager to take a moment to pause and reflect on God's bounty in this world. It's an ungrateful soul who can think of absolutely nothing to be thankful for."

Family. That was one of the things they were all supposed to be thankful for, the main thing her parents both said each year. Glynnis didn't totally get that. What choice did you have?

Right now, though, she was thinking of Carol, who might break down if she said she was thankful for family, and Alison and Sandy, who might not be able to say they were thankful for family, at least not without crying, and who might feel bad if they didn't say it.

"I'm thankful for disco," Glynnis said. "*Shake shake shake,*" she sang, twisting disco-like in her chair, "*shake shake shake, shake your boo-tay.*" The kids snickered.

"If you're going to make a farce of it —" Mr. Riggs said ominously.

"Sorry. Sorry. Sorry. Really, I'm thankful for my sewing licence." Now Alison and Hilda guffawed and Jay said, "What?" and Alison explained how they had to get a sewing licence in home ec before they could use the sewing machines.

"Fine. We'll drop it."

Embarrassed silence from everyone. Then Miss Balls said, "Well, I don't mind saying I'm thankful to be included in such a splendid gathering of family and friends, for life and health, knock wood, and all good things."

Carol gave Glynnis a quick, sad smile. "I am thankful for my wonderful family, my mother and father, my sister and brother, and Miss Balls and Mortimer and Alison and Sandy and Hilda, and the precious time given to us here on earth." Here she broke down. Sandy was sniffling, too, and Hilda. Glynnis' lip quivered, and Alison blinked rapidly. Soon they were all five of them crying openly.

"What on earth is going on with you girls?"

"Mass hysteria," Jay said.

"He's right, you know," said Miss Balls. "I've seen it at camp. Get a group of girls a certain age together and it doesn't take much to start them off. Why, we had whole cabins hyperventilating. Had to get them to breathe into paper bags."

"Carol? What is it?"

But Carol couldn't answer.

"Glynnis?"

Glynnis couldn't answer, either.

"I've had just about enough of this," Mr. Riggs said.

"I tried to warn you, Dad," Glynnis said.

"Warn me of what?"

"Thanksgiving … "

"I'm at sea. I'm completely at sea."

Mrs. Riggs said she thought they should be separated. She sent Carol to their bedroom, Glynnis to the cabin, Sandy to Miss Balls' room, Alison to Jay's, and Hilda to the living room. She visited Carol first, Glynnis later heard, and got it out of her. Then she gathered them all together in the living room and told them it wasn't true, Carol's heart was just fine and she'd die no younger than any of the rest of them.

"But Glynnis read it in a book," said Sandy.

"Then the book is wrong."

They could hear the adults in the other room laughing at them when they went back in. "You wouldn't think it was so funny if it was true."

"No, no, of course we wouldn't. But it's not. Just the sight of the whole lot of you, bawling away." Jay laughed and laughed.

"Ha ha ha," said Glynnis. She could see that Alison was as embarrassed as she was at having got caught up in it all.

Glynnis still wasn't a hundred percent sure her mother knew what she was talking about. How could that book be wrong?

But wait. Glynnis was a scientific genius. She would test the hypothesis. With mice. She would prove once and for all whether albinos die younger than non-albinos. What was the life span of a mouse?

She was in the library on Tuesday, looking it up, when Glynnis overheard Alison telling her friend Tracy Novak she'd flown up to Georgian Bay with Glynnis' dad, who was a pilot. "Totally decent."

"How come you were there? You're not friends with Pinkie, are you?"

"They're, you know, friends of the family."

"Weekend with Wimpy and Gimpy. Lucky you. What's the rest of the family like? Any Siamese twins?"

"Their mother's going to be a minister. She thinks I'm a bad influence."

"You?"

"Yeah, as if, eh? Smoke?"

Glynnis put the book up in front of her face so they wouldn't see her as they walked out of the stacks to the door. Afterwards, she wondered why it should be she who hid. They were the ones who should be embarrassed.

Miss Balls

AFTER HER SHOWER, straight to the typewriter. No more fretting and fussing. She snapped the shower cap round her ears and stepped into the stream of hot water. What a luxury. Hot water! She never failed to appreciate it. Sometimes she even stood an extra three or four minutes just to feel it coursing over her. Extra cost be damned.

Lemnos, as everyone who had been there reminded Beryl, had been a veritable desert island, requiring a donkey trek just to have a bath. Oh, the jolly sound of their voices in the showers at Etaples, remembering Lemnos, soap flying from their hair, screams when the cold water hit each in her little booth. Happy —

— times. What on earth? She was not — she was lying down. Silly Ballsie. You don't lie down to take a shower. Get up.

Yes, yes. I'd love to. I will. Only —

She'd never get it right, would she? Any of the things that had happened. That glorious day in Pop, laced with jealousy of the boys' prior claim on Bootsie's affection. The moment as she watched the brothers tease the sister that she realized what Bootsie's great appeal was, the thing that had attracted Beryl right from the start: she was well loved. Every word, every action was the word and action of someone well loved.

Shelled. Night after Neil's death. The operating tables full, the rain drumming down, the involuntary pause when the whine of the shell sounded before the boom of its landing. Back to work before the landing, the instruments rattling on their trays, bottles rattling in the supply cupboard. Here came another, very near, very near. The surgeons joking. Boom, smash. Rain of mud. A yelp.

In the morning, they fell into their biscuits, exhausted, Beryl almost asleep when she noted a clicking sound, what was that?

"Ballsie," said Bootsie. "I can't stop shaking."

The chattering of Bootsie's teeth, that's what it was. Blackie whined and licked her face.

Beryl threw her blanket over both of them, crawled in next to Bootsie and put her arms about her for the second time. Every muscle in her body was tense. Ballsie tried to get as much of her front against Bootsie's back as she could. Bootsie shook and shook so that Ballsie wondered if she'd ever stop. Gradually the shudders grew more intermittent, the muscles relaxed. And now it was an embrace, a real embrace. Ballsie realized it only suddenly, her nose in the nape of Bootsie's neck, Bootsie grasping with her hand the arm that held her. They fell asleep that way, tight against one another that night and all their remaining nights. The warmth of a human body, the greatest miracle.

Bootsie's letter was on the mantelpiece. What, what, what had she said?

Delicious warmth.

Only no, not any longer. Now it was cold, so very cold. Bootsie was gone. Bootsie was in the mid-Atlantic. Bootsie was on a lifeboat tossed on ragged waves thrown up by the lurching, shuddering, going-down ship. Ship looming close, close, no way to push away from it, oars broken. Sisters tense, calm, clutching seats, gunwales, one another's arms. Up, up on wave. Drop to trough. Spray. The ship lurching, shuddering. Midships going awash. Poop deck. Afterdeck. Ship gone. Up, up, up on whirlpool's rim. Marvel of nature. This giant vortex. Flip. Plash. Cold fills her ears. Cold cold water closes over her head. Gone. Gone.

Carol

THE SOCCER KIDS weren't playing anymore, so Carol had saved up enough to buy Mortimer a soccer ball. She'd got it from Hopkin's on her way home and then at home she pumped it up. She got her mother to give her a ride over to Miss Balls'. Now that Miss Balls' foot was a bit better, she always knocked before letting herself in. The door was always open.

Halfway up the walk, she could hear Mortimer, a series of short, sharp yaps, different from his normal bark. She knocked, but he didn't come to the door, even when she let herself in. His barking was coming from the bedroom. She knew right then what it was and she turned back out the door, but her mother had already driven off and she told herself, as her mother had told her after Thanksgiving, that she had a morbid imagination and that the premonitions she had of bad things happening were only a concoction of her brain. Carol walked slowly down the hall on tiptoe and stood outside the open bedroom door for a few seconds before peeking in. Miss Balls was not on the bed as she expected.

Mortimer was sitting outside the bathroom door, keeping up his yap. He saw her and didn't stop.

"Miss Balls?" No response. She went to the door and knocked. The water was running. What a relief. Her mother was right. Miss Balls was just having a shower and couldn't hear her. Mortimer stood, stopping his bark, waiting for her to open the door.

"Come on, Mortimer," she said. He followed her. "Look what I got you." She showed him the soccer ball and his ears shot up. "You want to try it out? Come on." They went into the backyard and Mortimer happily bonked the soccer ball with his snout. Carol waited to hear Miss Balls call out to them.

When, after some time, she went back in, she could still faintly hear the sound of the shower. Carol stood outside the bathroom door again. There was no other noise than the splashing of the shower.

"Miss Balls?" she shouted. "Miss Balls?"

A force field guarded the door handle. Carol's hand stopped an inch from gripping it. What if Miss Balls wasn't dead? You couldn't walk in on an old lady in the shower. Carol had that terrible feeling of intruding into adult territory when you can't help it, the territory of adult privacy, like a glimpse of your mother putting on deodorant, or what's between your father's legs when his bathrobe slips open and you can see through his skimpy PJ bottoms with the buckled-open fly. Still she pressed ahead.

What if she needed AR? *Use your first aid, Carol*, went Miss Balls' voice in her head, *use your first aid*. Then she dropped her hand from the air above the door handle and ran to the front door and outside and halfway down the walk. She stopped, panting. Her mother would not be home yet.

Neighbours. 911.

The neighbours' houses looked still as tombs.

She went back inside. Mortimer had started to bark again.

First aid, first aid, first aid, she told herself, and opened the bathroom door.

Inside was humid but not steamy. The steam had condensed and was running in droplets down the mirror.

"Miss Balls?"

The turquoise shower curtain was closed. Couldn't see through it. The feel of the air said cold water. It hit the curtain liner in plastic-sounding dops. Now the force field fronted the shower curtain. Carol thrust her hand through it to the left edge of the curtain and pulled it back just a few inches, turning her head away as she did, but still catching a glimpse of ... yes. Feet. One covered with a, it looked like a bread bag. With head still turned, she reached in and shut off the water. The handles of both taps were cold and water from the shower head fell on her wrist and hand. Cold. Freezing. "Miss Balls?" she whispered. "Miss Balls?"

And then she drew back the curtain from the right to the left and saw her laid out, pale as the underbelly of a frog, pale as herself, shower cap slipped up on the back of her head and down over her eyebrows. Steel grey pubic hair, small sacs sagging low on her chest that didn't even look like breasts. Mouth open, eyes wide and unblinking.

First aid, first aid, Carol told herself. ABCs. Airway, breathing, circulation. She put her hand in front of Miss Balls' mouth. No breathing. She put her middle finger on her throat. The body so seemed to radiate cold it almost stopped her from placing the finger, but she did. Nothing. She stood, walked out of the bathroom and to the telephone to call her mother.

"I listen to CHUM," said Glynnis.

"Is Mom there?"

Glynnis yelled and her mother came to the phone.

"Carol?"

"Miss Balls is dead."

"What?"

"Miss Balls is dead."

Her mother said she'd be there right away, and Carol slid down the wall holding the receiver, while Mortimer barked. "Mortimer," she wailed, and he came to her, crawled on her lap and licked her face and let her hold him.

THEY BROUGHT CAROL home bundled up in a blanket and fed her soup in bed like she was sick. Shock, Mrs. Riggs said. She got to stay home from school the next day. When she went back she was a celebrity, but she didn't want celebrity, she had had a glimpse into something far beyond the silly games of grade eight. She was serene. She did not need friends. She did not need Glynnis, with all her grabs for attention.

She did not need Lisa, but Lisa came to her. "Is it true you saw a dead person? What was it like?"

"Cold."

"Cold?"

"I felt like I was in a freezer." She shivered.

"Were the eyes open? Do you have nightmares?"

She did have nightmares, but she also had dreams where Miss Balls' eyes were closed in the tub and she was fully dressed and she opened her eyes and sat up when Carol pulled the curtain back and said, "Hello, there, dear, just taking a little nap." And then they would go for a walk in the woods, holding hands like Carol was five. She had dreams where Miss Balls did semaphore to her from across a great field, but she could not figure out the message.

It was like she had a foot in the underworld and people treated her that way, as if she were a mystical being and they were wary of bringing down her curse on their heads. She half liked it. She had pretended not to mind at John Fisher when everyone had run from her, but now she liked it. Now Lisa was getting her to talk to Jim Morrison on the Ouija board. Now Lisa was like her manager, her bodyguard. All of a sudden she was loyal. And Carol accepted it as right.

Part Three

AIR PHOTO -A21985-46
TORONTO, 1970
1:25,000
(FROM THE COLLECTION OF GLENN RIGGS)

THE DULLEST AND MOST uniform of his photos, barely worth a glance. And yet he looks. For anomalies. For things that were not there in the last photo. For things he never noticed before. For things he will never be able to find.

The 401 crosses the upper left of the photo like a ribbon around an LP all wrapped up for a present. Chaplin is the ribbon on the lower left corner. The rail line that opened up Leaside factories, the bottom right.

Yonge Street runs off the bottom of the page an inch left of where it started at the top and Bayview parallels it, with a little hump in the middle where it negotiates the river valley then makes its way back on course. South to north, Mount Pleasant tends to Yonge as the long, liney end of a parabola tends to the x-axis.

New bits jump out white: big white-topped houses on curvy streets north of earlier Hogg's Hollow's straight roads, a patch of streets just south of his own preserved from development until the last twenty years, still raw in the landscape. More of Don Mills burrowing like the termite of E.P. Taylor's brain into the heartwood of farmland.

The commercial buildings make a grey zipper of Yonge Street in the jacket of the city. He longs to unzip it. See what's underneath.

287

1982

Glynnis

THE RADIO CLUNKED and blared. Glynnis' hand flailed. Off. Off. Off. Ah. Thank you. Drift. Wait a minute. She slitted her eyes open. Gah! Camera-head on the bed. Tamara.

"Who let you in?"

They were doing a documentary. It wasn't, as far as Glynnis knew, supposed to start this early. She pretended to go back to sleep, for a moment or two genuinely dozing before the radio blatted again. She opened her eyes and looked at the camera. "Are you still here?"

Tamara backed away as Glynnis got out of bed.

"You ever notice how when you're lying in bed, the radio's really really loud, and when you get up, it's actually quiet? What is that? Some physical law, like the Doppler effect?"

Bathroom. Tamara backed now into the hall, standing aside for Glynnis to pass. The sound of CBC and the smell of coffee wafted up the stairs.

"I thought we weren't doing fly on the wall," Glynnis said. "I thought we were acknowledging the way the presence of the camera changes the scene. Because, you know, I don't usually talk to the flies on my wall." She had not anticipated how self-conscious she would feel in front of the camera. LIMP limp LIMP limp LIMP limp down the hall.

Carol's radio snapped on as they passed her room. Three radios, three different stations.

Tamara made as if to follow Glynnis into the bathroom. "What. No. You want to watch me pee? Okay." She let Tamara into the bathroom and sat on the toilet. "Here. I'm peeing. Peeing. Just as if I were alone. Pee pee pee." She was not peeing.

Tamara reached out with her left arm and turned the tap on. Glynnis peed. The camera panned down to Glynnis' feet. Right foot flat on the floor. Left foot dangling.

Glynnis tore off toilet paper and Tamara stopped the camera, hefting it down from her shoulder. "Jesus, this is worse than the flexed arm hang."

Back in Glynnis' bedroom with Glynnis partly dressed, Tamara shot more leg. Below two solid, muscled quads were matching knees. Below the knee the right leg continued to be well proportioned, with a high, well-defined calf muscle and a neat ankle coming to two points on either side of the leg. The left, by contrast, was thinner, the muscle scrawny, the skin scarred and puckered, the ankle huge and blocky, like worn wooden blocks in a nylon stocking. The left foot ended above the right foot's ankle. Glynnis turned it right and left to give a full view.

"Here, let's get this from a whole bunch of angles." Tamara lay on her stomach, knelt, zoomed in, zoomed out. Glynnis put on her orthopedic shoes for more shots. "You know, I'd like to get some bedroom slippers in this style. I'd like to get everything in this style."

She'd thought she was going to like this. She'd thought it would be funny. They were bantering — she was bantering — but it was not funny.

Downstairs, Mrs. Riggs said good morning to Tamara.

"Morning, Reverend Riggs," Tamara said.

"I'm not a Reverend yet."

"Won't be long. I'm just getting you used to it."

"Aren't we supposed to pretend she's not here?" said Mr. Riggs, looking up from the paper.

"It's not that kind of documentary."

"What kind of documentary is it?"

"I don't know, but not that kind."

Glynnis poured herself cereal. Mrs. Riggs made lunches. "You need something to eat, Tamara," Mrs. Riggs said.

"Breakfast is the most important meal of the day," said Glynnis.

"Funny, I thought coffee was the most important meal of the day."

"Can you tell me why you're doing this again?"

"Because Tamara can get an independent studies credit for making a documentary film."

"And this film is about?"

"Me."

Raised eyebrows. It occurred to Glynnis they might have to make two versions of the documentary, one for her parents to watch and one for everyone else. Her parents would not react well to *A Day in the Life of a Teenage Cripple*.

"*A Day in the Life of a Teenage Cripple*."

"Oh, cripes, Glynnis … You're not really, are you? That is offensive, you don't mean that."

"We'll talk about this later," Mrs. Riggs said, meaning not in front of Tamara.

God, they were so … respectable.

ON THEIR WAY to get fries and gravy to take to Vlad's room, Kelly from the swim team collared Glynnis. It's the camera, Glynnis thought.

"You'll join the synchro club with me, won't you, Glynnis?"

"But of course. Because I'm so graceful. And I always do what you say, Kel."

"See?" Kelly nodded round the table. "Now there's a true friend." Kelly waved a half-sandwich at Glynnis. "Tell them how fabulous it'll be, Glynnis."

"It'll be unbelievably fabulous. Unspeakably fabulous. Undeniably, unthinkably, un, un …" Well-timed pause. "It'll be really good."

Kelly nodded broadly again, holding her hands out toward Glynnis like a magician's assistant. "Anh? Anh? You see?"

Kelly's friend, Mish, looked up briefly from her textbook. "Compelling argument."

"I'm swayed," said Steph, stabbing a piece of romaine with a fork.

"I've got a whole routine planned."

"Of course you do," said Mish.

"Aren't you going to ask me what the music is?"

"What's the music, Kel," said Steph.

"'Thank heaven, for leetle girls …'" Kelly sang.

"Oh, Lord," said Deb.

Perform, perform. Glynnis put her face next to Kelly's and joined in. "'… for leetle girls get beeger' …" They paused, turned to each other and spoke the next line in the backs of their mouths with a Gallic r, "every day."

Glynnis and Kelly batted eyelashes, tossed their heads, clasped their hands and flung them and then finally — "For leee-tel girls" — laid their cheeks a-tilt on the backs of their hands. Kelly wanted someone to play off of? Okay.

Slow, scattered applause came from the surrounding cafeteria tables. Tamara trained the camera directly on Glynnis as if to say, "I'm waiiii-ting."

"You guys are, I don't know what you are," Deb said. "I don't even know you." She pitched her voice louder. "I don't know them."

"You're so —" Steph shook her head.

"Childish?" Mish said.

"We're obviously not exerting enough peer pressure here, Riggsie."

"Ah, they just don't know how cool synchro is, man. You want cool sports? Synchro. That's cool sports. You're a wienie if you don't do synchro. You're gay if you don't do synchro. Cool people? They wear sparkly bathing suits and nose clips and pile their hair into buns and bobby-pin little tiaras onto their buns and do the tap-crawl to 'Thank Heaven for Little Girls.'"

Kelly leapt up and yelled across the cafeteria. "Mac! Novak!" Alison MacDonald and Tracy Novak. "Synchro. You in?"

"What?" they yelled back.

Kelly whapped Glynnis' arm. They tossed their hands up, slathered on their best synchro smiles and began to spin, bending their knees as they went so they disappeared behind the table as if going under water.

"You know," Novak shouted as they popped back up again. "You guys are *so cool*."

Kelly bowed like the third-prize winner at the Salzburg Festival in *The Sound of Music*.

Tamara filmed.

"What's with the camera?" Kelly finally asked, off-handedly.

Cool. Very cool.

AT SYNCHRO WERE six serious people and six of their crowd, swim-team people. The serious people included twin grade twelves whose bathing suits matched, not Speedos but floral-patterned one-pieces with puckered chests and tie-strings that went around the neck. Chrissy and Cassy.

"Are they for real?" Mish turned to whisper about Chrissy and Cassy as they filed onto the pool deck behind them.

The group sat on the pool deck in front of Mrs. Snell, a trim, fifty-something English teacher with fading blond hair and lightly applied red lipstick. She wore a green tracksuit zipped up to the neck and sat lady-posture on a bench, back straight, knees and ankles together.

"My, this is wonderful," she said, counting with her head. "We've doubled our numbers from last year."

Mrs. Snell had competed in synchronized swimming, she said, way back when it was called water ballet. It must get in the blood because her daughter, now coaching a club team in Etobicoke, had been an alternate on the 1976 Olympic team when Canada had introduced synchro as a demonstration sport.

She gabbled happily on. The most important thing, she said, the thing above everything else, was that it be truly synchronized. The little things counted in synchro, posture, facial expression — here she took her index fingers and twirled them up from the corners of her lips as she burst into an enormous smile, looking briefly like the Riddler on *Batman*. It was a perfectionist's sport, she went on, it combined beauty and strength, or, as it was inscribed on the coveted Gale Trophy, named after Frances Gale of Montreal, the founding mother of our sport, "Graceful and Scientific Swimming." "Isn't that a riot? 'Graceful and Scientific Swimming.'" She gave a light pop of a laugh.

The swim-team people were bugging their eyes at one another. This was exactly what they'd come for. Much gayer than Glynnis had anticipated. She had taken synchro before, twice, and though it had been a little gay, it was nothing like this. Mrs. Snell was a special case. But Glynnis could not join into the eye bugging whole-heartedly. Mrs. Snell was clueless but some people belonged to the land of the clueless and there was an odd sort of beauty about those people.

Before they could get into the water, Mrs. Snell lined them up and showed them how to stand — back straight, head tall, shoulders back, derrieres in, and smile, ladies, smile — and how to walk —

arms loose, are we smiling? yes?, arms loose, toes pointed, right leg first, ex-teeend annnd step, extend-step, extend-step, very good.

And suddenly everything shifted.

"Right around the pool now, ladies, and–stay–in–synch. I want you synchronized at every step. When you enter the pool, when you approach the pool, when we're doing lengths, whenever possible. Soon you'll find you'll do it without thinking. You'll be synchronized in the shower!" Her pop-laugh again.

Chrissy and Cassy at the head of the line looked like perfect, fleshy automatons. Involuntarily, Glynnis rose up on her left toes to hide the limp. She felt blood rush to the surface of her skin.

"All right, now, our entry. Ready? Clean entry, no splash, and let's try a little arm motion, just a little forearms-crossed-in-front-of-you and then when you jump, bring them out and up. Ready? Arms crossed, and one-two-three in."

In the water, Glynnis' face cooled. But then Mrs. Snell wanted them to do heads up crawl, cupping their hands like little scoops. Little, gay, useless scoops. She wanted them to *place* their arms *neatly* and *precisely* in the water, with a slight pause before the stroke began to give them all time to synchronize and to create a visible rhythm to the stroke. She wanted them to bend their elbows. None of this windmill business, she said. "You, dear, the —" She had been going to say "Chinese girl" and then stopped herself. Lucky for her, Deb, who was actually Korean, looked up. "Yes, you," she said to Deb. "Bend the arm and place it, place it, place it. That's right."

Then it was tap-crawl, the same stroke, but with a little tap on the surface of the water after your hand left it. If this wasn't all the self-satisfied feminizing drill-mistresses Glynnis had ever encountered — in health, in home ec, in Sunday school, figure skating, all over — *now ladies, now ladies, now ladies, now ladies* — she could have been like Kelly, gaily tapping and scooping and placing and saying, "*Tap*-crawl, *tap*-crawl, *tap*-crawl," as she went. She tried, but an old feeling rose in her and even in the water her face burned. *You're clumsy, you're clumsy, you're clumsy, you're clumsy,* the stroke was really saying.

Next they sculled in place, toes pointed, body taut but relaxed, no water over anything, whole body on the surface. "That's right. Point your toes, there. Toes, toes. Toes. You there, toes." Then head-first sculling. "Let's have two lines now, two lines, and I want you to stay synchronized. Ready? First line, go, synchronized, synchronized, use that peripheral vision, that's it, no sagging in the middle there, up, up, that's it, toes pointed, pointed, toes pointed. All right, next group. Go."

Then it was reverse scull. "Toes. Toes. Point those toes. You there, yes, you, what's your name?"

"Glynnis."

"You don't seem to be hearing me, Glynnis. You must point your toes."

"I can't," Glynnis said. Except for Chrissy and Cassy, everybody stopped.

Mrs. Snell whipped her hands up to her ears and gave a gasp. "What's that? I thought I heard a four-letter word. C-A-N-T. We don't want to hear that, no, no, no."

"No, you don't understand, ze toes, zey do not point." Can't is a four-letter word. For fuck's sake. *Cant* is a four-letter word. C-A-N-apostrophe-T is a contraction.

"I've got a terrific exercise for ankle extension ..."

"No, I'm telling you, my ankle doesn't extend."

"Yes, and that's exactly what the exercise will —"

"Listen," Mac said, "the kid had a piano fall on her ankle. She's lucky she can walk."

"Oh. I see. Super. Right. Carry on, then."

The rest of the practice Glynnis couldn't help noticing the blunt barge of her foot plowing through the water in contrast to its slim, streamlined partner, and it felt like the Riddler had eyes only for the same thing, mentally clucking as she got them to do tubs — shins along water surface, knees drawn up to above hips, body forming a tub — and from the tub extending a straight leg up into 'the flamingo.'

Glynnis played Synchro Loser to "L'Amour Est Bleu," leaving her knee bent when it should have been straight and her foot at right angles to her leg instead of attempting to point her toes. She clutched at the water rather than sculling smoothly. This got a laugh from everyone except Chrissy and Cassy.

At the end of practice, Mrs. Snell told the others to feel free to practise on their own and called to Glynnis. "Come over here, dear. Get your towel. Let's see that ankle."

Glynnis held it out.

"Oh, my. Oh, dear. Oh, you poor thing."

"It's not that bad."

"But you understand, dear, you won't be able to compete ..." Her voice droned on. Glynnis could not believe it. She was actually suggesting that Glynnis might want to help her choreograph rather than swim. Why could Tamara not have caught this on video? This was exactly the kind of day in the life of a teenage cripple that Glynnis had meant when they'd first talked about it. She'd been saying that every day there was something. Every day. A look, a comment, sometimes innocent, sometimes not. And Tamara had said, "We should do a video." Now they had done the video and everyone had treated her like a normal person and she'd been embarrassed and wondered if she wasn't actually oversensitive the way some people had told her she was.

In the pool the people she had come with postured goofily.

"Mm? Would you like that?" prodded Mrs. Snell.

"You know? Actually? *Can't* is a contraction. *Fuck* is a four-letter word."

Glynnis limped down the pool deck. In the shower room she turned her face into the spray, letting the water pelt her eyes. She had a vision of melting into the tiles and fading away, but the feet of the others slapped into the shower room in an excited clump.

"Hoo, Riggsie!"

"Oh, my God, Glynnis."

"Did you just say what I thought you said?" asked Deb.

Glynnis turned, opening her eyes. She was not ready for them yet, but she tried anyway. "*Can't* is a contraction. *Fuck* is a four-letter word."

"Right fuckin' on," said Novak.

"Glynnis, you rebel, you," said Kelly. "What did she say?"

"Nothing."

"No, I mean before."

Glynnis talked through her nose. "'Now, *dear*, I'm sure you understyand, we have to adhere to the *styandards*, and well, of course it's not *me*, it's the *judges*, the *judges* have styandards and wayell, of course you're welcome to come *swim* with the rest of the team, but I'm afraid you won't be able to *compete*. Maybe you'd like to help me choreograph, mm? Dear, would you like that?'"

Guffaws, outrage, admiration all echoed through the tiled green room and still Glynnis would have preferred to be alone.

"She's got a point, you know," Chrissy or Cassy said. "You'd put the whole team out of the running."

"She's just thinking of the team," agreed the other, pulling her hair out of her bathing cap and tilting her head back to let it swing back and forth in the water. She stepped out of the stream to let her sister do the same, then they both wrung out their ponytails and high-stepped off to the dressing room.

"Somebody doesn't like us," Steph sang.

"Deer! That's what they move like," Novak said. "It's been bugging me."

"No," said the skinny grade nine in response to Steph. "They just, you know, care."

Everyone stared at her as if they'd forgotten she was there.

"Or colts," Novak said. "Maybe it's colts."

"About synchro," said the skinny girl.

"You mean people ..." Steph screwed up her face, "... *care*? About synchro?"

The girl shrugged. "Apparently."

"Colts," Glynnis said. Novak was right. Novak surprised her. Novak's was the only pure utterance of the afternoon, the only thing not said for effect. It took a certain security to make such an utterance. Glynnis liked to think she had it herself, but she didn't.

"It wouldn't be so bad if everything didn't have to be pretty-pretty," Deb said. "'Tap-crawl, tap-crawl, tap-crawl,'" she piped. "I mean, how about," she dropped her voice, windmilled her arms, "smash-crawl, smash-crawl, smash-crawl?"

"I like it," Glynnis said, still straining to match her mood to theirs. "Punk synchro."

Kelly made as if playing the opening bass line of "Rock Lobster." Deb did the smash-crawl against the water of the shower.

Then they were all doing it, eight girls in the shower smashing their arms through the water and bobbing their heads up and down and wiggling their hips. Something in Glynnis loosened.

"Oh, my God," Kelly said, stopping suddenly. "Oh, my God. This is brilliant. This is brilliant."

"Oh, my God, oh, my God," said Steph. "What?"

"Rock *lobster*? Rock *lobster*? It's a move, it's a move, the lobster, it's a synchro move, it's like this." She waved her hands in front of her as if sculling and hopped backwards on one leg with the other leg stuck out straight behind her. "And you go backwards. That's the Lobster. Forget 'Thank Heaven for Little Girls.' 'Rock Lobster' is mandatory. It must be done."

"I believe that'll go over well with Mrs. Snell," Mish said.

"Snelly? Who needs Snelly? We'll start our own club. Won't we, Riggsie?"

Carol

EVERY DAY, Carol thought about quitting school. She hated every-thing. The only people she didn't mind were the stoners. At the same time, of course, she longed for people to like her, or to refine, she had for so long longed for people to like her that the longing had slipped into despising. Her celebrity in grade eight from finding the dead body had unravelled until it had again become her fault that she had found a dead body.

Fault or destiny, hard to say. She had developed an idea that she had the touch of calamity.

Problem about quitting school, though, was what to do instead. She, like, wasn't going to be the next Barbra Streisand any more. Nice voice, sure. She had even written a couple of songs, but they weren't very good, at least she doubted it. Glynnis was no judge.

Once upon a time she had thought about being a nurse like Miss Balls, but in actual fact sick people didn't appeal to her and probably you needed better vision. If she could barely see to take out a splinter, how was she going to find a vein. Guidance counsellors were always saying think of your passion and then try to figure out how you can make it so you can do that thing. Which was pretty stupid when you thought about it. How many people were actually

302

going to be famous actors and actresses? Like, one? Hockey players? Race-car drivers? Nuh-uh. But sometimes she wondered if maybe she should be an undertaker, because really, wasn't that her passion? Death? Occasionally she had fantasies about there being a nuclear holocaust in which, somehow, she was spared, and there was one man who was also spared who was also an albino or sometimes just blind, and they began the job of repopulating the world. And then one night staying up late watching a movie with Glynnis while their parents were away, she was shocked because the movie was almost exactly like that except the albinos were all bad guys who came out at night and wanted to kill Charlton Heston. They were called The Family. It made her sick. She couldn't watch it. She couldn't not watch it. She stood beside the couch, always on the verge of leaving, arguing with the movie until Glynnis said, "Oh, just sit down."

The guidance counsellor had been taken aback when Carol said she wanted to find out what was involved in becoming an undertaker. But then he went along with it. And that's what she started telling anyone who asked her what she was going to be, not that anyone did except aunts and uncles. Aunt Helen had paused and then decided to take it as a joke. Carol's cousins were going to go to law school and accountant school and pharmacy school and art school. Carol wished she was good at art, but basically she could just draw a skull and crossbones. At that she was becoming quite accomplished. She did it on her jeans in marker. Her mother didn't like it. Her mother wanted her to cheer up. Her mother wanted her to have friends. Her mother wanted her to exercise and be well rounded. She wanted to watch TV and draw skulls and crossbones on whatever part of her she felt like.

It was acknowledged. She had become a problem.

Glynnis, on the other hand, won medals in swimming and played first trumpet and got good marks and had nice, bright, lively friends. A smart aleck, though. She'd be fine if she just shut her trap once in a while.

Still and all, Glynnis was one of the things Carol didn't hate. When Glynnis wasn't off being well rounded, they hung out at home and watched TV and ate junk food, hiding the empty packets from their mother, who, among other strange transformations, had gone health-food nutty. They wandered in and out of each other's rooms when they were supposed to be doing homework. Glynnis lay on the floor and read while Carol sat on the bed and played guitar. Or they'd both just lie there, listening to music, talking about the stupid things their parents had said and done. At night, when it was time for bed, Glynnis read aloud. Right now it was *The Clan of the Cave Bear*.

In Carol's lockable (laughable, Glynnis called it; the lock was a joke) pink five-year diary that she'd got when she was like nine, she kept a list of dead things she had seen. Miss Balls was first on the list. Then roadkill: squirrels, raccoons, a dog. When the seasons changed, fish. Frogs. Mice. She'd started out including bugs, too, but they were really far too numerous. Just running her hand over the outside of the screen door at the cottage she could kill thirty mosquitoes.

She'd be thinking her list was impressive and then all of a sudden it would seem paltry compared to all the death out there to discover and she'd be tempted to go to hospitals looking for dead people or to hang out outside nursing homes waiting for the residents to be wheeled out, but she made it a rule it had to be dead things seen in everyday life. Of course, if she worked at a funeral parlour, that'd be regular life.

She also kept a list of novel ways people had been killed. This was why she read the newspaper. Her parents thought she was taking an interest in current affairs. Industrial bread-kneading machine. Car accident, drunk teens on train tracks. Father and son, drowned while sailing on Lake Ontario. Three-year-old, fall from sixth-storey balcony. Woman, forty-six, drowned while feeding ducks.

She wondered how she herself would die. She preferred that it be somehow novel. She preferred that it not be in a bathtub.

⌐⌐

SHE HAD TURNED SIXTEEN. She had turned seventeen. Legally she could quit school, but even morticians needed high school.

And then she was smoking with Lisa Chivvers and her reason to stay in school walked by. Loped by. Her reason had hunched shoulders, hands stuffed in the rib-cage pockets of his jacket, boots eating up the pavement, and most fantastic of all, stupendous green spikes of hair raking an arc in the air with the bounce of his walk. Sleek equatorial lizard, all quickness and laze. Carol, who rarely lifted her eyes, lifted her eyes and outright stared. Fifteen feet away from them, not that he showed any awareness of their presence, he turned his head slightly and spat, a small, neat thwop of gob straight from mouth to gutter. His face was slack, but at the last second as he went by, Carol thought his lizard eyes flicked toward hers. She couldn't be sure — she was always seeing things that weren't there, or that were but were something else, poodles that turned out to be sweaters, three-year-olds in raincoats (fire hydrants), people on street benches (parking metres), people that were mailboxes, garbage cans, shadows. But this time she was pretty sure his eyes had flicked her way. And why not? People stared at him? People stared at her, too.

"What a case, eh?" said Lisa.

"Yeah," Carol said. Monotone voice, heart catapulting into her mouth.

She passed him once a day between third and fourth periods. He did not go to the cafeteria. She looked every day for a week even though it was nice out and she preferred when it was nice to take her lunch to a nearby parkette. When the weather was bad, she was forced into the caf like everyone else and she'd eat with Lisa and her guys, or with Glynnis, though more last year than this. Last year it had still bugged her to be alone. This year she'd realized there was honour in being a loner. Later, when she got out of school, she would meet other loners. They would be loners together. She had visions of this. They wore grey and were quiet and it was always winter in the visions. There were four of them and they loved each other.

ONE DAY AT LUNCH she followed him. Around the corner, down the street to Fran's, where she lost her nerve and let him go in without her. The next day and the one after, he went to the Yonge-Eglinton food court. He read the *Toronto Sun* and ate chicken chow mein and sat in the same seat. She bought a doughnut and took a table close enough to see and far enough away not to be suspicious. After a week or so, she decided she had to approach him, so she went up and said she liked his hair.

"Fuggaw," he said back, without looking up. Not lizard, scorpion: just a flick of words and she was stung, paralyzed. She fucked off.

Later, in the bathroom at school, she realized that he'd thought she was making fun of him. He'd thought she meant she *didn't* like his hair. Damn. She should have known. She'd seen the jock-boys call him Snot Head, like that was the most original insult in the world, she'd seen the stoners she usually thought were okay and who kept saying how laid back they were, bristle and call him a fuckin' freak. What she should've said was, "No, I mean it, I really do like your hair," and he'd have said, "Really?" looking up, and she'd have gone, "Really" and that would have been the start of it all.

She started recording in her dead things journal how many times people said, "Nice hair." A lot, was the answer. "Fuggaw," he'd say. He just kept loping along and saying "Fuggaw."

SHE'D BEEN NERVOUS at first about his finding out she was follow-ing him (though at the same time she half-wished for it, had fantasies about it), but it seemed that he was oblivious, as she herself normally was, except when her awareness was heightened by the need to watch him. And so she followed him after school. The first day was disappointing; he just went home, walked south on Yonge, cut up Balliol. But at least she now knew where his home was. The next time he took the subway south to Wellesley and walked over to Jarvis and disappeared into an office building. Only afterwards when she was heading home did she think she should've looked closer to see what kind of offices were there, like doctors or what. The day after that was the same until Wellesley, where just outside the station he met … shit … a girl. A punk girl, black hair like a thick Russian fur hat. They didn't kiss or anything, hold hands, but Carol felt sort of sick as she watched them walk off together. She let her stomach hit the turnstile and her body follow through. Her hand went up to her eyes against the light of the station, her feet kept on until out of the station and onto the sidewalk, where they halted. A man bumped into her and swore. Green hair, black hair, hitting the crowd on Yonge, disappearing.

The girl stopped Carol following him for a while, but it didn't stop her thinking about him. The girl was a revelation. How she dressed was *who Carol really was inside*. Black hair, pale face, black blobs of eyes, black lipstick lips. Army jacket, the short, khaki wool kind, some kind of short skirt, ratty leggings. *That's me. That's me.* Only, it wasn't. Yet. Her wardrobe at present was jeans and flannel shirts, a cowl-necked sweater or two. Her hair was so thin there was not much she could do with it: straight, shoulder-length, bangs. She had tried to feather it in grade nine to no good effect. She also wore oversize men's shirts with the tails out. Visible breasts meant audible comments. Boy 1: Did you know that barn owls are renowned *hooters*? Boy 2: Really, I thought hoot owls were bigger *hooters* than barn owls. Boy 1: Nope, barn owls are the *biggest hooters* of all.

Fuckers.

At the church rummage sale on Saturday, she found a rhinestone choker that was big and chunky and ugly-beautiful. "Where on earth did you get that?" her mother said. "Honestly. What you're wearing these days. It doesn't make you look attractive at all."

She went to the army surplus store on Yonge Street south of Wellesley, nervously, wondering if she'd see him on the way, and got two black T-shirts and an army jacket. She tried on boots but didn't have enough money. She needed a job. On Monday she looked up the phone number for the Trull Funeral Home but couldn't get up the courage to call and ask about work. She looked it up every day for a week, but only ever got as far as dialling the first three digits. She wrote the number down, though, and slipped it in her wallet.

At Shopper's she stole black hair dye and stored it at home in a drawer, every now and then taking it out and reading the label and wondering when she should do it. Not before Christmas. Maybe after. Maybe on New Year's Eve so that in the new year there'd be a new her, a new her who was more who she was than she was now.

CHRISTMAS WAS SOMEHOW actually not too bad. Her family was all sort of getting along. Jay was in journalism school and he brought his girlfriend home and they all loved her. Her parents didn't even object when it became evident that Jay and his girlfriend would be sharing a bed. The girlfriend was doing a PhD. She got presents for all of them, books. For Carol it was a memoir of a man whose family were undertakers in the American South.

After Christmas day, the whole family flew into their cabin at Rainy Lake and they cross-country skied, and Carol didn't think about the lizard boy so much, except to think she couldn't imagine him cross-country skiing or wearing a hat. She tried picturing bringing him home and it just didn't work. None of them would get him. At all. But of course it was stupid to even be thinking about that because as if it would ever even happen. He had a girlfriend already.

Who was cool. So, so much for that. She would just admire him from a distance, that's all she would ever do.

AND THEN GLYNNIS, with her punk synchro. One of those things she did with her loud, smart party people that she came home and told Carol about. Glynnis' stories were entertaining, like a soap opera or a movie. Though sometimes Carol felt like a shut-in, John Travolta as the Boy in the Bubble. Other people got to live. She got to listen. For punk synchro, Glynnis and Kelly had dressed up as Ike and Spike with, like, dog collars and fake safety pins through their cheeks and ripped T-shirts and jean shorts. They had everybody thrashing in the pool to "Rock Lobster."

"Then we hear this banging on the inside of the boys' dressing room and who comes out but Punker Guy. You know Punker Guy?"

Her heart stopped. Punker Guy. Her punker guy. Her lizard. At punk synchro. She nodded. Yeah, I know him.

"Him. We're like, does he know this is a joke?" Glynnis said.

"And? Does he?" Was she sounding casual enough?

"I don't know, I still don't know. I think so. I mean, how could he not? It's pretty obvious we're not all punkers. At first he didn't want to get his hair wet. And we're like, Grunt — good name, eh? — we're like, Grunt, this is synchro. Synchronized *swimming*. You have to get your hair wet. And then Mish, Smartypants, goes, I thought you said anything goes, which, it's true, we had said, and Kel's like, But how can you do the kip if you don't want to get your hair wet? How can you do the clam? How can you do the swirlina? Can you believe there's a move called the swirlina?"

"So did he get his hair wet?"

"Not once, the whole time, except for a little at the back so he had this, like, little tail, sort of dripping green down his back."

Carol could picture it perfectly. Green lizard tail.

"So what's his story?"

"Grunt? No idea."

"What's he like?"

"Personality? I don't know, I can't really tell. He doesn't say much. He grunts, he literally does grunt. It's kind of funny." She shovelled in her food. "How come you're so interested?"

"Just curious."

"Come to punk synchro. You can find out."

"Ha ha."

Come to punk synchro. As if.

OKAY. ESSAY. EUTHANASIA. What did she think? She supported it. For people. With inoperable things. Not for dogs with operable brain tumours. But for people. Sure. She sort of thought there should be suicide clinics, where anybody who wanted to could just walk in and say, "Yeah, I'd like to die, please?" There were too many people in the world, anyway. Maybe they'd have to, like, see a psychiatrist or something before they were allowed to do it. As a safeguard. As for people who were sick and old or quadriplegics or whatever, definitely they should be allowed to die. If you believed in an afterlife, then it only made sense. She didn't buy that suicides didn't get access to whatever heaven was. Murderers, okay, but suicides, they got in. They wanted it so bad.

She opened a drawer to get a pen and decided she needed to clean out and reorganize her drawers. Inside a tube of construction paper in the second drawer was the hair dye she'd shoplifted. She pulled it out and read the instructions again, then put it away, closed the drawer and went to watch TV.

THE NEXT MORNING, she was cruising the stretch of hall where Grunt had his locker, hoping for a glimpse, and found herself walking behind Glynnis, who didn't know she was there, and Glynnis' friend Kelly, who wouldn't have cared if she did. Up ahead were Alison MacDonald and Tracy Novak.

"You're coming to Alison's party, right?" Kelly was asking.

"I'm not sure I was invited."

"Of course you were. Are. Everybody is. This is the MacDonalds we're talking about. Hey, Mac," she called ahead, "Mac, Riggsie's invited to your party, right?"

Alison turned around and walked backwards. Carol ducked her head. "Nope. Everyone else in the universe, yup. Riggsie? No way, man." Was she going to invite Carol, too? No. No way, man. And who cared, because there he was, one boot forward, padlock in hand, twirling the combination with his fingers. Carol slowed.

Kelly grabbed Glynnis' arm and marched right up to him. "Hi, Grunt, how's things?"

He grunted. Carol stopped; then, realizing she had to make it look like she had a reason to stop, bent down to tie her shoe.

"Sure glad to see you at punk synchro yesterday," Kelly said.

He grunted again. She was making fun of him. And not.

"I'm just curious about one thing, though. What made you come out?"

He sniffed and swallowed. "Probation officer says I g-g-otta do more extra-cur extra-curriculars." A stammer. He had a stammer.

"You're kidding."

"What are you on parole for, if you don't mind my asking?" This was Glynnis.

"Nnnnot telling."

Carol tied her other shoe.

"Oh, come on. Please?"

"M-M-Man of mystery, aren't I?"

"Petty larceny?" Glynnis asked.

"Grand larceny?"

"B and E?"

"Simple possession?"

"Indecent exposure?"

"Manslaughter?"

"Not saying."

"Assault?"

"Give over," he said. That was it, they had found it, Carol thought. Assault. He'd beat up the fuckers who gave him shit over the stammer.

"Come on, Grunt, I'm dying here," said Kelly.

"Not saying." Grin in his words again. He shut his locker and loped off. His boots passed within grabbing distance. She could have reached out and locked on like a little kid playing British bulldog tackling his teenage cousin.

"You're bad," Glynnis said to Kelly. "Oh, hey, Crull. What are you doing?"

"My, uh, shoelaces keep coming undone."

"Oh. See ya."

"Come to Alison's party," Kelly said to Glynnis. "You must come, it's mandatory."

Why did Glynnis fall for these people?

EVERY DAY BETWEEN third and fourth periods, she had the opportunity to do what Kelly had done, just walk up and talk to him. Except she was with Lisa and Lisa was almost always blah-blah-blahing and it would be really weird — though satisfying, come to think of it — to just wander off and leave her talking, but she'd have to explain herself afterwards and Lisa wouldn't get it and would ridicule her and Lisa was all she had.

Twice she engineered a way to free herself of Lisa (bathroom, forgotten eraser) and still she couldn't do it. She could not go up and talk to him. She could make her feet take the right path along the hall to pass close to him, but after that, everything went wrong. She couldn't lift her eyes in time. She couldn't make her vocal cords work. Or she could, but too late. "Hi," she said to a baffled preppy girl as his shoulder passed her own.

"Hi, Carol," said the girl, Jenny Bird, from French.

Fuck.

There was always the food court. But she couldn't do it then, either. Today she couldn't even sit her usual three tables away. She stood in the middle of the food court like a dumb bunny, hating the oblivious postman in her seat, not knowing what to do until a woman in a red coat said, "Excuse me," and pushed past her. She turned and fled the food court, down the corridor and up the ramp into the mall.

Chicken, chicken, chicken, chicken, went her brain in synch with her footsteps. She got madder and madder at herself. She had to be able to talk to him about something. She had to be able to run into him naturally.

She went to Sam the Record Man and straight up to the guy at the cash. "It's my brother's birthday and he really likes punk. What should I get him?"

"What does he have?"

"Nothing."

"He really likes punk but he doesn't have any?"

"He's twelve." Man, she loved lying.

"Sex Pistols. Definitely," said another guy in the store.

"No way, man, Ramones."

"Pistols."

"Nuh-uh. Definitely Ramones."

"The Clash," yelled a guy from the back room.

Carol checked her wallet. She only had money for one. The first guy went and got a Ramones album. "Ramones," he said.

She bought it.

She didn't want to go back to school. Sixth period was French and she couldn't stand the thought of seeing Jenny Bird and having to pretend she'd meant to say hi to her. She walked home.

At Sheldrake and Mount Pleasant, there was a dead sparrow on the sidewalk and Carol realized her list of dead things was suffering for winter. That made her think once again of the lady in Alexander Muir Park, covered by snow for more than a month before being found. It did not freak her out in the same way it had before she found Miss Balls. Then it had terrified her, the thought of finding a dead body. Now it just made her feel cold. She rolled the sparrow over with her toe, wondering if it had frozen to death or what.

Her mother, she knew, was out. She liked the house quiet. She liked breaking the quiet with her new album. She turned the volume up to four, louder than she normally played it. The music made her want to jump. She turned it up to six. The drums resonated in her chest. She jumped. The record skipped. She bobbed her head instead and retrieved the bottle from the tube inside her desk and went to the bathroom. Two hours it had to stay in. She listened to the album three times.

Gabba gabba WE accept you WE accept you one of us, a song went, not the song, exactly, a sort of chant at the beginning of the song before the guitars started. She lifted up the needle and played it again.

Gabba gabba WE accept you WE accept you one of us.

She had heard right. A secret message.

It was one of the best afternoons she'd ever spent. Why didn't she do this more often? She listened to music and lay on her bed reading old Archie and Veronica comics, waiting for the dye to take, waiting for her life to change.

Carol was just packing up her bathing suit and towel and almost out the door when she heard the car door slam. Shit. Fuck. Shit. She

had to get out the door. She had to. Maybe if she went out the basement door while her mother came in the front door ... or vice versa.
She waited at the front door for a second to hear where the footsteps
were going. Up the walk. Front door. She tore down the stairs and
raced to the door. Perfect timing. Front door opened, basement door
opened. Then both shut together. Give her mother thirty seconds to
take off coat and boots and go to kitchen, then boldly out the driveway. Don't look back. The Ramones pounded in her chest. *I don't
want to be a pinhead no more.* At the end of the driveway, she couldn't
help herself, she ran. She almost laughed aloud. Her black hair
whipped across her face.

Rowena

ROWENA TURNED from draining the carrots and saw Death.

Turned, natural as can be, humming even, that contented, turned not even to look at the girls coming in but just as part of her task and there over her shoulder in the kitchen doorway was a walking corpse with clear plastic glasses.

Carol. Her daughter.

She let the pot of carrots drop heavily on the counter. The girl was determined to ruin herself. "What have you done?"

"What does it look like?"

"Oh, Carol," Rowena said slowly, continuing the sentence in her head. You stupid, stupid girl. Beyond that, Rowena could not muster words. Something took her over. Cold fury.

She moved the carrot pot so it would not burn the counter and left the room. The girls followed her with their eyes.

"Uh-oh," she heard Glynnis say.

Bedroom. Den. Rec room. No place in the house was the right place to be. Out was the right place to be. She got her coat and tam and scarf from the front hall closet. Just as she was reaching for the door handle, the door opened and Glenn was stepping through, yodelling his three hellos, though he stopped in the middle of the second one and pitched it lower, to her, warmly. Her former feeling, the amazing catch in her chest like the strike of a fish at the fact of his coming through the door, was barely a tug of the lure through a weed.

"Hello," she said briskly. "I am going. For a walk."

"All right." Humouring.

"I do not know how long I will be."

Now he clipped his words, too. "We'll expect you when we see you." You've no reason to be mad at me, the undertone said.

Oh, yes, I do, she answered mentally, stepping out the door and down the walk, although she didn't. A cold wetness rose from the snow, freshening the air. She drew it in through her nose as she marched through the night. Beneath her feet the hardening slush flattened.

Why did they make her so mad?

What was wrong with her?

She doubted, again, her suitedness to the ministry. She was too sharp-tempered. She was not wise enough. She was not wise at all. Compared to Milt she was about two years old. *Could* she be ordained with this fury in her? The date was three months off.

The fact she was asking the question meant she thought the answer was no, she could not. Should not.

She stopped at this thought. Felt the light, cold wind on her face, looked up to the streetlight shining against the black of the tree branches, the purple-grey of the clouded sky. Inside her was a great, silent roar. For a while she walked with no articulate thought, just her whole body clenching.

Eventually, to the rhythm of her footsteps her mind went *What are you do*ing, Carol? *What* are you *do*ing? Then it was just footsteps, left right, left right, just being out in the night, cold air on her nose, cheek, stockinged legs. And then again, What are you doing? Left right, left right, lef — Have you any idea how hideous you look?

Left right left right. A glance, only, had shown the patches of dye on Carol's scalp. On the hairline, small black globules. Carol had not only dyed her hair, she'd done a bad job, like a mentally retarded child had found the hair dye. *That* you could merely shake your head at. *That* child didn't know any better. But Carol. Carol.

Three short months. She must talk to Milt. She must contain herself or, or, bust herself open, immolate herself and be reborn, who knew what she had to do. Something. Something.

Carol was trying to turn into one of those grim creatures one saw on the subway, white makeup, black eyes and fright wigs, the pink of their tongues shocking against the black lipstick, the white face. One had stuck that pink tongue out at Rowena and waggled it. *I can make you turn away,* said the tongue. Rowena had stared right back.

Carol might put on the clothes, but she could never *be* what they were. It was not just stupid to try, it was suicide. Oh, God, please God, let Carol not be suicidal. So mopey and sulky and unknowable and *stupid*, that look, that dye job — no one could take it seriously, it was embarrassing.

The children that Thanksgiving all boo-hooing round the table, convinced Carol would die young. Oh, how they had laughed later, she and Glenn, laughed until they cried. But that's what she'd been afraid of even then. That Carol *would* die young. Not of heart failure. Of her own hand.

Dear God, she prayed, pausing for a moment as if establishing a connection, as she did when praying with real intent. When she felt the connection — really her own commitment to fully be with God as she prayed — she went on. Help me to help my children. Help me to help myself. Help me to understand and forgive others, help me to understand and forgive myself for jumping to conclusions, for sitting in judgement on my fellow man, for riding a wave of arrogance before you …

She would humble herself and go home. But not just yet.

Instead, she walked a giant square that took her at last to the Rosedale Golf Club. Slowing by the gates, she thought of her father, who had liked to dine here, always just one side or the other of tipsy, and his father, who had mapped out some of these streets and lost a bundle and then made it back. What a mess families were. Why had she thought hers would be any exception?

She walked farther east, looked through the trees at the light grey of the snow-covered dips and rises of the course, heard laughter spill through the air toward her. Nighttime laughter on a winter's night. There. On skis, three of them, racing and shouting, three young girls. They could be Glynnis' friends.

Her walk had warmed her enough to stand a good long time, long after the teens had passed from sight and hearing. She wished she had skis to kick and poles to pole until she was worn right out. How long it had been since she and Glenn had been truant on a weekday, put their skis on the car, driven out of the city and stopped at the first promising woods. They'd once done it regularly.

If she wanted, she could march over the hills right now, down to the creeky Don, follow it under the Bayview bridge, all the way to Glendon, then up the hill, and back up the streets to her house. It called her. Adventure. She stepped off street, into snow. She had not taken twenty steps when she thought, *Who am I trying to kid?* Clods of snow fell into her wet Wallabees. She buttoned her coat again, trod back up Riverview past the palatial estates that you'd never know were there if you drove along Mount Pleasant, toward her own home, with its difficult tenants. She *could* go home now, her body allowed it. The fury had shrunk. It was a pea deep in her belly. She had only to tense to keep it down.

Glenn had his feet up in the den. He folded the paper and waited.

"I get so mad," she said.

"Did you work off some steam?"

"Yes. I think so. I don't know what it is."

"She looks like a sick crow."

"It's more than that."

He did not seem too concerned. The pea bulged. Tense. There.

"She wants to shock us," he said, flapping open the paper again.

"Well, she's doing a good job."

"Not really. She can make us mad. She can't shock us. Not truly. If she didn't look like such a cheap vamp, I'd laugh."

"I don't find it funny at all."

"Well," he said, shrugging, and lifting the paper. So be it, said the shrug.

"OH, LOOK, it's the grim reaper," Glenn said in the morning when Carol slunk into the kitchen. "Morning, Grim," he said brightly.

Carol said nothing. Rowena said nothing. Carol poured a glass of juice, watered it down as usual, drank it, then poured a cup of coffee, added milk and sugar, stirred, left the dirty spoon on the counter and slunk out again.

"Thanks for brightening our morning," called Glenn.

Rowena decided to work downtown.

On the subway she tried to break the problem down. Two moods, irritable or furious. When furious, it was a fury that made her wonder if she had the temperament after all to be a minister, despite the Discernment Committee's assessment that she did, despite her list of the call of gifts. What was the cause of her fury? Well, cause she couldn't say with certainty, but its trigger was family. If her fury at her family kept her from being ordained, the result was a greater fury. So she refused to consider not being ordained, but remained furious and therefore, possibly, unfit. Round and round.

As she got off the subway, as she took the stairs two at a time, as she swept along with the other pedestrians, breaking from them round the corner, up the steps and into the church, her fury seemed to vanish. The church smelled so *churchy*. She drew air in like it was blessing her lungs and took the inside stairs two at a time. Light fell through the tall windows in pleasing angles. Milt was at his desk, on the phone, waving at her as she passed. She waved back, having a hard time recollecting now feeling anything but this hopeful vigour.

She studied the text for her sermon — John 1: 1-18. *In the beginning was the Word.* She read it out loud — *and the Word was with God and the Word was God* — letting the words bob up in the air from her mouth and then fall, settling all around her like the peaceful snow of God. The fury was a passing phase, not an obstacle. Not if it dissipated like this, not if the pea was — it was, wasn't it? — gone. Or was that it, there, sunk low, low, low?

Glynnis

THE MACÐONALDS' parties were legendary for the usual reasons parties were legendary — the amount of booze consumed, the amount of noise produced, the number of times the cops came — but the MacDonalds' parties went one further. They were the kind of parties at which people broke their backs diving off the garage into the neighbour's pool or put their fists through windows upon learning their best friend had died crashing into a tree at Georgian Peaks or aspirated on their own vomit.

Glynnis had been at the aspirating vomit one back when she was at Glenview and Jeff was the host. This was right after Dr. MacDonald had decamped and while Mrs. MacDonald was still at Homewood in residential treatment. Jeff was ostensibly looking after Alison and Sandy, which meant that every once in a while he drove them to the grocery store for more Kraft Dinner, cereal and milk. Sandy couldn't believe he was going to have a party while their mother was in detox. "Hey, we gotta get rid of the booze in the house somehow, right?" he'd said. Alison thought this was funny. Sandy wanted to pour it all down the drain. Instead, they put the plug in the tub and filled it with ice and the four flats of Carlsberg that were in the furnace room. The dining room table they covered with three-quarters-empty bottles they'd pulled out of an amazing number of nooks and crannies. Sandy's eyes filled up with tears. She took Glynnis to her room, vowing not to come out until everyone had gone. Glynnis didn't even have a chance to snag the Carlsberg she'd been counting on, which would have been her first whole beer. They played Labyrinthspel, a Swedish balancing maze game, and listened to the *Hair* soundtrack on Alison's record player to block out the noise until they heard the sirens and Alison burst into the room going, "Shit, shit, pretend we're asleep." But it was an ambulance, not the cops, they saw, watching out the window. Jeff's girlfriend had actually scooped vomit out of the mouth of Laura Primeau and called 911. She was kicking everyone out and later, when they'd left, she was breaking up with Jeff. "You are such a fucking idiot, I can't believe you," they heard her shout at him against the clink of beer bottles being cleaned up. But she was there in the morning and made them pancakes and sausages.

Now Sandy was at school in Switzerland, Alison was the party's host and Glynnis had been invited by a relative stranger, Kelly, who, apparently, had not bothered to come herself. Not that Glynnis had taken her literally. "You must come, it's mandatory" was a line — its point was effect, not content. But they'd been setting up punk synchro together, they'd been planning their routines, refining their personae, they'd been busting their guts over the swirlina. Glynnis would've sworn she was safe in interpreting "You must come, it's mandatory," to mean a loose "It'd be nice to see you there," or a "You're all right. If you come I promise not to ignore you."

At any rate, Glynnis had come.

First she'd had to go to a doughnut shop. Glynnis' mother had a notion that one didn't leave the house past nine o'clock. No matter if you returned at precisely the same time you would have had you left at eight, nine o'clock was too late to go out.

So Glynnis had bundled up at eight and trudged over to Yonge Street. Her foot functioned as a crude thermometer. If it went numb in less than a block, it was exceptionally cold. Tonight it went numb after four houses. She huddled herself down into her scarf, tasting wet wool and cedar through it. A light new snow dusted the side streets. Main streets were a dry, salt white. It was impossible not to wonder how anyone survived this climate before cities and central heating, impossible not to marvel that there was a city here at all, that cities were built this far north. And farther north. Ottawa. Moscow. Winnipeg. Edmonton. Yellowknife.

But cities made you value the wrong things, for of course if you did think of this place cityless, you recognized how livable it was. Snowshoes. Fur. Deerskin. Moccasins. Small dwellings.

She warmed inside her coat, inside her hat. Her foot stayed numb.

The doughnut shop was grey and depressing, a holding tank for losers before they died of cancer — old woman with huge drop of snot looming over her *Toronto Sun*, two paunchy men, arms across their bellies, mute. At the counter, a woman with badly home-frosted hair told the waitress how many times she'd been to the chiropractor since her accident and how much it cost and how the insurance was saying they weren't going to pay for any of it.

Glynnis read *Macbeth* and ate crullers, chilled and jittery about the party. What if someone came in here on the way there and saw her, intuiting immediately — as they would indubitably do — that she was killing time until it was okay to show up, that she had had to deceive her idiot mother and play sneaky-sneak games like a twelve-year-old? She would die of embarrassment. She would stay here all night and then walk home. "How's the party?" Carol would say, and Glynnis would say, "Great," because although she could talk to Carol about most things, she could not admit even to Carol that she was as much of a loser as she was.

An hour later, with Macbeth dead and Malcolm about to be crowned, she tugged down her hat, rewrapped her scarf over nose and mouth, buttoned her coat and stepped out into the cold.

By Mount Pleasant she began to warm again and on the other side, as the sound of the busy street receded, she slowed, listening. The squeak of the snow underfoot leapt up at the streetlights like white line-drawing animation overtop live-action film. It was the kind of frozen night when the air is so clear and crisp it feels like if you could tap it with a steel hammer it would ring and ring and ring.

She looked up at the stars through the bare branches of maples. The strip of sky seemed black and far away and vast and reaching almost right down to her but stopped by the human layer, the trees, the streetlamps, the houses with smoke coming out their chimneys, the bright snow on the ground. Lady Macbeth seemed as impossible when you stood here as northern cities had seemed earlier. She could not exist. In a November-cold castle in Britain, okay, sure. Here? No. This was an odd thought, that a fictitious character did not seem able to exist simultaneously in two climates — it was not as if she *could* exist in a November-cold castle in England *while* Glynnis stood in below-zero weather in Toronto, but rather that in Toronto in this weather she could not exist, period. Her truth depended on where you were.

Glynnis walked on, enjoying her solitude now, not nervous anymore about the party. She stopped again half a house shy of the MacDonalds', just at the point when she became aware — or would have done had she not already known — there was a party. Something about approaching a house where a party was going on on a winter night demanded stopping. Outside, from a distance, all the houses seemed alike. Then, as you drew closer, you became aware that one house was more alive than any of the others. There was more movement inside. Lights seemed to burn more brightly. Noise spilled out in a bright, appealing tinkle, and all that was possible at a party twinkled inside, was held within the house as within the covers of a book or within some kind of reverse Pandora's box. Glynnis had not been to many parties and had not really enjoyed the ones she had been to, but that feeling of potentiality remained, and though she had the urge to maintain her solitude and walk on into the quiet night, so she feared not to know what she might have had had she gone in.

As she walked up the driveway, the noise rose like an orchestra warming up before a concert, discordant, individual. She stopped again to listen.

A car — no, a van — turned onto the street, slowing to a stop as it neared her, and this, the anticipation of people getting out and seeing her standing there like some weird, nervous loser, propelled her partyward. Up to the side door. Open it. Full in the face — steamy warmth, light, full blast of noise after the quiet cold of outside, three times louder than you expected. Yes, houses do insulate.

She walked up the steps into the kitchen. "Riggsie!" The kitchen was crowded, smoky, warmly lit. "Spike!" Her punk synchro name. Alison had a greeting as warm as the light. "The Spike Who Came in From the Cold! We're having glühwein. Want some glühwein?" She snapped her fingers at a tall, lank-haired guy wielding a ladle at the stove. This was Beatty, a titular attendee of their high school, but one rarely in attendance since he was on the national ski team and spent most of the year in Europe. He had the highest cheekbones Glynnis had ever seen on a man. At the stove he looked ordinary and domestic and knowable, and the promise Glynnis had sensed while standing outside the house seemed on the brink of breaking open. They were in a warm house on a cold night drinking hot white wine from plastic thermal mugs like jovial and innocent European Alpine youth of ... one generation ago? two? Whichever generation hadn't known war or Nazism. Yet. She'd been invited by someone who'd said, "You must come, it's mandatory."

And then the next person entered and Alison ran through the same routine again — "Brody! You made it!" — only this time, instead of turning their heads briefly from their conversations and then back again, the boys high-fived the newcomer and the girls began to flirt and Glynnis noticed for the first time that they all wore turtlenecks and ski sweaters, they all had straight teeth. She was in a kitchen full of skiers. *Back away slowly*, she thought, and wondered if Kelly would laugh at that or not.

Where was Kelly? Glynnis took her plastic thermal mug of glühwein — hot white wine, what a weird concept — and went downstairs to dump her coat. Kelly wasn't in the downstairs hall, wasn't in the rec room, wasn't in the furnace room where Novak was playing caps with a skinny yearbook photographer, two stoners and a beefy girl from the volleyball team. "Riggsie. Fuckin A," she said.

"Fuckin fuck."

Novak threw her cap and missed. "Fuckin *fuck*." She took a swig of the beer between her legs.

"Fuckin A," said one of the stoners.

"Fuckin A," said the beefy girl, flicking her cap, nailing the target.

"Fuckin fuck," said Novak.

"Seen Kelly?"

"Point."

Glynnis had not said 'fuck.' "Why the fuck are we playing this fuckin game?"

"Fuck if I know."

"Can we fuckin stop yet?"

"Fuck, no."

"You guys say fuck a lot," said the beefy girl drunkenly.

"That's really fuckin observant," said Novak.

"Fuckin A," said the other stoner.

KELLY WAS NOT in the dining room, not in the living room, not in the upstairs hall, not on the stairs, not in the lineup for the bathroom. *It's mandatory, you must come. I, of course, can come or not, depending on my whims.*

Feeling a little like Scrooge accompanying the ghost of Christmas present, Glynnis continued to meander through the house. She found herself writing letters to Sandy in her head.

Dear Sandy. I'm in your basement. Two semi-wasted guys with perms (guys with perms: survey says?) are trying to play ping-pong. It's not that they're so bad, just that people keep bumping into them, putting their drinks on the table. Oh, oh, wait, these guys are actually funny, they're playing Film Speeds Ping-Pong. Slo mo. Fast forward. Now they're trying to figure out reverse. Ah. Make a lot of sucking noises while drawing the paddle back before a shot. Okay, maybe I can forgive them the perms.

Remember when we played with racing helmets instead of paddles? Those were the days, eh?

They seemed like the days now. They hadn't so much at the time.

What is it, something in the air? Or the natural outcome of parties in rec rooms? It's like Games Night down here. There's the ping-pong. A game of caps in the furnace room. Guys playing table hockey. And this group of semi-dressed-up people — two girls in, like, skirts, and two guys in suits from the Sally Ann — very intently playing hands down as a drinking game.

Over at The Bar-n (this was what they called the barn-wood-covered bar Mrs. MacDonald had had installed in the basement before she stopped drinking), *the guy who always wears the Hawaiian shirt and the porkpie hat is playing bartender. Seriously, it's like he's ten, and he's just found the coolest toy — a real bar. He's pouring drinks, he's handing out beers from the fridge, opening them with a flick of the wrist. I think he's even trying to get people to tell him their troubles. He should get Steve Keddis down here. There's some big drama going on with him and Laurie Frye. Last time I was upstairs there was this, like, pack of sympathetic girls around him, sending emissaries to Laurie, who was sucking back the Canada Coolers and coming onto a guy apparently in love with his own chest (his shirt's open to his navel and he keeps checking it out while he's dancing). Apparently Steve made out with three different girls at some*

Jarvis party last week when Laurie was away and she found out and dumped him. There's another group of girls trying to keep Laurie from drinking too much and doing something stupid with Mr. I-Love-My-Chest. Mike Fisk is taking actual bets on whether they get back together tonight or not.

Dear Sandy. I'm upstairs now. Laurie is crying in the dining room with her coterie around her and Steve is I don't know where, out for a toke maybe. Somebody's saying, "Should I go get Steve? Do you want me to get Steve?" and she's wailing, "No. I don't ever want to see him again in my life." It's not looking good for the reunion backers.

Alison's serving Glue-vine (sp?). Of this I have never heard. I get the impression it's Scandinavian, but how can that be? It's not like you hear a lot about Scandinavian wines. Do they even grow grapes in Scandinavia? Is Glue-vine made from grapes? Or is it made from pine sap and apples as the taste would lead you to believe?

I wonder what you would make of this. I recognize a lot of people but don't really know anybody. It's weird walking around your house when all these strangers are here and you're not. The ski people make me nervous. They're too good-looking. Too square. Not my dad's 'I know you think your old Dad's a square' square, I mean square — their teeth are square (or, okay, rectangular, but close enough), their shoulders, their faces, their jaws, their hands, their brows. You ever notice that? Everything except their noses, which are pert. Plus, they only associate with other good-looking people. Beatty seems different, though. Maybe it's his nose. His unpert nose. His pugilistic-looking nose that was pert once, now no more.

If you were here, what would we be doing? Maybe we would be at my house, avoiding the whole thing. Maybe we would be playing hands down as a drinking game. Kelly Eberhardt was supposed to be here. Ike. (I told you about punk synchro, right?) She's all, "You must come, it's mandatory." And so I come and where is she? Pas ici.

You know what's really weird? That we're the same age now as all those people at Jeff's parties. Oo. Freaky, man. They were, like, grownups, as far as I was concerned. They seemed so big and important. Maybe it was all the moustaches and mascara. Now it's Blues Brothers suits and, I don't know, Danskins.

There's this guy here, looks sort of like a teddy bear, going around asking people to sleep with him because it's his eighteenth birthday — that's his line, "My eighteenth birthday today. I'm legal. Can't drink" — and here he hides his beer inside his jean jacket — "but I can vote. People want to sleep with voters, I've heard. How 'bout you? You want to sleep with a voter?" And I think, "Eighteen! That used to seem so old." And now it's only sort of oldish.

Eventually it occurred to Glynnis that the sensible thing to do, the thing she would really enjoy, would be to go to Sandy's room, find some paper and actually write the letter. *Dear Sandy,* she wrote in her head, threading her way up the stairs between seated figures. *I've been writing you a letter in my head for the last hour and I finally decided I should write you a real one. Where am I? In your room, where else?* Not yet, actually. She was squeezing past the people in the bathroom lineup. *Yes, your room. Alison's having a party. Your mother's still in Europe, I think. Wherever she was going after visiting you. And Alison's having a party. Is it as wild as Jeff's and Rob's and Mary's? I don't know. Hard to say. My perspective has changed. Cops haven't come yet. No one's had a near-death experience yet.*

Now she was down the hall outside Sandy's closed door. All the bedroom doors were closed. She glanced around, not wanting people to see her going into a bedroom and thinking they could, too (she was different, she was family), and ducked in when the coast was clear.

Her first impression was of peace. The noise was shut behind her almost as it had been shut inside the house when she'd stood in the driveway.

And then a rustling from the bed made her stomach leap. Somebody was in here. Making out. Ack. *Get out, get out,* the stomach told Glynnis, while her brain stem said *Sorry* to the making-out people. *Sorry, sorry.* The handle of the door she'd opened and shut so smoothly seconds before eluded her for several uncomfortable moments. Then she found it. Turned. Opened. An arc of hall light swept across the bed. She stepped out and closed the door behind her.

Wait a minute.

'Sorry'? Who was making out in Sandy's bedroom? In Sandy's bed? They should be the sorry ones. She contemplated going back in, opening the door and exposing them, whoever they were. But her mind reran the image of the triangle of hall light. The back of the head, blocking her view of the other person. She knew that head. It belonged to Alison.

Okay, Alison. Not some gross stranger. Alison. Okay. Her heart was beating more quickly than she liked. She told herself to get a grip.

Just then the door to the master bedroom opened and Novak came out. She made a wincing face. "There's hanky-panky going on in there."

"I know, I know. In there, too." Glynnis inclined her head toward Sandy's room. She leaned forward and said behind her hand, "Alison."

"What?" said Novak, apparently astounded.

"I'm pretty sure."

"And who?"

"Didn't see. Just the back of Alison's head."

"Hah," said Novak in a funny sort of way, as if she were a spy and Glynnis had just inadvertently given her good information. They both stared at the door for a while until Glynnis shifted. "Let's stand here and watch," Novak said.

"Nah." Glynnis couldn't imagine meeting Alison's eyes.

"They've got to come out sometime, right?" said Novak.

"What if they don't?"

"They've got to. They will," she said with certainty.

"Are you seriously going to stand here and wait?"

"I'm seriously going to stand here and wait."

"That's a little weird."

"I don't mind being weird."

Glynnis went down the hall. Maybe she would just go home. She didn't feel like finding someone to talk to, and the party was at that point where people were getting seriously drunk. She herself was only a little tipsy. She'd had two glasses of glühwein.

As she passed the bathroom door, out spilled the guy whose eighteenth birthday it was. "Change your mind yet?" he asked her.

"Give it up, Mike," she said.

"Okay," he said, following her down the stairs. He used her shoulders to steady himself.

"All right, Mikey," said a guy on the stairs as they passed. Other people around the guy clapped.

"Please," said Mike. "I've matured. Eighteen and —" he counted on his fingers, "half a day. I'm a changed man. My intentions are honourable. Fathers, your daughters are safe with me."

"Okay, you can let go now," Glynnis said at the bottom of the stairs. "Here. Lean on the newel post."

"The what?"

"The newel post. This thing."

"Is that what it's called? Wow. How do you know that?"

"It came to me in a dream. What do you mean how do I know that? You just know things."

"Or, in my case, you don't." Mike looked genuinely sad about this. He clasped the newel post, leaning his face against it, and gazed at Glynnis. His cornflower blue eyes were ringed with a starburst of black lashes. "You're funny." He blinked. "You want to have a meaningful relationship with me? I'm okay with the limp." Glynnis was blindsided. He meant it nicely, but fuck, you just never expect these things.

Alison appeared on the stairs. Behind her was Brody, the guy who'd come in after Glynnis. Behind Brody was Novak. The light in the hall was dim, but it was obvious that Alison was sway-on-your-feet drunk.

"Fuck off," Glynnis said lightly to Mike.

"Wo," Alison said, teetering to her left and almost sitting on someone. Both Brody's and Novak's hands shot out to catch her.

Suddenly Glynnis knew what was going on and somehow the three of them appeared in sharper outline despite the dim light. Novak's eyes were bright. Brody's were clear, his step peppy. Alison's eyes were the dull bulbs of the intoxicated. A terrible drama was unfolding. A terrible, terribly private drama. Only Alison and Novak knew, and Alison had taken herself out of the equation with drink.

Alison had been making out with Brody not just because. She had been making out with Brody to prove she was not gay.

But she was. She had been. With Novak. Glynnis knew this with the certainty of the right answer.

And it came to her more slowly but just as certainly that she herself was like them. With that, something came alive in her stomach. Not butterflies. Dragonflies, maybe. Small birds. Small, tense hopping birds. Singing.

"Poll," Mike said to Alison, who ignored him, so he redirected his question to Brody. "What's this called?" He pointed to the newel post.

"I don't know. A stair post?"

"Poll," he said to Novak, who stopped, watching Brody and Alison move on toward the kitchen. "What's this called?"

"The newel post?"

"Damn. How do you know that?"

Novak's eyes flicked at Glynnis. Her mouth smiled though nothing else did. "I'm a fuckin genius." She followed Alison and Brody into the kitchen. Glynnis couldn't help herself, she followed too.

"Out of our way," Alison said, waving her arms. "We are fetching

333

the marshmallows. We're on a quest for marshmallows. We're going to find the marshmallows. We're going to light a fire. We're going to roast them and we're going to eat them. Aren't we, Brody?"

"Yes. We are."

Acting as if she had no agenda other than getting herself a beer, Novak went to the fridge.

Glynnis made for the glühwein. Beatty sat on a stool next to it. "Man, she's wasted," he said to Glynnis.

"You can say that again."

"Man, she's wasted."

"That joke never gets old, does it?" Glynnis said.

"Never."

"Is there any more glühwein?"

Beatty shook his head.

"Just as well."

Alison and Brody had found the marshmallows. They were now leading a group of people downstairs to light a fire in the rec room fireplace. Novak meandered over to Glynnis and Beatty as if she hadn't noticed and didn't care.

"What is glühwein?" asked Glynnis.

"Mulled wine," said Beatty. "Ancient family recipe."

"Scandinavian? It tastes Scandinavian."

"Cherman. I always wanted to be Scandinavian but ve ah Cherman."

"You look Scandinavian."

He shook his head. "Not blond enough."

"Those cheekbones, though." She was flirting with Beatty. How easy it was.

"Slavic," Beatty and Novak said at the same time.

"I wanted be Scandinavian so I could ski everywhere," Beatty said.

"I used to want to skate everywhere. Like Hans Brinker." When I could still skate, Glynnis thought.

"Yeah. With your, like, hands clasped behind your back, just sort of …" Here he made a leisurely skating motion.

"Exactly. Does it ever occur to you that somebody invented skates?"

"I know, I know. Skis." He shook his head.

She was charming him, she could tell. He was lovely. She imagined being married to him, the lovely world-class ski racer. They would entertain and watch everybody else and make wry comments.

"My father skied out of Czechoslovakia during the war," said Novak. "He still has the skis."

"Really?" Beatty turned to Novak with interest. The same interest. Okay, she wasn't charming him. Not particularly.

"He'll tell you about it within half an hour of meeting you."

"Must be a great story."

"It's very *Sound of Music*. Except the part where his entire family gets sent to concentration camps."

"I didn't know you were Jewish," Glynnis said, wishing she could clamp her hand over her mouth and take it back. Why would that even be worth commenting on? Glynnis wondered if this was the whole of life, moments of pleasure interspersed with a crawling sensation in one's innards.

"It wasn't only Jews that got sent to the camps." In her ignorance, Glynnis felt culpable.

A pert-nosed girl interrupted them, grabbing Beatty's hand and saying he owed her a dance. "You've been hiding in here all night."

Glynnis watched him good-naturedly let himself be pulled and thought of the girl's happiness and expectancy — he would marry someone like that — and of Novak and Alison's whatever-it-was.

Novak saw the look on her face. "You have a crush on him, don't you?"

"What? No."

"Yes you do."

"Shut up, I do not."

"You do, you do. Riggsie loves Beatty, Riggsie loves Beatty."

"Fuck off." She said it because she could, because their game allowed it.

Suddenly, Novak turned aggressive. "What's your problem with me, Riggsie?"

"What?"

"What's your problem with me?"

"What are you on about?"

"You have a problem with me."

"No, I don't."

"Yes, you do."

"No, I don't. What's your problem with me?"

"I don't have a problem with you."

"Yes, you do."

"Okay, my problem with you is you have a problem with me."

"Oh, for Christ's sake." Glynnis wanted to say she *knew*, she sympathized, Novak did not have to suffer alone. Also: Novak was completely gorgeous — that was Glynnis' problem with her at the moment. She had always considered Novak good-looking, but now she was struck dumb by her beauty, making it difficult to remember that she did in fact have a problem with Novak, she'd had a problem with her since grade seven.

Sirens sounded.

"Fuck," they said together.

⌐

AFTER THE COPS LEFT, Glynnis and Novak put Alison and Brody to bed, Brody in a separate room, and consigned Mike to the care of his less-drunk buddies and Laurie to the care of her less-drunk girl-friends. They found Steve Keddis passed out in the backyard, not yet hypothermic but getting there, kicked out just about everybody else and cleaned up chip bowls and ashtrays. There were about six of them left — Beatty, Glynnis, Novak, the guy in the Hawaiian shirt and a handful of others. They lay around the fire in the basement. Hawaiian Shirt quietly played guitar. They'd passed the tired stage and now were wide awake and bonded, unwilling to part. It was two-thirty in the morning. Glynnis was supposed to have been home by twelve.

Finally Glynnis roused herself and said she had to go.

Novak accompanied her to the furnace room and as Glynnis bundled up, said, "So what *is* your problem with me?"

And Glynnis paused a minute, then did up her coat and pulled on her hat. "Glenview. Grade seven. You're in grade eight. You're in the library. Alison's in the library. I'm in the library, only you don't know this. Alison's parents have just split up and she and Sandy have spent the Thanksgiving weekend at the cottage with my family. You ask something like What'd you do on the weekend? and she says she was at our cottage and you, you call my sister and me Wimpy and Gimpy. You say, 'How do you know Wimpy and Gimpy?'"

"Oh, yeah. I remember that."

"Well. There you go."

"Not that particular incident, but Wimpy and Gimpy, I remember that."

"There you go," Glynnis repeated, folded her scarf over her face and knotted it behind her head. Novak was tying her boots.

"Sorry."

"Yeah."

Glynnis headed out.

"Good night. Thanks for —" Novak suddenly looked uncomfortable, as though she'd just realized that thanking Glynnis for anything was like thanking her on behalf of Alison, which would reveal that she had a special tie with Alison, which she was afraid to reveal. She shrugged. "— everything."

"Yeah."

Out in the cold, her shoes loud in the frozen street, Glynnis trotted along with her hands in her mitts inside her pockets, marvelling at all the people sleeping, warm, inside the houses, and at the stars and at the coldness of space.

No. Not all sleeping. Carol was watching a movie. "You owe me," she said.

"What."

"I covered for you. Mom hears me and goes, 'Glynnis, is that you?' and I go, 'No, it's me, Glynnis is already asleep,' and she goes, 'Okay,' and goes back to bed. How was the party?" she asked, flipping off the TV.

"Alison got wasted, the cops came, Keddis passed out in a snowbank. You know. The usual." Glynnis wanted to be alone, to keep the time-slowed-down feeling of the last five hours, in which she seemed to have lived years.

"Bedtime story?"

"Aw, I'm really tired."

"Come on. You owe me. Two pages. One page."

Her acquiescence was grudging, but then, as they shared the bathroom, brushing their teeth, peeing, as Carol brought her pillow in and a blanket and settled herself on the floor, as Glynnis opened the thick paperback and began, at three in the morning, to read, an odd joy filled her. She couldn't have said about what.

Carol

SHE WOULD NOT let her eyes drop. She would look right at him. Right at him. And say ... God, "hi" was such a stupid word.

But what else was there to say? They had sculled, their two bodies feet apart in the pool, they had splashed in the water and done gay synchro moves. It still gave her nothing more to say than "hi."

Here he came. Was he looking at her? Impossible to tell. Was he? Didn't matter. Ready?

"Oi," he said. To her.

"Hi," she said back, her head on swivel. His back! His lope! His hair! Rake rake through the air. *Hi* was a brilliant word.

Lisa couldn't believe it. "You know that guy?"

"Yeah."

"You *know* him? How do you know him? *You* know him?"

Carol shrugged.

"Come on. You gotta tell me. You know the fuckin lunatic loser punk guy?"

Carol shrugged again. "He knows my sister."

"Oh. Well. That makes more sense." Three seconds later: "Are you turning punk on me? Is that the thing with the hair? It is, isn't it? You *like* that guy, don't you. Oh my God, I don't even believe it.

You *like* the scummy loser punk guy. You're nuts. You think he's even going to look at you?"

"Shut up. He said hi, didn't he?"

"Nice little, quiet little Carol Riggs?"

"I'm not nice. I'm not little. People've been calling me Killer since I was eight years old."

"It creeps me out to even think about getting close to him."

"Yeah, well, you're not me, are you?"

SHE FOLLOWED HIM to the food court. Walked right up and sat with him. "Hi."

Nod.

"You probably don't remember but one time I came up to you here and I said I liked your hair and you thought I was joking, but I wasn't, I really do like it, I think it's amazing. Is it okay if I sit here?"

He shrugged in a yes kind of way. He kept eating his lunch.

Say something, say something. "So, like, what groups do you like?"

"Groups?" Only the way he talked, it sounded like Erp?

That was the wrong word, groups. Shit. "Do you like the Ramones?"

He made a noise like the beginning of, presumably, a Ramones song. She didn't recognize it.

"I only have one album, but I think it's great." *Great. Great.* Might as well have said *I think it's neat. I think it's groovy.* Fuck.

He didn't say anything for a long time. His knee jiggled. The flee impulse suddenly kicked in. He'd seen through her. Seen that she'd bought a Ramones tape yesterday and that the dye was crap and looked like crap and was not only crap but was bullshit, that here was a girl who until last week would have said Barbra Streisand was her favourite singer. But now she'd put herself there, she didn't know how to extricate herself. *Well, see ya around,* she rehearsed in her head. *Nice running into you.* No.

Later. Too preppy girl.

Sayonara.

Or just get up and leave. *Sorry to have bugged you. Am I bugging you?*

He swallowed his food. "I'm unna start a band," he said. (*Band.* That's the right word.) "Got a name. Scumbuckets." He scooped the last of his chow mein into his mouth. "Need a the?"

"*The* Scumbuckets?" She knew him instinctually, what he'd meant.

"Yeah."

"I like just Scumbuckets better."

"Yeah."

"Where are you from?" she asked.

"London." He paused. "Ontario." He grinned. His teeth were small. You could see his gums. "Year in Manchester, though. Grandparents." His lips were plump in the middle, like worms, and thin at the sides. Worms. Ha.

"You sort of have an accent and sort of don't."

"Yeah. Had to come back."

"You didn't want to?"

"S' dead here."

"Yeah." Carol had only a vague idea what he meant.

"I mean, not completely dead. S' changing."

They walked back to school together. Carol thought she'd die from happiness. He played drums. He'd been in a band before but it didn't work out, they didn't get any gigs. He needed a guitar player. Who could maybe sing.

Click. Her. That was her. "I play guitar," she said.

"Do ya," he said. Nothing more.

They parted at the second floor. "Wool," he said. "See ya."

See ya. Was that just a way to get away? Or did he mean it? Like he *wanted* to see her? Had she blown everything by saying she played guitar? He'd be looking for someone to play electric guitar — Scumbuckets wasn't going to have some girl up there with an acoustic guitar playing, like, Joni Mitchell songs. Duh. Gradually she convinced herself she'd ruined the whole encounter. And then she'd remember his smile and wonder.

Catalyst. That was the word.

THE NEXT DAY he was there again. To make it look more natural, she went and bought herself food, a soup from the deli, and carried it on a tray in his vicinity as if by accident. "Oh, hi," she said. "Okay if I sit with you?" She couldn't believe herself.

He didn't tell her to get lost, not that day, or any of the days after that. She kind of thought he was glad to have someone to talk to. He asked her if she thought he should put up signs for his band or advertise in the neighbourhood paper. Signs, she said, though really she had no idea. Then one day he asked if she'd help him put up signs, so they put them up around the school and on telephone poles in the neighbourhood and at the other high school down the street. WANTED: bass player, guitar player/singer, for punk band, with his number on tear-off strips. She surreptitiously tore off one of the strips for herself and tucked it in her wallet along with the number of the Trull Funeral Home. She played along with the Ramones album. All the songs had, like, three chords and the strumming was all basically down-up-down-up-down-up-down-up. She'd crank the stereo so the acoustic guitar didn't seem to ring so and just go, bopping her head in time. The only trick was keeping up. They were fuckin fast, man.

The end of the following week, he said, "'M having auditions Sunday." He played drums with his chopsticks. "Wanna come?"

Carol thought she'd hyperventilate. "Sure. What time?"

Four. Four o'clock Sunday. Wait a minute. Was he asking her to audition? Should she bring her guitar?

For the next four days, every minute she was alone in the house she practised "Blitzkreig Bop." When she wasn't alone, she sat on her bed and played her own songs. "That sounds wonderful, Carol," her mother said, too enthusiastically. "Are you finished your essay yet?"

NOON SUNDAY, she extricated herself from the post-church discussion of her mother's sermon ostensibly to go work on her essay at the library but really to go kill time until she could unembarrassedly show up at Grunt's house. If anyone asked why she was taking her guitar she'd just say she was, um, meeting Lisa, who wanted to borrow it.

But no one asked. No one noticed. "Don't forget to ask the librarian for the vertical files," her mother called out from the dining room.

The day was cold and pale. Bright, but not aviator-glasses bright. Her regular shaded glasses would do. Her guitar case bounced against her leg as she walked. She wished it did not have flower stickers on it from when she was twelve. She wished she did not have to carry it at all. Carrying her guitar made her self-conscious and was in fact part of the reason she had quit guitar lessons. (The other part was the teacher, a paunchy hairball who would not have been bad if he hadn't kept telling her about things he had at his place that she'd one day come and see.) But better to have the crutch of the guitar than to show up without it and look like she thought Grunt had asked as a friend or even more than a friend and not as just a possible guitar player.

She was too shy to ask the librarian anything, and spent the three hours depressing her callused fingerpads against page corners of books she was not reading.

Then she went into the washroom, put on her rhinestone choker and applied the black lipstick she'd got at a costume store on Friday. She kept worrying someone who knew her would come in, one of her mother's friends, but when no one did, when she stepped back from the mirror and saw a black-haired, black-lipped, black-lashed vision, a rush of excitement took her and she felt like Wonder Woman, spinning out of the library and charging off into the sky. Subway. Even better. Not Wonder Woman, Underground Woman. Lurking in the tunnels, frightening all good citizens of the city.

Of course she was early and had to walk around the block. Her hands in her black wool gloves were numb when she knocked. Her heart threw up a thing, a bubble, into her throat that made her wonder what a heart attack felt like.

"Hi," she squeaked to Grunt's mother, a woman with a dark swoop of hair who gave the impression of a character in a movie with subtitles. (Carol could not read subtitles, the type was too small and disappeared too quickly, but she sometimes watched the movies anyway, trying to guess what the people were saying. If it was late at night, she did it out loud. — Oh, Etienne! How cruelly you treat me. — But Stephanie, my little cabbage. You must stop throwing yourself at me.)

"Is —" But the woman — Grunt's mother? really? — was stepping forward, directing her back down the steps and up the narrow driveway to the garage at the back of the lot. Carol could hear him, a little thuddy-thud like someone was tapping a knife on an empty margarine container, every now and then a tinnier sound like a pie plate.

The woman closed the door, incurious.

Carol found a door on the side of the garage and knocked on it, doubtful he'd hear her, but the drum sounds stopped. He opened the door. "Lo," he said. "Cm in."

Outside it was a rickety garage. Inside it was a sea of grey. Carpet, she now saw. Floor, walls, ceiling, the back of the door, everything. Grey. It felt like she'd stepped into a scene from a futuristic movie, like she'd stepped into a cell, a cocoon. There was a bank of wide shelves along one wall, also carpeted, that held the usual garage-type things — lawn chairs, boxes, golf clubs — and a drum set on the floor.

"Brought your guitar," he said, going to the drum kit.

The world sounded different in here.

"I, yeah, I didn't know if — I wasn't sure if — I thought I —"

He pressed his lips together to say something and then there was a pause during which it didn't get said. It seemed to make him angry that his words were stuck and she could not help feeling he was angry at her.

"Play," he said, finally. He held his drumsticks in his right fist and had his fists on his bouncing thighs, waiting.

"Really?"

He nodded.

She had imagined jumping up before the first note of "Blitzkrieg Bop" and bringing her hand down on the strings as her feet hit the floor (she had been practising this) — she had imagined this impressing the hell out of him — but now that she was here, what her fingers started to play when she closed her eyes (they closed on their own) after she tuned was a song she had written called "Hello There, Death." She heard her own voice like a separate thing, high and sweet and clear. *You might not believe it but we'll all die and so will I, so will I.* A folk singer's voice. All wrong. But there was nothing she could do about it now. *And I say, hello there Death, how do you do, you know I think I've seen you befooore.* Strum-strum strum-strum. Big, ringing chords she'd once loved that now sounded ostentatious. Fingerpicking. *Hello, there, Death, how do you do, don't just stand at the door, stand at the door. Come on in* strum-struck-a-strum-struck-a *(there's some people that I'd like you to meet). Come on in.* A light cymbal began to keep time. She relaxed a little. *(If you like them wouldn't that be sweet.) Come on in —*

She sang the song through, relaxing into it more and more, starting to like her guitar again, feeling the ting-ting-ting-ting of the cymbal like a touch on her spine. Getting that playing-together feeling that was centred in the spine, too, the kind that gave you shivers. Like they were talking to each other except it was a deeper communication than talking. Back to the chorus: *Hello, there, Death, how do you do, don't just stand at the door, stand at the door, Come on in (there's some people that I'd like you to meet), Come on in (All the better if they fall at your feet), Come on in —*

The door, at this moment, opened.

Carol stopped singing. "Wo," she said.

A large figure stood in the light of the door.

"Hi, Death," said Grunt, and despite the smile you could hear in his voice, Carol felt a sense of foreboding, as if it really were Death, there at the door.

"Come on in."

Death ducked his head sheepishly as he moved into the light, and Carol saw his round baby face.

"Hi, Death," Grunt repeated, laughing so hard he had to clutch his sides and bend over his drums. Carol too. She put her arm under her guitar to hold her stomach.

"What?" Babyface kept asking, smiling and blinking.

They waved at him, shook their heads and kept laughing. Another two guys poked their heads through the door.

"What's so funny?" a guy with sticking-up hair and an old man's grey winter coat said. The others shrugged. Grunt and Carol now were trying to wind down, trying to stop, but every time they did, they set each other off again. "Hi, Death," they repeated in breathless voices. "Come on in."

"So what's the deal, here, man?" asked the tightly wound one. Grunt waved his hand in front of his face, wheezing.

"Okay, we get it, something was very very funny, but like are we going to like jam or you want to like hear a solo or what?" He started taking out his electric guitar. "I thought this was going to be a punk band," he said disdainfully, nodding at Carol, or maybe just her guitar. "Or is she your girlfriend or something?"

Carol's face went hot. She took off her guitar and put it in its flowered case.

Grunt's voice came behind her. "Are you my girlfriend?"

What? Was he joking? She flipped shut the snaps. Did he know this guy? He had to be joking, he had to be calling her his girlfriend like he called the other guy Death. Right? Should she say something? What? On her face was, who knows, some bizarre crooked smile. Stand up, turn.

That's it. Smile.

Enigmatically.

And then Grunt was trying to say something again. He made about six attempts, then finally said, "Punk's punk." And then he nodded at Carol, but she couldn't tell if he meant she was punk or she wasn't punk.

"Who does it? That song?"

"You should audition the real people."

"It's b. It's b. It's brilliant." He took his drumsticks in both hands. "One. Two. One two three four." Two bars of eighth notes on the tom-toms, then, "Death." Wham. "Death." Wham. "Death death death death. There's one thing you get when you are born, you know that you're going to die." He was shout-singing it, putting a little turn in die, *die-ie-ie*. "You might not believe it but you'll all die and so will I-ai." Then he stopped. "Who does it?"

"Nobody. I do. Me." Again she blushed. She was packed up now. Wound-up guy was plugging in a little amp he had. The next thing to do was go.

"Well," she said. "Bye."

"Fuggin brilliant," he said again, now lightly tapping out the same rhythm on the drums.

She closed the door behind her, shutting the sound away. From the house came the faint strains of opera. She stepped out into the freezing evening with a sense of relief that the sun had gone down and a sense that what she'd just experienced was not real, was an alternative universe like she'd always sensed right next to them, portals everywhere and only chance to keep them from stepping through at any time. The ravine at Glenview had felt like that. Was it the vagueness of her vision that tended to see things in blocks with entries as dark holes in the trees or bright squares in the buildings? Or were there really alternative universes?

Are you my girlfriend?

BY THE TIME she got home — she'd had to stop in the washroom at Eglinton station to wipe off the lipstick and modify her garb — she was certain she was not Grunt's girlfriend. The question was just him, what he'd say, part and parcel with the way he rarely gave a direct answer, but gave an answer parallel to the question. She was also certain that when it came to putting a band together, Grunt would pick a wound-up, punk-looking guy with an electric guitar over a folk-singing girl with an acoustic guitar.

But. Then again.

She stepped through the door and here was her family, Jay's voice rising, then her father's, the sounds of cutlery being laid out in the dining room, her mother's voice telling Glynnis not to forget the buns. She was home. Where she lived. Once, she had come home each day with a feeling of her life beginning as she stepped onto their property. Away from home, her life was on hold. Home, it unfolded.

Now it was the opposite. The second she entered the door, her life was on hold.

"Did you get good information from the vertical files?" Mrs. Riggs asked.

"I forgot to ask," she said.

"Oh, Carol. I specifically reminded you before you left."

"Rockin' hair, Crull," said Jay.

"Ix-nay on the hair-nay," Glynnis said.

"Sore subject around here," said Mr. Riggs.

"Good pig Latin, Glam."

"What, you can't just add 'nay' to any word? Really?"

They barely noticed she was there. They blathered on about Trudeau, whether he was just legacy building or blah blah blah. Normally this made her feel like a fish in a fish tank, like the air was thick and if she opened her mouth, bubbles would come out. Glub. Glub. But actually it was not so bad being talked over and ignored. She could think about Grunt. She could relive the afternoon. Once she looked up and saw Glynnis eyeing her and realized she had been smiling, almost laughing — "Hi, Death. Come on in." Glynnis widened her eyes questioningly. Carol looked down at her dinner and smirked.

EXCUSED FROM the dishes to work on her essay, she closed the door to her room and picked up her guitar, quietly strumming the punk version of "Hello There, Death," hearing Grunt's voice in her head.

When she heard footsteps on the stairs, she raced to her desk and bent over her essay, rereading what she'd written. "Euthanasia, meaning good death, is the practice of helping people die. We do it to dogs all the time, why not people?" Mortimer had had a brain tumour the year before and her parents said he had to be put down. They do brain surgery on people, she'd argued. Why not dogs? But it would cost thousands of dollars, they said, and he was only a dog, and besides, it might not help. "It didn't help my mother," Mrs. Riggs said. What could you say to that? 'Well, try it with the dog, maybe it'll be different'?

"It's not fair," Carol had wailed to herself in her bedroom, "it's not fair." First Miss Balls and now Mortimer. For a few days, she'd gone around saying if they killed Mortimer, they'd have to kill her, too. And she had felt that way, she had meant it, she had thought they could go together, she and Mortimer, a little injection and they'd drift off into whiffs of smoke through black air. They'd whoosh through the atmosphere, and then through space for a really, really long time, sort of dreaming, until it seemed that they'd drift and dream forever and then they'd land on a place like a new planet and wake up as a sort of hybrid human-dog because their spirits had mingled on the way, and ... here things sort of trailed off. She didn't know what would happen after that, and anyway, she hadn't been allowed to find out. She woke one morning to find her parents had hoodwinked her. Mortimer was gone. Forever.

"Everything I love dies," she'd wept, "everything."

Her mother had sat down with her, taken her arm and said very seriously, "Yes. Everything we love does die. It's the way of the world," and there was so much sorrow in her mother's eyes that Carol had been madder than ever because now she was not even allowed to whine. She had lost an aged friend and a dog. Not a mother. Not a brother. Not a friend in the prime of life as Miss Balls had.

Her mother did not understand that there was something special about Carol that made it dangerous to be around her. Carol felt it in the core of her being. So far her parents had not died, so far her siblings had not died. But Glynnis had sustained a major injury. Glynnis had been maimed.

What it really was, Carol thought secretly, was that she *was* meant to die young, only the extra years given to her were being taken off the lives of the people she loved.

A new pit of dread opened up in her stomach. Grunt. If she loved him, he was on the list.

Glynnis tapped at the door and slipped in. "What was that about, at dinner?"

"What was what about?"

"You know." Glynnis hopped onto Carol's bed, then lay down with her arms behind her head.

"No. I don't know."

"Yes, you do. You were smiling to beat the band."

"To beat the band? To beat the band?"

Glynnis shrugged. "So. Tell me you really went to the library today."

"I really went to the library today."

"Yeah? With your guitar?"

Oh. Hot cheeks. But the involuntary smile was back. Glynnis was onto her. Glynnis had already bugged her about liking Grunt when they'd walked home from punk synchro.

— Say you like him.

— Shut uuuup.

— Say you like him.

— Shut uuuuup.

— Say you like him.

— Shut uuuuup.

— Carol and Gru-unnt, Carol and Gru-unt.

— Shut uuuuuup.

She had whapped Glynnis' arm and they had run down the cold, dark street, whapping and laughing until they were panting. Then they'd gone in to The Inquisition.

"Okay, I went to the library. And then I went to Grunt's. Shut up. For auditions. He's starting a band." She told Glynnis everything. "It has to be a joke, right. 'Are you my girlfriend.'"

"Well, maybe, but it's a pretty good warm-up, I mean, there's definite flirtation there."

"Really? You think so?"

"Oh, for sure. No question."

A will-o'-the-wisp of well-being danced around Carol, shimmering just there, just here. The way he'd laughed. The way he'd wanted to know who did that song like he liked it. The he'd said fuggin brilliant.

"Play me the song," said Glynnis.

"Where's Mom?"

"I don't know. Den, probably."

"Okay." She played it both ways as quietly as she could. Her version and the punk version.

"When did you write that?" Glynnis said.

Carol shrugged. "Last year sometime."

"Who did you want to die?"

Carol shrugged again uncomfortably. "Nobody in particular." This was not true. She had been thinking of her entire grade eleven homeroom class.

After Glynnis left, Carol tried to work more on her essay but got nowhere. The will-o'-the-wisp sank down into the ground. Everything she touched did turn bad. Everyone she loved, she hurt. The world was lead. Nothing mattered. People died. Nothing good happened. Everything good ended. The end.

Waiting for tomorrow was agony. She didn't want it to come. She didn't want confirmation that the other guy was in. That she was not his girlfriend, that he had been joking. She said she was staying up to finish her essay. But what she did was go back and forth, back and forth, watching the tabs on her clock radio flip over to a new number. She couldn't wait to know. She didn't want to know. She couldn't wait to know. She didn't want to know.

Dawn found her face-down on the desk, drool marking the two typewritten pages beneath her cheek. She looked up at the page still in the typewriter. HE WAS JOKING, HE WASN'T JOKING, HE WAS JOKING, HE WASN'T JOKING, all the way down the page until the final words ran off the edge of the paper. HE WAS JOKING, H. Which did that count as? He was joking? Or he wasn't?

SOMEHOW SHE GOT through the first three periods. The bell rang. She and Lisa slung their purses over their shoulders, lifted their books to their chests, filed out of class as usual. Her heart was going crazy. Look up, look up, look up, look up.

He might not say anything. He might just say hi and keep on walking.

But no, he'd say something. If he didn't, she'd ask. Fuck it. Better to risk looking stupid than stay like this.

They approached the stretch of hall in which they usually passed. He was not there. She turned and scanned. No. Definitely not there. No green mohawk in any direction. Just Lisa, beside her, yammering.

At lunch, on her way to the Yonge-Eglinton Centre, she heard some of the smokers.

—Yeah, he totally had it coming, man.

—What, cause he's a punker? That's bullshit. Live and let live, man, that's what I say.

—What I heard, I heard he beat up Pakis.

— On the subway. Last year? Year before?

— Hey, good for him.

— Fuck off, that's sick, you're sick.

— So why's Walker suspended?

— He totally broke the guy's nose, he like smashed his face in, guy had to go to the hospital. It was kind of sad, actually. Guy didn't even fight back. He's just, like, curled up in a ball and Walker's, like, 'Get up, ya punk. Get up so I can nail you.' Fuck.

— Fuckin Walker, man. Fuckin lunatic.

— Walker's just Walker, man. Guy beats up Pakis, he fuckin deserves it.

— No way, man.

What hospital? Sunnybrook? The Wellesley? Toronto General? At the mall she called them all from a pay phone. No, no Grant

Bulvey had been admitted. He had to be home. It was the only place she could try. She dialled the number from the strip of paper. The woman with the accent answered. "Is Grant there, please?"

"May I ask who's calling?" Carol hung up. She had just recognized that feeling in her stomach. Responsibility. She had been right. Everything she loved got hurt. She had to stay away. She had to end it before it started. She could never see him again.

GRUNT WAS NOT at school for three days. The first day, Carol felt strong. She would not see him. Even if he said she was in the band, even if he said, "Are you my girlfriend" every day, she would be strong, she would spare him, for she knew and he did not that her touch was the touch of death. Never would he know of her sacrifice and she could not tell him, even if he declared his love, for he would not believe her and would insist, and she would have to lie and say she liked him as a friend, but only a friend.

The second day she thought it would kill her not to see him. But she still had to be strong.

The third day, she thought if it would kill her not to be with him, and if being with him would kill him, then maybe it would be better if they both died young, if their love burnt out in a big giant flame. And really, what kind of fucked-up mumbo jumbo was she spouting, anyway? Did she honestly believe she had the touch of Death? Come on. She wasn't that important. She was just a wildly unlucky person.

She went to his house. Standing on the doorstep, she thought, Fuck, what if. And then he opened the door. First thought she had was he was wearing a mask, his eyes were that black and swollen. There was tape on his nose. His hair was down, falling over one side of his head like a mane.

"Hi," Carol said. "You okay?"

He shrugged. "Broken rib." He stepped back from the door so she could come in. She couldn't believe how easy it was. "Broken nose. I've been in worse."

"Really?"

"Oh, yeah."

"I knocked a piano on my sister once," said Carol, as she followed him down the hall. Hot face. Where had *that* come from?

He turned to her with his eyebrows raised. Then they were at the back of the house in the kitchen and she sat on a stool at a counter while he put the kettle on and waited for it to boil.

She told him the story, how Glynnis had taken her to show-and-tell and had taken Alison away from her. "I just ... lost it. I went bonkers. There was no stopping it. I mean, and all I did was just kick once. I, like, knew I couldn't kick Glynnis. But I had to kick something. So I kicked the closest thing. If the piano hadn't moved I would've just kept kicking and kicking and kicking. But it moved, it went bam. And I could see Glynnis was badly pinned, she was screaming. I thought she'd have, like, a broken leg. Miss Balls — she was this old lady who was like our aunt — she was certain it'd have to be amputated." She realized as she drew to a stopping place (she could go on and on; she had never, ever told the story before, not to anyone) that he was very still, that he was paying very close attention. When she stopped, he turned his face away again.

"It turned out they didn't, but, well, you've seen it. She's crippled for life anyway."

"Never really looked," he said, pouring hot water into two glass mugs.

"She was in the hospital for more than a month." Carol went on, told him everything. How they'd called her Killer, how they ganged up on her, how she'd gone to the new school and how it had followed her there. How she'd learned to use it. If people were scared of you, they didn't bug you so much.

"Fuckers, eh?" he said, handing her a cup of tea and heading for the door to downstairs. She followed him.

"Who?"

"People."

And he told her his story. Stammer. Speech pathology. Beaten up every week: scrawny kid, couldn't put out a sentence. It built up. Built up. Built up. You could hear it even now in his voice.

Skip a bunch of years.

Parents split. He gets sent to boarding school. Meets somebody named Doof. Really Duiffenhuiser or something. Doof. Big, dumb, no one likes him, either, but Grunt doesn't know that yet, he just knows he's got a buddy, somebody looking out for him. Then New Year's Eve, he's fifteen, Doof's sixteen, they're back in Toronto, going to a party. Preppy boys. Ralph Lauren shirts. Khakis. Topsiders. They're already a little drunk, they feel important, and Doof starts giving this guy on the subway a hard time, calling him names, telling him to go back where he came from. Guy says leave him alone, he's done nothing to them. Doof says more stupid shit and the guy calls Doof a very rude boy and gets off. Doof's all like, "Call me a boy? Call me a boy? I'm a man, you piece of shit. You call me a man." Doof starts hitting him, he starts hitting back, and that's where Grunt must have started in, though he didn't remember that, he didn't remember how his first blows fell, he only remembered that once they were falling it was like she said, there was no stopping it, there was no thought involved whatsoever, there was just the kicking, just the punching, just the "Yyyyyah." Just the "That's right, fucker. Fuckin take us on see what happens."

They were charged with assault. They did time. Grunt got sent to wilderness boot camp after juvie and met Hugh. Best thing that ever happened to him. Hugh: worker. Anarcho-pacifist. Fired. Let them have a hoot on a canoe trip (Lisa's kind of hoot, not Glynnis', Carol gathered). Refused to use holds on them when they ran away. "Some dumb-ass was always trying to run away. Like where you going to go, dumb-ass, all you know is fuggin Scarborough." Hugh was into smashing the state, not people.

"Now I look like I beat people up and I don't, and they beat me up 'cause I look like I beat people up." He snorted. Slurped the last of his tea. When he tipped his head back, the light caught his eyes. Shiny. He squinted the tears away. "That guy, that guy, he'd done nothing. He was like me getting b-, getting b-, getting beat up as a kid. He got it because he was there, because we could, because it was all about, it was all about, it was all about power and right then we had it. Fuck." The longest string of words she'd heard him put together. His voice was haunted. For a moment she thought of the man they had beaten. Then she thought of Miss Balls' captain, shooting the dog. The men drowning Emanuel Jaques in the sink. Herself, kicking the bricks. Vile. Vile. Human beings were vile.

He was still on probation. Four more months. The severity of the crime. It was starting to get to him, driving him crazy, what he couldn't do. He was no threat to society. He was a fuckin pacifist. But as long as he was on probation, he had to go to school, he had to be home by ten, he couldn't drink, he couldn't smoke drugs and he wasn't supposed to see Hugh, but he did anyway.

They were in the grey garage, sitting on the floor, leaning against the carpeted wall. Their hands were close together on the floor between them. She didn't get that last bit, why he couldn't see Hugh. "'No fraternizing with known criminals.' Load a crap. Soon as probation's over? Mout of here."

They sat silently for a while. At first Carol was uncomfortable, but then she began to listen to the silence. She got the sense that he was listening to it, too. Then she felt his hand over hers. He drained his teacup, squeezed her hand and jumped up, going to the drums.

"Hey," he said. "Scumbuckets. You. Me. Death."

A shiver ran down her spine.

She said she should go, and he said okay and he came close to her and took her hands and looked at her lips and then kissed them, darting his tongue through like the lizard he was. The effect was flame-thrower — whoosh down the core of her. Heart in her mouth. Die young, die young, who fuckin cared, it'd be worth it. They kissed for a long time. She had to take care of his nose. She felt as if she had never been kissed before, though she had, at parties by friends of Lisa's boyfriends, thick-tongued guys with something ugly about them, glasses as thick as hers, or acne or just a bad face. This was completely different. When he put his hands on her boobs, she didn't want to move them, she wanted him to bury his face. And then he did. Bliss. And recoiled. "Ow, ow, ow," holding his nose. Laughing.

"I should go."

"We're, like, the same, aren't we," he said. "Dangerous." He grinned.

Her heart erupted, heart-lava cascading into her chest cavity. Yes. Yes. She knew exactly what he meant. They weren't dangerous, they were totally innocuous. But then again, they were.

"Are you my girlfriend?" he said.

She smiled and bit her lip and went outside.

Glynnis

ON MONDAY, in her locker, Glynnis found this, written in red ink on loose-leaf paper:

Once upon a time in a small village near a glen, lived a handsome princess, only she didn't know she was a princess because she had been stolen away from her family as an infant and raised by marmots. Unfortunately, her marmot family was killed one day in an avalanche, and she was left all alone in the world.

The handwriting was unfamiliar, the story unsigned. She assumed it was from Kelly, some sort of apology for not having come to the party.

One day, weak with hunger (for she had kept alive by eating grubs and mites (roasted, the grubs were delicious, crisp on the outside and tender and gooey inside, but unfortunately she had no way to roast them and so had to eat them raw)), she stumbled into the village, where she was taken in by the bossy miller and his wife, who fed her pancakes and sausages until she was well again. She could only talk in Marmot, a language of hoots and whistles, and they thought perhaps she was an idiot, for they did not know the Marmot language.

Not really Kelly's style. And why come up with a new, fictitious explanation when the real one involved a toy poodle bitten in half by a Great Dane?

Glynnis skipped ahead in the story, searching for clues. Near the end of the last page she found one. The story was from Tracy Novak. She read on.

"My dear," said the bossy miller to his wife. "I think we've taken in an idiot. All she does is hoot and whistle. Here, you," he said to the handsome princess who didn't know she was a princess, "sweep up, now. Do the dishes."

The handsome princess had no idea what he was saying. "Thank you for the delicious meal," she whistled and hooted. "It makes a nice change from grubs and mites."

"My dear," said the miller's wife. "You are quite right. She is a complete idiot. She is not even grateful for the delicious meal we so graciously offered to share with her." Actually, the miller's wife had been about to give the extra pancakes and sausages to their pigs when the handsome princess who thought she was a marmot came along. All their children had grown up and moved away and they wanted someone new to boss around, which is why they had taken her in.

"Well, my dear. What shall we do with her?"

"Perhaps she's had a spell cast on her. She is rather handsome, underneath all the grubs and mites. Let's send her to the Spelluncaster."

"My dear, you are quite right," the miller said. "Get thee to the Spelluncaster," he said to the handsome marmot, who merely whistled in reply.

"My dear," said the miller's wife. "I think perhaps you may be an idiot, too. Can't you see the idiot doesn't understand you? We must take her to the Spelluncaster ourselves."

Although they were quite unused to doing anything except making pancakes and sausages, they managed to take the girl to the Spelluncaster.

"Glippy-glap-gloopy," the Spelluncaster said, waving her hands around in the air, "libby-lubby-loopy, la la, lo lo. Haba tibby saba, ooby-dooby daba I forget how it goes."

"Hoot, hoot," went the marmot-girl.

"Sorry. Can't do anything for you," said the Spelluncaster. "This girl was raised by marmots."

The Millers decided they could boss her around anyway and took her home. In hopes that she would one day learn to obey the bossing instead of merely whistling and hooting, they sent her to school. Neither of them ever did what the other told them to. "Pick up your clothes," the miller's wife would say to him and he would go on shaving. "Clean the bathroom," he would say in response and she would fan herself and eat another pancake. Their house was a mess. The handsome marmot princess began to clean up out of habit, as marmots are tidy folk, and the millers thought that she must be learning something in school, although they were a bit puzzled as to what, because when they said, "Feed the chickens," she would wash the dishes and when they said, "Wash the dishes," she would clean the hair-brushes and when they said, "Empty the ash can," she would beat the rugs, and when they said, "Beat the rugs," she would butt heads with the goat, whose head actually didn't need butting.

But that's neither here nor there.

She went to school, where in response to the teacher's questions, she hooted and whistled as any good marmot would. The children, however, thought she was being funny and they laughed and applauded her cheekiness. They began to hoot and whistle at the teacher, too, but they made very little sense in Marmot. "Toasty toasty bedbugs!" she heard them say. And then, "Spread my soul on the floor and salt it." She was excited finally to be amongst people who spoke her language. She thought perhaps they were talking in code or were reciting avant-garde poetry. But when they said, "Alabaster coon turd" and "my soul is a salty toasty spread" and "coon turd bedbug" and so on, she realized that not only did they not know what they were saying, they were saying it with a very limited vocabulary. She remained popular, however, although quite lonely, even when she gradually came to learn some of their language.

She looked longingly at two sisters, who, for some reason she could not discern, were not popular, though they could speak the regular language every bit as well as the rest of the children, while she herself could not.

There were several words that got repeated over and over again, and on her way to and from school, she practised these. Her mouth was unused to making these foreign shapes, but she practised hard and soon she was able to say them. "Decent!" she said. And, "thatizsogay!" She tried them out at school and they were well received. She used them on every occasion. "Decent!" she said, when the miller's wife plopped pancakes and sausages down in front of her, and "Thatizsogay!" when the miller proposed that she bake a strudel.

She continued to look longingly from her big crowd of children to the two sisters, playing on their own in the deep mud of the schoolyard. She listened carefully for their names so that one day she could call them and they would all play together, and she practised their names just the way she had practised her first two words until she had perfected them. Then, on a damp, foggy day, she called out. "Wimpy!" she called. "Gimpy!" she called.

Glynnis felt her face flush. Even now the words stung.

The two sisters turned their heads and her heart leapt with joy, for she thought she would now find true friendship.

Then they looked at each other and with one accord, turned and fled and never came back and from that day to this, the handsome little marmot has been as lonely as a grain of sand on the moon.

This was a different Novak than the one she knew. A Novak she'd never imagined. A Novak *lonely as a grain of sand on the moon.*

GLYNNIS READ THE STORY another three times lying on her bed after dinner, a weird careening feeling barrelling through her, and then she went to her typewriter.

Once upon a time in a small village near a glen, lived an ugly stoat, who thought, for some strange reason, that she was a handsome marmot princess. Her parents, who were also stoats, but thought they were a bossy miller and his wife, sent her to the village school.

The careening feeling subsided. Words spilled out.

"Hello, how do you do," she said to the teacher. "I am a handsome marmot princess."

"Hello, how do you do," she said to the other students. "I am a handsome marmot princess. You do not understand me because I speak only Marmot, a language of hoots and whistles."

Because the miller and his wife were really stoats, everyone was afraid of them. You see, the people were all rats, and as everyone knows there is nothing a stoat likes better than to get its teeth into the neck of a nice fat rat and shake it until it is dead. And so nobody told the ugly stoat that she was not really a handsome marmot princess, but an ugly stoat, and that really she spoke only ordinary language, not Marmot at all.

Then one day, a handsome marmot family moved into the village. The two marmot sisters went to school, as good, honourable marmots do, and were only mildly taken aback to find that their schoolmates were a pack of rats and a stoat. As their teacher was a duck, they thought it was all just par for the course in this funny new town, where the rats and the stoats and the ducks lived and learned together as one.

They thought the stoat was joking when she said, "How do you do, I am a handsome marmot princess." They laughed their heads off.

"What is so funny?" the stoat asked.

They couldn't answer, because their heads had rolled down the hill, and as everybody knows, heads don't work unless they're attached to bodies.

"You probably don't understand me because I speak Marmot, a language of hoots and whistles."

The marmots ran after their heads so they could answer, but they didn't know where they were because of course their eyes were in their heads and their heads were in the dirt and not attached to their bodies. They fumbled about in the dirt until they finally found their heads and put them back on.

Then they laughed their heads off all over again, for they realized they had put on the wrong heads. Finally they got the right heads on the right bodies.

The marmots, who were perfectly bilingual, and perfectly honest, said, "You are not a handsome marmot at all, you are an ugly stoat."

The stoat said, "I am not. You take that back."

"Well," said the older marmot. "Really 'ugly stoat' is just a figure of speech. Not all stoats are ugly, in fact, some are quite handsome, though not as handsome as marmots, that goes without saying."

"You are right," said the other marmot. "You're not an ugly stoat, you are just a stoat."

"I am not a stoat, I am not a stoat," the stoat whined. Just then a small kindergarten rat sped by, and the piqued stoat unthinkingly snatched it up and sunk its teeth into the poor little rat's neck, shaking the unfortunate rodent back and forth to its death.

"See? You are a stoat. You just killed that rat."

"I did not."

"You did, too. It's lying there limp and lifeless."

"Is not," said the stoat, poking the dead rat with its toe. "See? It just moved."

"That was you poking it."

"Oh, I am terribly, terribly sorry. You must be right. I am a stoat. I am an ugly stoat." And the ugly stoat, who was really not so very ugly, began to cry and cry.

"I know," said the younger marmot. "Is there a spellcaster in this town?"

"No," said the weeping stoat, "but there's a Spelluncaster."

"Let's go see the Spelluncaster. Maybe she can help."

So they went to see the Spelluncaster, who, after they had explained the problem, waved her hands in the air and said, "Shameezle, shamozzle, sossa-pepper incorporated, one two three four five six seven eight, shameezle, shamozzle."

Nothing happened. "I don't think your spell worked," the older marmot said.

"Oh, bless me, that wasn't my spell, I just have a cold."

"Well, do you have a spell that would turn our friend the stoat into a marmot?"

"My goodness, no, where on earth did you get such an idea? A stoat can't be turned into a marmot. A stoat can only be turned into a boat, or a moat, or a goat, or something that rhymes."

They pooled their resources and went through all the words they could think of that rhymed with stoat. When they had run out of words, they asked the stoat, "So, would you like to be an oat, a boat, a moat, a goat, a vote, a dote, a rote, a float, a bloat, a gloat, a note, a zygote or a compote?"

"Can't I be a marmote?" the poor stoat asked.

"Only if you speak with a Hungarian accent the rest of your life," the Spelluncaster said.

"I'll do it!" cried the stoat determinedly.

"All right, then," the Spelluncaster said. She waved her hands in the air around the stoat's head, then drew them quickly back when the stoat tried to bite them.

"Sorry," the stoat said. "Instinct."

"Manamana, bup-doo-be-doo-be," the Spelluncaster said. "Manamana, bup-doo-be-doo. Manamana, bup-doo-be-doo-be be-doo-be be-doo-be be-doo-be-doo-be doop doop doobee do."

She clapped three times and presto, the stoat was turned into a marmote, who, though of course infinitely more attractive than a stoat, was nonetheless somewhat ugly as marmots go.

Glynnis nestled the letter in her knapsack the next morning to plant in Novak's locker before stage band. The halls were empty, there was no danger of being seen, but still her heart thumped as she approached the bank of lockers. She threw glances over both shoulders like a cartoon spy before sliding the fold of paper through the vent slits. At the last second, she panicked, pinching madly at the falling paper. Did she have the right locker? She pressed her cheek up against the metal, peered through. Phew. Novak's striped towel. Her shoes. She let the paper drop.

"Ransom note?" a voice said behind her.

She jumped.

"Love letter?" It was her history teacher, Mr. Humenick, one of the ones who took a special interest in Glynnis and who thought she wasn't living up to her potential but understood why because he had been like that as a student. The history office was right behind her. The door had been closed.

"Just a regular note note," Glynnis said when she'd recovered.

"Yeah, and I'm the pope. Come on, who's it to, who's it to?"

"Nobody." If it really had been just a note note — and it was, it was — wasn't it? — she would have taken his own tone and said, "Oh, yeah, like I'm going to tell you."

"But it's just a note note."

"I'm, uh, going to band," Glynnis said, and left as quickly as she could.

She did not go straight to band but into the washroom, where she sat on a toilet seat and lightly banged the side of her head on the side of the stall. Fu-uck. She had a crush on Novak. It was obvious. It was pathetic. She felt vaguely sick. How had this happened? Her stomach floated balloonlike in her belly, her cheeks were hot. In grade eight she and Tamara had entertained themselves with preteen advice books from the library. "A crush on older girls or women is normal and nothing to worry about. Before you can say, 'I adore my camp counsellor' you will grow out of it and find your crushes placed firmly on 'dreamy' boys." But Glynnis would not grow out of this because she had never grown into it, it had always been there. Alongside, it's true, crushes on boys. But those were different crushes, the ones on boys. Social crushes. I-know-you-like-me-so-why-won't-you-ask-me-out crushes. You-fit-my-conception-of-my-social-worth crushes. This was a heart-thumping, tongue-tying crush precisely like every puppy-love gush story she'd ever pretended not to read in the corner of the library.

How was she going to be able to see Novak again? How was she going to be able to look her in the eyes?

Stage band let out at quarter to and Glynnis could not help herself, she had to walk by Novak's locker, walk down the hall, la-la-la, looking without really looking like she was looking. Novak was talking to football guy, he had the locker next to hers. Look down, look down, no, look ahead, far down the hall, look abstracted. You're thinking. You're having deep thoughts. You're barely aware of your surroundings.

"Hey, Riggsie."

Novak's locker was open, she was hanigng up her pea jacket. Had she found the story yet? Couldn't tell. Maybe. No, there it was, there on top of the basketball shoes. Bit of white. So she hadn't found it yet.

"Oh. Hey. Hey. How's, uh, how's Alison? She recover from Friday?" Football guy was standing there, waiting to resume their conversation. Humenick stepped out of his office.

"No idea."

Huh. Keep moving, don't stop to talk. "See ya." No idea, eh. Huh.

Would she think it was weird Glynnis hadn't said anything about getting *her* marmot and stoat story? Well, if she did, she wouldn't when she found Glynnis'. And she could've just asked. Could've said, Hey, did you get that story I left in your locker? And Glynnis would have said, Ohhh, that was you. I didn't know who it was from, well, I sorta knew, I guessed, but ha ha uh I didn't know for sure.

God. Good thing she hadn't asked. Pa-thetic. Drown her in a bag with six other kittens.

In history, Humenick winked at her. *Now. Now. Drown me now.*

Not until punk synchro when Novak hooted and whistled through practice, did Glynnis get confirmation the tale had reached its audience.

"What's with the whistling?" Mish said in the dressing room afterward.

"Private joke," said Novak, flashing a smile at Glynnis.

After that, nothing. A nod here, a hi there, a hoot, a whistle, a nothing, Novak was with the guy in the Mexican poncho and big hat, she was with the fat girl in drama, she was with brilliant acne boy, she was with football guy, she was with Mish or Steph, she was with Grunt and Carol? Yes, Grunt and Carol. Wow.

She was not with Alison.

She was not with Glynnis.

Before, Glynnis would have said the wide cast of Novak's net was all about show, that she cultivated acquaintance with such a range of souls so that people would notice and say, Wow, look at the surprising people she knows! She must have so many sides! So much depth!

So thorough had been her impression of Novak's essential fraudulence that it was strange now to start seeing the possibility — the likelihood, even — that there was something genuine at the core of it, a genuine interest in people, an abhorrence of confinement to one or two social groups, a love of non-conformity that did not exclude a love of one or two conformists. Like what Glynnis herself pretended to aspire to, while in fact being seduced into aspiring to membership in a group like Kelly's.

Glynnis wanted to throw herself in Novak's road. *Hey! Cultivate acquaintance with me.* Instead she had to pretend to have her own life that was just as full and interesting as Novak's seemed to be. This should not have been hard to do. She had band, she had Tamara, with whom she was editing the boring video of her unremarkable life, she had Stephen and the video of his life, she had Kel and punk synchro, she had classes and homework and her own circle of acquaintance. But the whole time she had visions of embarrassing scenes where she burst into song and dance like Judy Garland in a vaudeville finale, arms and legs windmilling, Look at me!

Look at me!, of implausible scenarios where, injured somehow —
diving into the pool? clipped by a car at a crosswalk? squashed under
another piano? — she lay near death and Novak, seeing this, suddenly realized that lying here was her one true love. She bent over
Glynnis, smoothed her hair away tenderly and promised never to
leave her side.

Novak did not seem to miss Alison too badly, she was not dragging around in a big mope. Possibly this was a good cover-up job.
Possibly Novak was happier without her; possibly Alison had limited
her, kept her from her net. Glynnis had seen Alison standing apart
impatiently while Novak chatted up a pal, had seen Novak say, I'll
catch up to you later, or Alison say, I'm going on ahead. At the time
she'd thought Novak was the rude one, making Alison wait while
she made random conversation with unimportant people, but now
she saw that the problem was Alison being stuck up and unfriendly.
Novak was better off without her.

But Novak was so convincingly unaffected that Glynnis began to
wonder if she had misread the whole situation. Maybe Novak and
Alison were just friends and Glynnis had made the whole lesbian
thing up. Maybe she had based her own conviction that she was a
lesbian — icky word, she wished there were a better — on something
that had never existed, like a Peanuts strip she remembered. Lucy is
bent down looking at something small on the sidewalk. Linus walks
by and she says, "Sh, a butterfly. Did you know that some butterflies
migrate all the way from Brazil?" Linus says, "That's not a butterfly.
That's a potato chip." And Lucy says, "I wonder how a potato chip
made it all the way from Brazil."

A thought once thought could not be unthought. Even if wrong,
a misapprehension, it was there. There. Like a crystal ashtray on a
table in a dark room under a beam of bright light.

"WANT TO GO see a movie?"

Oh, God. This was like one of her fantasies. Yes. Yes. "Okay," Glynnis said.

"All righta. Let's go."

"What, now?" It was just after lunch.

Novak was leaning against the next locker. Her pea jacket was open, her arms were folded across her chest, her feet in their perfect-shade-of-tan Grebs were crossed, her faded jeans hung low in front, higher in back. She wore a Cowichan tuque. Glynnis had never before been aware of such perfection in a human being, not in the clothes themselves but in the wearing of them, in the pose, in the skin they covered, the muscle and bone the skin covered, the heart beneath it all that pumped.

Yeah, now.

Okay. Chuck books in locker. Ow. Fuck. Not cool. Pick up dropped *The Living Environment*, 3rd Edition, put back on shelf. Take out coat. Be cool. Move slow. Try not to shake. "So. Do you do this a lot?"

"Skip school to go see matinees? I sure do. Matinees are what I live for. Matinee. Matinee." It was like she was licking the word. "Isn't that the best word? Morninged."

"Wouldn't it be more like 'of the morning'?"

"What, you're Sheila Fischman all of a sudden? I like 'morninged.' 'Gad, I've been morninged.'"

"We're about to be morninged."

"We are. We're about to be morninged in the afternoon." She hooted and jumped up, swiping at a parking sign with her hand. It was cold out, her jacket was open. Cooking.

They bought their popcorn, found a spot in the middle of the almost empty theatre, settled in with their feet up.

Glynnis had to tell herself to be herself over and over. She felt brittle and giddy and not precisely sure who she was. "Well. Here we are. About to be morninged. I feel kind of nervous. I've never been morninged before."

"What? Never?"

"Well, not since I was little. Then I was morninged a couple of times, but I didn't know its true significance."

"You're going to love it."

"I know I am."

My God, what was going to happen? Was she really going to be morninged?

The lights went down, the coming-soons began. Novak tilted her face to the screen, tub of popcorn on her belly, hand moving from tub to mouth, tub to mouth. She was gone, lost in the screen. Or was she? Did she feel Glynnis' upper arm? There? Was she aware of that? And pretending not to be? No. No. Not aware. Accidental touch, circumstantial touch, it meant nothing to her.

Glynnis could not move. If she moved, Novak would feel her move and *become* aware of the arm and then, well, who knew what then, but something, she'd move her arm and the warmth would be gone. Or not move it. Or …

Watch the screen, she told herself.

"Are you cold?"

"Cold?"

"You're kind of shaking. Here, put my coat over your knees."

"Thanks." Don't shake. Do not shake. Relax. There. Relax. Watch the movie.

The coat was warm as a morning bed.

The movie started. A man playing a woman berated the Wise Men, who had announced themselves to a baby in a dim byre. "What are you doing creeping around a cowshed at two o'clock in the morning?" squawked the baby's mother. "That doesn't sound very wise to me."

Novak snickered. Glynnis snickered. She relaxed a little. With the next laugh, she relaxed more. Midway through the following scene they were laughing so hard, they were grabbing each other's sleeves. Come the stoning, a few scenes later, they were rocking back and forth. As the film rolled on, they sank in their seats. Rose again. Leaned on the armrest between them, whole upper arms touching. Laughed with their heads close together. Laughed with their heads turned away. Laughed their way into intimacy.

"Wow," said Glynnis at the end. She handed over Novak's coat, just as warm as when she'd received it. Felt its absence like a draught. "Being morninged is very good."

Walking out into the dark in a different part of the city than she was used to being in, going on the subway to a home where no one knew how she'd spent the afternoon, Glynnis felt like her world had cracked open. She had a secret life.

Rowena

ROWENA HAD TAKEN a morning at home to iron her clothes and pay the bills. Now, on the bus on the way to her noon meeting, her lunch flashed in her mind, sitting on the counter at home. She opened her briefcase. Darn. What a waste of good food.

Was there time to dash into the Dominion at Yonge and Egg and grab something? Yes, barely. Bagel, cream cheese, yogurt, apples. Granola bars to share. She trotted down the brown tunnel of the lower level of the mall. Out of the corner of her eye, she spied teenagers in the coarse embrace they somehow got away with these days, the boy against the wall with his legs apart and the girl right in between them, pressed up. The boy had green hair in a stegosaurus strip down the centre of his head. The girl had a leather jacket with graffiti on the back.

Something bothered her while she shopped, a feeling of having missed something. She kept going over her mental list — bread, cheese, fruit, yogurt, cookies — and finding nothing missing. Even after exiting the store and squeezing past a large woman with a shopping cart who did not bother to stand right on the escalator ramp, she worried it in her head. As she got off the ramp and followed the flow of foot traffic toward where the boy and girl had been standing — they were gone now — she realized what it was. Nothing on her grocery list.

The force of the realization stilled her feet. She gaped at the empty wall. The girl in the leather jacket had been her daughter.

The big woman nearly bumped into her. "Whatsa matter, the race called off?" Lunch-hour traffic streamed around her, women's heels clopping, teenagers' unlaced boots slapping the floor.

She had not recognized her own daughter. But also she had. It was just that her mind, finding the two categories, Carol and girl seen, mutually exclusive, had simply refused to see. The girl was a punk, was a slut, was shameless, was mixed up, was misguided, had bad parents, came from a broken family, was trying to prove something, was being used, was stupid, bitter, twisted, angry, was tough, hard-bitten, brazen, low, a delinquent.

Carol as Death. Carol as Harlot. What next? One did not expect one's children to grow up to be archetypes.

"Rowena?" said a surprised voice, as if to say, Why would *you* be standing stock still like a crazy person in the middle of the underground thoroughfare?

"I forgot something," Rowena said. It was her neighbour, Leona, a blabby woman she'd been on parent-teacher committees with years ago. "At Dominion. And then I forgot what I'd forgotten and I was just standing here trying to figure it out."

"Oh, I know," Leona said. "That happens to me all the time." Leona looked like she might launch into a story about a time she'd forgotten a jar of mayonnaise to make that dip, you know, the one with the —

Rowena had to jump on it. "I think I'll just …" She gestured and began to hurry back toward the ramp up to the main level.

Leona nodded. "Good luck," she said. "Nice to see you," she called after her.

Cast adrift from the ramp, Rowena floated through the mall, appalled.

Should she storm over to Carol's school, drag her out of class, take her home and keep her there?

No. It was lunch hour anyway; Carol would not be in class. Her daughter and the stegosaur had gone somewhere else to continue their make-out session (this gave her a sick feeling). She could search for them, but what would she do if she found them? Grab Stegosaur by the ear like a Victorian schoolmarm? If only she could. If only.

No. She should go to work. Calm down. Think things through. Good heavens, she was a single parent. Glenn should be a part of this, too. They were not a bad team, but Glenn was only a part-time coach. The easy fellow, lately. Unpopularity fell to her. Well, whatever else, Carol was grounded. As for the rest, they'd see.

She was late for her meeting, which was being held in the church itself so that they could see a projection of the sculpture at the approximate size and in the approximate place that the Arts in Worship Committee proposed to put it. *Crucified Woman*. Rowena winced whenever the name was given, it sounded so much like aggrieved feminists crying, *Poor me, poor me.*

Margaret was just finishing her presentation as Rowena entered. "Art should provoke. Art should make people think. And church should provoke. Church should make people think. People shouldn't turn off their brains simply because it's Sunday."

Barry Oliver sputtered, but Milt waved him off until Margaret had wrapped up.

On a screen set up next to the pulpit was a side view of sculpture and sculptor, with the sculptor not paying attention to the camera but looking at the sculpture's feet, or base perhaps. Rowena barely noted it — she had seen pictures already — except to remark to herself how ordinary the sculptor looked — an ordinary middle-aged woman. She could have met her at a party and never have known she was an artist, let alone one who would sculpt a crucified woman.

Barry was rebutting. A linguistics professor, he spoke well and passionately to the small crowd, but Rowena could see students spending a whole session staring in horrified fascination at the foam that accumulated between his molars and his cheek.

Carol! In that jacket. His jacket, she now saw in the way it had slumped on her shoulders.

Rowena's heart filled with fear.

"Bring in the sculpture," Barry said. "Just don't bring it into the church." Spit flew from 'church.'

She agreed with Barry. If art was going to provoke, it needn't do it in the church proper. One could provoke just fine thank you from the narthex.

Fear that this whole generation would just turn off from the world, that they would create an apocalypse of their own without even needing a bomb to go off. Her mind served up a decrepit world with hard-faced, spike-haired youngsters squaring off against one another, bottles in fists, swigging and hurling. No compassion left, only anger and destruction. And her daughter — *her daughter* — among them.

An old man with his hands on his cane claimed not to like having any kind of crucified figure in the church — "There's no Christ on our cross. The cross itself is enough. We're not Catholics" — after which a mild little woman with hair straight as falling water hestitatingly proffered evidence that women had historically been crucified, a fact people deserved to know, a fact that challenged the notion of men being at the centre of the world's suffering. Barry disputed this loudly. And so it went.

She must save Carol. Carol must be saved.

Glynnis

COME ON, Novak would say.

Come on, we're going to the art gallery.

Come on, we're going to synagogue.

Come on, we're going to Chinatown.

And they would pick up that jokey intimacy, that not needing words, and toss it around between them like a football.

They had not been to one another's houses — "Who *is* this person you're spending so much *time* with?" Glynnis' mother kept saying — and Glynnis wanted to keep it that way. It was too good for houses, it was too big for houses. It was something their families didn't know. It was their lives.

They did not much allude to it when with their other friends, either, at punk synchro or elsewhere. They did not hide it, exactly. But there was a privacy to their adventures that Glynnis savoured.

At the art gallery, they made up art criticism. *Beyond the obvious sexual pose, the grotesque bulges of bronze symbolize the grotesquerie of the human heart thudding in its fleshy prison, while the stippled effect on the surface, or 'skin', if you will, reflects the pimply, essentially pustular nature of human emotions.*

In Chinatown, they were Harvard and Buck, barbecued ducks

who didn't know they'd been barbecued. "Hey, Harv, that's quite a sunburn you got." "You're one to talk, my friend. You're burned to a crisp, Bucky-boy." "Remember the old days, at the pond, Harv? Those were the days, eh, Harv?" "What's happened to us, Buck? When did we get so old?" "Old! Old! I feel half-dead!" "Like someone roasted you on a spit?" "Yeah, yeah, like somebody roasted me on a spit!"

On Bloor Street West they'd found nothing more interesting than an IGA store, where a faded little bucking bronco gave a surprisingly brisk ride for a quarter, until an apologetic-looking four-year-old winced as his mother reamed them out.

Novak was a toucher. Glynnis had never noticed this before. Some people were and some people weren't. Touchers touched you on the arm to emphasize a point, they grabbed your bicep when something was funny, they whapped your thigh to get your attention on the subway, they leaned their elbow on your shoulder when they were tired, they leapt up in the air with their hands on your shoulders when they were hyper. They did this very easily and naturally.

At every touch, Glynnis' heart hopped from perch to perch in her chest like an anxious sparrow.

"COME ON," Novak said one Tuesday afternoon at Glynnis' locker. "We've got to make a dish for a potluck."

Glynnis was supposed to be going to driver's ed. "A potluck?"

"A potluck."

"Okay." She packed up her knapsack. "Who's having the potluck?"

"LOOT."

"Loot?"

"LOOT."

"Loot."

"The Lesbian Organization of Toronto."

Glynnis felt quivery as a caught frog, pulse throbbing in her throat. "Natch," she said.

Novak grinned as if the Lesbian Organization of Toronto were hilarious. Which it was. LOOT. Ha. But there was a matching pulse in Novak's throat, she was sure of it. It bumped her voice up a tone in pitch.

"I'm thinking vegetable stew," Novak said. "All the lesbians my mother knows —"

"Eat vegetable stew?"

"Are vegetarians."

"Right. Vegetarian lesbians." Glynnis pictured women with large ruminant teeth. Lank hair. Sloe eyes. "How many lesbians does your mother know?" (It was the first time she'd said the word out loud since thinking she was one. It felt thick on her tongue, like molasses.)

Novak's mother was a city councillor. Her father was an abortion doctor. They were often in the news and not often home. Novak was free to come and go as she pleased. Their house — which Glynnis was thrilled to be coming to (really, the thing that she liked was that their friendship did not intrude into her own home) — was a house that seemed to live in the past, remembering its former bustle like an aged great-aunt. The dining room was Mrs. Novak's den. The buffet, the dining room table, every surface was covered in stacks of papers. When they had dinner parties, Novak said, they had to eat in the living room with the guests balancing the plates on their knees. Glynnis loved the house, but when she imagined being alone in it, *Lonely as a grain of sand on the moon* was the phrase that went through her mind.

"I don't know. Three?"

"That's a representative sample."

Being invited into the Novak home did not violate Glynnis' sense of their friendship being outside family life but instead hinted tantalizingly at a whole unknown side of Novak — Novak the Novak. Novak the youngest child, Novak the daughter of a war refugee,

Novak, daughter of parents who dared put their beliefs into public life, Novak, daughter of history. There was something vulnerable about Novak at home, as if she might inadvertently reveal too much of herself.

Glynnis wanted to see everything. The den. The skis Novak's father had skied out of Czechoslovakia on. Photo albums. The medicine cabinet. Novak's room. Where she watched TV. Instead she meekly stood loose-handed while Novak dropped the groceries and ducked out to put on music that Glynnis didn't recognize, jazz with sad vocals piped into the kitchen over hidden speakers so that when they began to chop, the music was like a soundtrack. This was the anticipation scene in which they were spotlit in companionable activity while the music told you what to feel, what was to come. This music told you that if they ever got together, they did not stay together — one of them died or got married. This music said, "One of these people will end up alone." To reflect Glynnis' true feeling, the music should have been saying, DON'T OPEN THE FRIDGE, THE KILLER'S IN THERE!

They were going to a lesbian potluck. Aaaaaaaaaaagh.

Glynnis' mother knew some lesbians, too, Glynnis suddenly remembered. From church. They were middle-aged and stout. One of them wore a suit jacket and slicked back her hair. The other had fuzzy hair and wore makeup. Her mother thought it was sad the way they mimicked sex roles. Glynnis thought it was sad they were so old. Oh, my God. What if they were there? What if they were potluck-goers? Agh.

"Are you nervous?"

"No." Obvious lie. "Are you?"

"How many of them will there be? What will they look like?" Novak slid the eggplant from the cutting board into the pot. "They'll probably think we're lesbians, too. I mean, that makes sense, if you show up for a lesbian potluck, you're probably a lesbian."

Are you? Glynnis wanted to ask. Are we?

"So we'll have to pretend," Novak said before Glynnis could find the courage to speak. "Remember how we'd do that in grade seven? 'Lesbe friends and go homo'? And you'd, like, put your arm around the back of the other person's head with your hand over their mouth and kiss your own hand?"

"Nobody talked to me in grade seven, remember?"

Glynnis did remember. She could picture Mel doing it with Sandy, Toby doing it with Janet Green. Novak doing it with Alison. How soon afterwards had the hand slipped? How soon had they really kissed? As soon as that? Grade seven? Or had they danced around it for years, like the two of them were doing now?

"Here. Like this," Novak said, wrapping her arm round the back of Glynnis' neck and planting her palm on Glynnis' mouth, then dipping her like a ballroom dancer and smooching her own skin. Her eyes looked unreadably into Glynnis'. They said nothing, they were simply beautiful and Glynnis thought she was going to do it, she was going to use the same method on Glynnis as on Alison. Yes. Yes.

Glynnis was spun upright again. Let go.

She could only try to match her grin to Novak's, agree not to acknowledge that they could do this — put their faces so close — only if they pretended they were pretending.

They played air hockey in the rec room (she got to see the rec room!) while the stew stewed.

It took them less than fifteen minutes to get to 342 Jarvis, an ordinary brick row house with no distinguishing features. They sat in the car, looking across the street at it, at the people passing. No one went in or out of the building.

"Is it seven o'clock yet?" Novak checked a piece of paper, a flyer folded up in her pocket.

"On the nose."

"It's kind of like Willy Wonka's. 'No one ever went in or out.'"

"Are there even lights on?"

"You want to just leave?"

"Do you?"

"No. No way. We're here."

They got out of the car, Novak holding the casserole in its bag, and crossed the street. When they reached the other side, Novak took Glynnis' hand, threading her fingers through Glynnis', and swinging it between them as they walked up the stairs and knocked. Glynnis' heart hopped, hopped, hopped. Their joined hands felt like gigantic flashing neon balloons. Weirdly, passersby barely remarked them.

There was no response for a long time. Novak checked the address on her sheet. Yup. 342. The house even matched the picture on the flyer. They were definitely in the right place. Glynnis had an urge to drop the hand now, but Novak held on. Their cold hands were warming.

Finally, the door was opened by a grey-haired woman in a flowered housedress and cardigan. "What you want?"

"Uhhhh, is there a potluck here tonight?"

"Potluck? No potluck," she said. "Always people knocking on my door."

"Are you sure? We have a flyer," Glynnis said, dropping the hand and plucking the flyer from Novak's jacket pocket.

"Of course I am sure." She made as if to close the door.

Glynnis and Novak looked at each other and shrugged.

"Would you like a casserole?" Novak said, just before the door closed. "Here. It's vegetarian." Glynnis looked at the flyer. 1980, it said.

"Take food from stranger, no."

The door shut. They were left on the stone steps in the cold. Novak looked at the flyer as if she wanted to pluck it back.

Just as she had been suddenly certain Novak and Alison MacDonald were lesbians, Glynnis was certain that Novak had had this flyer since 1980. She'd found it and folded it and tucked it into a book, and for two years, the first Tuesday of every month, Novak had wondered about the lesbian potluck. Who was there. Should she go.

And finally, finally, she had gone.

And there was no potluck.

Glynnis felt something plummet in her, as if the hopes had been her own.

They got back into the car. "They must have moved or something," said Novak. Her eyes were glassy and to avoid looking at Glynnis, it seemed, she leaned over and dug around in the glove compartment.

Now was the time. Right now. *That's too bad. I was really curious.* Or *Have you ever thought you might — ? Were you and Alison — ? I know you and Al — ... You don't have to ... pretend.* But there she was herself, pretending, and not able to stop it. Novak, too, apparently, who was so bold in other instances. Who went up to total strangers and, well, offered them casseroles. And who right now was delicate as ice forming on a black pond.

"Are you hungry?" Novak said. "I'm hungry. Aha. Here it is." She flourished a plastic fork retrieved from the glove box.

Steam from the ripped foil of the vegetable stew clouded the car and fogged the windows. They passed the fork back and forth. After a certain point, the lesbian question didn't seem to matter anymore.

"Let's go see if it's too late to get into Second City," Novak said.

Carol

.

WHAT CAROL learned about Grunt: His mother was manic-depressive and lived in London, Ontario. The woman in the house was his step-mother. She was Danish. His father had met her skiing in France. Carol thought she seemed lonely. Grunt's father was not home much. Grunt would not say what he did, except that he was a capitalist pig. Carol gathered he was some kind of executive. He was also a member of AA. As a sort of joke, he always said, upon seeing Grunt, "Grant me the courage to accept the things I cannot change." As if Grunt was something he would change if he could.

He was the kind of man you would wonder the first time you met him why anyone would ever hate him and later you would wonder how you never noticed that he treated everyone other than himself as a bug.

"So this is the girlfriend," he said when he first met Carol. He stuck his hand forward. "Nice to meet you. I'm Grant's father." He was handsome and had dimples and a tan and nice smile wrinkles. "Make yourself at home." He did not mean this. He meant, *Confine yourself to the garage and the basement.* Usually they were entertaining guests. That was the one thing that seemed to make the stepmother happy, cooking meals with many elaborate dishes. Grunt never expected to be invited to eat with them. He would come in and get the plates that waited for them and take them back out to the garage. At Carol's house they would have been forced to eat with the guests and socialize. Here it seemed less like freedom than exclusion.

The person Grunt looked up to most in the world was Hugh, the fired leader from DARE, whom he was not supposed to see. Hugh was twenty-five and did a punk show on Ryerson Radio. They met him sometimes at a pool parlour on Queen Street or at the arcades on Yonge Street. He loved to play Pac-Man and talk. He had a girl-friend, Mariellen, the girl she had seen Grunt with that time she had followed him in the fall. Carol liked Mariellen. She wasn't sure about Hugh. Why did he want to hang out with people so much younger than him? It reminded her of her guitar teacher.

Carol did not know what Grunt thought of her except that they were the same. That they were dangerous. That she was more sexu-ally experienced than she actually was. Though it made her nervous, she liked this.

Her actual experience consisted of seven or eight episodes of mostly unpleasant kissing, four or five of which included awkward groping, and one of which included jerking a guy off. But she had listened to Lisa and learned. Lisa read *Playgirl* magazine aloud, Lisa read out *Penthouse* fantasies, Lisa editorialized. Carol listened, a heat between her legs.

With Grunt, all he had to do was walk close to her and she felt the heat. They were not one of those couples who were touching each other all the time. When they walked, it was not hand in hand. When they sat, it was not with arms around one another. That was, Carol sensed, too football-star-cheerleader for Grunt. Instead, they walked separately. She walked and he loped. And every now and then Grunt grabbed her hand and pulled her to him to plant his tongue in her mouth. Flamethrower all over again. He'd do it irreg-ularly, when they were walking down the street, when they were on the stairs in the subway and people had to squeeze around them, when they were outside the principal's office. The way her body felt, she would've had sex right then and there every time they kissed. She loved it when he sucked her neck. She had an actual orgasm the first time he put his mouth on her breast.

What was the point of waiting? She'd been wanting to sleep with Grunt for almost six months, ever since she had first seen him. Her inclination was to lose her virginity and get it over with, move on, but the *Playgirl* advice was that you keep their interest longer if you make them wait, and there was an answering instinct in her that confirmed it.

He liked her. She knew that much. He liked having her around. He'd come up when school was over and sort of nod his head toward the door. He didn't object when she said she couldn't, her parents would be wondering where she was. But he always did that nod. When they weren't making out they listened to music or played music or went to the arcade or punk synchro. And if she didn't know how he felt about her, she knew exactly how she felt about him. Gaga. She loved every hair on his chinny-chin-chin. His prominent Adam's apple, his smooth chest, his small teeth, his pink gums. His laugh, his sideways way of looking at things. His grunts.

The word *alive* had whole new meaning. She was alive. All her cells were awake for the first time. She went to bed thinking of Grunt. She woke up thinking of Grunt. In between she thought of Grunt.

This alone would have been all she needed. But to top it off, there was Scumbuckets. How their days went was: school, the garage, kissing and groping, blow job, Jonathon's arrival, Scumbuckets rehearsal, dinner, home. Or rehearsal, home.

When she played, Carol started out self-conscious but there was something about playing really loud and fast that made your heart go crazy and everything bust loose so that you'd do almost anything. Thrash the hair, thrash the neck of the guitar, jump, jump, jumpjumpjumpjump, shout things out, groan, roll your eyes, go mad. Carol took off her glasses to play, so she was blind, and this helped, too. Grunt had a flask that Hugh filled with Scotch, which also helped.

⌐

"LET'S GO OUT for dinner," her mother said one night when her father was on block and Glynnis was out. This made Carol suspicious but she couldn't see a way out of it, given that she had already concocted two major social studies projects with Lisa that had needed nightly work for weeks. They went to Oliver's Fish House on Yonge, where she had loved to go when she was younger because there were booths. Tonight, all the booths were taken. They had a table by the window instead.

"Well, isn't this nice," her mother said. "We haven't done this in forever."

Once they had ordered, her mother began talking in a mild voice, the voice that signalled trouble, the laying-a-trap voice.

"So, Carol, how are you? We haven't seen much of each other lately, have we?"

Is that a problem? Carol wanted to say.

"I have so many things in the evening, we just hardly ever see each other and I wanted to check in with you to see how you are doing."

"Fine."

"How is your math? Are you getting along better with Mr. Rose?"

"House on fire, Mom."

"No need to be sarcastic."

"I'll never get along better with Mr. Rose, he's an asshole."

"Language."

Yes, I'm using it, she wanted to say. She was starting to say more of the things she thought of saying, but she was not saying them all yet.

387

"Now how about boys." Carol became aware of the people at next table, a middle-aged couple who ate without speaking.

"How about boys, Mom."

"Are there any boys you're interested in?"

"Mo-om."

"I'm only asking because, well, this is the time of life these things happen. I know you've been interested in boys for years now and you might be ready to date. I'm not sure you'd tell me —"

What was her game here? Should Carol invent a boy to be interested in? Her instinct told her not to tell the truth.

"Uh, there is one guy I sort of like."

Her mother shifted back a little in her chair receptively.

"His name's Jonathon. He plays double bass in the stage band." Once begun, lying was so easy, so good, so much fun. "We're not exactly, like, dating, but he did invite me to a movie on Friday and I'd kind of like to go."

"What does he look like? Is he handsome?"

Oh, how sad it was. Her mother was trying to talk girl talk.

She screwed up her face. "I don't know if you'd say handsome. He's okay-looking, I guess."

"Is he tall? Short?"

"I don't know. Average height."

"Skinny?"

"No. He's more chunky than skinny. Mom, what's with the —"

"Does he have nice hair?"

"What?"

"What kind of hair does he have?"

Huh?

"I don't know. Regular hair." As she was saying regular, she got it. Fuck. "You know exactly what kind of hair he has."

"This is not the way I — "

Mrs. Riggs stopped abruptly and looked down at the table.

"Here we are," said the waitress, setting down the plates.

"Lovely," said Mrs. Riggs, smiling, actually smiling up at the waitress. Unbelievable. The waitress left. "This is not the way I meant things to go. I am worried sick about you, Carol. I'm just worried *sick*." She said it in her dire voice, her things-couldn't-be-worse voice. She went on to describe how she'd seen them in the Yonge-Eglinton Centre, how she hadn't even recognized Carol at first (to which Carol could not help smiling), how pro*found*ly *sha*ken she'd been when she had, how *des*perately *wor*ried she was that Carol would make a wrong turn now and regret it the rest of her life, how com*mit*ted she was to helping Carol through this *dif*ficult, *cruc*ial time, blah blah blah. She spoke for a long time and then finished off with, "Well, what do you say?"

"What do I say to what?"

"Are you with me?" She swung her fist. God, her mother was such a Girl Guide.

"Together we *can* prevent forest fires," Carol said, taking another mouthful of trout.

"Carol. I am serious. You could start by according me a little more respect."

"I don't need help, Mom. I'm fine. I'm great. You can help me by just staying out of my life."

"I'm your mother. I'm in your life whether you want it or not."
Great.

"Now, I'm not saying we'll forbid you to see this boy —"

"Good, because you can't, anyway."

"I don't like your tone, thank you very much. I'm not going to forbid you, because I want you to learn responsible behaviour and you don't learn that sitting home hating your mother for keeping you from seeing your friends. But we are going to set some limits. Your father and I want to meet this boy before you see him again."

"Oh, for Christ's sake, Mom —"

"Language."

"— people don't do that anymore."

"Well, anybody who wants to call me old-fashioned is welcome to do so, but I do want to meet him. I want to know what kind of a person you are spending time with. He did not make a good first impression, but I'm willing to concede I could have judged too quickly."

"Mom, this is stupid. There's no point. I'm going to see him tomorrow at school. You're not going to meet him between now and then."

"Why not? We could drop by his house on the way home."

"Are you kidding? I don't think so."

"Well, I was kidding, actually. I do have a sense of humour."

"Oh, yeah, you're a scream."

"I am trying to hold it together here when what I really want to do is paddle your bottom like you were a little girl and put you to bed without any dinner. This is dangerous, what you're doing, dangerous and harmful and just plain stupid. You're putting on this costume for this boy, you're acting like a, like a, an s-l-u-t, frankly, and let me tell you, you are going to pay for it later. You need to be yourself and be proud to be yourself, not try to turn yourself into someone else. You may think you're épater-ing the bourgeoisie, but frankly, the bourgeoisie has seen it all before and it all ends in the same place — with you hurt and miserable and who knows what else. I only have your well-being at heart, Carol."

Carol had no idea what her mother was talking about with the French and she had no comeback, except to say, "You're wrong," with her arms folded.

Mrs. Riggs looked around and said, "Let's go." Carol had finished half of her dinner. Her mother had barely touched hers.

Walking into the house, Mrs. Riggs said, "We are not done with this discussion."

"Oh yes we are," Carol muttered.

She wanted to phone Grunt but she had never phoned him before and he had never phoned her. She didn't know if he even knew she had his phone number. He'd be in the garage, anyway, where there was no phone.

When she saw him the next day, she couldn't figure out how to even bring it up. *My mother saw us yesterday ...* She didn't want to use words for what they had been doing, for any of the things they did with their bodies. Embarrassing, to speak of her mother. Embarrassing not knowing what words to use.

So she said nothing.

"C'mon," he said, after school. She was supposed to go straight home.

They went to his place, as usual, into the garage, where he plugged in the heater and grabbed the old brown sleeping bag off the shelf and wrapped it around them while they kissed and felt each other, whatever parts felt right to feel. Normally this led to a bump and grind with her back against the four-by-four strut of the shelf, to his fingers cupped around the outside of her pants, the heel of his hand rubbing, and then to her kneeling down in front of his open fly.

Once, Jonathon had walked in before they were done. They had all stopped and stared for a heartbeat, then he'd walked right out again, and Grunt had done up his pants, and she'd wiped her mouth. Grunt had been like a gleeful leprechaun the rest of the afternoon and Jonathon had blushed every time he looked at her and she'd gone from feeling mortified to sort of proud.

Today, instead of kneeling, she leaned forward with her hand around his balls in their underwear and said, "Fuck me." What she was going to do about the blood she didn't know.

She was close enough to see his eyes go big and he had to back off not to come right there. Oh. So this is what Lisa had been talking about when she'd said, "You gotta learn to use your power."

Carol must have looked blank, because she'd added, "Your power over their dicks."

There was no furniture in the garage except for lawn chairs. The floor was too cold. His eyes landed on the lower of the two wide shelves that lined the wall. It was stacked with boxes of Christmas lights and stove fuel and old suitcases. He cleared off a space for them and found another sleeping bag to cushion the plywood. Carol climbed up, not quite so sure now that it was about to happen, now that she was laying herself down for him. To get the feeling back, she said, "Fuck me," again and it had the same effect on him as before, a slackening and a gathering. He was at her mercy. He reached for her jeans behind the flaps of her open coat. Undid the fly, began to tug them down uncertainly. She wriggled, pushed the underwear with the pants, had already taken off her boots. She'd never felt so naked as now, in a cold snap in March, naked from the waist down. He took off his jacket, pulled down his suspenders, pushed his pants down to his thighs, put the jacket back on and began to try to find her vagina with his penis. She was ready for magic, she was ready for pain. He tentatively worked his way in, groaned and withdrew, then thrust barely a dozen times before lurching forward and gasping just as she was starting to think, *Oh, I see how this could feel good.* Her own fingers went in smoother and not as deep. But she could see getting to like this.

Jonathon tapped at the door. They dressed again, opened the door and let him in.

She felt no different and completely different. No longer a virgin. But the same. And not the same. A circle. Round and round.

Rowena

AS ROWENA DONNED cassock and surplice over skirt and blouse, there was a feeling of quiet excitement in the air. She and the others dressed in the choir room. The vestry was too small for twelve ordinands, three ministers and the moderator. Twelve ordinands like twelve apostles. How the link went back through time to the most basic of basics — the people drawn to one man, the people drawn to those people. Simple people spreading the Word simply, even despite the enormous complications of the Church, of churches. This twelve had among them five women. This twelve would be ordained by the first woman moderator of the United Church of Canada! The links went forward in time as well as back. They were bringing the church into modernity. It had to keep up with modern life, it had to, or it lost its relevance. She, too, had to keep up with modern life.

The twelve joked quietly amongst themselves like surgeons before an operation. How about that. The extraordinary was come ordinary. Well, life was full of marvels. She would never have thought, at age thirteen, that she would be here today, walking up the stairs now to gather in the narthex; it had been beyond the scope of her imagining (how sad that was, and how revolutionary the changes being wrought by feminism). Even three months ago, she would not have believed that when this day came she would feel so well, so happy and balanced and renewed. Of course there was a tremendous sense of renewal in the very fact of what was happening today. Today she was formally committing to a new life, one already begun, but today formally sanctioned and blessed.

She had, too, a new understanding of her daughters. The extra time with Carol was really paying off, and last week's school open house had been nothing short of revelatory.

Here, now the organ was starting, the congregation rose, the ordinands processed. In the large church, the people she loved raised their hearts to God, or she hoped they did, and she trusted God to see them and forgive her teenagers their adolescence. Her heart beat, proudly humble, as she walked up the aisle. She looked ahead to where the *Crucified Woman* used to be. She missed her.

Celia had wanted to see the sculpture after hearing Rowena describe the controversy, the meetings, the soap opera of characters, the final decision, yes, to take the daring course and put her in the church. (They had long lunches, she and Celia, once or twice a month. Rowena felt guilty about their length but they were always worthwhile.) So Rowena had brought her friend, and looked, really looked at the crucified woman for the first time. She was skinny. She was naked. Her breasts pointed different ways, one slightly up, one slightly down. Rowena had noticed this already, but Celia pointed it out. "Look," she said. "Mine do that, too." The woman's head drooped. Her nose was prominent in her face. Her hair hung. Her hips bespoke her womanhood just that touch beyond the usual depictions of the hips of Christ. Rowena realized that what she had not wanted to look at before was the sculpture's nakedness, her ordinary, unidealized human body.

"Huh," Celia had said, walking round and round.

"What do you think?"

"You know, I honestly don't know. I suppose it does make you think."

"She makes me uncomfortable."

"*Crucified Woman*, not female Christ."

"True."

"Were women crucified?"

"Apparently there's no evidence either way, but a little philosophy professor in our congregation thinks that there must have been. Slaves were the people crucified most. She thinks women slaves must have been, too."

"What for, I wonder."

They came to no conclusion that day. But Rowena found herself going into the church each day to sit with the *Crucified Woman*. And when Glenn began putting forth the same arguments she had used in February, she found herself sounding like Margaret. Glenn thought it presumptuous either way — if the woman was supposed to *be* Christ, well, that was just silly, because there was a historical personage and that historical personage was male; and if she was supposed to represent the suffering of women, well, did Rowena really think that all women had it worse than all men?

If you put it that way, it did feel presumptuous. Rowena didn't personally feel oppressed, exactly. That was not the point. The point was to get people asking questions. *What if* Jesus had been a woman? *What if* God were female? And to say, too, yes, women have suffered, physically, for the sins of the world.

The figure was not Christ, but it brought Rowena closer to a physical sense of Christ than she had ever come before. Other Christs were generalized. The not-Christ crucified woman was specific, a real woman. It was the breasts that did it, their asymmetrical pointing. Christ, too, must have been that particular.

The crucified woman was gone now, but she remained in that

Rowena would never return to her older version of Christ. She would always now be able to sense just beyond the reach of her senses the physical Christ, His skin, His finger-hairs, His ear-pattern, all unknowable but real and particular.

Now, the Right Reverend Wilson greeted the congregation. "Ministry is the work of God, done by the people of God." She smiled warmly at the ordinands, and went on. "We are here today to ..."

Rowena tried not to find her family right away, to wait until her eyes lit naturally on them. Ah. Easy enough. Carol's awful hair. Glenn beamed at her — how lovely, he was proud! — and winked. Ugh.

She'd been annoyed with him for not being there last week to accompany her to the girls' open house. Irrationally annoyed. He never missed anything he could help missing. He'd catch up with her as soon as the flight log was entered, as soon as he could make the drive from the airport.

In the meantime, she'd had to watch Glynnis' video alone.

The screening was in the drama room, a classroom made over to resemble a Bohemian rehearsal hall. Floor lamps lit two living-room-like corners with couches, beanbag chairs and carpet. The middle of the floor was bare.

The drama teacher walked with a literal swish, his pants were that wide. "Mrs. Riggs, how wonderful, hello, hello, welcome. Where's our young star, is she with you? No? Ah, here's the director, where's Glynnis, where's Stephen, they need to mix." Then he was off greeting the next parent, Stephen's mother.

They had made three videos, not just one, none of which Rowena thought was quite as offensive as *A Day in the Life of a Teenage Cripple*. *A Day in the Life of a Teenage Asthmatic*. *A Day in the Life of a Teenage Neurotic*.

Here was Glynnis, nervous and trying not to look it. "Hi, Mom." With her was a girl (a girl? yes, a girl) with a tuque on. "Novak," Rowena surmised, about whom she had heard so much.

The tuque seemed odd, some kind of affectation.

The room swelled with students, a few sundry parents, Tamara's mother, who, without meaning to, always made Rowena feel stodgy.

The teacher clapped his hands.

How is he *allowed* to teach, Rowena wondered as she had for the last three years. He is *so* effeminate.

The principal arrived, making Rowena blush the more for the swishy teacher. He didn't *need* to do any of it.

"I have the most terrific pleasure," he said, resting his chin on his folded-together hands, "of introducing three videos by Tamara Byrnes. *A Day in the Life of a Teenage Neurotic. A Day in the Life of a Teenage Asthmatic* and *A Day in the Life of a Teenage Cripple.*

Rowena winced, she could not help it. She wanted to shout out, *She's not a cripple, what an awful thing to say.* But Glynnis was the one saying it and Glynnis was undisturbed, chatting to her friends, settling into a beanbag chair with that Novak, determinedly not looking in her mother's direction. Rowena understood but felt shut out anyway. They had become distant.

Oh.

Because Glynnis talked — she was always talking, making editorials, cutting up, arguing — Rowena had not noticed that they did not really *talk*.

Rowena tried to spread her time around, she really did, but it was Carol who'd needed her most this last while. They'd gone to movies. They'd gone to the art gallery. They'd gone to the symphony. Just the two of them. Glynnis had been so busy. She never had time for more than the most token bits of family time. Glynnis would be her next project, Rowena decided.

The sound quality on the videos was patchy. You saw Stephen wake up, wheeze, go to the bathroom, not let the camera follow him in. You actually saw the jostle as he put out his hand to stop it. Then the camera watched the door and you heard Stephen's voice saying,

"What you're hearing is me turning on the taps. It is *not* me peeing."
The kids laughed. They loved this. Stephen's mother laughed, too,
loudest when she saw her loud American self in bright flowered robe
saying "Morning, sweetie," and Stephen rolling his eyes at the plush-
ness of her affection. You saw Stephen going to school. Saw girls say
hi to him, saw boys look away or sneer. "What's with the camera,
Wheeze-Box?" You saw him take puffs here and there from his
puffer. Later there was an out-of-time sequence that showed all
the puffer uses. "God, Wheeze-Box, you're such a fag."

The teacher definitely ought not to be teaching.

"I'm an asthmatic."

Rowena snuck a look at Stephen's mother, but she did not seem
upset. "You tell him, honey," she called out.

The same routine was repeated with Tamara, only she was awake
already when the camera came in (she had not slept). The camera
followed her into the bathroom and turned away from her as she uri-
nated — there was no nudity, but the sound was uncomfortable,
Stephen was right to run the taps — and showed her using an astonishing amount of toilet paper, wrapping it right round her arm so as
not to get any drips. Afterwards, she washed her hands for a very
long time before picking up a towel, about which she asked off-
screen if it was clean. In the kitchen, her mother smoked and read
the paper, while Tamara made herself a sandwich, "untouched by
human hands!" Later the video showed her eating the sandwich
from its bag, fingers on the plastic, declaring again that it was
untouched by human hands. Rowena was shocked. She'd had no
idea that Tamara's cleanliness obsession was so severe. She needed
help. But here, too, Tamara's mother, like Stephen's, was laughing
and shaking her head.

Glynnis was next. Rowena's palms were sweating. She wiped them
discreetly on the arms of her sweater. There she was. Asleep. What a
long time since she'd watched her children sleeping. Sometimes they

fell asleep in the car or on the chesterfield, but she had fallen out of the habit of really looking, of using that chance to simply love the face, unconscious of any gaze under which it changed. Then Glynnis' radio snapped on and she woke with a start. And there. Just there. There it was, the change, from innocence to savagery. From blank slate to broken slate, cynicism clattering from the corners of her mouth. Rowena felt it like nails on a chalkboard, the difference between what Glynnis could be and what she was trying to make herself be. Then there they were in the kitchen, she at the coffee pot, Glenn at the table with the paper. How old they looked, how like *parents* they sounded. How poorly that discussion had gone, the one about this video she was now watching. Her face felt hot. What the scene did was criticize her, and what it criticized her for was nothing other than being who and what she was. It was not fair.

Now here was Glynnis back in her bedroom, showing off her leg, the scars and the skin grafts, the stiff ankle, the difference in leg length. Again Rowena wanted to call out. For heaven's sake. Did Glynnis not see all she had? *Stop being sorry for yourself, young lady. Stop feeling hard done by. There are people worse off than you by a good long shot. You're not making it any easier by dwelling on it.* At the same time, Rowena was remembering the tiny crushed leg on the gurney. So small! A stick. Glynnis had been so little. So young. She had not had enough time to enjoy that body, whole. She *had* lost something. She'd lost something most people took for granted.

Then came the rest of Glynnis' day, a day that seemed to show how well regarded she was by staff and students alike. Teachers turned to her in class, students laughed at her answers, which were wry and right. Students called out to her in the halls, in the cafeteria. She was a *presence*, bobbing down the hall with her limp. Couldn't she see this? No. There was that sneer.

And now she was at home again, getting undressed. "You know what this," she gestured at the camera, the person behind it, the video, "made me realize? My life is really boring. Like, *nothing* happened today. But okay, here's the other thing. People treated me differently. They saw the camera, they went, 'Oh, better act like we like her.'"

No! Glynnis. No! They like you. Believe it.

"God, I sound so sucky, don't I? I'm not really this much of a suck. I'm not. Shut up.

"This one time? In grade seven? The year had started really badly. I walked in on the first day and I was wearing The Shoes." She held up a pair of oxfords with the built-up heel. "Not these ones, but a pair just like them. They were brand new, I'd never worn orthopedic shoes before, I'd had this big fight with my mother about them, and she made me promise to wear them. We have this thing in our family where a promise is, like, sacred. If you promise something, that's it, you do it. Anyway, they're new, I'm not used to them, they have these really friction-y rubber bottoms that, like, grab the floor, and the left one has an inch-high heel, which I'm also not used to. So I walk into the first day of grade seven and I'm sauntering to the back because all the cool kids sit at the back and I'm a cool kid, that's where I belong, so there I am, saunter saunter, and then, *bam*. The sole of The Shoe grabs the floor and, like, pitches me toward the wall. Okay, that's not so bad. I try to recover, I make a joke, I call them Frankenshoes. But nobody laughs. They just look at me like I'm not even there.

"It was like that all year. This one time, I overheard these people talking about me. Not just anybody, these were my friends, well, not all of them, three of them were and one was someone I didn't really know. And they were going — this is a direct quote — 'She's really not that bad, you know. She just tries too hard.' 'She's not that bad. She just tries too hard.' Trying too hard: the cardinal sin. Then they have this debate about whether they should tell me or not. That's such a girl thing, isn't it? 'Someone should tell her.' 'Yeah, right. Who's going to tell her? Not me.' 'I'll tell her.' 'Right. You're going to go up to her and say, Um, Glynnis, I know you really want to be cool but in case you haven't noticed, you have a limp, and, uh, well, a limp just isn't cool, so when you try to be cool you just make yourself look more stupid."

Who? Rowena wanted to know, boiling. Which of Glynnis' friends had said that?

"Well," said Glynnis, and paused. "Thing was, they were right. There was this girl at summer camp — same summer, this is, like, two months before — who was a Thalidomide baby. She had only an upper arm. Ends at the elbow. And I had actually had the same thought about her they had about me: 'She's trying too hard.' 'Why does she have to wear a tube top?' 'Why does she have to be so angry?'

"And then, like two months later, I'm like, Aha. This is why.

"I actually felt like I was going to die that day. What I would do, I would close my eyes, turn off my heart, dissolve in a molten pool of self-hatred. The End.

"I went around in this, like, stone box for about a month. And then I got mad. Fuck 'em, I thought. Fuck 'em. Fuck 'em. Fuck 'em.

"The girl at camp? The reason I thought she was too angry? One day she'd taken a marker and on the front of the arm, on the front of the stump, she'd written *Fuck* and on the back, she'd written *you*, so when she waved it back and forth, it said *Fuck you Fuck you Fuck you Fuck you*. She walked into her cabin and she just stood there in her tube top, waving it back and forth. *Fuck you Fuck you Fuck you*."

Glynnis sat there looking at the camera with a smile on her face. She held The Shoe lightly in her hand and smiled at the camera with a kind of mad peacefulness.

"I mean, that's fuckin brilliant."

The room had gone still. It was the kind of story that did that. Barely even a story at all, and it stopped people, arrested them. Rowena had to hold back a sob. Here was a whole person she did not know! Same revelation about Glynnis as about Carol in the mall. She did not know her own daughter. She bit her lip. She knew no one. Not her husband, not her son, not her friends. No one. We're all sealed up inside ourselves and only reveal certain bits in certain ways. Thank God for God.

She wanted to hug Glynnis, to tell her how proud she was. But Glynnis slipped out before she could catch her.

⌐

"HERE IS MY servant whom I uphold." The Old Testament lesson was from Isaiah. Maybe she should have asked Jay or Glynnis to read after all. "I have endowed him with my spirit that he may bring true justice to the nations."

Rowena bowed her head. True justice to the nations. Such a large responsibility she was undertaking.

"Faithfully he brings true justice; he will neither waver, nor be crushed until true justice is established on earth ..."

What inspiration in this book. *I will neither waver, nor be crushed.* Like Milt. Like Desmond Tutu. Like Gandhi. Like Christ. *I will neither waver, nor be crushed.*

⌐

GLENN HAD FOUND HER at the open house in the hall. He was uniformed still and prominent, and the sight of him had its usual effect — that catch in her heart. Hooked. She leaned into him briefly before they proceeded down the hall and she tried to explain the video, how she'd seen Glynnis as a separate individual entirely, little known, unknowable, but also so like herself in looks, still in so much danger of staying angry and bitter for life, despite that end note of — what was it? — acceptance of non-acceptance? He put his arm around her, he leaned down to listen, and she felt completed. He was there.

In the viewing stands for the swimming pool was an enormous crush. This was a much more popular event than the videos. The parents were crowded into a back corner, where one couple argued in low voices: But it was a pregnant shark. Why get squeamish about fetal pigs? You're happy enough to eat bacon. *You're not logical,* the man was really shouting. *You don't listen to me,* said the woman. They sounded as if the thing they really wanted to do was annoy each other, it had become their goal in life. Rowena hoped she and Glenn never became like that.

A big man in a crumpled fine grey suit joked his way through the students, then greeted the group of parents. "I'm told not to expect Esther Williams," he said. "Hi, Wilf Eberhardt." Kelly's father. They shook his hand and introduced themselves.

"Where's the punker? Kelly told me there was a punker."

"There? With the shaved head?"

No, that was Glynnis' friend, the one with the tuque. A familiar-looking woman shook her head and rolled her eyes. "That's my daughter. Any opportunity to make us crazy." Ah. The city councillor.

Around them students chattered, found ways to gain each other's attention. Boys stole hats or doo-dads, girls shrieked. Rowena had never been one of those girls. She had not liked those girls. They seemed harmless enough now, but she was glad she did not have to prance and grab, glad she had a man at her shoulder, glad she was not young, sorry for her children that they were, sorry for all the pain they would have to go through. Not that she would take their youth from them — just its pain. But of course they went together, they would always go together. Joy, too.

Over the PA came a blur of static, a flitting up the radio dial through half-tuned stations until it rested in a mildly static groove.

Two girls — ah, Glynnis and Kelly — bustled out in old-fashioned bathing suits, loud, flowered bathing caps, bright lipstick and reading glasses. "Good evening," Kelly said in a nasal voice. "I'm Betty J. Vickers and this is my sister, Bobbi R. Vickers. You may have heard of us. We're the Vickers sisters, 1965 Synchronized Swimming Champeens. We're here today to introduce you to an exciting new art form and sport that I fully expect to see integrated into the next summer Olympics. Now we were a little skeptical at first, I admit, but our young friends Ike and Spike convinced us — before they overdosed — that punk synchro was the new wave, so to speak, of synchronized swimming, and, well, after just one week of coaching these talented swimmers, we agreed." They whipped off their bathing caps, formed their hair into points, put giant safety pins in their cheeks.

Then the music began — the three ascending notes on a bass guitar that Glynnis had imitated in the kitchen continuing under the weird sci-fi vocals — and the kids bounced out from the dressing room like strangely clad pogo sticks. They were in torn T-shirts and cut-offs held together with safety pins. They spread themselves out around the pool.

The students around them roared.

The punk boy — they had met him, at last. Meeting him had been such a sticking point. Carol had refused point blank at first but then when she had neglected to be home on time the very next day after their first talk, Rowena had insisted on a name, address and phone number, and if Carol wasn't home when she said she would be, Rowena would be calling and embarrassing Grant until she did get home. She had threatened to go find them at lunch or after school, to descend unannounced. So Carol had brought him home, this Grant. He had flat eyes that revealed nothing. The eyes of the stupid or the very hard-shelled. No excitement, no nervousness, no fear. He'd been like a board. Yes. No. One-word answers to everything they asked. It was very hard after meeting him to okay Carol's seeing him. He was a blank page. An empty vessel. But they had met.

Now. His skinny chest, ribs showing. Young. He was a young kid, like Carol. He was figuring himself out. Here he was having fun, he was grinning like a kid, he was doing all the moves. And Rowena's opinion of him began to change. She saw how it could all be a protective shell, all of it. Glynnis told her he had a stammer, which was why he spoke so little. Carol alluded to a mean father.

How badly hurt children can be. We think they are resilient. We think the things that happen to them don't matter. But they do. All we can hope for is not to do too much damage. Despite our best efforts, every single one of us is damaged. Why, she herself. Glenn. June. Everyone she knew was affected by the things that had happened to them as children, the parents they had had. A lucky few had had wonderful parents and were wonderful themselves. A marvellous many overcame it all to become the basically good people of which society was made. Some few were damaged beyond repair. Her children seemed to think they were the very first ever to have such miserable parents. They didn't know how good they had it. Glenn's father got himself killed in the war, his mother had been an overcompensating smotherer. Her mother had gone mad and died, her father hid and drank and her grandmother slapped her for no reason at all.

Carol and Grant and Glynnis and the girl who had shaved her head, they did not look damaged beyond repair. Not at all. God grant that none of these children were, neither the ones who looked frail not the ones who looked strong. God grant.

Their routine was silly and inelegant and the teenagers around them ate it up. Rowena felt like smacking her head with her hand. All this time she'd been seeing it wrong. It was a comedy routine, a parody, a skit, a skit in water, just like the skits they had done at her high school. They had picked the music, done the costumes, worked out a routine and were performing it. They were exactly like the members of her glee club, though they would protest loudly if she ever made the comparison to them.

So much that she was afraid of she didn't need to be afraid of. And how wonderful that Carol was part of it, for once.

⮌

THE RIGHT REVEREND Wilson spoke to them now, as they stood in a row in the weak light of the May morning. "Sisters and brothers, you have been called to an ordained ministry. Remember that you are called to serve rather than to be served, to proclaim the faith of the church, to look after the concerns of God above all. So that we may know you believe yourselves to be called by God and that you profess the Christian faith, we ask you: Do you trust that God has called you to the life and work of ordained ministry?"

"I do so trust," said Rowena, with the others, tears of joy behind her eyes.

"Are you persuaded that the holy Scriptures contain all things necessary for eternal salvation through faith in Jesus Christ?"

"I am so persuaded, by God's grace," they said.

"Will you be faithful in prayer, in the study of the holy Scriptures, and with the help of the Holy Spirit continually rekindle the gift of God that is in you?"

"I will, God being my helper." Rowena thought of Brownies. Of the afternoon she prayed that the hurt child not be Carol and not be someone else's and the gift God had given her out of that ill-formed, illogical, unfair prayer. Out of that *human* prayer. She almost wept.

After the moderator had laid on hands and addressed them as ordained ministers — "Rowena Riggs, we recognize you as an ordained minister of the United Church of Canada" — a solemn moment during which Rowena was filled with joy, Rowena looked again at the congregation and found her family, all smiling at her, even Carol.

She herself was beaming, filled with the greatest sense of well-being she had felt in her life. The communion followed — her first communion as an ordained minister. There was a special smile on Milt's face as he pressed the cube of bread into her hand. She bent her head and prayed. Oh Lord, thank you for all your blessings. For my children and the chance to raise them, for this call and this new career and the chance to serve you. She raised her head. The communion was being offered to her family now, the bread and wine passed along the pew. Glynnis joked with Jay, flicked her eyes at Rowena, almost raised her Dixie cup. Glenn ate solemnly as he always did, then flicked the little cup of juice like it was a holy chaser. And Carol — what was happening with Carol. Her hand was over her mouth. She was running out. Tearing out. Oh, how too bad. The poor girl was not feeling well.

Carol

MAYBE SHE WAS still a little drunk. Should've been sleeping. Sleeping during the day was magic, especially during a day of blazing sunshine. Fuck the sunshine, give me the dark. The dark's way better 'cause it's ... 'cause it's dark dark dark. Come with me and we'll sit in the park duhnuhnuh. The dark's way better 'cause it's dark dark dark. Come with me and we'll sit in the park duhnuhnuh. We'll sit in the park and we'll grope and paw. Just don't bring the law law law. You could be as stupid as you wanted in lyrics, it didn't matter.

Instead of sleeping the day away, she was in church. Watching her mother get ordained. Who else did this happen to? It was surreal. Grunt'd be sleeping. Till noon. Or two. She thought of his sleeping body, of sleeping beside him, which she had never done for more than an hour. After the gig last night they'd gone to a party somewhere, she didn't even really know where since she'd got there in the back of Jonathon's van with the equipment. A squat. People he knew lived like this, not in houses with their parents but in abandoned buildings. She suddenly saw they had a whole separate city that she hadn't even known existed. An underworld. Where she belonged. He'd been wired, still, jumping up and kicking the wall out of pure excess energy. And she'd had to get home for her mother's ordination.

She almost laughed out loud in the middle of the service. They had no fucking idea, none, none of these people. Someone was reading the lesson now. It was about sheep. The lesson was always about sheep. They were sheep. All of them, the whole congregation, following along, bleating. And she was the black one. She almost laughed again. Her stomach felt funny. Glynnis smirked alongside her. Glynnis had been there. Glynnis knew. She was glad Glynnis knew. She was glad someone who'd known Carol knew Skunk, that there was someone to take back to the old world news of the new one, even if only in her head.

Glynnis leaned into her ear and said, "Edmund Fitzgerald got wrecked."

Carol had to hold her sides.

She was a different person than she'd been yesterday. Yesterday she'd been Carol. Today she was Skunk. It wasn't just a made-up name anymore. It was who she was. Scumbuckets had performed. Skunk had performed. Skunk lived.

Jonathon's brother's girlfriend's cousin was the booking manager at the Pontiac on Sherbourne. Jonathon had been bugging him and bugging him to listen to their two-song demo and finally he'd booked them in to cover for a band from Manitoba that was supposed to open for the Bopcats but that had had to cancel because their van had broken down outside of Thunder Bay. They'd only had, like, two days' notice, and they had barely enough songs to make a set. They'd had to fill out their set list with covers. "God Save the Queen" had been done before, they couldn't do that. Or "My Way." They tried doing "Feelings," but it sucked too badly even to make into a joke. Then they were joking about long songs to fill up the time and Carol said "Wreck of the Edmund Fitzgerald" and Grunt went, "Edmund Fitzgerald got wrecked got wrecked, Edmund Fitzgerald got wrecked" and then Jonathon (whom Grunt called Boy Death) went, "Edmund Fitzgerald broke his neck broke his neck,

Edmund Fitzgerald got wrecked," and Grunt went, "My mom said, Let this be a lesson, son" ("Edmund Fitzgerald got wrecked," went Skunk and Boy Death). "Don't drink and drive or you'll end up on your bum" ("Edmund Fitzgerald got wrecked"). Fifteen minutes later they had another four minutes' worth of set. They did a punk "Georgy Girl" and a ska "I Am Woman," which Boy Death and Grunt both sang along with. They tried a punk "Snowbird," but it just didn't work.

Carol had felt like a zombie before the gig, she was that nervous. But then they did the sound check in the afternoon and it was nothing, all she had to do was take off her glasses, that was it. She was Skunk. (Her hair was growing back in so she had a white stripe down the middle of her head.)

Grunt introduced her that way, and with the name came a new power she hadn't known she had. Skunk could do things Carol would never do. Skunk could do things Carol was too chicken to do. Skunk could do any-fuckin-thing in the world. Skunk was afraid of nothing. Skunk could drink guys under the table. Skunk used half a bottle of hairspray and made her hair stick out. Skunk let her heartbeat lead her where it would. Skunk threw herself around on stage like a crazy person. She bent over and yelled into the mic, she flung herself backwards. "I'm Skunk. And I'm rrrrrabid," she said.

If these people in the church knew, if they knew, they'd shit their pants, that's what they'd do. She heard it in her head as a song. If these people kne-ew, if these people kne-ew, they'd shit their pants, that's what they'd do-o.

She smiled again. Glynnis whapped her thigh and nodded at the front of the church, like, Pay attention, only she didn't mean it.

Sermon now. About "the call," and the three levels of "the call" and God's work and people's work and blah blah blah. "You're born, you live, you die. It's chance that the human race is here at all," Hugh had said last night. "Life at all. Right batch of chemicals, right distance from the sun. Coulda happened, coulda not. But it happened. And what people *do*, well, doesn't matter at all. We'll die out sooner or later." Mariellen had tried to object to this, but it was hard to refute in the end. Her argument was, Well, we *are* here and we *have* feelings, so why not try to be, you know, sort of decent to one another.

"But that's just it," Hugh had shouted. "Most people aren't decent. They want to look decent, but they aren't. They hurt each other the way they would either way and then they cover it up with something that excuses them and lets them think they didn't hurt anyone or if they did that it was justified." And Carol remembered a conversation with Miss Balls where she'd said the same things. She thought about herself and Glynnis and how they both made excuses, even about little things, but about the accident, there they did it on a large scale. Glynnis excused herself for being mean to Carol while sucking up to Alison, and Carol excused herself for lashing out at her. Mr. and Mrs. Riggs excused themselves for killing Mortimer. Miss Balls excused herself for calling two black girls pickaninnies, which had got her booted out of the Girl Guides. Whoever killed Emanuel Jaques probably excused himself, whoever killed the lady in the park.

Life was meaningless, people hurt each other, that was that, and here they were going on about God is Good, God is Love. God is nothing. There's just people, and people suck. Except for a few. So why not have a good time? She could think all this almost gleefully. It was not depressing. It just was.

Now they were being ordained. Her mother looked short up there, with the minister passing in front of her and putting her hand on her head. She was too far away for Carol to read her expression, but her posture seemed fake to her, the bowed head, the hands with the fingers entwined, false humility, although for an instant her certainty of her mother's falsehood flickered and was gone and it seemed possible that she truly was humble and putting something bigger before herself.

The communion came around, the little cups of grape juice and the square of bread. She ate and drank without thinking and then people were standing up and turning to the people around them and shaking their hands and saying "The peace of the Lord." All these people, all these gestures, hollow.

She'd got home at four in the morning. Opened the door normally, confident, somehow, that it was so late everyone had to be sleeping. They'd have thought Carol had come home with Glynnis at one or whenever and anyway, what the fuck, she was Skunk, what were they going to do, kick her out of the house? Fine.

She was right. They were sleeping. Even her mother, who had said the day before she didn't know if she'd be able to sleep a wink.

Suddenly Carol's stomach heaved and her face flushed and she knew she had to get out of there. Luckily she was on the end of a pew. The person at the end of the pew behind her held out her hand as if that's what Carol had meant to do, come give her the peace of the Lord, and she brushed by the hand and held her breath. Out in the hall, she ran for the exit, burst through the doors and around the corner and barfed into the bushes with her hands against the wall of the church.

Fuck.

She wondered how Grunt was feeling this morning. She had to see him. Had to. Right now. Because how she felt was, well, physically crappy, okay, but happy. Crappy and happy, crappy and happy. Everything was a punk song.

"Carol?" said Glynnis.

"Snot my name anymore."

"You okay?"

"I am so okay. I am pretty fuckin okay."

"Okay. Good. 'Cause it looked like you were barfing."

"I love barfing."

"Where are you going?"

"See ya."

"Carol. For fuck's — you can't just take off."

"See ya."

"You are so dead, you know that."

"Bye."

"What do I tell Mom and Dad?"

"Sayonara."

Glynnis

THEY HAD KISSED. She tried to maintain her outer composure but her whole body was smiling. They had kissed. Finally. In the back hall of the bar, beside the stack of beer cases. A malty kiss. A backdoor kiss. A fleeting, lippy, soft-lip kiss. If she closed her eyes, tuned down the lesson — "He summoned his twelve disciples, and gave them authority over unclean spirits" ('unclean spirits,' ha! went a corner of her mind) — turned up the soundtrack in her head (high-speed Scumbuckets even though they'd finished their set at the time of the actual kiss), she could almost feel it again. Lips against lips. A completely singular feeling, there was no comparison. She'd had no idea. None.

"First Simon, who is called Peter," went the lay reader, someone's daughter, a girl who licked her lips nervously and raced over groups of words then paused as if waiting for everybody else to catch up. Rowena should have got Glynnis to read, only Glynnis was a non-believer (fingers crossed, warding away the devil). "Go to the lost sheep of the house of Israel," the girl continued. "And as you go, preach, saying, 'The kingdom of heaven is at hand.' Cure the sick, raise the dead, cleanse the lepers, cast out devils." Glynnis pictured her mother pulling a palm off a supplicant's head, yelling like a TV preacher. "Demon come out," she whispered to Jay.

Carol last night. Man. Unbelievable. Carol last night was a cast-out devil, she was a fury. "I'm Skunk. And I'm rrrabid-uh." She was brilliant. Glynnis knew her better than anybody and even Glynnis hadn't known she had it in her.

Glynnis had been worried about getting in. She'd never been to a bar before. Tamara had put eyeliner on the corners of Glynnis' eyes to make her look older and made her a drain-chain necklace and bracelet to make her look more punk. Kelly wore Chinese slippers and pajama-y pants, men's shirt hanging overtop. Except for Tamara, who wore pointy boots and leopard skin every day, and Stephen, in his mod sixties suit, and Novak, who'd shaved the head again and wore a white T-shirt and jeans with skinny black suspenders, their costumes were all visibly inauthentic. But they let them in.

They not only let them in, they offered them beer, pitchers of it. It was bland and drinkable. They drank. The bar filled. The band came on — Glynnis hadn't seen Carol up till then, they must have a back room or something — and surprised the hell out of them by being actually pretty good. Glynnis would never have known that Grunt was that funny. He was, like, either Mr. Deadpan or a big goof at punk synchro. But the biggest surprise was Carol. Carol taking over the stage like Carole Pope. For a minute everything was so different about her that Glynnis didn't notice the obvious thing. Carol was not wearing her glasses. She was blind up there, she was blind as a bat. She was working like a bat, on radar, zinging herself up and down and forward and back on the stage, always swooping back to the mic just before she needed to, to yell-sing the next song. This was not the Carol Glynnis heard singing in her bedroom at home. This was —

"I'm Skunk," Carol said. "And I'm rabiiiiiid-uh!"

— a rabid skunk.

Glynnis didn't notice getting drunk. But she danced in public for the first time since grade seven, when a gigantic group of kids at the first dance had gone, "Do the Glynn-is!" instead of "Do the hus-tle!" If she was dancing in public, she had to be drunk. They were all dancing, everyone in the bar, practically, was dancing, the dance floor was packed. Everyone was sweating and hooting and a couple of guys were slam dancing and she and Novak started slam dancing too. Jump jump jump, bam, shoulder check. Jump jump bam. Bam. And then the punk guys. Bam bam. They hit hard, harder than she and Novak. Bam. After the first time, she was ready. Bam. It was satisfying, it was visceral, it was kinetic beauty. It was some kind of weird and perfect human connection. Total strangers bouncing off of each other like a mock fight, the one that would avert the real fight. Late in the evening, the punk guys disappeared, Bopcats were playing rockabilly and she and Novak were still slamming each other. Bam. Bam. Once, they missed, their timing was wrong and they glanced off of each other. They were down on the floor, Novak was crossways on top of her and they were laughing but time elongated, their eyes locked, and ten minutes later they were in the back hall in a little U in the middle of three stacks of two-fours, feeling lip on lip and body against body. And then there was a flick of movement in the corner of their eyes — waiter coming back with another case of empties — and then it was closing time and they were out of there, outside, heat coming off them in waves in the cool spring air, off the big gang of them, loud and drunk. Glynnis had tried to find Carol. She'd congratulated her as soon as their set ended but lost track of her when the Bopcats came on. Oh well. She was a big girl. She'd find her own way home.

Now here they were in church. She almost laughed out loud. Carol, too, was giddy. Nobody here had been where they'd been, nobody knew what they knew. She had never felt closer to her.

As they stood up to exchange the peace after communion, Carol pushed past her and hurried out the back of the church. Glynnis wanted to follow, but you don't just run out of church. Unless your sister does, and she might need you.

Outside, Carol was straightening up beside a flower bed, pulling her hair back from her face and wiping her mouth. "Are you okay?" asked Glynnis. She had not heard Carol come in last night. Thankfully, their mother hadn't either. Let's hope she hadn't noticed Carol having to run out and barf in the middle of the ceremony.

"I'm so okay. I'm really fuckin okay."

Wait a minute. Carol was leaving. She couldn't leave. She couldn't do that.

But she was.

She was breaking all the rules. She didn't know when to stop. It was one thing to drink and smoke and stay out late. It was another to leave your mother's ordination. Glynnis was in awe. The magnitude of what Carol was doing!

It made Glynnis feel terribly young, a child frightened of her parents' anger, while Carol was beyond that. Grown up. She felt, glancingly, as if she had lost something irreplaceable. Dragons live forever but not so little boys.

~

DAZED, GLYNNIS made her way back inside. The service would be over soon. A reception would follow the ceremony, upstairs in the hall. They were supposed to stay for a short while before heading home for the garden party her father had planned. Glynnis meandered up. Two women bustled in the kitchen, getting out coffee cups and trays of goodies. She felt again the contrast between last night and this morning. Beer fumes and church coffee. The feeling of the kiss was back. Lips against lips. *Novak*, her heart cried out inarticulately. *Novak*. What she meant was *I love you*. All those months of agonizing, of mute pining, of seesawing wildly from day to day and hour to hour, of pretending they were just friends while being certain they were more than that, of being certain they were just friends while mourning not being more, over. O-ver. They had kissed. She could hardly wait to see her again — tonight, maybe? Could she somehow get away? Tomorrow, certainly.

People began to mill into the hall. Her brother found her. "What happened to Crull?"

"She had to puke."

He smirked. "Hungover?"

"Very."

"Who's hungover?" a beatific Mrs. Riggs said.

"Oh, shit," said Glynnis, and watched her mother's face slump like a cliffside in California rain.

"Oh, no," said her mother. "I thought she was —" Her eyebrows set into a line. "Oh, no."

Now Glynnis had to tell her mother, too, that Carol had walked away from the church, that Carol was not, presumably, coming to the garden party their father had planned and had catered, the party that was waiting for them at home.

Ever since she'd first glimpsed her mother crying at the hospital, afraid the accident had been her fault, Glynnis was attuned to vulnerability in her mother. Sometimes she turned a blind eye toward it, saw it and then pretended she hadn't. Today her heart broke for the woman. Minutes earlier Glynnis had never felt closer to Carol. But Carol. By walking away, Carol had broken a contract she and Glynnis had signed by being born a year and a half apart. Null and void.

Carol

THE FATHER ANSWERED the door this time. "Looking for Loverboy?" he said. "Your guess is as good as mine. Gonzo. AWOL. Didn't come home last night. Not home by tonight, guess I'm calling the probation officer. Dumb little fuck. He's got two months left. Two months."

Carol was not expecting this. She did not have enough money for the subway. She had no idea where the squat was. There was nothing to do now but walk home.

It shouldn't have thrown her as much as it did. Big deal. He'd be home later.

But she had the feeling that he wouldn't. That having missed his curfew, having broken his probation, he had broken it fully. He would not come home. He'd stay at the squat. With his buddies. Who all seemed like complete strangers now, though last night they'd felt like her most intimate friends. What did she know about having friends, anyway? He wanted to be free. He was free.

And she. She was a poseur. (She thought of the X-Ray Spex song. Fuggin brilliant.) Her mother's ordination. A garden party. Well-heeled middle-aged people eating vegetables and tiny quiches. The pilots and their wives. They would call her dear and ask what her favourite subject was.

Death.

Well, isn't that interesting. Roy, Carol's favourite subject is Death. I didn't know it was a subject. Is that an elective, dear, or is it a required subject?

Luckily they were all in the garden. It was not hard to sneak in the front door and hide out in her room.

She lay on her bed. After a time, she opened the bottom junk drawer in the cupboard. Hey. There were the tapes she had made with Miss Balls when she was walking Mortimer, before Miss Balls died. She had not listened to them in years.

She took out a tape and popped it in the tape deck.

"That war was declared on my eighteenth birthday seemed terribly significant to me. I thought right away I would play a part in it. We heard the news not long before noon. My brother Tom and I were out for a tramp. Tom was about to go up to Oxford. A boy called out to us, a boy sitting on a stone fence. He called out to anyone who passed by. 'There's going to be a war!'

"Well! It changed everything. Tom didn't go up to Oxford, he went to Sandringham. Monty was suddenly our neighbour on Salisbury Plain. Papa didn't go back to Toronto with me and his new wife so I could 'come out' as he wanted me to — this would have been after I did a tour of the continent with Aunt Charlotte and Emily — he rejoined his regiment. His wife stayed with us at Aunt Charlotte's.

At Christmastime, Papa and Monty were home on leave — Tom had just died, we were all grief-stricken, it was quite the awfullest Christmas ever. My cousin Freddy, just a little younger than me, declared his intention of lying about his age and joining up come the new year. Papa hated lying. I thought he'd pounce on Freddy, who had only to wait a few months for his eighteenth birthday. But Papa seemed to approve. So I said I'd do the same, I'd lie about my age and join up, I'd join a VAD."

Here Carol's younger voice broke in to ask what a VAD was.

"Volunteer Aid Detachment. They were run by the Red Cross. They did all sorts of things, ran canteens and so on, hospitals, but it came to mean a volunteer nurse, VAD.

"Didn't we have the biggest row. We'd already had great fights about my becoming a nurse, but this was the biggest of them all. Oh, I can't even begin to tell you. Women had no place in war, he said, VADs were ninnies, trained nurses were donkeys. No self-respecting lady would put herself in a position to see the things a nurse saw. It might be all right for the lower classes, but ... Well. You get the picture. Tom would have defended me. Monty was no help at all.

"Trouble was you had to be twenty-three to be a VAD. I looked old for my age, but I didn't think I looked twenty-three. You only had to be twenty-one to begin training as a Nursing Sister.

"As I lay in bed that night in the pitch black, I resolved I would do it. I would do it when Freddy did it, first thing in the New Year. I was meant to be a nurse. I felt it in my bones."

Carol could see Miss Balls' gesture here, her bent elbow and clenched fist as if her bones were feeling it even then. "Every time I encountered something injured, I felt a thrill, a physical pull, a fascination and a curiosity about how best to make it better. I suppose I might have thought of becoming a doctor if I'd been a bit more imaginative. But there was Miss Nightingale, and Miss Wetherby-Simms —" (that was Miss Balls' Girl Guide captain) "— and they made me very set on nursing."

"In the new year I went up to London, I took a bedsit with the little money I had, and I went straight to the London and Miss Luckes and presented myself as a candidate for training.

"Oh, I'll never forget how it felt to leave. I hadn't realized it, but Aunt Charlotte's *had* become my home, despite my thinking it wasn't all those years. I told Aunt Charlotte, in case I was turned down, that I was visiting a school friend in London. I packed my case with little more than a change of clothes — if I was a nurse, I'd spend

most of my day in uniform anyway, I didn't need a lot of clothing —
and off I went. My heart had never pounded so hard, and I'd never
been more determined or more convinced that I was stepping into
my destiny. I remember. It was a feeling all up my spine that this was
the right thing to do. I thought I might throw up it went so against
my grain to disobey my father. But the rightness was there in my
spine. And Tom agreed. Tom was on my side."

Tom was dead. How could he be on her side? Carol listened to
the old woman (young woman, then! Eighteen! Like Carol in about
a month) stand her ground in front of the intimidating Miss Luckes,
listened to her read the copy she had kept of the letter she'd written
her father, listened to the stories she told about training, the times
she thought she'd never make it through the day, she'd never wash
another inch of linoleum (they used the practitioners as 'general
dog's-bodies,' Miss Balls said). She flipped the tape and listened to
Miss Balls walk straight up to another intimidating matron and
request entrance to the Canadian Army Medical Corps, and get it.

And she knew what she would do. She would go directly to the
funeral home on Monday morning. She would take her resumé, with
its one summer of day camp and its odd jobs. She would walk in and
insist on a job. She'd clean, she'd do windows. She'd do anything.
"This is what I want to do," she'd say to the man. (She should re-dye
her hair.) "I want to work in a funeral home."

"Well," he'd say. "I admire your chutzpah. Let's see what we can
find for you." She would apprentice and get really good and he
would deed the business to her when he died.

And maybe, she'd have another life as Skunk. Scumbuckets would
cut a record and become a cult hit. They'd never make a lot of money,
which was why she needed the funeral home.

TINK TINK. Tink. Tink tink.

Her eyes flicked open. Tink tink. Tink tink tink. Tink.

Pebbles at her window. Carol was flooded with happiness. There was someone who would throw pebbles at her window past midnight.

She opened the window, shout-whispered that she was coming.

Outside by the garage door, she took the lapels of Grunt's jacket and pulled them toward her. He had not abandoned her. She put her forehead on his chest and breathed in. How could she have doubted?

He was not going home. He was staying with Hugh.

"I'm coming, too."

He didn't object.

She went upstairs and packed lightly, like Miss Balls. Her electric guitar was still in the van. A knapsack. Her guitar.

She did not need to go to school. She did not need to write essays on whether it was right to mercy-kill people. She did not have to sit and glub like a fish just because her family treated her like a guppy. She did not belong here. She had never belonged.

She left a note. "Good-bye. I am leaving home. Carol."

Rowena

DUPED. She had been feeling *sorry* for Carol. Her heart had gone out to her. When actually, her underage daughter had run out of her mother's ordination because she was hungover.

Oh! Driving up to a houseful of well-wishers. She would have to smile and chatter and listen and talk when all she wanted to do was throw herself on her bed and break open, let the hurt come crashing out. She wondered if she should tell people, if that would make it easier, rather than pretending, but she thought she'd break open all the sooner if she told.

Once she was inside and the guests had started arriving, it was not so difficult after all. She fell into a mode she recognized as the one she'd used when her mother went mad, the one that let you go on as you needed to go on when things had fallen apart around you. She let people congratulate her and ask her about her plans, whether she had a congregation yet, whether they would move (as if Glenn would consider moving!). She let them tell her about ministers they had known, good ones and bad ones. She asked them about their lives, what their children were doing, where they were going on their next trip, whether they had finished their dissertation yet, or their watercolours course, or their marathon training. Everyone asked where Carol was and she said as naturally and easily as she could that Carol was at a friend's.

It was a brilliant day, as Glenn had hoped it would be, and they spent most of the party in the garden. The magnolia blossoms were almost visibly opening right beneath their noses, a glorious day. Toward three o'clock, as people were starting to think about leaving without yet announcing their intentions, as couples and families were giving one another signals, Rowena thought she saw a face at the dining-room window. She raced in, but no one was there. June MacDonald emerged from the powder room. "Did you see anyone here just now? I thought I saw Carol."

"Where *is* Carol?"

"Oh, June," Rowena said, almost breaking down right there. "I don't know. She's got this boyfriend —"

June took her arm. "We are going to get everyone out of here and you are going to tell me all about it."

June stayed until five, sitting with Rowena and Glenn in the den while Glynnis and Jay and Marnie cleaned up. June had had a daughter go astray also and knew what it was like. Afterwards Rowena felt exhausted and went upstairs to lie down. There was a sound from Carol's room, a voice not Carol's. The radio must have come on somehow. Mis-set alarm. She opened the door to turn it off and there was Carol, sitting on the bed, tears streaming down her face. What was that voice? Rowena recognized it. Beryl's. Mother and daughter froze. Two rabbits. Two hunters.

"… the most terrific storm," said Beryl.

Why had they never listened together to the tapes before?

Rowena took a breath.

"I'm not going to apologize," Carol said, turning off the tape. "So you can save your breath. I'm not going to say what I did wrong. I'm not going to make up a punishment for myself. I'm not going to do that whole charade. You always made us do your job for you."

Wordlessly, Rowena backed out of her daughter's room. She went to her own room and bit a pillow as she wept. She missed her mother, the old one before the madness. She missed Beryl's awkward good nature, her kindness. The simplicity of it all. Oh it was complex then, everything had been. But it was not like this.

IN THE MORNING Carol was really gone and Rowena cursed herself for giving in to her own pain, for not going into Carol's room, sitting on her bed and waiting for her to talk as she'd done after the accident. Carol always would talk, eventually. If someone was there to listen.

Glynnis

HER PARENTS hovered by the phone all day. Glynnis could not phone Novak, not for two seconds. She rode her bike over instead. Her parents didn't want her to go, but she insisted she would only be a short time. She was a little disappointed Novak hadn't tried calling her.

A little kid with shoulder-length hair and a bow tie answered the door wearing a party hat. "Is, uh, Tracy here?"

"Aunt Tracy!" Party sounds trickled out of the living room. Glynnis could only see the hall.

"Hi," Novak said, surprised. "What are you doing here?" She had a plate in her hands. Some kind of salad.

"Sorry," Glynnis said. "Family drama. Didn't know you had a —" She waved at the party.

"Birthday party," Novak said. "My niece is turning one." She leaned in the doorway and took a mouthful of salad. She was acting like before. Before before.

"Oh."

"Want some?" Novak offered a forkful. "It's spinach salad."

"No thanks."

Glynnis could hear a deep voice, booming inside, though she could not hear what it said. Novak's father. Glynnis had seen him once or twice, he was a tall man who started out wide at the top and tapered to a pin at the bottom. He always looked annoyed to have a stranger in his house.

"So what's your family drama?" Novak asked.

"Oh. Nothing. Carol just left home."

"What?" Novak stepped outside. "What happened?"

Glynnis had been dying to tell someone, she realized. "First we're at the ordination, right? And —"

The kid came outside and said, "Come on, Aunt Tracy, it's time for cake. Aunt Tracy shaved her head, you know."

"Yeah, I know."

The kid disappeared inside.

"I should let you go," Glynnis said.

"Okay. Tomorrow. Tell me all about it."

How could this be? They had kissed, for God's sake. Everything had changed.

Except that apparently it had not.

At school the next day it was like they'd gone back in time even further, to when Glynnis was imagining herself doing song-and-dance routines in the middle of the hall to attract Novak's attention.

Glynnis didn't have the guts to say, "Hey, what's going on?" She rehearsed it. Daily. Hourly. She would find Novak after school. She would say just that, *Hey, what's going on?* like Novak had asked her at Alison's party, "What's your problem with me?" Maybe she would say that next. *Hey, what's going on? What's your problem with me?*

Or she'd go to Novak's house. *Hey, what's going on? What's your problem with me?*

Or she'd call her on the phone.

Or she'd wait until Novak came up to her locker again and said, "Want to get morninged?" and then just casually work it into the conversation as they went to the movie.

Or she'd say nothing at all and let what was be. They had kissed.

Novak had gone weird and distant. Novak wished she hadn't kissed Glynnis, that seemed plain. Glynnis wished they'd kiss some more. What point was there trying to change that?

It was no different with girls than boys. She was not love-object material.

⌐

ONE DAY IN JUNE just before exams, Lisa Chivvers came up to Glynnis in the hall and said Carol wanted to meet her the next day at Fran's.

Carol was in a booth at the back. Glynnis had not seen her in almost six weeks. Her hair was now almost half-blonde and half-black. It looked freaky and very punk. But she wore her old glasses so her eyes bulged in the usual uncool, non-punk way. She seemed thinner. They looked down and up several times.

"Do you know what you're doing to Mom?" Glynnis asked.

Carol burst into tears. She pulled a hank of serviettes out of the dispenser and boo-hooed into them while Glynnis shifted uncomfortably in her chair, wondering what she was witnessing.

Finally Carol shoved the wad of serviettes under her glasses and wiped her eyes. "I'm pregnant," she said.

Glynnis drew her head back. "Oh." It was the most obvious possibility, but somehow it had not occurred to her. She had thought that maybe Carol needed money or something from home. "Does Grunt know?"

"He doesn't want it." Here she sniffled briefly. Glynnis swiped another wad of napkins for her. After a while, Carol composed herself. "I was wondering if you could ask Novak about getting an appointment."

"Oh." Glynnis had barely spoken to Novak for weeks. But what was she going to say to her distraught sister — no? "Okay. Sure."

Carol sniffed and wiped her eyes. "Thank you."

Now Glynnis was shredding a napkin. The waitress came and filled Carol's coffee cup. Glynnis ordered a grilled cheese. "You want something? Grilled cheese? Hamburger? It's on me."

Carol shook her head.

"Um, Crull. Are you sure about this?"

She nodded.

"You've, you know, thought about it?"

"Oh, like I can think of anything else."

"Okay, okay, I just had to ask." Glynnis leaned back in the booth and clasped her hands in front of her. "So," she asked in a bright voice. "How's things?"

It worked. Carol laughed. They both laughed until they were wheezing and then Carol was crying again. "Oh, God," she said. "I'm a wreck."

She ate half of Glynnis' sandwich when it came. She had found a job, in a doughnut shop, but it was only part-time and minimum wage and it was Land of the Scuzzbag when it came to customers. Grunt had got a job as a short-order cook. They hadn't had any new gigs yet, but they were supposed to be opening for another band the week after next. "So Mom's upset?"

"I don't know. Yeah. I mean, of course she is. She's trying to be Zen about it. Or, like, Christian about it, like accepting, and having faith. But she thinks she's a bad mother. She thinks she, like, did something wrong."

"Do you think she did?"

Glynnis shook her head. They were talking about the accident.

"Me neither," said Carol. "Well, I mean, she could've not freaked out about Grunt. But, like, big picture? Naw."

They were saying what they'd always said. They'd brought it on themselves. Their mother had nothing to do with it.

"What's it like being away from home?"

Carol nodded as if convincing herself. "It's great, it's great, it's, yeah. Listen, I should go, I gotta get to work."

Carol gave her the number for the doughnut shop. Where she lived had no phone. Glynnis promised to call her on her shift the next night.

⌒

GLYNNIS CALLED NOVAK. "My sister wants an abortion."

"How many weeks?"

"I don't know, I didn't ask."

"Phone the clinic. Make an appointment."

"Couldn't you just ..."

Novak sighed. "I'm not a broker, okay?"

"She's underage, my parents can't know."

"You should tell your parents. She should tell your parents."

"It'll kill them."

"It won't. It generally doesn't."

"They'll want her to keep it."

"It's her decision."

Glynnis waited.

"'Kay, I'll talk to him. But he'll say, Tell her to make an appointment."

She phoned back later that night. "Yeah. I was right. 'Tell her to make an appointment.'" Glynnis understood then that Novak was intimidated by her father, that it had not been easy to ask him. That he had considered it an interruption. "How've you been?" Novak asked.

"Great. Good. I've been fine."

"Good. Okay."

"How do you think I've been?"

"I don't — That's why I —"

"What's your problem with me, Novak?"

There was another pause. "It's not you."

431

"That's not how it feels."

"Yeah. I know. I'm sorry."

That was that. Glynnis didn't say any more.

GLYNNIS LOOKED UP doughnut shops in the phonebook and found the one that matched the number Carol had given her. It was one without an ad, just the shop name in little type, "Delish Donuts," on Dundas, west of Bathurst, a part of Dundas Glynnis had never been on before.

The shop was one of the ones you know just by looking the doughnuts are going to be stale. Glynnis got there soon after Carol's shift had started at four. Carol looked surprised to see her, and nervous. She kept eyeing her boss, an older woman sitting on a stool visible through the door to the back. Glynnis sat at the counter. Carol poured her a coffee. "We've got to call the clinic ourselves, Novak says. She says you can lie about your name and age and they probably won't ask."

"I don't get a break till six-thirty."

"It'll be closed then. Can you use the phone here?"

Carol shook her head. "There's a phone booth on the corner."

"Can't you ask for, like, five minutes now?"

"I just started."

"I could cover for you."

"You phone."

"When can you go?"

"Anytime."

Glynnis went to the phone booth, pulled the number out of her pocket, dialled. She couldn't believe how nervous she was and it was not even her going to have the abortion. Pregancy. Abortion. They were like these big zeppelins of the worst things that could happen. Everybody would know. But, like, how did that make sense? "Clinic."

"Ah, I'd like to make an appointment, please."

"How many weeks are you?"

"Oh, um, I don't know —"

"When was your last period?"

"Last week," Glynnis almost answered before realizing she was supposed to be Carol. "I'll have to, I'll have to call you back."

Now the boss woman was behind the counter and looking at Glynnis suspiciously. A scuzzy man asked for a refill and the boss said, no refills, you want more coffee you pay. Glynnis had to line up and order a doughnut. She leaned forward. "How many weeks are you?"

Carol's cheeks pinked. She looked left and right. "Honey glaze?"

"Yes, please."

As Carol handed her the donut, she said, "Eleven weeks. I think."

"Thank you." Eleven weeks. Glynnis counted in her head. That put it back before she'd left home. Oo. Weird. Her sister had been having sex and, like, talking to her the very next day.

Glynnis made an appointment for Carol Morgan, (fake) birthdate May 8, 1961, for one week from today, two in the afternoon. She wrote all this information down and passed it to Carol, who tucked it into her pocket. Glynnis left, feeling slightly exhilarated, like a spy. Carol ran out after her. "Will you go with me?" she asked.

"Won't Grunt go?"

"Too? Will you come, too?"

"Of course." They made a plan. Harbord and Spadina. Quarter to two.

Glynnis ate the donut waiting for the streetcar. It was stale.

Carol

CAROL HAD A HEADACHE. She felt sick. She felt hollow.

She was not hollow. She was far from hollow. Inside her was a thing she was about to get rid of.

But she was a hollow person walking down a street. The crazy-person street, the street they lived on, every block three or four of them. Hugh liked that, being amongst the crazy people. Carol did not. The crazy people terrified her. Not that they might hurt her. She was terrified that it would turn out she *was* one.

Up the blunt street, across the narrow street, up the broad busy one with the low brown sides.

He'd been picked up. He'd taken off. He'd been picked up. He'd taken off.

Hadn't called the shop, hadn't shown up for work, hadn't called work, hadn't called his dad, hadn't called his mom. Picked up by the cops, parents would've known. So. Taken off.

But he'd left the drums. He'd never leave the drums. Would he leave the drums? Hadn't left the drums last time.

Would he leave Hugh? Guru Hugh? Hugh Guru? Would he leave and not tell Hugh? What he'd do, he'd tell Hugh, tell him to not tell Carol.

He'd taken off.

Why? Why? Why? Why?

Oh my God, crazy person, she *was* one. She was saying it out loud. Only noticed because of the way people cut an arc around her.

The mom could be lying. The dad could be lying. Coulda paid his bail and taken him home and locked him up and kept him from calling.

No. His dad, to Mariellen: "'Grant please' has departed for parts unknown. If he ever comes back, I'll let him know you called." His Mom: "You're looking for Grant? Well, aren't we all." And then, with urgency in her voice: "If you see him first, will you call me? Will you? Please? Please?"

He'd taken off.

One-fifteen. Down the street with broad sidewalks. Up the narrow streets with narrow houses. He'd taken off. She was too much. She wasn't enough. She was a loser. She was blind. She was ugly. She was boring. She was a fake. She was cursed. She was a curse.

She should never have showed up that day at his house. But she'd had to. She'd had no choice. She could not *not* see him. So she had herself to blame for both of their downfalls.

First week she'd barely gone outside. The apartment was a storefront with the front window painted black, mattresses on the floor, bookshelves made out of fridges, lamps made out of dolls' heads. There were about eight of these. She later found out it was how Mariellen made a living, making doll's-head lamps. They sold for thirty dollars each at shops farther east on Queen.

They went out to get booze cans, they went out to get smokes, they went out to get food. They smoked drugs and had unbelievable conversations. They listened to punk. They played punk. And then they were all out of money and had to find jobs and they made a pact to go get them and keep them for two weeks. So she called Trull Funeral Home and borrowed a hat for a disguise and went back uptown for an interview and the guy said, "Look, we don't hire people with death obsessions," so she'd applied at the first doughnut shop that had a sign and got the job. They had grown-up conversations. They slept from four in the morning till noon or two. They smoked and read the newspaper. "Injured sailor," she wrote in her laughable diary, "drowned in sinking helicopter." "Two mountain climbers on Everest." "Two hundred and fifty Lebanese. Bombed." She had a hard time getting used to hearing Hugh and Mariellen. Unh, unh, oh baby, yeah, fuck me, yeah, yeah. She and Grunt did it silently, his eyes popping out when he came, breath held.

He'd taken off. Gone to England. Changed his name. Gone to Manchester.

Only … if he hadn't taken off, if he hadn't been picked up, if he was in an alley somewhere, in a dumpster, in the lake … Beat up, knifed. Run down. Someone would, someone would have found him, someone would have called his parents.

Taken off.

Where? Why? What had she done? *He* had come to *her*. Wasn't like she forced him into anything. But he'd acted like she had, like she was to blame for seducing him, like it was her fault she had got … what she had got.

He didn't want a baby. There was no room in his life for a fuckin baby. He didn't even, he didn't even, it never even crossed his mind she'd do anything but what she was doing. And that was just sad, that was just fuckin sad. 'Cause it meant, well, she didn't know what it meant. What it felt like it meant was he didn't love her, they weren't fuckin Sid and Nancy after all, he didn't actually give a fuck about her. He never said, "I love you." He said, "Yeah."

She could not believe it was only weeks since she had left her parents' house. Felt like half a year at least. She'd been riding this amazing high, it had all been fabulous up until she realized she hadn't had her period for two months. She had to borrow money from

Mariellen to go get the test, though she didn't say what the money was for. And finding a time to tell Grunt wasn't easy. She had to do it one afternoon when they woke up. "So, um, there's this thing —" "Yuh." "There's this thing I gotta tell you." "Yuh," he said, lighting a smoke. "What is it?" "I, uh, did this test? And, uh, I'm pregnant."

"Ah fuck."

"Yeah."

"Ahhhh, fuuuuck."

"Yeah."

"Ah, FUCK."

"Yeah."

Up street with streetcars' deep steel-on-steel roll, street with buildings growing up from the sidewalk. Cross at lights by high school. Past tough-looking boys outside corner store, black, Italian, Portuguese, calling things out, Hey, baby, wanna do me, making the other guys laugh, all about making them laugh, all about making themselves look better than someone. Old, old, old.

Now a crowd of girls, black girls, white girls, brown girls, girl loud.

— No, not like that. Give it to me, give it to me. Like this.

— Give it back.

— And then he.

— Can you believe it?

—What you say?

Past them down the quiet-seeming street, neighbourhood-seeming now, brighter seeming. Past restaurant, past bakery, flowers out front corner store, past laundry. Where? England? Would be better without her. He'd be freer. No money for a plane ticket. Maybe a freighter in Halifax, Liverpool-bound. Hair cut, sailor suit on, waving to shore. Goodbye. Goodbye.

Another crowd on the sidewalk. Sale. Or opening. Or picket, teachers on strike, CUPE, OPSEU, walking a circle. Waving to shore. Goodbye. Goodbye. A man reading the Bible. Crazy street preacher.

No. Protect the rights of the unborn.

Oh.

Well, at least she was in the right place. She kept walking, with her head down, her face hot, her arms prickling, right through to Spadina. Now what. She was here. She was early. She was tired.

North on Spadina was a bus stop with a bench. She sat down, closed her eyes, listened to the traffic. Wanted to beat her head against something. He'd been picked up. He'd taken off. He was in a dumpster. He was on a freighter.

Three days ago, he'd been gone when she woke up. Not so unusual. He'd nip out for the paper sometimes, for some eggs from the corner store, for smokes. But this time he hadn't come back before she had to go to Land of the Scuzzbag. Not there, nobody at the apartment when she got off at midnight. First time she'd been there alone. She turned on the TV, watched the one channel. The doll lamps creeped her out now that she had a thing dolls were modelled on inside her. She fell asleep around two, heard Hugh and Mariellen come in around four, heard them drop into bed. Hugh snoring. She was up at eight, looking through Grunt's stuff. Nothing conclusive was gone. His ID he had. His army surplus knapsack. The notebook he put stuff in, song lyrics, poems he'd written for her. Drum sticks. Jacket. But those were things he always carried with him. Only other things he had were a row of books, an army surplus sweater that was missing, some long underwear shirts, some extra socks. She went out to work again. Nothing changed. Nothing else went missing. Nothing else showed up. Hugh was convinced he'd be back in a week or thereabouts. As long as he was alive, Carol thought, a flame searing her chest. She'd gladly give him up as long as he was alive. She called the hospitals again, like last time. She got Mariellen to call the dad.

He'd been picked up. He'd taken off. He was in a dumpster. He was on a freighter.

She couldn't go on like this, not knowing.

Gone either way, went another part of her.

But it makes a difference.

He's just as gone either way, it insisted.

But alive or dead.

Gone either way. Almost like a song. She'd write it, later. *Six leagues to sea or six feet under, He's gone either way.*

No, she thought. Not the same. If he was dead, she could chase him. If he was on the freighter he was really gone.

Where the fuck was Glynnis?

Come on, Glynnis. Come on, Glynnis. Come on come on come on.

Glynnis

"WELL, WELL, WELL, Glynnis Riggs."

Shit. Mr. Humenick.

"And where are you off to this fine afternoon?"

"Doctor's." Glynnis walked backwards as she spoke. "Just hurled in the girls'. Feel like crap. I'll get a note, don't you worry, Mr. Humenick."

"This is the exam, Glynnis. You can't miss the exam."

"Yeah, I know. Rare blood disease. Very sick. Gotta go." She turned and walked on, but he trotted lightly to catch up and then walked beside her.

"If you're kidding, it's not funny. If you're not kidding ... You are kidding. Aren't you?"

Glynnis saw his eyes light on something at the end of the hallway, something he took to be of significance. Novak. Who was pausing at the stairwell door, as if she might be waiting for Glynnis. Ah, fuck. He thought she was skipping the exam to hang out with Novak?

Go, Novak. Get out of here. Fuck off.

"Why don't we go along to the office and just let them know about your appointment, eh?" said Mr. Humenick. They were in hearing range now, Novak could hear this. She fucked off.

"I really don't have time ..."

"Oh, doctor's offices, they're always running behind, you'll be fine."

"No, really, I don't have any, I have to be there on time."

His tone changed. "Glynnis, you're a good student. I don't like to see anyone put their future in jeopardy, but I especially don't like seeing good students put their future in jeopardy."

"That's really ... I appreciate ... Look, I really have to go." Glynnis and her teacher pushed through the doors.

"There comes a time when somebody's got to put their foot down," he said. "Now, I don't want to be the heavy, but I don't believe you're sick, you clearly don't want me to phone your mother, and I think it's time you were held accountable. When a good kid starts missing a lot of classes, I start looking out for them. I've been looking out for you, Glynnis. I see things. That letter. Whose locker. You know what the nuns call it, don't you?"

They were at the bottom of the stairs. Glynnis never heard what the nuns called it. She ran. "I'm phoning your mother," he yelled.

She was almost at Yonge Street when Novak caught up to her.

Novak: "What was that about?"

"Humenick thinks we're —" She waved back and forth as if to say "we're an item."

"You and me?" Novak feigned surprise.

"No, me and the Pope."

"Where'd he get that idea?"

"Fuck, Novak. I don't have time for this. I gotta meet Carol in ... Fuck. Five minutes." Glynnis had received a phone call that morning from someone calling herself Kelly but actually named Mariellen. Grunt had bailed.

"I'll drive you." She paused a minute, then added, "Fuck," like they were playing the game again.

"Fuckin okay, let's fuckin go," said Glynnis.

But when she got to Harbord and Spadina, Carol was not there. It was quarter after two, she was not that late. Carol must have gone in. Glynnis had Novak drop her off.

A small knot of people with handmade placards walked in a circle in front of the building. They seemed almost mechanical until one woman, seeing Glynnis turn off the sidewalk and up the walk, roused herself to outrage and cried, "Shame, shame," at her back. Inside the front door was an intercom to get through the inner door. She buzzed. "Hi, I have an appointment at two o'clock. Carol Morgan?"

The receptionist buzzed her in and asked her to fill out a medical information sheet and asked if she had someone coming to pick her up. "No, actually, it's my sister who has the appointment. I was supposed to meet her outside and she's not there, so I wanted to see if she'd come in yet."

"I'm sorry, I can't release that information."

"You can just tell me whether she's here or not, can't you?"

"Our patients' confidentiality is of the utmost importance."

"But I'm the one that made the appointment, she was too chicken. I was supposed to come with her. If she's not here, I've got to know."

"I'm sorry, I can't give out that information."

"Look, if she is here, you can just go ask her if it's okay to tell me, right?"

"I'm sorry, I can't do that."

"Why?" No answer. "She's not here."

"You're welcome to wait."

Novak came in just at the end of this. "Oh, hi, Tracy," said the receptionist with surprise.

"Hi, Claudia." Novak waltzed right in and was back out in no time. "She's not here," she said to Glynnis.

"Tracy —" chided the receptionist, but they were already heading out the door.

"Then where is she?" Glynnis said outside. She looked left and right. Across the street. Left and right again. The protestors called out slogans.

"Come on, let's just go down the block here. Get away from the lunatic fringe."

They found a stoop to sit on.

"Fuck," said Glynnis. "Fuck."

"So she decided not to come." So what? said Novak's tone.

"Or she came and left again because I wasn't here." She explained how desperate Carol had sounded when she'd told her Grunt had gone AWOL. "Fuck fuck fuck."

"Well. Let's wait."

Glynnis let out a long breath.

"What's the big deal?" asked Novak. "Why are you responsible?"

"I don't know. I just am." Glynnis leaned forward and scanned the street again. "Because she's my sister," was all she could think to say.

They debated Grunt's basic character — scaredy-cat or rebel? Damaged soul or deep waters? Glynnis tried to explain Carol, her thing about death, how even though their parents had set up an appointment expressly for the doctor to explain to Carol and Glynnis that the textbook had been wrong, albinos did not die young, Glynnis thought Carol retained the idea that she would. Novak talked about her father, the death he averted as a young man, the death threats he got now.

Carol did not show.

Glynnis ran a hand over her face. "Humenick's going to call my mother. I should have covered better." She pressed on her eyelids with her fingertips. "Oh, my God, my life's gone down the toilet in one afternoon."

"You can always say he's wrong."

"He may be wrong in deed but he's not wrong in spirit."

Novak said nothing.

"What *happened* to you?" Glynnis asked.

Novak seemed for a moment like she might try to answer, and then the silence lengthened. That might have been a shrug as she ran the tread of her high-tops over the brick of the building next to them, or not. Hard to tell.

When five o'clock came and went with no sign of her sister, Glynnis got Novak to drive her by the coffee shop. Six scuzzbags, no Carol. They drove down Queen Street looking for a storefront that people might be living in. One right across the street from the mental hospital had silver windows. "There! There!" They parked, got out and knocked. No answer.

They walked farther west and found one with black windows. They stopped and knocked again. Tried to peer through scratches in the black paint. Thought they saw a fridge. A TV. Dolls' heads. "This has to be it," said Glynnis and they camped out outside the door until it got dark. At nine o'clock, Glynnis thought to phone her parents. They'd be wondering where she was like she was wondering where Carol was. She could not do that to them. Across the street was a phone booth with the door off. It smelled like pee. The receiver smelled like barf. Glynnis held it gingerly to her ear. No dial tone.

Carol

AFTER A TIME, Carol heard someone sit down next to her on the bench. A clatter. Roar from the street. The hiss of the bus door as it opened.

"Here's the bus, dear," an old woman's voice said.

Carol opened her eyes and stared straight ahead. She didn't move. She shut her eyes again. She hadn't been called dear in a long time. Old people did not think she looked dear these days.

"Don't you want the bus, then?"

Carol had an instinct to answer. To be polite. She bit it. The bus doors hissed closed.

"I like that. Both at a bus stop, neither wants the bus."

Carol heard a sound of paper ripping. Lifesavers, she thought, and couldn't help opening her eyes to check but when her eyes were open, she thought she was having a vision. On the other end of the bench, Miss Balls popped a lifesaver into her mouth.

She turned to Carol. "Lifesaver, dear?"

Not Miss Balls' voice. Trust the voice. Not Miss Balls. Of course not Miss Balls. But the look was startling. Carol found it hard to look away. She took a lifesaver. "Thank you."

Carol checked her watch. Two o'clock. Appointment time.

She got up and walked to the corner of Harbord. Four protestors. No Glynnis. Spadina and Harbord. They'd been clear about that. She went back to the bench.

"Waiting for someone?"

"Mm."

She lit a cigarette and sat back down, sneaking glances at the lady. The hair was the exact same steel, the exact same style, basically the Queen's. The glasses were the exact same grey cat's-eye. The lips were the same thin lips.

Pardon me, she wanted to ask. Your last name isn't Balls, is it?

"My poor feet need a rest," the woman said. She put them up on the bench. "Only for a minute, mind. I've been out here six hours a day for two hundred and three days and I'll be here 'til I drop. They can arrest me, they can detain me, but that's the only thing that'll keep me away."

The shoes were the exact same shoes. It all seemed to say, yes, he too is dead, when you find him, he will be dead.

"My goodness, dear, what's the matter?"

Carol shook her head and kept crying. She hadn't cried in a long time; she had trained herself out of it. She thought of Miss Balls saying, "My, you are a crier, aren't you." Which was when she'd stopped being one. She cried harder.

"Whatever it is, it's nothing that the Lord can't fix."

Then Carol put it together. The placard, the lady's words.

She got up again, went to the corner again, hugging herself. No Glynnis. She felt trapped. Couldn't go forward to the clinic, couldn't go back to the bench with its Miss Balls look-alike. She sat down against a brick wall, gravel digging into her butt.

"You're here for an appointment, aren't you?" the lady's voice asked.

Carol nodded.

"And the boyfriend didn't show."

Carol shook her head.

"Never mind. I'm going to get a cup of hot soup. Would you like to come? It's not a long walk."

IT WASN'T THE SOUP. It was the promise of a place to pee. She had to pee. When she'd peed, it didn't feel like she could leave without drinking the soup. And when she'd had the soup, it didn't feel like she could leave without going to the evening service, and after the service, they offered her a coffee and a bed and there was Miss Balls, no, not Miss Balls, Mrs. Sarinen, saying, "You know, dear, it *is* a sin, you do know that, don't you?"

And she bawled and bawled and bawled and promised to take Jesus into her heart and by God, she meant it, she did. This was what her mother was always talking about, about faith. It was something that you *felt*. You could feel God, there, just behind your shoulder. Jesus be my guide, she whispered.

"That's right, dear."

"Jesus be my guide." Louder. *Gabba gabba WE accept you WE accept you one of us.* "Jesus, be my guide!" she cried. Yes. Yes. Tears rolled down her face.

It didn't last. She was left thinking again about the people she loved and what had happened to them.

She loved Glynnis and Glynnis had almost lost a leg.

She loved Miss Balls and Miss Balls had had a stroke in the shower.

She had smiled at Emanuel Jaques and he had been drowned in a sink.

She had loved Mortimer and he had been euthanized by her parents.

She had loved Grunt and he had been beat up. And then he had disappeared.

She was about to make the thing inside her die.

Wait.

No, actually.

She wasn't.

Rowena

ROWENA WAS TRYING to be okay. Her internship was over. She had not been shortlisted for the first two ministries she had applied to. While waiting to hear from a third, she had nothing to do but wonder where her daughter was and what exactly she had done wrong.

She joined the Church's Refugee Sponsorship Committee. She joined Amnesty International. Still she had time on her hands.

Glenn was gentle and kind. One day late in May after they had told themselves they needed to try to live their lives, he woke her with coffee at six-thirty. "Let's go to Rainy Lake." They had not been since Christmas. They had not flown anywhere, just the two of them, in Rowena didn't know how long. No. She did. Not since their twentieth anniversary. Almost three years ago. Early on she had found it the most deliriously romantic thing, flying off to a little cabin on a lake you couldn't get to by road. They had gone practically every week. Rowena would fly, Glenn would take pictures out the windows of the plane, or Glenn would fly and Rowena would marvel at all that lay below them. They would land, swim if it was warm enough, fish from the point or take out the canoe, light a fire for their lunch. Sometimes they would stay and cook the trout in the cabin, open a tin of peas, sleep out under the stars. Then came the children and an end to their extended honeymoon. Not altogether, not right away. They brought Jay for a time, but he was a fussy baby and it was not much fun to stay on shore and jiggle him while he cried and Glenn was casting from the rock. When the girls came, it became not worth it, not for just a day. They took to going to her family's cottage on Georgian Bay for longer stays. They never really went back to their Rainy Lake days, even when the children were in school and they could if they had wanted. Her pilot's licence lapsed. They took shorter trips. The Bruce Trail. Albion Hills. Oak Ridges Moraine. Serena Gundy, Glendon College, Wilket Creek. Scarborough Bluffs.

Over the soothing roar of plane engine, Glenn shouted, "Fly!" She shook her head and looked back out the window.

"Fly!" he shouted again.

It took her another several minutes to reorient herself before she could take the controls. Tachometer. Altimeter. Air speed. Heading. My goodness, she had to think again! Her heart beat harder. It was a warm, clear day. Thermals buffeted them as they flew over fields. Glenn hooted happily. He was very good at keeping an eye on all she did while seeming not to. He had been, she remembered, a very good teacher. She remembered her first flights, the giddiness of altitude mixed with the giddiness of his presence. Oh, the promise! It was enough to make her cry. The beauty below, too, was enough to make her cry. Fields gave way to shield, and soon there was their little lake, an elongated puddle in the glacier-scraped landscape. She bit her lip, gave the controls back to Glenn, who landed them easily on the lake and taxied them to the bay. Rowena stepped out to fix the rope and hop in the water to wade to shore and was immediately assaulted by blackflies. She tied up the plane and trotted to the cabin for bug hats and rods and tackle. Glenn flipped the canoe from beneath its shelter and they were off, out into the blessed bugless breeze, stopping briefly to put their lines in the water, then trolling lazily in the mild May sun.

A tenderness between them. A sort of apology from him.
Here they were, together still.

⤙

ROWENA'S CHIEF relationship when at home was with the telephone. She waited for it to ring. It obliged on its own time, at irregular intervals. When it did, she gave herself completely to it. She
dropped things, let them burn, overflow. She ran. The phone, deadpan, revealed nothing. She trembled before it. She picked it up.

"Hello?"

And wanted to bash it, bash it, bash it against the counter. It never
gave her Carol. Today it gave her Glynnis' history teacher, of all
people. Was Glynnis sick? he asked. No, not that she knew of. The
tub was running, she'd been in the middle of cleaning it. She was
wasting water. No, Glynnis didn't have a rare blood disease.

"No, I didn't think so. She's, well, she's rather blatantly skipped my
exam," he said. "It seemed, it looked like, it looked exactly like she was
meeting someone, meeting someone, a girl, Novak, Tracy Novak."

"Yes," said Rowena slowly.

"She was skipping my exam to meet Novak. I, I, I, I, I hesitate to
say this, but I have my suspicions about, about Glynnis and Novak.
They are very — close. They are too — close. If you know what
I mean."

"Yes. Yes. I think I do," said Rowena. "Thank you, Mr. Humenick,"
said Rowena. She hung up on whatever he said next, teen melodrama
something something, and went back to the bathroom, turned off
the tub.

Novak this, Novak that, for months. Then suddenly, after the
ordination, no Novak. The difference had not registered with
Rowena before now. She had attributed Glynnis' moroseness to the
same cause as her own.

How far had it gone? How close was "close"? Novak in the tuque, Novak's bald head in the pool. A horror filled her. Revulsion. *Both* her girls in the apocalypse. She knelt at the edge of the bathtub with her rag, then dropped her forehead on the edge of the tub. She lifted her head and brought it down again, lightly.

Blind. Selfish. Unvigilant. Blind. What worth her career now? Her non-career, her nowhere career.

The rest of the afternoon she cleaned. Every now and then she stopped and sat in the living room, looking out the front window. By five, when Glynnis ought to have been finishing her exam, Rowena was getting the ladder out of the garage to clean the outsides of the windows.

By eight o'clock she had clean windows and no daughters at home. Glynnis had not called, even with an excuse, which since Carol's departure was unlike her. Home a great deal, she had been extra careful to call when she was not. She had been lovely. She had kept Rowena company, made her play chess, taken her to the nursery for bedding plants. Only because she was on the outs with Novak? The thought was a knife.

At nine, she heard the door open. What would she say to Glynnis? What on earth would she say?

"Hi, Mom," said Carol.

Glynnis

NOVAK DROVE PAST Glynnis' mother's church.

"Shit. Fuck." The wrath of Rowena. What was she going to say? *Uh, oh, yeah, I just, uh, heh heh, didn't feel like going to the exam. No big stink. Nope. Nope. Wasn't doing anything special, just, uh …* "He phoned. I know he phoned. Did he say anything? What did he say?"

"Whatever he said, all you have to do is say he's wrong. He's got no proof. He wasn't at the bar. So he's blowing wind out his hole."

"Oh, that's what I'll say to my mother. 'He's blowing wind out his hole.'"

"Okay. 'He's mistaken.'"

"But he isn't."

"He is. We were drunk. It was one kiss."

"Fuck, Novak." Glynnis shook her head. She put her elbow on the car door and chewed on her thumbnail. They turned onto Dupont.

"What?"

Glynnis said nothing along Dupont. Nothing all the way up Poplar Plains. Nothing on St. Clair. On Mount Pleasant, she said, "You know exactly what."

"No, I don't."

"Yes, you do. You've had that flyer for, like, years."

"What does that mean? What —"

"Don't say 'What flyer?'"

"— flyer?"

"The flyer, the flyer. The one you've had since 1980, the one you've secretly consulted the first Monday of every month since 1980, thinking about the first Tuesday of each month and whether you've got the guts to go, the one for the lesbian potluck, the one you took me to that we 'pretended' we were lesbians for."

"Oh, thaaaat flyer."

They were at Glynnis' house. Novak pulled over and put the car in park. "So I had the flyer."

"So you had the flyer, so … you and Alison were a couple, so at the party, you — so, you and I … so when you finally admit that something is going on, when we finally, like, kiss, the next day you act like nothing happened."

"Oh. That." Novak seemed genuinely tongue-tied. She made several attempts to speak, to explain herself. Then she let them drop.

"Tell me you weren't just pretending to be pretending," said Glynnis.

"I wasn't just pretending to be pretending."

"No. I mean it. No joke."

Novak pulled at white threads on the knee of her jeans. "I was pretending to be pretending," she said to the steering wheel.

"Thank you! That's all I wanted to hear." Glynnis pulled the lever on the door.

"Wait. You're just going to go?"

Glynnis stopped. She waited. *No. If you ask me to, I'll stay.*

"I'm, uh. I'm, uh. No. Go. Forget it. I'm sorry." Novak shook her head self-critically. Glynnis waited some more. "I'm just, I'm kinda, you know me, I'm just kinda … superficial. I do stupid things and then I … Serious things scare the shit out of me." She put on her rueful charm look that seemed both transparent and actually quite charming. Her hair was growing back, a fuzz around her head.

She looked like a handsome eleven-year-old who knows he can smile his way out of trouble.

"Can I feel your hair?" Glynnis asked.

Novak bent her head down and Glynnis ran her palm from back to front. It felt like the pelt of some soft creature. "Wow. That feels great."

"Yeah. It does, doesn't it?" Novak grinned.

"I gotta go," Glynnis said.

"Yeah."

"Thanks."

"For what?"

"I don't know."

"What I'm here for." Novak grabbed Glynnis' hand, ran it over her head again. Leaned down and waved out the window as Glynnis backed off. Waited while Glynnis went up the walk and into the house.

"Hello?" Glynnis said.

"We're in here," said her mother.

Oh, great. Her father was home. The two of them were sitting there, waiting. *Mr. Humenick called today*, they'd say. *He had a very interesting hypothesis. I wonder if you'd care to illuminate.*

What *did* the nuns call it? Glynnis wondered, trudging into the kitchen.

The "we" was not her parents at all. Carol sat at the kitchen table, eating a slice of toast with peanut butter. Her mother sat across from Carol with a cup of tea.

Glynnis covered her eyes with her hand and walked up and down in agitation. When she took her hand away, she found she was weeping. Her mother put her arm out, and Glynnis walked into it, taking the seat at the end of the table. Carol put her hand on Glynnis' other shoulder.

The front door opened again. "Hello, hello, hello," said their father.

His three hellos. Their three voices: "We're in here."

AIR PHOTO A20187-9
TORONTO, 1969
1:30,000
(FROM THE COLLECTION OF GLENN RIGGS)

THE NEW CITY is just about all here now. Off over there, the suburbs begin, began years ago. Don Mills plots its Aboriginal art patterns on farmland. The horses are gone from Windfields farm and under-construction subdivisions whiten its southeastern corner. South of the new CNIB complex on Bayview lie the neatly ruled lines of North Leaside, decades old now, looking fresh as 1950. A little bit north and a little bit west, the slightly less neat line of his own street — about as old as he is, about as raggedy — fits into the corner made by Lawrence bending down to Bayview.

In this picture, you cannot see anyone, but they are there, like people in books. Open the pages and you will find them. His wife, in a sleeveless dress, with shapely arms, tremendous legs and a smooth brow. A smile on her face, a skip in her walk, a heart like the wind you fly into. His young son, poised to turn ten, bright as a penny, curious as a fifty-cent piece. His little white-haired daughter, her gay, trusting face. And his littlest laughing, blue-eyed darter, who runs in circles with her arms outstretched, who runs and runs and runs until she drops like a puppy into sleep.

Appendices

War Time Hospital: a play by Glynnis R. Riggs

Elwood Glover's Luncheon Meat: a video by Glynnis R. Riggs

Miss Boothson's last letter to Miss Balls

Three Scumbuckets songs

"Mystery: The Heart of Beauty or God Is Beauty":
a sermon by Rowena Riggs

War Time Hospital

BY GLYNNIS R. RIGGS, ESQ.

Scene 1

Boots:	Good morming, Bbootsie.g
Balls:	Good morninf, Ballsie. How did you sleeep?
Boots:	Very well, thank you. How did you sleep/?
Balls:	Like the dead.
Boots:	Oh, Ballsie, do not say that, it gives me thw shivers.
Balls:	Sorry, Bootsie, I don't mean to scare you.
Boots:	we are around enoug dead people without you going and saying you sleep like them. It's not good luck to say things like that.
Balls:	I said I'm sorry
Boots:	You don't know what it is like finding those poor sweet boys dead in theiir beds in the morning.
Balls:	No, you are right, I do not. I am new here. I am the yYoungest Nursing Sister on the Front.
Boots:	Don't worry, Ballsie. I will protect you.
Balls:	Will you, Bootsie?
Boots:	I will, Ballsie. Bootsie and Ballsie forever.
Balls:	Hurrah! Bootsie, are you married?
Boots:	No, I am a nurse.
Balls:	I am a nurse, too. I will never marry.
Boots:	Some nurses do marry. Some girls even become nurses just to find husbands. Imagine!
Balls:	Then some girls are not true nurses, are they? True nurses are born to it, like you and I.
Boots:	Say, Ballsie, has the new doctor arrived yet?
Balls:	I hope so. Old Pea seems to be going off it.
Boots:	You mean Old Peanut.

Balls:	No, I mean Old Pea.
Boots:	Going off what?
Balls:	His nut!
Boots:	Ha, ha, ha, you are so funny.
Balls:	Yes I am. He is off his nut though. I am afraid he is going to cut off the wrong leg of somebody.
Boots:	He's not that bad
B&B:	Yet!
Balls:	Uh-oh. Here comes Head Nurse Matron Bats.

Enter Bats.

Bats:	Ladies!
B&B:	Aye, aye, sir!
Bats:	Caps straight?
B&B:	Aye, aye, sir!
Bats:	Aprons clean?
B&B:	Aye , aye, sir!
Bats:	Boots polished?
B&B:	Aye aye, sir!
Bats:	Fignernails cut?
B&B:	Aye, aye, sir!
Bats:	Boogers wiped?
B&B:	Aye, aye, sir!
Bats:	Then don't delay, let's start our day!
B&B:	Aye, aye, sir!
Bats:	Hup-twothree-four, hup-two-three-four.

Scene 11

Dr.Peanut:	Ah, Bats, there you are!
Bats:	Yes, here I am.

Dr. Pea:	Ah, Bats.
Bats:	Yes, Dr. Peanut.
Pea:	Beautiful Bats.
Bats:	That's me.
Pea:	Marvellous Bats.
Bats:	Dr. Peanut.
Pea:	My dear dear Bats.
Bats:	Dr. Peanut we have work to do.
Pea:	Do we Bats?
Bats:	Yes, Dr. Peanut, we do.
Pea:	What kind of work my lovely Bats?
Bats:	Lovely amputations, Dr. Peanut.
Pea:	What's that you say? Combinations?
Bats:	AmpPUTATIONS.
Pea:	Ah. How many?
Bats:	Three legs and four arms.
Pea:	Three heads and four barns? Let's get to work then, shall we? Where are the patients, darling Bats? Is that them?
Bats:	No, that's not them. That's nursing sister Boots and nursing sister Balls. They will assist you.
Pea:	I will miss you too, Bats.
Boots:	If the new doctor doesn't come soon, we are in trouble.
Balls:	You can say that again.
Boots:	If the new doctor doesn't come soon, we are in trouble.
Pea:	Bring in the patient.
Balls:	Okay, here he is.
Pea:	What is wrong with him?
Boots:	His right foot was blown off, poor boy.
Balls:	Ew, gross.
Boots:	Don't say that, Ballsie. You will scare the patient.
Patient:	Aaaaaaaaaaugh.

Pea:	Where's your foot, soldier?
Pat:	Aaaaaaaaaugh.
Pea:	Don't know it. Never been there, I'm afraid.
Boots:	Here, bite this bullet.
Pat:	Thanks.
Pea:	Scalpel?
Boots:	Scalpel.
Balls:	Excuse me, Dr. Peanut.
Pea:	Suction.
Boots:	makes sucking noise.
Balls:	Dr. Peanut.
Pea:	Saw.
Boots:	Saw.
Balls:	Dr. Peanut, shouldn't you be cutting off the wounded leg?
Pea:	Are you telling me how to do my job?
Balls:	That's his good leg.
Pea:	Doesn't he want a matching set?
Pat:	Nooooooo.
Pea:	Oh, all right. There we go then. All done.
Balls:	What do I do with this bloody stump?
Boots:	In the incinerator it goes.
Pea:	Next?

Scene 3

Boots:	Well we made it through another day.
Balls:	Gosh, I'm tired. I could sleep like the dead.
Boots:	Donot say that!
Balls:	Gosh, I'm tired. I could sleep like the amputated.
Boots:	That is better.
Balls:	Whatis that noise?

Boots:	That//? That is just the shells exploding at the front.
Balls:	No, not that noise, that noise.
Boots:	You mean the rats squeaking?
Balls:	No.
Boots:	Batsy snoring?
Balls:	No.

Bootsie sniffs air.

Boots:	Oh, no! Gas attack! Quick, get your gas mask.
Balls:	What is it? Are the terrible Huns gassing us?
Boots:	No. The terrible Batsy is gassing us. That noise is her big fat farts.
Balls:	No!
Boots:	Yes. Hurry up. put your gas mask on or you really will sleep like the dead, because that's what you will be if you sniff too much of Batsy's farts.
Balls:	Oh, what a terrible war.
Boots:	Yes, there is danger everywhere, even here in our biscuits.
Balls:	No fair, Bootsie. Do you have cookies in your bed that you are not sharing with the whole group?
Boots:	Oh ho ho. You are very green, arent you, Ballsie. No, Ballsie. Biscuits is what we Nursing Sisters calls these flat things we sleep on.
Balls:	Oh ho ho, silly me. I have so much to learn. Will you teach me, Bootsie?
Boots:	Of course, Ballsie. We nursing sisters have to stick together, come hell or high water.
Balls:	Good night, Bootsie.
Boots:	Good night, Ballsie.
Balls:	Bootsie, whats that noise?
Boots:	What noise?

Balls:	That noise that sounds sort of like a —

A big bomb falls.

Balls:	— bomb.
Boots:	Help help, I'm trapped under an elephant.
Balls:	Thats not an elephant, thats Matron Bats.
Bats:	Help help , I can't feel my legs.
Balls:	Oh no, what do I do?
Boots:	I cant breathe!
Bats:	I cant feel!
Balls:	I ll save you, Bootsie!

Ballsi tries to pull Batsy off of Bootsie.

Bats:	Dont move me! I think my back is broken.
Balls:	But your crushing Bootsie. Oh no , this is terrible.

Enter Dr. Gorgon.

Dr. G:	Never worry, never fear, Doctor Gorgon will soon be here.
Balls:	Are you Dr. Gorgon?
Dr. G:	Yes.
Balls:	Then youre here already.
Dr. G:	Oh right. Never worry, never fear, Dr Gorgon is … now … here. Rex Gorgon, at your service.
Balls:	Do you have a backboard?
Dr G:	Let me check my utility belt. Yes, I have the Acme Expandable Backboard.
Balls:	Help me put Matron Bats onto it.

Boots:	Hurry!
Dr G:	Hark. Is that a cry of a maiden in distress?
Balls:	Its my bosom buddy, Nursing Sister Bootsie. Matron Bats is crushing her.
Dr G:	Oof.

They get Batsy off Bootsie.

Boots:	Oh my saviour! My saviour!
Balls:	It was nothing, Bootsie.
Boots:	My saviour, my saviour!

Bootsie kisses Dr. Gorgon.

Boots:	You saved my life.
Dr. G:	It was nothing. A trifle. All in a days work. Would you marry me?
Boots:	I'd love to.
Balls:	But Bootsie, you said you would never get married. You said you were a true nurse.
Boots:	Oh. Right. I forgot. Dr. Gorgon, my love, I renounce you forever!
B&B:	Bootsie & Ballsie forever! Hurray!

The End

Elwood Glover's Luncheon Meat

A VIDEO BY GLYNNIS R. RIGGS, ESQ.

GRADE FIVE ENRICHMENT

Camera shows Elwood Glover behind his desk.

ELWOOD

>Good day, I'm Elwood Glover. Welcome to Elwood Glover's Luncheon Meat.

Widen to show chair next to desk. Zoom in on open-face sandwich on chair, with macaroni and cheese loaf. Zoom back out.

ELWOOD

>This afternoon I'm interviewing my lunch. Welcome. So, Mr. Macaroni and Cheese Loaf, tell me, where did it all start for you?

The Meat just sits there.

ELWOOD

>Ah yes, the Maple Leaf factory, you must have fond memories of those early days at the factory.

Meat says nothing.

ELWOOD

>I know I have wonderful memories of my early days. It was the Boring Lunch Show Host Factory in Udora, Ontario. Oh, we had swell days of sitting behind our desks and asking our imaginary guests about their early days, when they were tykes.

Meat sits there.

ELWOOD

> Now your family is a little bit different from the average
> run-of-the-mill luncheon meat.

Zoom in on sandwich.

ELWOOD

> I mean macaroni and cheese! Wow! That's daring in a lunch
> loaf.

Nothing. Zoom out.

ELWOOD

> Um, so are you doing anything later? You want to go for
> lunch?
>
> Say, how do you feel about ketchup?

*Elwood pulls a bottle of ketchup out of his drawer. Puts ketchup on the
luncheon meat.*

ELWOOD

> Well, it's been a pleasure talking to you. Our guest today has
> been the very eloquent, the very gracious Mr. Macaroni and
> Cheese Loaf. Tomorrow on Elwood Glover's Luncheon
> Meat, meet that underdog of the luncheon world, Bologna.
> Why's it called "baloney" and spelled "bologna"? And what
> really is in it? Is it true there's pig's hooves and intestines in it?
> Find out tomorrow on the next exciting episode of Elwood
> Glover's Luncheon Meat. So long.

June 12, 1918
Halifax

My darling Ballsie,

I hope this finds you much improved and back on your feet. I know how you hate to be idle. We have had two days in Halifax while stocking up for the return journey. Quite a different pace from the No. 7. Same patients for six whole days! Some quite well, but for bits missing and so on. We have entertainments every night, quite like a luxury liner — scenes from Hamlet, a nocturne or two, music hall numbers, ragtime, pantomime, all sorts. Some awful, naturally, some of it quite good. Everyone so d—ned glad to be headed home.

Lost two en route. One to kidney failure, another to what we thought was tetanus and turned out to be meningitis. Oh, I hate it every time.

Mother and Norah and boys have come down to meet me. Wonderful reunion. Father's presence missed, but he was not feeling well enough. His absence covers for the more keenly felt absences, however. Mother covering up a fair bit, I think, about Father's health and difficulty of things at home. Wanted to hear all about Neil's last hours. Told all I could, leaving out bit about Lindsay's head, naturally. Do you know, I see it, at night? Now that I'm safe from bombs and shells I find I'm getting right 'windy'. I don't know how they stand it, some of them. Oh, this war! It must end!

Willie has grown about a foot. He was a little boy when I left. I didn't realize until seeing them all how much I am losing of their growing up. If the war lasts another year, Simon will be able to join up. He plans to just as soon as his birthday rolls around.

Oh, I can't get enough of them. We stayed up very late at the hotel, and woke early to squeeze in every single minute we could.

I can't tell you how nice it is to be back in Canada, all the little familiar things, I can't even tell you what they are. Money. Ways of saying things. "Well, holy smoke!" I heard a man say on the street. Now maybe Americans say "Holy smoke," too. They must. But it made me feel very at home.

The team on board absolutely wonderful. Matron the calmest soul alive. Making many firm friendships, but I do miss you awfully, dear.

With much love,
your
'Bootsie'

Three Scumbuckets Songs

Hello There, Death

LYRICS AND MUSIC BY CAROL RIGGS

I read the papers,
people are dying every day
everywhere every way

It's the one thing you get when you are born
you know that you're going to die
you might not believe it but
you'll all die and so will I
so will I

so I say
hello there, Death, how do you do
you know I think I met you before
hello there, Death, how do you do
don't just stand at the door
stand at the door

come on in (there's some people I'd like you to meet)
come on in (if you like them wouldn't that be sweet)
come on in (there's some people that I'd like you to meet)
come on in (all the better if they fall at your feet)
come on in

You Fuck Me Up

LYRICS AND MUSIC BY GRUNT BULVEY

You fuck me up,
I'm a fuckup
I fuck you up,
you're a fuckup.

We're a couple a fuckups
a couple a fuckups
a couple, couple, couple fuckups
and that's all right with me

We get fucked up
We are fuckups
We get fucked up
We are fuckups.

We're a couple a fuckups
a couple a fuckups
a couple, couple, couple fuckups
and that's all right with me

Edmund Fitzgerald Got Wrecked

WORDS AND MUSIC BY SCUMBUCKETS

Edmund Fitzgerald got wrecked, got wrecked
Edmund Fitzgerald got wrecked.
Edmund Fitzgerald broke his neck, broke his neck
Edmund Fitzgerald got wrecked.

My mum said, 'Let this be a lesson, son'
(Edmund Fitzgerald got wrecked)
'Don't drink and drive or you'll end up on your bum'
(Edmund Fitzgerald got wrecked)

Edmund Fitzgerald got wrecked, got wrecked
Edmund Fitzgerald got wrecked.
Edmund Fitzgerald broke his neck, broke his neck
Edmund Fitzgerald got wrecked.

I drank two mickeys and I hopped into my car
(Edmund Fitzgerald got wrecked)
I revved the engine but I didn't get too far
(Edmund Fitzgerald got wrecked)

Smashed into a lamppost
Smashed into a lamppost
Smashed into a
Smashed into a
Smashed into a

Edmund Fitzgerald got wrecked, got wrecked
Edmund Fitzgerald got wrecked.
Edmund Fitzgerald broke his neck, broke his neck
Edmund Fitzgerald got wrecked.

Mystery: The Heart of Beauty or God Is Beauty

BY ROWENA RIGGS

FEBRUARY 21, 1982

"IN THE BEGINNING was the Word, and the Word was with God, and the Word was God."

This, for me, is one of the most beautiful and mystical passages in the Bible. It's beautiful in part because it's both decipherable and unparaphrasable. That is to say, we can figure out what it means, but we can't say what it means any other way than the way it already says it and still have it mean precisely the same thing.

Which leads me to wonder: Is mystery always at the heart of beauty? What is beauty? Why does beauty exist, why does it matter to us?

But let's go back a minute to the question of what the passage means.

"In the beginning was the Word, and the Word was with God, and the Word was God.

"He was in the beginning with God."

Before there was anything else, there was the Word, and the Word was with God, and the Word was God. (See? There's the bit there's no other way to say.)

With. Was. They are separate. They are the same. Separate. The same. Like soap bubbles merging and splitting. Only not like soap bubbles. Like nebulae or galaxies. Snowflakes falling and joining snow on the ground. Or like nothing we can fully imagine, only something we sense.

And now there's a "He." "The Word" is now a "He." "He was in the beginning with God." Which seems to imply, again, a complete being — soap bubble A, galaxy alpha — existing alongside God — soap bubble B, galaxy omega.

"All things came into being through Him; and apart from Him nothing came into being that has come into being."

All right. Here, he seems to be one again: God, Word and He, all at once. One giant soap bubble.

"In Him was life; and the life was the light of men." Oh, my goodness. What a leap we've made. Word. God. Him. Life. Men.

In fifty-six words we've gone from nothingness to men. Wow. <u>Four lines</u> encapsulate a philosophical and religious framework for our entire world! Again: wow. That's beauty!

But it doesn't stop there.

"In Him was life; and the life was the light of men. And the light shines in the darkness; and the darkness did not comprehend it."

Well, duh, as my kids used to say. We are daily at the task of trying to comprehend what is beyond comprehension — who we are, why we are here, what is God, what role does God play in the world, why do bad things happen. No wonder the darkness didn't comprehend the light. How can darkness comprehend light? Light does not exist in darkness.

Another eight lines on, the Word becomes flesh. The light of men becomes <u>a</u> man. That which existed before anything else becomes the thing that we are — a human being. The biggest, most eternal thing in existence becomes one of the smallest, most evanescent things in the universe. Miraculous. Darkness comes to know the Light.

When I feel I can't make sense of anything, I come back to this passage. I read it out loud and galaxies explode. I read it out loud and snow floats down. I read it out loud and understand without knowing precisely *how* I understand. I read it out loud and know beauty.

Beauty in its sense, its meaning, yes, but beauty in the passage itself, also in the balance of the phrasing — in the three-part beginning, each of the three parts leading one from the other: "In the beginning was the Word, and the Word was with God, and the Word was God" — in following a three-part beginning with a simple

476

one-part statement employing repetition of and variation on what's come before: "He was in the beginning with God." — in the balance in cadence between the third verse and the fourth verse: "All things came into being through Him; and apart from Him nothing came into being that has come into being" and "In Him was life; and the life was the light of men."

This beauty, this balance, this euphoniousness, this harmony is like the beauty of the natural world, like the beauty of the sun, like the beauty of the moon and stars. The beauty of Bach and Beethoven. The beauty of Joni Mitchell and the Beatles. Of Rembrandt and Da Vinci and Michelangelo. Of Jackson Pollock and Henry Moore and Almuth Lutkenhaus. We can never explain or define it for once and for all. But there is something in it that is constant. This is why, I think, that people over and over and over have said that God is Beauty. They are an equation. They are the same thing. They are both knowable and unknowable. Simple and complex. Eternal. Paradoxical. Mysterious.

"In the beginning was the Word, and the Word was with God, and the Word was God. He was in the beginning with God. All things came into being through him; and apart from Him nothing came into being that has come into being. In Him was life; and the life was the light of men."

Snow falling, settling on our shoulders, lining the ground.

Hallelujah. Amen.

Acknowledgements

My thanks go to Pat Fleming, Zsuzsi Gartner, Anna Nobile, Alison Pick and Marg Scott for reading early versions of this manuscript. Also to Cindy Holmes for helping me carve out time and space to write, to Steve Galloway, quite importantly, for lunches, and to the Canada Council and B.C. Arts Council for financial assistance during the writing of this book.

For help in research, I want to thank Dr. Barbara Mortimer of the nursing history department of Queen Margaret University College, Edinburgh, as well as the Imperial War Museum of Britain, which provided me with copies of unpublished nursing memoirs. *Lights Out: A Canadian Nursing Sister's Tale*, by Katharine Wilson-Simmie, was a great help, as was *Our Bit* by Mabel Clint. Dr. Stephen Tredwell of B.C. Children's Hospital provided guidance on medical matters, but any errors are mine, not his.

The perspicacious reader will notice certain historical liberties taken. *Crucified Woman*, by Almuth Lutkenhaus, was exhibited at Bloor Street United Church in 1979, not 1982. Fourteen nursing sisters died in the sinking of the *Llandovery Castle*. The fictional Helen Boothson makes fifteen.

ANNE FLEMING's first book, *Pool-Hopping and Other Stories*, was a finalist for the Governor General's Award for Fiction, the Danuta Gleed Award and the Ethel Wilson Fiction Prize. Her recent short fiction was selected for the 2004 *Toronto Life* fiction issue and won the 2003 National Magazine Award for Fiction. Anne Fleming grew up in Toronto and now lives in Vancouver, British Columbia.